THE OTHER WORLD

ABBIE EMMONS

For Katie,

my lighthouse through the storm

PROLOGUE

My father always told me that there are two worlds.

Our world, and the Otherworld.

Our world is simple. It is the island. It is the lighthouse. It is the endless waves of ocean stretching in every direction. It is the soft, thick blanket of clouds rolling across the sky, carrying rain and sometimes snow.

The Otherworld is out *there*.

Beyond the edge of the ocean.

I wouldn't have known it existed had I not asked my father when I was eight years old.

"What is out there, Papa?"

With a smile, he answered, "More ocean. Thousands of miles of it. Waves and waves into infinity."

"Infinity," I whispered, reaching my hand out as far as I could.

We were standing at the railing around the top of the lighthouse. I spread my fingers and watched infinity fill the spaces between them.

"And what's that, Papa? That land way out there?"

Papa's face went pale and quiet, like the breathless calm before a storm. His sharp eyes looked past the fog to the distant shapes of islands like ours.

"That is a whole other world," he said, placing a weathered hand on my shoulder. "It's where most people live."

"Why don't we live there?"

"Because we have our own world, little Orca." His gaze floated across the silver-crested waves as they danced closer to our shore. "The other world is full of danger and darkness."

"Like thunderstorms?"

Papa nodded. "Like thunderstorms. But not the thunderstorms you've seen. These thunderstorms are inside people. They *are* people. They're dangerous… mostly because you can't see the storms coming. People can change from light to dark in a moment, without warning."

I didn't understand what he meant. But I thought about his words.

I thought about the other world.

The Otherworld.

Papa knew it well. He'd lived there for a long time before he came to the lighthouse. But I couldn't remember ever seeing the Otherworld, and I longed to know more about it. Papa's natural history books talked of rainforests sweet with nectar and fizzing with tropical birdsong. Deserts as wide and lonely as the open seas. Mountains so tall they were never without snow.

Earth wasn't the problem, Papa said. It was the people who caused the problems.

The thunderstorm people.

But even thunderstorms have another side to them—a terrifying sort of beauty, when rods of white lightning split the sky into pieces and flash on the swells of the black ocean below. I used to sit by the window and watch such storms with Papa at my side. When the thunder roared and shook the sea around us, I would snuggle close to Papa, and he would tuck me into the side of his overcoat. He smelled of rain and salt and hard work. Our dog, Lucius, didn't care for stormy nights. He would lie across Papa's feet and whine until the thunder ceased.

Our island is small enough to circle in a day's light on foot, a coastline of hard gray beaches and jagged black rocks slick with sea mist and vibrant green moss. If you walk straight across the island instead of around it, you come into a thick gathering of trees—stout junipers, sticky hemlocks, and paper birches—thousands of branches reaching up to the sky and blanketing the mossy forest floor in golden leaves come autumn.

But of all the sights and wonders our world has to offer, none is more familiar to me than the lighthouse. Her whitewashed tower stands proudly on the island's northern tip, crowned by a glass-walled lantern room, sea mist worshipping at her feet as she sends light across the water to infinity.

At times, I have glimpsed lights from the Otherworld, too. Little pinpricks of light, as if some stars had fallen out of the night sky and landed in the water—twinkling for a moment on the horizon before the waves swallowed them up.

What is it like out there? Will I ever know?

When Papa spoke of the thunderstorm people in the Otherworld, he emphasized how much we don't belong there. How much *I* don't belong there.

"You're a very special, kind soul, Orca," he'd say, looking deep into my eyes from across the dinner table. "People aren't kind in the other world."

"None of them?"

"Not many of them," Papa said. "You're like… a delicate and unique branch of coral. You belong far away from the violent crashes of the waves on the rocks. You see, corals can't survive in the tide. That's why they flourish in a reef, on the ocean floor. Out of harm's way."

I understood what he was saying:

I wasn't strong enough for the Otherworld.

According to Papa, it would smash me and destroy me.

Year after year, I helped Papa keep the light. Occasionally, boats and planes would cross paths with us, always miles out of reach—traveling in too many directions to determine where they came from or where they were going. I amused myself by making up stories about the people in those planes and boats. Where they might be traveling to, and what kinds of lives they led.

Every three months, a coast guard boat would come to our island and moor off the east side. Two men would carry out a routine inspection to ensure the lighthouse was up to standard. Our only other visitor was the supply man, who came twice a year to deliver us essentials we couldn't grow or build ourselves. Knives, new flint, ointment, fresh rope, yellow wax candles, sacks of flour and rice, and fat bricks of soap. I loved to examine the new supplies piled up in our living room, studying them like treasures from the bottom of the sea. My only taste of the Otherworld.

When the supply man left, I would watch his boat through Papa's spyglass, squinting hopelessly through the eyepiece until the small craft vanished into the distance.

Season after season, year after year, the Otherworld remained a mystery. The only evidence that it existed at all lay in the ropes and the wax and the knives.

And the pinpricks of light.

And the look in Papa's eyes when he remembered it.

THE LIGHTHOUSE

June 14, 1997

STRANGE TREASURES

orca

Every year on my birthday, Papa carves a new driftwood orca whale and leaves it on my nightstand. It's the first thing I see when I open my eyes on the fourteenth day of June. I know exactly which piece of driftwood Papa used for this one. He's made it a thing of beauty— sculpting away the gnarls and knobs of the branch to release new life from its soul: an orca whale breaching high from a wave of driftwood, its pectoral fins like wings in flight.

I turn the carving over in my hands, marveling at Papa's talent before I place it atop my dresser with the others. There are big ones, little ones, males with tall dorsal fins, and females swimming beside their babies. Today, I have a pod of eighteen orcas porpoising across my dresser.

Eighteen.

I've waited an eternity for this day. To finally step over the threshold of childhood and embark on a new chapter of my life. In the Otherworld, eighteen means something. It means you are no longer a little girl in need of protection. It means you are an adult, capable of making your own decisions.

It means anything is possible.

I twirl over to the window and throw it open. Briny, sweet sea mist billows inside, fluttering the papers pinned to my walls—ocean charts and illustrations from marine biology books. Seashell garlands sway and clink jovially in the breath of a new day. I lean my elbows on the windowsill and peer across the water to the mist-shrouded islands in the distance.

So many adventures, waiting to be had.

So many mysteries, waiting to be discovered.

So much *more*, just beyond my reach.

Today is the beginning of it all.

I wrap myself in my crocheted shawl and head into the living room. Lucius lifts his scruffy head upon my entrance, romping over for a good-morning hug. I kneel on the floor and loop my arms around his neck, planting a kiss on top of his head. He is a sandy, salty mess of a dog—another outcast from the Otherworld. Papa found him at a harbor five years ago, whimpering in a box marked "free to a good home." He was the only puppy in the box, and there was no telling if he'd had any brothers and sisters taken before him. The fact remained: Lucius was all alone. Perhaps they didn't like his mismatched eyes—one was brown and one was blue—but I always thought it made him more beautiful. Papa didn't have the heart to leave him behind, so he tucked him into his raincoat and brought him to the lighthouse. He's just the right sort of dog to have on the island—a mix between "some kinda collie and some kinda shepherd," according to Papa's analysis. I think he may be part bloodhound because he can smell a good meal cooking from half a mile away.

"Today is the day, Lucius," I whisper conspiratorially into one of his floppy brown ears. "I'm going to ask Papa to take me to the Otherworld. He can have no possible reason to object now that I'm eighteen—"

"Orca?" Papa's warm, mahogany voice calls from the kitchen. "Is that you?"

I pat Lucius's head as I climb to my feet. "Come on, boy. Let's go."

Papa's eyes light up when I step into the kitchen. "Happy birthday, my sweet girl."

I dash across the room and pull him into a hug. "The carving is beautiful. Thank you, Papa."

He murmurs a humble laugh against the crown of my head. "I'm glad you like it, Orca."

"I love it."

Reaching over the sink, I push open the window and invite the morning breeze inside. Beyond the window, a knoll of soft young grass slopes down to the land's end where massive, craggy rocks meet the sea. My gaze follows a pathway of golden sunlight glittering on the high tide like crushed diamonds. Waves crash, and seagulls cry.

Our world carries on, ever the same.

But today is different.

The aroma of chamomile and lavender fills the kitchen as Papa strains freshly steeped tea into two ceramic mugs for us. A sickle of morning light crests the side of his face, contrasting with the scruffy, salt-and-pepper beard that lines his jaw. Steam curls around his weathered hands as he pours the tea, his gray eyes solemn and thoughtful.

"Everything feels so much more *alive* now that I'm eighteen," I begin, sitting in my usual spot at the table and settling my chin on my fist. "I almost feel like a new person. Older. Wiser."

"Mm," Papa murmurs, taking a seat at the other end of the table. "I'm glad to hear it…" But his voice could no more be described as *glad* than a rainy day could be considered cheerful.

"Papa? Is everything all right?"

His somber eyes meet mine. "I hope so, Orca."

"What do you mean?"

"Well, it's just… I received a phone call yesterday."

"A phone call?"

The satellite phone is our only connection to the Otherworld, and I've never used it myself. Papa has always told me that the phone is not a plaything and should be reserved for emergencies if we need to reach the coast guard.

Or, in this case, when the coast guard needs to reach *us*.

"They've summoned me to the mainland," Papa says quickly, as if the words sting and he needs to get them out in a hurry.

"The mainland," I echo, a thrill of hope awakening in my chest.

The Otherworld.

"Why?"

Papa draws a deep breath and stares into his mug of tea. "It seems there are some changes to be made around here."

"What sort of changes?"

"Modernization," Papa says with a sigh. "All the lighthouses across the country have been fully automated for years now. Ours is the only one that hasn't been converted to the new system."

"What's the new system?"

"One without lightkeepers."

I frown. "But how is that possible?"

"Technology has changed a great deal since the last light was installed in the sixties. The new lanterns they make now can be controlled remotely by the coast guard. There's no longer any need for a middleman."

"Does that mean we'll lose our place here?"

Papa shakes his head. "I've been told we can stay on. The grounds and tower will still need upkeep, which we will continue to manage…" A weak grin tugs at the corner of his mouth. "Don't worry, sweet girl. It won't make much of a difference to us. If anything, it will give me more free time to spend with you."

I shake my head. "I'm not worried, Papa. On the contrary, it sounds exciting—*modernization* here at the lighthouse. And what a lucky coincidence that you just happen to be summoned to the mainland on the very day I turn eighteen!"

Papa regards me with a curious frown. "A lucky coincidence?"

"Yes! Because it's a special birthday, isn't it? I mean, in the Otherworld, eighteen is the beginning of adulthood. It means I'm older and wiser and…" I clasp my hands together in my lap, my chin tipped up with confidence. "Well, the truth is, I was planning to ask you to take me to the Otherworld. For my birthday. But I was worried it might be a bother. And now—" I laugh, a giddy rush of excitement flurrying through me. "Well, now I don't have to worry about that at all because you need to go to the Otherworld anyway, and—"

"Orca." Papa's voice is quiet, but firm enough to stop me mid-sentence. The sorrow in his eyes is outmatched only by his unwavering resolve. "You won't be coming with me to the mainland. Not this time."

My heart sinks. "Why not?"

"Because I need you to stay here, to keep the light and look after things. And take care of Lucius, of course."

At the sound of his name, Lucius trots over and pushes his head into Papa's lap.

"Lucius could come, too," I offer, though I only half-expect him to take this suggestion seriously. I lean over the edge of the table to say, "Would you like to see the Otherworld, Lucius? I know I would—"

"No, Orca." Papa gives me a stern look from across the table. "I need you to stay here. I trust you to take care of things; it's no small task. Do you think you can handle it?"

"Of course I can handle it, Papa. But I wouldn't be any bother if I *did* come with you. And I'm sure the lighthouse would be fine for a day without us."

"I'll be gone for more than a day," Papa returns decidedly, those first three words burning me like a bee sting.

I'll be gone.

"How long do you suppose it will take?"

Papa sighs, rubbing his beard. "I hope no more than three days."

"*Three days?*"

"These government matters can take time. I don't like it any more than you do, Orca. But I promise I will return to you as soon as possible."

My gaze drifts down to the cracks in the old kitchen table. I know every line and scratch, exactly how it got there. This one from the bread knife I dropped a few weeks ago. This one from the year I learned to write the alphabet and accidentally scrawled past the edge of the page. This one from Lucius's claws, attempting to steal a cooling pie before I wrestled him to the floor.

Eighteen years I have sat at this kitchen table and looked across at Papa's sweet, familiar face.

Six thousand, five hundred and seventy days.

Perhaps I was foolish to hope, to wait, to expect that one of those days would be *the day.*

The day Papa told me I was old enough, strong enough, wise enough to go to the Otherworld with him.

I swallow the pang of disappointment knotted in my throat and manage to ask, "When are you leaving?"

"A boat will come for me first thing in the morning," Papa says. "I hate to leave you like this, my sweet girl. But you'll be strong for me, won't you?"

I nod, proving it now—if only to myself—as I blink back the stinging tears. "Of course, Papa."

"IT'S NOT FAIR," I grumble, trudging down the flagstone path to the green-house, my harvesting basket slung over my shoulders and Lucius trotting at my side. "My whole life, I've been asking Papa to take me. Now, the perfect opportunity arrives and what do you know? I can't go with him. Even *you* have seen more of the Otherworld than I have, Lucius."

He sneezes with an air of smugness.

"Well, you don't have to rub my nose in it."

I open the door to the greenhouse and step inside, Lucius close at my heels. A riot of color surrounds me—greens and reds and yellows and purples. Morning glories ribbon up the support poles, pressing their faces toward the ceiling in search of the sun. Beds of romaine lettuce grow in different stages of readiness. Feathery carrot tops drape from deeper beds of rich soil, and heavy vines of tomatoes cling to stakes, covered with small fruit. A long trough of strawberry plants follows the wall at my eye level— red jewels dangling from tender green leaves. Sugar snap peas tangle play-fully around everything in their reach, and the pepper plants sit stoically, watching their wild fun. Butterflies dance to and fro, fluttering from blossom to blossom in darting glimpses of yellow and orange and blue and white.

My favorite part of the greenhouse is the very center, where a circular opening in the roof allows rainwater to filter down and collect in a basin. Colorful orchids hang from the ceiling, their roots twisted acrobatically around the opening. Papa designed it that way to give the orchids a moist habitat while collecting the rain in a convenient place for the rest of the plants. I whisper hello to the orchids, and they reach out as if to shake hands, their painted faces smiling with shy elegance.

I lift a clay pot from the side of the basin and fill it with rainwater, tucking it against my side as I circle back through the greenhouse to water the plants. Lucius sniffs the ground for fallen berries, occasionally sneezing on the dirt.

Tomorrow, Papa leaves for the Otherworld.

And I stay behind.

All these years, leaning as far as I can over the lantern room railing with Papa's spyglass. All these years, squinting through the fog into infinity, hoping to glimpse just a fragment of the Otherworld. All these years, poring over Papa's maps and learning the names of our neighboring islands: San Juan, Lopez, Whidbey…

Yet Papa won't take me with him.

"What have I ever done, Lucius?" I say, returning to the basin to scoop up more water.

Lucius glances up from the green bean beds across the row. His snout is dusty-brown from sniffing the earth, and his ears are perked, waiting for a command or food—I can tell he hopes for the latter.

"What have I done to make Papa think I'm so weak? So… incapable?" I sigh, watering the tomatoes and the peppers. "What have I done to make him mistrust me?"

Lucius whimpers and lies down. Very helpful.

I shrug my harvesting basket off my shoulders and open the woven lid. I start by twisting the biggest heads of romaine from their beds and shaking off any excess dirt. Next, I move on to the tomatoes—plucking off only the roundest, reddest fruits and gently laying them in my basket.

"Maybe it's not just me," I murmur, running my fingertips over the long row of strawberries. "Maybe it's because of Mama. Maybe he blames the Otherworld… for what happened."

I've lost track of how many times I have pulled back the curtains of my past memories, searching for a glimpse of Mama—a trace of a voice, a smell, a touch. But each time, I find nothing. I was only two years old when she died, too young to remember anything about her. Trying to summon a memory feels like pushing my arms far down into sand, digging for something that isn't there.

It wouldn't be half so disheartening if Papa would tell me about her— if he would share some of his memories with me. But he never speaks of Mama, and I learned many years ago to keep the subject off my lips. Every once in a while, I see the light in his eyes change from present to past, and I wonder if he's thinking of her. I've never seen a picture of her, so I don't even know if we look anything alike. But it's impossible to mistake the sadness in Papa's eyes when he looks at me sometimes, and I know that I remind him of Mama in those moments.

Lucius whines at my feet, waiting for a strawberry. I carefully pluck the sweet rubies off the plant, collecting them in a separate, smaller woven basket so they won't be crushed among the other vegetables.

"Or," I add, "maybe I just haven't done anything to *prove* that I'm capable."

Lucius watches me roll a berry between my fingers.

"What do *you* think?"

He paws my leg and shimmies an inch closer.

I pop the berry in my mouth.

He looks so devastated, I can't help picking another plump strawberry and tossing it to him. He catches it in midair and immediately wants another.

"No, we can't eat them all here." I turn back to the trough and continue harvesting. "Anyway, back to what I was saying. Maybe Papa *would* let me go to the Otherworld if he saw that I'm much stronger than he realizes. Maybe I can find a way to prove it to him… Any ideas?"

Lucius tilts his head as if thoughtfully considering the question.

"I know what you're thinking," I say, lowering my voice to a doleful doglike grumble. "'Orca, you've complained to me about the same thing over and over again. You just can't stop talking about the Otherworld! I'm tired of hearing you go on and on about it.'" I sigh, popping another strawberry into my mouth. "I know, Lucius. And I'm sorry to dump all this on you… but you're my only friend."

I lower into a crouch, cupping his dusty, speckled face in my hands. He stares at me with those beautiful mismatched eyes, as if he can read my thoughts.

"I wish I could talk to Papa about this. But he doesn't understand… and I don't want to upset him. He just doesn't know what it's like. He's had his adventures; he's lived in the Otherworld. For so many years, I've looked out over the sea at night and watched those lights from the Otherworld and wondered what it's like out there. I've wondered what my life might have been…" My throat tightens as the ache of tears chokes my voice. "It's a kind of grief, Lucius. I can't describe it, but… it's like mourning something you never had. Something you *could've* had. If only things were different."

Unbidden tears begin to fall, spilling from my eyes. Lucius dips his head down and licks them off my cheeks, startling a laugh out of me. I slide my arms around his shaggy neck and clutch fistfuls of his fur.

"Oh, Lucius. You always know how to make me feel better."

BY MIDAFTERNOON, THE SUN tucks herself behind a blanket of clouds and leaves the rest of the day smudged in shades of gray. While Papa goes fishing at the cove, I sneak off to walk the beach and collect shells, my linen pants rolled up to my knees and Lucius tromping at my side. He loves to splash through the surf and bark at seagulls, making them scatter.

The tide is going out, leaving behind all sorts of new treasures. Thanks to Papa's books and charts, I can identify most of the shells I find: silky white scallops, gnarled gray oysters, ribbed brown *Astarte*, and one huge empty *Macoma* that opens up like a pair of butterfly wings.

Then, lodged between rocks in a tide pool, I spot something unusual:

a thin bronze chain coiled around a fat strip of kelp. I reach down, sifting through a tangle of seaweed, and pull it out.

It's a compass, small and finely crafted, strung on a chain and dripping with saltwater.

Where did it come from?

I look to the horizon, squinting to see if there's anything else unusual in the receding tide. But there are only gray waves upon more gray waves. My gaze slides back to the beach, where Lucius hops over driftwood, barking happily at the gulls.

That's when I spot something ahead washed up on the sand. From here, it is nothing more than a black lump that the tide is beginning to release from her frothy fingertips.

A dead seabird, no doubt.

"Lucius, come!" I holler, gripping my handful of shells and running down the beach toward him.

Lucius has a habit of putting nasty things in his mouth. He also has a habit of defiantly running away from me when he thinks I have a mind to deprive him of fun. He looks back at me with a crazed spark of adventure in his eyes and bolts down the beach for the dead bird.

"Lucius, *come!*"

I sprint after him as fast as I can, splashing through the shallow water and dodging branches of driftwood. As I draw closer, I see it's not a dead seabird.

Lucius trots to a halt and sticks his nose in the black lump, sniffing and sneezing ferociously.

"What is it?" I say, slowing to a stop.

It looks like a sack of some kind—battered and black, strangled by a long string of kelp. Zippers and buckles are stitched into the bag, and two long straps hang off one side, reminding me of my harvesting basket. Perhaps it's designed to be worn on the back?

I peel the kelp off the sack and turn it over in my hands, undoing one of the buckles and pulling the zipper open. To my surprise, the interior is completely dry. Feeling around, I find a flashlight, a clear bag with fishing lines and hooks, a tiny box of matches, and a fold-out knife.

Then, without warning, the sack begins to vibrate.

"Holy mackerel!" I gasp, dropping it as I jump back.

MMM-MMM-MMM, hums the sack.

"What on earth?" I whisper, creeping a few inches closer. Whatever is making that strange noise, I'm more curious than I am afraid of it.

Moving carefully, I pull back the zipper of the top pocket and peer inside. A small rectangular device hums at the bottom of the pocket. Just as I pull it out into the light, the vibrating stops. Lucius prowls closer with caution, sniffing as if to ask whether the object in my hand is edible.

"Is it… a phone?" I murmur, turning it over in my hands. The little device has an antenna sprouting from one side, but there is no number pad. Only two strange words written on the side: **Motorola StarTAC**. "It doesn't look like any phone *I've* ever seen."

I pull the compass out of my pocket to take a closer look at it. Could these strange treasures be related? Have they come from the same place?

I lift my eyes to the gray horizon once more, my heart racing with a thrill of anticipation.

They *have* come from the same place.

They've come from the Otherworld.

YOU'RE ON YOUR OWN, SUPERMAN

jack

Altitude: 1,200 feet.

Ocean: gray, empty, unforgiving.

Sky: dark, angry, preparing to storm.

Fingers: freezing, stiff, wrapped around the yoke.

Heart: pounding, pounding, pounding.

I sweep my gaze over the waves below, searching desperately. The coming storm has made the whole world go dark. A mass of black clouds churns in the west, flashing with rods of white lightning.

"Come on, Adam, where the hell are you?" I rasp, scanning the swells below.

Finally, I see something:

A familiar de Havilland Beaver, half-submerged in the cold, black water.

My stomach plummets. I force myself to breathe. I need to land, but the seas are rough—getting worse by the minute. One wrong move and I could catch a wing or dig my floats, tip my plane, and get swallowed by the ocean.

It's a risk I have to take.

Banking hard left, I start to descend—my heart lifting into my throat as I watch my altimeter spiral down, down, down. Within moments, my floats are skidding over the tops of the frothing waves. I slow to a stop about fifty feet away from the wreckage. Close enough.

Shoving open my door, I scramble down the ladder and dive into the next swell. I barely feel the cold, though the water must be fifty degrees. My lungs burn as I stroke through the waves, arm over arm, kicking hard against the current. Finally, I make it to the cockpit of the wrecked float-plane and claw my way through the torn-open door.

That's when I see him slumped over the copilot's seat. His face is submerged in the water, his arm twisted behind his back.

"Adam!" My voice tears out of my throat as I lunge forward to grab him.

His skin is as cold as ice. There's a deep gash in his chest, wet with more than water.

I pull my hand back.

Blood.

I jolt awake, sweating and gasping for air, my bedroom spinning around me—

My bedroom.

I'm dreaming.

I was dreaming.

It was just a dream.

I'm still gasping, hyperventilating, shaking—

Breathe, Jack. It was just a dream.

I clutch my wet face, digging my fingertips into my hair. The bed-sheets are stuck to my arms and chest. My stomach is doing somersaults, and all I can see in my mind is blood, Adam's blood—

I look at my trembling hands.

It was just a dream.

But could it be true?

I squeeze my eyes shut and breathe deeply for a few moments, trying to calm my racing heart. When I open my eyes again, my gaze lands on the other bed.

His bed.

It's still neatly made. Hospital corners. The faded quilt folded twice at the end. His desk, his dresser, his books—frozen in time.

Frozen, like his skin was.

Face in the water.

Gash.

Blood.

"No," I say, my voice like sandpaper in my throat. "No, no, it was just a dream."

I force myself to look away from his side of the room and climb out of bed, feeling gutted as I walk to the door. The sound of my parents' hushed voices drifts down the hallway from the kitchen. I duck into the bathroom and turn the shower on to the coldest setting, bracing my arms against the tiled wall as the icy water rushes over me.

Colder, colder.

Is this fifty degrees?

The coast guard has a method for calculating the likelihood of survival when someone is lost at sea.

The survival rate for a twenty-eight-year-old man in fifty-degree water is one hundred percent in the first two hours.

Three hours and it falls to seventy percent.

Six hours and it falls to five percent.

I'm so cold now, I can barely breathe. I reach down and shut off the water. I stand shivering and gasping for a long moment, my forehead pressed against the shower wall.

It's been three days.

Not hours.

Days.

I throw on a pair of jeans and a T-shirt, running a towel through my wet hair. The voices of Mom and Dad become clearer as I drift down the wood-paneled hallway toward the kitchen. Their conversation dies as soon as I step into the room.

"Jack," Mom says from the table, where she sits across from Dad, "are you okay, sweetheart?"

I look at Adam's empty chair.

"I'm fine," I whisper.

Silence while I shuffle over to the coffee maker and pour myself a cup. Silence while I watch the black liquid swirl and steam. Silence while I walk to the table and sit down.

My gaze slides between Mom and Dad. I want to ask if there is any news, but at the same time, I don't want to know. Dad stares into his coffee cup, and Mom presses her lips together. She's been crying.

I look at Adam's empty chair again.

"I'm going outside," I mutter, standing up.

"Wait, Jackie."

I look at Mom, but she only stares at me like she doesn't know what to say. She tucks a strand of hair behind her ear with one trembling hand. "We want to talk to you."

Those words hit me like a punch.

Adam is dead.

I swallow, gripping the back of my chair. "Did you hear from the coast guard?"

Mom nods slowly, her gaze drifting down to the table.

No, no, God almighty, no.

My stomach twists into a knot, and my throat closes up. I want to run.

I don't want to hear this.

I would rather shoot myself than hear this.

But for Mom and Dad's sake, I don't leave. I stay where I am and try to act like a man.

Like Adam.

At last, Dad looks me in the face. "They still haven't found him."

Relief rushes through me, and strangely enough, my first thought is, *Thank God.*

Because if they haven't found him, he could still be alive. They don't know.

"But it's not a rescue anymore," Dad says, a dark cloud passing through his eyes as they lock on mine. "It's a recovery."

Mom starts to cry again.

The words "rescue" and "recovery" seem so similar to me. For a second, I don't register the difference. Then it hits me.

You rescue a person.

You recover a body.

I shake my head, feeling like I'm still trapped in a nightmare. "They're giving up?"

Mom wipes her tears with the edge of her sleeve.

Dad takes a deep breath and meets my gaze again. I can see my pain reflected in his eyes. "This is the last day."

The last day.

Those words make me want to punch a hole through the wall.

"No," I rasp, shaking my head firmly. "No, they can't give up."

"They can't look forever—"

"It hasn't been forever!" I explode, slamming my hand on the table. "It's only been three days—"

"The coast guard has done everything they can," Dad says, his voice steady but shuddering underneath. "They said at this point the chances of survival are almost zero, and their efforts are no longer fruitful."

"So they're giving up," I repeat, anger boiling inside me. "They're giving up, and Adam is still out there. He's still alive—"

"Jack—"

"He's still alive!" I shout over him, rage flaring in my chest. "I don't care what you say, and I don't care what they say! He's alive, and they're doing nothing. They're going to let him die out there!" I kick my chair and turn to storm out of the house.

Dad jumps up in a flash. His strong hand locks around my forearm, halting me right where I stand.

"Jack," he says, that cloud of pain still heavy in his eyes, "we have to accept the truth."

I stare at him, feeling like there's another hand wrapped around my throat because I can't speak. I want to yell in his face that he's the one who has given up. Mom, too. They're both giving up. They're both sitting here mourning Adam like he's already…

I rip my arm out of Dad's grasp and shove the door open, bolting outside. I hear Dad shout my name, but Mom says, "Let him go, John." And he does.

I race across the driveway to my Mustang, diving inside and starting the engine. It's foggy as hell this morning, so I have to drive slower than usual to the port. Blankets of mist wrap every tree in sight. It's cold for June. Or maybe that's just my hands gripping the steering wheel. Knuckles white.

Memories rush back to me as I drive down the familiar winding road.

It was sunny that morning. Adam drove because I didn't have my license yet. He rapped his fingertips on the steering wheel in time with "Fortunate Son" playing on the radio. We both wore aviator shades. Windows down. Sunlight on the dashboard, on the veins in his arms.

I hang a right, swerving into the driveway for the port. Everything is quiet, frozen in time. I check the dash clock. 8:34.

Hangars loom like watchmen in the fog, which is slowly thinning out. I park my car and get out, slamming the door shut. The sound is like a gunshot in the quiet of the sleepy port. Seagulls cry in the distance. Tidewater laps against the docks. Adam's keys jangle in my hand.

"Let's get up there," Adam said, grinning as he slapped my shoulder. He was only two inches taller than me. Fifteen had shot me up to his level. I liked it there.

His de Havilland Beaver was already waiting for us, tied to the dock, her blue pinstriped wings ready to take flight. We'd done this so many times, the walk was routine. I'd been up there for dozens of hours, Adam, my instructor, telling me what to do—guiding my hands over the instruments. The more we went up together, the less he did for me, the less he even had to tell me.

I felt good. He made me good.

The dock bobs up and down as I walk out to Adam's other plane—the one he uses for passenger flights. I stop at the end of the dock and gaze out over the water. Endless gray waves roll into the fog.

I wish I could believe the sun is burning it off, but there's no way to know for sure. If I take off, pushing the weather, and the cloud base drops any lower…

I don't care. I'm going up.

I need to.

Before I can change my mind, I start untying the Beaver from the dock, my hands slick with cold sweat.

I pulled open the door, sliding in first so Adam could sit beside me. But he hesitated. While I slid the key into the ignition, he just clung to the ladder, watching me with a knowing grin on his face. Standing there in that bomber jacket, he looked like a fighter pilot from World War II.

"Are you getting in, or what?" I asked.

Adam lowered his shades and looked at me, his blue eyes lit up with a spark I hadn't seen before. "No… You're on your own, Superman."

My heart stopped. "W-what? No, wait—"

"First solo flight," Adam declared.

My stomach somersaulted.

"Now? Today? You didn't tell me—"

Adam laughed. "Of course I didn't. You'd be a nervous wreck."

Too late. My heart was pounding double time. "But I can't," I stammered. "I can't do this, Adam. I need you."

Adam shook his head. "No, you don't," he said. "You got this." And he shut the door.

Slam. I'm alone inside the Beaver. I take a deep breath, sit back, and try to focus my mind.

Ignition switches: on. I listen as the engine rumbles to life. The propeller spins in front of me, slicing the fog. While waiting for the engine to warm up, I go through my checklist. Fuel levels, oil temp, pressure gauges, tank feeds. Everything is good to go.

I glance out the window at the empty dock.

Adam stood outside on the dock, his arms crossed over his chest, still grinning in the sunlight. A six-foot-one mountain. He always called me Superman, but it was a joke. I knew who the real hero was.

"Good luck," he mouthed, and gave me a two-finger salute.

I saluted him back.

My heart races as I buckle up and slide my fingers to the worn grooves of the yoke.

I feel possessed—like some unseen force is controlling my body. It's crazy to go up in this kind of weather. Visual flight requires a minimum of one mile horizontally and five hundred feet vertically. I'm lucky if I'm looking at three hundred feet right now—and distance is even weaker. There's no telling how thick the fog will be once I'm over the straits.

"Oh, screw it," I mutter, reaching for the throttle.

I powered out to the broadest part of the harbor, lining up the flyway ahead of me.

"Okay, this is fine," I told myself. "Relax—you're fine. You're just flying solo. Holy shit—"

I wrapped my fingers around the throttle, keeping the yoke straight.

Inhale. Exhale.

"Here we go."

The engine roars, gray waves blurring underneath my floats; curtains of white fog whip across the windows. My heart pounds harder and faster as I work the throttle with one hand, pull the yoke with the other, and lift off.

It's the best feeling in the world: the moment your floats leave the water and gravity falls away, and all of a sudden—

You're flying.

It feels like actually being Superman.

As I climbed into the cloudless sky, the shimmering tops of the waves shrank farther and farther away. It seemed like the world was opening up to greet me, glistening in the sun and humming with life.

Altitude: 2,000 feet.

I eased the throttle down and pushed the yoke to a neutral position. The world sprawled beneath me, a thousand colors glistening in the sunlight. I knew it all like the back of my hand, but it looked like a brand-new world that day. The shapes of the islands. The thick forests of evergreen circled by rocky beaches. Deception Pass Bridge, arching over the water like a giant steel hand clutching the last strands of fog.

I banked to the left, soaring over the pass. Tiny boats streaked through the water two thousand feet below me, leaving star trails in the blue. I brought my gaze back up, about to say something to Adam—then I remembered he wasn't beside me. He was back on the dock, all the way down there. And I was all the way up here, on my own. Solo. Free.

I started laughing, unable to control the euphoria that exploded inside me like fireworks.

I threw my head back and hollered, "WOOOOOOOO!"

Altitude: 1,000 feet.

I was wrong— the fog isn't thinning. There's no sun to burn it off. I know my flight path like the back of my hand, and I can see the shapes of the islands around me, but the waves are hidden under a thick sheet of white.

Damn it.

I bank shallow to the left, watching my compass. 250, 240…

The islands slowly drift away and vanish in the fog. All around me, above me, and beneath me is white. I catch glimpses of waves far below and the darting shadows of gulls, like ghosts between layers of mist.

A crosswind comes from the north, dipping my port wing as a blinding fog swaths my windshield.

I can't see a damn thing.

Cussing under my breath, I push the yoke out and drop down fifty feet, seventy feet, a hundred feet… trying to escape this fog.

But I can't. It's everywhere.

My pulse starts racing again, blood rushing through my ears as I remember what Adam used to say: *Bush pilots who get stuck in clouds usually get stuck in granite.*

What the hell am I doing out here?

Do I seriously think I can do a better job searching for my missing brother than the coast guard can?

I'm out of my mind.

Banking hard to the east, I watch my compass do a one-eighty, leveling out between sixty and seventy. Altitude: 800 feet.

Just get back to the port, you idiot.

I'm flying below the minimums until the islands come into view again—dark, rugged lumps rise out of the fog like the backs of sea monsters. When the shore of Whidbey comes into view, I start my descent, keeping a close eye on my altimeter. Moments later, my floats skid across the water, sending up a spray of white.

I ease the throttle down and let the tide sail me into port, remembering what Adam taught me: never approach the dock faster than you want to hit it. I make a U-turn and slide up close to the dock, then shut down and hop out to grab the ropes.

My hands tremble as I tie down the plane and walk back to the parking lot, where my lonely Mustang is waiting. For a breathless moment, I sit in the driver's seat, listening to my pounding heart.

I press my forehead to the steering wheel and feel the burn of tears in my eyes.

"I can't do this, Adam," I whisper to the silence. "I need you."

I STAY OUT ALL DAY. Just driving around, nowhere in particular. Eventually, I pull into the Deception Pass state park and sit in the parking lot. I try calling Adam's cell phone again.

No answer.

I know it's selfish of me to stay out on the worst day of my parents' lives. But I can't stand to look at them, to see the grief in their eyes.

I fall asleep at some point and wake up to a late afternoon shadow. That's when I realize what a coward I'm being. If it were the other way around, Adam would be home right now, comforting Mom. Never leaving her side.

I wish it *were* the other way around.

That thought is enough to motivate me to drive back home. It's six o'clock by the time I pull into the driveway. The house looks quiet. Dad's truck is gone.

I walk through the front door and slide off my shoes. There's no one in the kitchen, nothing on the stove.

"Mom?"

That's when I hear it.

A sob.

A sniff.

She's crying.

That sound is a jab in the ribs, enough to knock the air out of my lungs in this house where it's already so hard to breathe. I steel myself and walk down the hallway, nudging open my bedroom door.

Mom is sitting on Adam's bed, her shoulders shaking as she silently cries into her hands. I hate the sight of it so much I want to smash everything in the room—

No. Control yourself, Jack.

What would Adam do?

I walk straight over to Mom, sit on the bed, and wrap my arms around her. She crumples into me, sobs rushing out of her, tears melting into my shirt.

I feel like I'm in a dream. Like this is all some sick, twisted nightmare, and my alarm's going to ring in a second—*beep, beep, beep*—and I'll smack my hand over on the nightstand and shut it off and open my eyes, and there will be Adam sitting on his bed in the morning light, pulling on a T-shirt, saying, *Get your ass out of bed, Superman.*

"Shh, Mom, it's okay…" I whisper, pulling back to look her in the face. "You can't lose hope. Not yet."

She shakes her head, swiping her tears away. "Jack—"

"Don't say it, Mom. *Don't*. He's coming back. I don't care what the coast guard says."

She stares at me, her wet cheeks glistening in the light from the hallway. "I can't go through this alone, Jackie. I need you to help me bear it."

I shake my head. "You're giving up on him."

"Do you think I want to?" Her voice strangles in her tears, and she stops, pressing one hand to her chest—like her heart is breaking. "Your father says we have to accept this. Maybe he's right."

"Well, I won't accept it," I snap, jolting to my feet. "You and Dad can believe what you want, but I'll never give up. I'll *die* before I accept this. In fact, I'd rather have that, okay? I'd rather die. I'd rather *die*—"

"Stop it!" Mom stands to face me, tears quivering in her angry, grieving eyes. "Don't ever let me hear you say that again."

"I mean it, Mom. I wish it were me and not him who went down out there."

"Jack—"

"If anyone should be here, it should be Adam. He's worth ten of me—"

Mom slaps my face. "How dare you say that to me! Don't you realize how much that rips my heart out? Don't you realize *you* are all I have left to live for? My boys are everything—I already lost Adam, and now here you are, saying you want to die, too?"

My throat locks up, hot tears sliding down my jaw. "I can't do it, Mom… I won't give up on him."

"He's gone, Jack." She cups my face in her hands. "Sooner or later, you're going to have to accept that. He would want you to be strong. To help *me* be strong."

My stomach tightens into a knot, my whole body going hellfire and brimstone. I shake my head firmly. "No. No—"

"Jack—"

"No!" I knock Mom's arm away and rush out of the room. I can barely see through my tears as I storm down the hallway and out the back door, Mom's words chasing me like demons.

He's gone.

Choking on air, I race across the driveway and duck into the shadow of our woods. Sappy wet pine branches slap my legs, my face. I don't know where I'm going, but I know I can't stay in the house for one more minute with Mom's grief hanging in the air.

He's gone.

My hands shake uncontrollably. I squeeze them into fists. Out of breath, I stop behind the barn—where I first caught him kissing a girl, where he first caught me smoking cigarettes. There's no place I can go to get away from his memory.

He's gone.

Rage wells up in me like a dam about to break. I can't hold it in any longer.

I curl my fist tight and punch the wall as hard as I can. The shock of pain actually feels good—something real to rattle me out of the black abyss of *acceptance.*

"Damn you, Adam!" I roar, punching the wall again and again and again. "Damn you!"

SLAM, SLAM, SLAM.

The pain is nothing compared to the war inside me.

"I hate you!" I shout over the voice in my head, his voice.

"You're on your own, Superman."

"I'm not Superman! I can't do this. It's too hard—I'm not *you!*"

My final blow cracks the wall. My wrist crumples, and I howl in pain, yanking my hand back. It's covered in blood. I whimper like a wuss, cradling my hand and slumping back against the wall.

"I'm not you," I gasp, shivering in the dark, tears running down my face. "I can't do this…"

The demons whisper, *Mom is right. Dad is right.*

We have to accept the truth.

He's gone.

I stand on the edge of a precipice, staring down at the endless void of a life without my brother. If I dive headfirst into that nightmare, there's no going back. I'll be falling forever. I'll be trapped in hell.

I'll never wake up.

That's when my phone starts ringing in my pocket. It's probably Dad, wherever the hell he is. I reach into my jacket with my uninjured hand and pull out my phone. Blinking back the tears, I peer at the number displayed on the tiny screen.

It's Adam.

Holy shit, *it's Adam!*

My bloody hands shake uncontrollably as I answer the call and press the phone to my ear.

"Adam!" I shout hoarsely. "Adam, are you there?!"

There is a long whoosh of white noise; then a girl's voice crackles through the phone.

"Hello? Hello, is this… Superman?"

THE BOY

orca

Papa is still out fishing when I return to the lighthouse. I hurry inside with the mysterious sack, Lucius clicking at my heels. He seems just as curious as I am to investigate what's inside—but I don't open the sack until I am back in my room.

"Shh, shh," I chide Lucius. "Papa can't know about this. We have to be quiet."

Lucius sits back, watching me intently as if the sack will produce some fanciful new food for him.

I begin with the top pocket. Though the outside of the sack is soaking wet, everything inside is dry. I pull out the strange rectangular object from before. It hasn't vibrated since I first found it, but I'm sure I will puzzle out its purpose in time. I set it on my bed and continue exploring the sack of strange treasures.

Besides the flashlight, fishing line, matches, and pocketknife, I find a small bag of extra batteries, packaged food that looks like nothing I would eat, and a small leather wallet containing a pilot's certificate and a photo ID.

"Adam Stevenson," I read under my breath.

Tucked inside the wallet is a color photograph of two young men standing in front of a floatplane, grinning in the sunlight. They're nearly the same height but not the same age. One looks distinctly older—Adam. I recognize his face from the photo ID, though he looks much happier in this picture. The sunlight catches in his dark brown hair and highlights the shadow of stubble on his sharp jaw. He's wearing a bomber jacket with sunglasses clipped to the collar, and he has one arm slung over the other boy's shoulder as if to show off the imperceptible height difference between them.

There's a wild excitement in the younger one's eyes, like he either just had the most thrilling experience of his life or he's about to. The sunlight makes artwork of him, too, etching the lines of his jaw, shoulders, and forearms.

Looking at the photo is like gazing through a magic spyglass into the Otherworld—catching a glimpse of a life I know nothing of. It feels almost… intrusive. Yet I can't stop looking. I can't stop studying every detail of the photo, committing it to memory.

The last thing I discover hiding in the bottom of the sack is a little black notebook filled with writing—different color ink throughout, but always the same penmanship. I spread the book open to a random page and begin to read.

02/22/97

If trust is earned, why are children so trusting? If I were born and immediately adopted by another family and grew up knowing them to be my family, I would not question it. I would completely trust that they were telling the truth. But if later I discovered that they lied to me and were not my biological family, this would lead to feelings of betrayal, and only THEN would I have trust issues. So perhaps it's not that "trust is earned"… it's that mistrust is learned. Children are born telling the truth. They cannot understand the concept of disloyalty or deceit until they are introduced to it by others.

A bang from outside jolts my attention away from the journal.

Papa's back.

I snap the book shut and stuff it back into the sack along with the other treasures. My hands tremble as I zipper the pockets shut and slide the whole thing under my bed. The mystery device is the only thing I keep out—tucking it under my pillow before I rush out of the room.

PAPA AND I MAKE dinner together, as we always do. He cleans the fish because he knows I'm not too fond of that part, and I prepare the vegetables I harvested this morning. Lucius watches, hopeful of scraps. Meanwhile, Papa talks me through the duties I'll take on tomorrow when he leaves for the mainland.

As the night goes on, he keeps remembering things to tell me—about the light, the weather, and the satellite phone. I nod receptively at all the information, though most of it I already know. I'm so closely acquainted with every inch of our island, the lighthouse, the tides, and the rain-clouds… I couldn't forget a single detail if I tried.

"Do you trust me, Papa?" I ask when we are seated across the table from each other.

He regards me with a furrowed brow. "Of course I do, Orca."

"So you think I'm capable."

Papa nods. "Very. I think you won't have a problem with anything while I'm gone."

The flicker of hope in my heart wanes a bit. I suppose I should be glad that Papa trusts me to manage things here on my own. But I wish he trusted me enough to go to the mainland with him.

That's going to be the hardest part. Watching Papa journey to the Otherworld and leave me behind.

Watching from the lantern room.

As I've done all my life.

At least I have my new treasures from the sea to keep me company. That fascinating notebook full of strange handwriting.

Where did they come from?

I ask myself that question again and again. I know the sack belongs to a pilot named Adam Stevenson, but how did it come to be in the ocean? The more I think about it, the more anxious I become to solve the mystery.

"So," Papa says, pulling me out of my thoughts, "you walked the beach earlier?"

I stop chewing to stare at him. "How did you know?"

Papa smiles softly. "Lucius's paws."

I look down at the mongrel napping on the floor. Sure enough, his legs are still damp and sandy—evidence of a seagull chase through the shallows.

"Yes," I admit. "We thought we'd sneak away while you were out fishing."

"And did you find anything interesting?"

It's a question Papa often asks me after my shell-collection walks. But this time, my heart stutters over a beat.

"Uh… no," I say to my plate, shaking my head. "Not particularly."

AFTER DINNER, PAPA GOES up to the lantern room, and I return to the mystery device I hid under my pillow. Upon closer examination, I discover a tiny hinge on one side—a mechanism to keep two parts clamped together. After a bit of prodding and prying, I manage to flip the device open.

"So it *is* a phone," I breathe in astonishment, tracing my fingertip over the number pad. "A phone that flips open… Extraordinary."

The tiny screen flashes, displaying a scrolling message.

47 missed calls from Superman

Who is that? And why has he been trying to call Adam Stevenson forty-seven times?

Better question, where *is* Adam Stevenson?

A chill ripples down my spine as I remember where I found his belongings—washed up on the beach. Was their owner lost at sea, too?

There's only one way for me to find out.

After much clueless fiddling, I pull up the number for Superman and press the call button to dial him back. For a long moment, I wait—listening as the phone rings.

"Adam!" a young man's voice shouts, muffled and tinny through the speaker. "Adam, are you there?!"

My jaw drops, and for a second, I can hardly believe someone has answered. "Hello? Hello, is this… Superman?"

The question is followed by a long silence, every bit as stunned as mine.

"What the hell? Who is this? Where is Adam?"

I pull the phone away from my ear, staring in awestruck wonder. He can hear me, and I can hear him! I'm talking to a boy from the Otherworld. I can't believe it…

"Hey! Who are you? Answer the question, damn it!"

I snatch the phone up and hold it to my ear. "My name is Orca Monroe, and I don't know who or where Adam is, but to answer your question, I live in a lighthouse on an island in the middle of the ocean, and I've never seen a phone like this before, so you'll have to forgive me if I seem a little surprised by the strangeness of it all."

Superman's voice comes back, sputtering, "What? Wait, wait, wait. Just… start at the beginning. Where did you find this phone?"

"On the beach. It was inside a big sack that had washed ashore—"

"What beach? Where? Where the hell are you?"

"I told you, I live on the island with the lighthouse."

"Well, that narrows it down, Sherlock," he snaps. "Which island? Anywhere near Whidbey?"

"Whidbey… Is that where you are?"

"Yeah. Now how close by are you?"

"Uh, I'm not sure exactly. I can get a map, but they're all in the lantern room, and Papa's up there right now, and if he sees me talking to you on this device, he'll take it away because I'm not supposed to talk to people from the Otherworld and—"

"LISTEN," Superman cuts in roughly. "My brother is *missing*. He's been missing for four days now. His plane went down somewhere off the coast of Whidbey. I need to know where you are!"

"Your brother? Is he… Adam Stevenson?"

"Yeah. Have you seen him?!"

"No, and stop shouting." I wince, holding the phone a distance away. "You're hurting my ear."

Superman mutters a foreign word under his breath. "Listen, I need you to tell me more about where you are. Where exactly you found his backpack."

"Backpack?"

"The big sack!"

"Oh. Right, yes. I found it on the beach. I told you that already."

"Yeah, okay, but where is this beach? What's the *name* of your *island*?" He emphasizes the words like I can't understand English.

"I… don't think it has a name."

"How can it not have a name?" Superman sighs. "Who else lives on this island?"

"Nobody. It's just Papa and me."

"You're shitting me."

"I'm *what*?"

"Okay, let me get this straight," he says. "You live in this lighthouse on this uninhabited island, and you have no clue where you are in relation to the rest of the San Juan Islands."

"I *do* know where we are. It's just I don't have exact coordinates at the moment."

"Whatever. I don't even care about that right now. I just need to know if you found any evidence of a person. Footprints or anything like that?"

"I don't think so…"

"Anything at all. THINK!"

"No!" I snap, my face growing hot. "I didn't find anything except the sack."

"Well, you have to look for him. You have to search the island—you have to find him. He's alive. I know he is! Everyone thinks he's dead. The coast guard quit the search, and my parents are giving up. They think he's dead, but he's not, *he's not*—"

"Okay, calm down," I tell him, my heart pounding faster. "If your brother is here, I can find him. I know this island like the back of my hand."

"When can you start looking? Now?"

"Uh… it's getting kind of dark," I say, pointing out the obvious. "But I suppose if I told Papa, we could search with flashlights—"

"No. Don't tell your father. Don't tell anyone. Nobody can know that I asked you to look. They think he's gone, and that I'm just going crazy and won't accept it. Your father won't let you search the island, and then Adam really will die, and—"

"All right," I cut in, "I won't say a word. It's probably better that way. Papa's leaving for the mainland tomorrow, and he'll be gone for a few days. I can search the island while he's gone, and he won't be here to stop me."

Superman doesn't reply. I hear him gasping for breath on the other side of the phone like he's halfway to a breakdown.

"It's okay," I try to comfort him, though my voice is unsteady. "If Adam is here, I *promise* I'll find him. I'll start looking as soon as Papa leaves in the morning, all right?"

"All right… Thank you."

"Of course."

"What did you say your name was?"

"Orca."

"Like the whale?"

"Yes. What's wrong with that?"

"Nothing's wrong with it. It's just… uh… unusual."

"Not as unusual as Superman."

He breathes a sad little laugh. "My name's not Superman. That's just what Adam calls me. I'm really Jack. Jack Stevenson."

A little glow warms up my heart. "It's nice to meet you, Jack." I can't help but smile. "That's the first time I've ever said that. You're the first person I've ever spoken to… from the Otherworld."

Jack falls silent for a long moment before saying, "You're shitting me."

A World Without Video Games

jack

This is by far the weirdest conversation I've ever had, and it's only getting weirder by the second. The girl with Adam's phone is talking to me like I'm an alien from another planet—but really, it's the other way around. *She's* the one from another world.

"So let me get this straight," I begin slowly. "You're telling me that you've never… met another person in your life?"

"Well, if you don't count Papa and the coast guard and the supply man who comes twice a year."

"Wait, what? Hold on, my phone's about to die."

"Die? What do you mean *die?*"

"I'll call you right back, okay? Don't go anywhere."

There's no avoiding Mom when I walk through the front door, still cradling my bloody, busted hand. She freaks out when she sees it, dragging me over to the sink to wash the wound as if I don't know how to do that myself by now.

"What on earth happened to you?"

"Nothing, Mom. I'm fine, really. I need to charge my phone."

"Your phone can wait." Mom runs cold water over my bloody knuckles, and when I look into her exhausted, red eyes, I can see that she needs this—she needs to take care of someone, to put something right. So I let her wash my hand and wrap it in a clean towel.

"I'm sorry for yelling," I whisper, kissing the top of her head.

She squeezes my arm. "It's okay, sweetie."

In my room, I pull my phone charger out of the mess on my nightstand and plug it into the wall, stretching out on Adam's bed so I don't have to look at it. Poor Adam always kept his side of the room so shipshape but had to look at mine, which is almost as much of a wreck as I feel. I see clothes I keep forgetting to put away, my backpack slumped beside my bed, books spilling out to join the VHS tapes and video games on the floor, most of which are in the wrong cases. My sneakers kicked far away from each other, my aviator shades ready to fall off the edge of the dresser, and my bomber jacket left on my unmade bed.

I wish I'd been as tidy as Adam was.

Did I just say *was*?

I curse under my breath, picking up my blood-smeared phone and calling Adam's number again. For the millionth time, I listen to it ring, ring, ring. I know it won't be Adam who answers, and that knowing is a knife in my chest because all I want is to hear him pick up, to know it's not true, he's not—

"Jack Stevenson?" Orca asks.

"Hi, Orca." My voice breaks like a thirteen-year-old's, and goddamn it, I am *not* going to cry, not on the phone with this girl.

"Are you all right?"

"Yeah, yeah, I'm fine. Tell me more about your island."

"What about it?"

"Anything. How big is it? What's the terrain like? How long does it take to get around it?"

"It's not very big," she says. "I can walk around the whole thing in less than a day. Some of the coastline is sand, and some of it's rocky and steep. You have to climb when you get to those places if you're walking around the perimeter. It's not hard, though. I'll go out looking tomorrow after Papa leaves for the mainland. Lucius can help me search."

"Who's Lucius? I thought you said—"

"My dog. He's a good tracker, and I have some of your brother's stuff, so he'll be able to pick up a scent."

My racing pulse begins to calm. Not because of this tracker dog, but because of the way Orca says it. With hope in her voice. She's the only one who still has hope. I know she's naive—for god's sake, I'm probably the first person besides her dad that she's carried on a real conversation with.

But she has hope.

When no one else does.

"Thank you," I whisper, my voice in tatters.

"Of course. It's no trouble at all."

"No, I mean, *thank you*… for believing. You're the only other person besides me who has hope that he's still alive. I can't tell you how alone I feel." I press my eyes shut, pulling in a deep breath. "Tell me something else about you."

"About me? Like what?"

"I don't care. Anything. Just keep talking. What's your favorite color?"

"Um… indigo."

A sad laugh tumbles out of me. "Indigo."

"The color at the very edge of the sea when the sunset has faded. Did you ever notice it's not really blue? It's indigo."

I've never noticed.

"What's *your* favorite color?"

"I don't know. Red, I guess."

"What kind of red?"

I look down at my busted hand wrapped in the towel, a circle of blood seeping through the fabric.

"You know, actually, I think I like indigo better." I realize that I'm going to have to ask her some better questions. "What's your favorite movie?"

"Movie?"

"Yeah. Or do you not have those on Recluse Island."

Orca giggles. "No, we don't."

"You're kidding. TV?"

"What?"

"Do you have a *television?*"

"Papa has a tele*scope.*"

"No, no, not a telescope. TV is like… it's on a screen. And you can watch shows and movies and play video games."

"What is a video game?"

Okay, now I *really* feel like I'm talking to an alien.

"I don't even know how to describe them to someone who doesn't know. Have you *seriously* never seen a movie?"

"No. What is it like?"

I shrug. "It's like… moving pictures. Like you're watching a story in the format of scenes captured and playing inside the screen. It's so hard to put into words 'cause you have to *see* it."

"I guess so."

"Do you even have electricity?"

"Yes, of *course.*"

"Don't say it like, 'oh my god, that's so obvious, Jack, you dummy.' So far, you sound like you're on a different planet."

Orca grunts. "I could say the same of you, boy."

"Boy? When did I become 'boy'?"

She laughs. "To me, a boy is as strange as movies or video games. I've never seen one before."

A grin tugs at the corner of my mouth. "Well, I'm technically an *adult* now, thank you very much. I turned eighteen in April."

"I just turned eighteen, too," Orca says.

"Really?"

"You sound surprised."

"Just thought you were younger. You sound younger."

"Well, so do you."

I scoff. "Hey—!"

"It's not a bad thing! Papa says it's good to seem younger than you are. That way, when you're old, you still look young."

"Your papa sounds like a controlling jerk."

"What?"

"I mean, he doesn't let you have any fun? No friends, no movies, no video games?" I shake my head. "You've probably never had pizza, either."

I'm being sarcastic, expecting her to come back with, *Of course I've had pizza, you dummy.*

But then she goes, "What's pizza?"

I blink. "You're joking."

"No, and I'd rather not hear about any more things from the Otherworld. I can't have them, so—"

"The *Otherworld?*"

I'm probably going to wake up in a second and find that all of this has been a dream or a hallucination. There's no way this girl is real.

"The mainland," Orca explains. "I call it the Otherworld. Because it's all the way out there, and I'm all the way out… here. Alone. Like you said. No friends, no movies, no pizza. But Papa is good. He loves me, and he wants me to be safe."

"By keeping you like a prisoner on Alcatraz?"

"He doesn't like the Otherworld. He thinks it's full of dangers and evil and that it's better to stay away."

"Well, that's fine for him if he wants to live like a hermit. But what about you?"

Orca falls silent for a moment. "He thinks I'm not strong enough to handle the real world."

"That's bullshit. I don't even know you, and I know that's bullshit."

Another pause. Then Orca replies innocently, "What's 'bullshit'?"

I can't stop myself from laughing. "Anything that isn't true."

It feels good to laugh again.

It feels good to have *hope* again.

Orca is going to search the island for Adam tomorrow. And if he's there, she'll find him.

Thank you, Orca. Thank you for being my lifeline.

THE SEARCH

orca

I've never seen Papa scared. Not even in the blackest storms, when the wind blows so fiercely it seems like the waves could reach up and swallow our lighthouse whole. When I was younger, I would run from the loud cracks of thunder, run to Papa. He would hold me and tell me stories about the orcas, how they watched thunderstorms from under the waves. He would secure the shutters and wait out the storm with me. And never once did I catch a glimpse of fear in his eyes.

Until today.

I sit in the living room and watch Papa slide his last few supplies into his messenger bag. Dark clouds of anxiety gather in his eyes as he scans the room.

"I'll be fine, Papa."

"I know you will," he says, but the fear still lingers on his face. He checks his pocket watch. "The boat should be here in ten minutes."

I nod solemnly. "Okay."

I'm not afraid to be alone. I feel wholly capable of managing things while Papa's away. The lighthouse, the chickens, Lucius, the shutters if it storms. I know it all so well, I could manage it in my sleep.

No, it is not the fear of being left alone that has twisted my stomach into a knot—it's the fact that I haven't told Papa about Jack Stevenson or the lost pilot or the strange treasures that drew me into this bizarre predicament.

I have three very good reasons for not telling him.

First, because Jack asked me not to. And the strange boy sounded so desperately sad, so out of his mind with grief and fear—I couldn't deny him my secrecy. I know nothing of the foreign ways of the Otherworld; perhaps his people really would have forbidden the search for his brother if I'd told Papa.

Second, I don't want to burden Papa with anything else. If he knew about the missing pilot, he might call off the whole trip to the mainland, invoking some nonsense about my not being strong enough to handle a stranger from the Otherworld.

Which leads me to my third and most important reason:

The search for Adam Stevenson, if successful, could be the solution to all my problems. Nothing would make Papa see my true strength and capability quite like rescuing a stranded pilot, completely on my own with no help from anyone.

This, I decide, could be the true test of my fortitude. The proof that I *am* strong enough to handle the Otherworld. So I keep it a secret.

I follow Papa out to the beach, where a boat pulls up ten minutes later. The man on the boat is gray-bearded and half-hidden behind sunglasses. Papa wraps me in a fierce hug, and I breathe in the scent of rain and salt and hard work.

"Goodbye, Papa," I whisper.

His strong arms hold me a moment longer, then fall away. "I will come back to you as soon as I can, my sweet girl." He smiles softly, but the fear still lingers in his gray eyes.

It's not until Papa is on the boat, streaking off across the waves, shrinking smaller and smaller as the fog spirits away the small craft—

It's not until he's gone that I wonder:

Perhaps it isn't me he's afraid for, alone on the island.

Perhaps he's afraid for himself.

Alone in the Otherworld.

"LUCIUS, COME!"

The sound of dog nails scrabbling on wood echoes through the house as I tie my cloak around my neck. Lucius skids to a stop beside me, eager for food.

"No, you already had your breakfast. Now listen."

He sits. Ears perked.

"We're going out to search for Adam Stevenson. He looks like this." I hold up the photograph I found in Adam's wallet. "He's the one on the right"—indicating the older one, with the dark hair and the sharp jawline—"and he smells like this." I open the sack and let Lucius take a long sniff of the interior.

"Lucius," I say, command in my voice, "find."

He romps out the open door and down the steps. I fly after him, into the misty gray morning. Lucius always gets excited for the first part of a "find." Eager to prove himself, he voraciously sniffs the world as if his next meal depends on it… until he picks up the scent of some delicious distraction, and I have to call him back for another command.

I've decided the best course of action would be to follow the coastline. If Adam endured a roughhousing from the ocean, he could be stranded on the beach or perhaps the rocks. I've mentally prepared myself for the possibility that he might be in bad shape—recalling the first aid guides Papa made me commit to memory when I was old enough to "stomach such things." We both needed to learn basic medical procedures in case the need ever arose. Today I am glad of my knowledge.

Steeling myself with as much confidence as I can muster, I set off with Lucius by my side. We skip down the big rocks to the hard gray sands below, whitewater crashing on one side and skinny pines reaching up on the other. The shoreline stretches out ahead of us, so tranquil and familiar— yet today it looks more lonely and desolate.

I've spent countless mornings wandering these beaches with Lucius, my feet sticky with saltwater, my pockets stuffed with shells. I'm used to these long, lonesome walks on the strand, yet somehow it feels so different knowing that Papa is not back at the lighthouse.

I shake my head to dispel the shadow of fear creeping up on me.

I want this. I want to prove to Papa that I can handle a challenge; I can cope with the dark parts of life. I am not like a delicate branch of coral; I am like an orca. The top predator of the ocean.

Pulling the hood of my cloak up over my head, I whistle to Lucius, who has forgotten that we're tracking a human, not a squirrel. He bounds back to me obediently, sand spraying.

"Lucius, find."

We trek onward, Lucius sniffing furiously, me scanning the ground for any trace of human life.

For the first hour, we find nothing. I've long since lost sight of the lighthouse over my shoulder, which makes me wonder:

If I *do* find Adam out here, and he's unconscious, how in the world will I get him to the warmth and safety of the lighthouse?

Lucius stops at that very same moment to look at me, as if also questioning my ability.

"Oh, I'll think of something," I mutter. "Let's just find him first."

That's when I spot some unusual indentations in the sand up ahead. I quicken my pace, taking note of the tide lines. The markings begin where the wet sand ends, staggering between rocks and knobs of driftwood. Even up close, I can't confirm they are footprints—and Lucius trotting past this evidence without a backward glance quashes my small flicker of hope. Still, he's not *really* a tracker—and perhaps Adam's shoes don't smell anything like the inside of the backpack.

I examine the mysterious prints, following them to a weather-beaten log, where they abruptly end. I examine the log for any disturbance from a pair of boots, but there is nothing.

Lucius barks, light-years ahead of me.

"Coming, coming," I huff, hopping off the log.

I reach into my pocket and take out the finely crafted compass I found in Adam's backpack. The needle quivers as I walk, ever true to the north.

Everyone thinks he's dead. Jack's panicked voice echoes through my mind. *The coast guard quit the search, and my parents are giving up. They think he's dead, but he's not, he's not...*

Poor Jack. I barely even know him, yet my heart aches when I remember the way his voice trembled through the phone last night, so desperate, so broken. So close to slipping off the edge of sanity.

He must love his brother very much.

THE DAY PASSES SLOWLY. Side by side, Lucius and I scout the entire coastline of the island—picking our way through fields of driftwood, climbing up rocky slopes, edging along the tree line to peer down at the tidewater smashing against the shore. My legs grow tired of hiking, and my eyes grow weary of surveying the landscape, but my heart never ceases to anxiously press against my ribs, thudding with equal parts hope and dread.

I still haven't sorted out what I'll do if he's badly injured or unconscious. Or even worse, *what if he's dead?* I couldn't leave him wherever I found him—but I couldn't drag his body back to the lighthouse, either. How would I manage?

How would I tell Jack?

The lighthouse is coming back into view now—rising from the northern tip of the island to shine courageously across the dark gray sea. The clouds at the horizon have split open to allow the sun her one and only appearance of the day, skipping orange flares across the tops of the waves before the ocean swallows her up.

Lucius pants beside me, his pink tongue unfurled and his eyes dewy with fatigue.

"You did good, boy," I say, scratching his head. "We'll both sleep well tonight, huh?"

As I climb the small grassy knoll up to the house, I wonder what Papa is fixing for dinner—but then I see the unlit windows and remember: Papa is gone.

It's such a strange and lonely feeling, stepping into a dark, cold house.

I shiver and turn on a few lamps in a small attempt to gladden the empty living room.

Lucius sprawls out on the kitchen floor with a great sigh and waits for his supper. I feed him first, then start fixing something for myself—shoving a chunk of bread in my mouth to kill my hunger pangs. The wood stove has gone out, so I forgo cooking and instead toss a variety of fresh vegetables into a wooden bowl: sweet young peppers, chopped tomatoes, strawberries, snap peas, and a few cold potatoes baked to creamy gold perfection.

I hum every song Papa ever taught me while I prepare the food, keeping myself company as best I can. But it's not the same as having Papa here. I never noticed how much space one soul can fill.

When I sit down at the table to feast, the silence is deafening. Lucius has already passed out, and even when he *is* awake, our one-sided conversations aren't exactly satisfactory.

I take Adam's phone out of my pocket and flip it open. As much as I hate to be the bearer of bad news to poor Jack, I know I should update him on the search. I need to let him know that I tried, and that I haven't given up.

The phone only rings once before Jack's voice bursts through the speaker. "Did you find him?!"

My heart flinches. "No, Jack. I'm so sorry. I did look, though! I walked around the whole island and searched the coast very thoroughly. Lucius helped me too. But we didn't find Adam."

There is a long, sad silence; then Jack's voice returns. "Not even… a trace of him?"

A sharp pang of sorrow clutches me. "I'm going to look again tomorrow."

"You already looked, Orca—"

"But I didn't search the woods! I didn't have time. I'm going to look there tomorrow. He may have gone to find shelter—"

"He must've been injured in the crash. He couldn't have gone that far."

"You don't know that."

"I *do* know that!" Jack roars. "He crashed his plane, for Christ's sake. I saw it! It looks like it went through a goddamn war, and it's going to be a miracle if he's alive! It's going to be a miracle…" His anger burns off abruptly, leaving nothing but ashes of grief in his voice.

"Don't say *if*, Jack."

He remains silent.

"I promised you last night, and I'll promise you again: if your brother is on this island, I *will* find him."

A sharp inhale. He's crying.

"And for what it's worth," I add, "I believe he *is* alive. I have a sense about it."

"What, do you have ESP or something?" Jack questions, his voice wobbling with tears.

"ESP?"

"Extrasensory perception. Like, you know something without hearing it or seeing it."

"Yeah," I say, nodding. "I do. Don't you?"

"No."

"You don't ever just have a feeling about something in your heart? Like a frequency that only you can hear?"

"I don't know. Sometimes, I guess."

"So, in your heart… do you *really* feel that Adam is dead?"

There is a long silence; then Jack whispers, "No."

A weak smile touches my lips. "There. ESP."

MORTAL WEAKNESSES

jack

She's so strange.

But at the same time, so cool.

Probably the strangest, coolest girl I've ever talked to.

I still haven't told anyone about her; I'm afraid that Mom and Dad will think I've gone nuts. Afraid that I actually *have* gone nuts and I'm just hallucinating Orca and none of this is real.

But I'd rather live in a fantasy than accept that Adam is gone.

My parents' acceptance has already choked the air out of our home. I can't breathe when I'm there. I can't look Mom or Dad in the face. I can't talk to them about Adam. But I can't talk about anything else, either. What the hell do you talk about when your only brother is missing, presumed dead? The weather?

I've spent the whole day at the port, cleaning up his hangar (which was already clean, go figure) and examining the damage to his Beaver. Sitting in the pilot's seat and asking myself what could have happened before he crashed. Wondering how Orca's search was going. If it hadn't been so damn foggy today, I could have flown out there myself and helped look for him. When Orca finally called and told me that she'd found nothing, it felt like another punch in the gut.

But still, she believes he's alive.

She believes, and she makes me realize that I still believe, too. I still feel it in my heart, like she said—a frequency only I can hear.

She's right.

We can't give up.

I *won't* give up.

I'm sitting outside the hangar, my back against the wall, looking out at the twilight. Docked floatplanes rock gently on the low tide as fingers of fog wrap around them, night settling in. Orca, my lifeline, is still on the phone with me.

"Maybe it would help you to talk about him," she says softly.

"I don't think so."

"Why not?"

"Because I… I just get angry."

"Don't think of him as gone," Orca says. "Just tell me the good things. How old is he? I don't think you said."

I take a deep breath, tipping my head back against the wall. "Twenty-eight."

"Oh wow. So he's much older than you."

"Yeah. He's like… my second father, to be honest. Even when I was a little kid, he seemed like a grownup. He was always my best friend, though. Bossy older brother, of course. But he made me feel like a man by hanging out with me. He taught me everything. How to fish, how to shoot, how to drive… how to fly. Couldn't teach me to clean up my side of the room, though."

Orca hums a laugh. "Ah, so you're messy?"

"I think I'm just human. Adam is… a god. But he puts up with my mortal weaknesses. With a little correction. I don't mind. He's right, most of the time. And I'd give my left arm to hear him scold me again."

"Your left arm?"

"I'm left-handed. It's an expression."

"Ah. Otherworlders have a lot of expressions, don't they?"

A surprised laugh stumbles out of me. "Uh, yeah, I guess we do."

"So what are these 'mortal weaknesses'?"

I frown. "Wait, what? Mine?"

"You *are* the mortal here."

I laugh, feeling a blush race up my neck. "Uh, I don't know. The usual. Laziness. Arrogance. Losing my temper. Flirting too much."

"What's flirting?"

That one throws me. I hesitate, not sure how to describe it. "Flirting is… just talking, really. Making jokes and… saying things. When you're attracted to someone and you want to get to know them better. Just have fun with them, you know?"

She doesn't know. The only "someone" she's ever known is her father. Clearly, he's done a good job of sheltering her.

"So," I say, changing the topic, "your dad left for the mainland this morning? Does it feel weird to be all alone?"

Orca sighs wearily. "Yeah, it does, actually. I thought I wouldn't mind it, but it's so… lonely. I keep thinking he's up in the lantern room, and then I remember that he's gone, and it's such a cold, sad feeling. You know?"

I press my eyes shut. "Yeah. I know."

"I want this, though. I want the chance to prove to him that I *am* strong. That I have what it takes to handle the Otherworld."

"You shouldn't have to prove it, Orca. Your father should let you come to the mainland if that's what you want. You're an adult now—he can't keep you prisoner."

"He doesn't keep me prisoner."

"Really?"

"Yes, really."

"So you *want* to stay on Recluse Island for the rest of your life?"

"No, of course not! I want to see the mainland, I told you that. I just…" Orca takes a deep breath and lets it all out again. "I don't want to hurt Papa. He's a good person, and he just wants to keep me safe."

"Yeah, well, there's a difference between *safe* and *suffocated.*"

"I know," Orca murmurs. "And I think I can make him see that, in time. It's been such a relief to be able to talk to someone about it. To be able to talk to *you*, a real person from the Otherworld! Sorry, you must think I'm so odd."

"Are you kidding? You're cool. You're... unlike anyone I've ever met. Just because you don't know what video games and movies are doesn't make you *odd*. You probably know more about survival than I do. That's badass, Orca. I think probably everything about you is badass."

"What does 'badass' mean?"

"You know, like, cool. Strong, confident. Awesome."

Orca falls silent for a moment. "Are you flirting with me, Jack Stevenson?"

"What? No."

She bursts out laughing.

"No, I'm *not*," I insist.

Damn it.

I want to know what she looks like.

We say goodbye after that so she can get some rest and start looking for Adam again first thing in the morning. For a while I just sit on the ground outside the hangar, watching darkness fall.

Thinking about Orca.

THAT NIGHT, I CAN'T SLEEP. I lie awake, my gaze drifting lifelessly over Adam's empty bed. Finally, I push back my sheets and cross the moonlit room, stopping in front of the bookshelf. It's loaded with his books, boring stuff like philosophy and business. Propped up in the gaps are a few pictures Mom put there forever ago. The basketball team photo from my junior year. Dad with Adam at the 1979 all-star baseball game in Seattle back when he was ten years old, grinning from ear to ear.

And then, me and Adam—the day I got my wings.

We're standing on the dock in front of his Beaver, squinting into the sunlight. I was fifteen, on top of the world—literally. He was my hero. So high above me, even if it looked like only two inches to everyone else. His arm around my shoulders, his aviator shades clipped to his bomber jacket. He laughed as Mom held up her camera and told us to smile. *Jack can't stop smiling*, he said. I shoved him. But he was right.

"God, Adam," I whisper now, alone in the darkness. "Where are you?"

I slide out one of his philosophy books, just to flip through the pages and look at his annotations. Highlights, underlines, ideas scribbled in the margins. His handwriting.

Eventually I climb back into bed and watch the moonlight slide down the wall. It makes the dark less black and more blue.

Indigo.

I shut my eyes and think about how I would describe Orca to Adam if he were here right now.

"She's, like, the purest person in the world," I murmur to the empty space where my brother should be. "She's innocent and naive, but she's also funny and smart and way stronger than she thinks. She makes me laugh when I feel like I'm falling through the bottomless pit of hell." I pull in a shaky breath and let it rush back out. "And with any luck, you'll meet her before I do."

TENENS INFINITUM

orca

I overestimated my ability to sleep.

The house is so terribly quiet. Every gust of wind seems to howl louder than usual. Every crash of the tide on the rocks could be construed as distant thunder. Every occasional snore from Lucius startles me. *Was that a knock on the door?*

I'm fidgety and restless, tossing and turning in the moonlight until I finally realize that I might as well turn on a light. Somehow, insomnia in the dark is much more unsettling than insomnia in the golden glow of a bedside lamp.

My body is sore from trekking around the island, but my mind is still racing. I know it's Papa's absence setting my nerves on edge, but there are reasons beyond that. Reasons to do with Jack Stevenson. I succeeded in taking his mind off his troubles—in getting him to laugh, even—but I have not succeeded in the task I undertook so boldly: to find his brother.

The failure eats away at my conscience like a receding tide eroding the shoreline.

I must try harder tomorrow. I must overturn every stone in search of evidence. Jack is right; I do have extrasensory perception. I can sense that I'm not alone on my island.

Adam's notebook lies on my nightstand, untouched since I first picked it up and read that rather strange notation on trust and mistrust.

I wonder what else he wrote in here.

Unable to resist my curiosity, I open the journal to a random page and begin to read.

01/14/96

The butterfly effect

Butterflies and hurricanes: what do they have in common? We're always asking ourselves that, but about "real-world problems." And it seems there is no urgency to connect the dots—to understand how our infinitesimal decisions might impact the world in massive ways. Good and bad. Innocent or intentional. Even the butterfly cannot turn back time.

Tenens Infinitum

And speaking of time...

Does it even exist? Humans look for patterns in order to make sense of chaos (even chaos must have a THEORY—see the butterfly effect). Thus, we find patterns in the seasons, which repeat themselves. On and on, ad infinitum, with no contextual numbering system to record the PASSAGE of time— humans invented that. So time, then, is infinite and immeasurable without our computations.

But theorists would argue that time must progress because there are such things as the past, the present, and the future. The past is gone, and the future isn't here yet, which means you can only live in the present, correct? Maybe not. When we go back to the past and vividly remember something or speak about that memory with someone else, we relive it. We even say, "Don't relive it," for negative memories. Most people think that is just a figure of speech, and maybe that's how everyone uses it. But on an anatomical level, it's literal. If you go back (in your mind) and vividly remember an event, the same mental and emotional reactions are occurring in your brain... the same neurons firing and wiring together, creating the same physiological responses in your body. So on a cellular level, we ARE "reliving it."

Or perhaps we're returning to that moment in time, LITERALLY, transcending the human-made constructs of Time and Space to access something beyond the third dimension.

At this point, I am lost. Still, the words draw me in like a spell, releasing my mind from the grip of anxiety and pulling me into a world beyond the mainland—the world of Adam Stevenson's mind.

I turn the page and continue reading.

01/22/96

More than one universe?

They say the universe is infinite. But how far does infinite go? To infinity, obviously. We can't even imagine infinity because our brains are finite. Yet we can conceptualize infinity—funny. Anyway, before the discovery of quantum mechanics, the top-dog physicists pretty much closed the book. Nothing new to see here; move along. Or keep studying atoms. But someone dared to ask, "What's INSIDE an atom?" And now we have quantum mechanics and string theory.

The question unlocks the door, not to the answer but to exploration.

The exploration ends when we decide on the answer.

But is there only ONE answer?

Is there only ONE universe?

continued

On his deathbed, Copernicus publicly released his controversial work that proved the sun, not the earth, is the center of the solar system. At the time, it was considered heresy. Now we can't imagine a time when people believed anything else.

Perhaps one day, we won't be able to imagine a time when people thought there was only one universe.

Theories differ, and I don't know which one seems most likely. But the idea that we exist in another universe, in another world, and have made a completely different assortment of decisions that have set us on the course of a completely different path in life... It's almost not so freaky as to be outside the realm of possibility.

Quantum physics allows this. So who are we to call it an impossibility?

scientia corrumpitur
knowledge corrupts

SOULMATES

"According to Greek mythology, humans were originally created with four arms, four legs, and a head with two faces. Fearing their power, Zeus split them into two separate beings, condemning them to spend their lives in search of their other halves." –Plato's The Symposium

I always thought the concept of soulmates was ludicrous. It's obviously a construct of ancient mythology, an explanation for the unexplainable—a feeling you have when you meet someone and feel like you've met them before. Like you've not getting to know them for the first time but rather remembering who they are... from another life.

Or perhaps from another universe?

I think people want to believe in soulmates because

That's where the entry ends, as if he was interrupted while writing the conclusion of this musing. And now, here it lies in my hands, unfinished. I have no idea what some of these words mean, like *Infinitum* and *Copernicus* and *soulmates*, but I enjoy the vicarious romp through someone else's thoughts. Adam's writing is so different from the perfectly polished science and biology books I grew up reading.

There are many previous entries in the journal, some of which are entire pages filled with words I can't read—another language. My eyelids grow heavy with fatigue, and eventually, I surrender to close them for a moment.

SOMETHING WARM AND WET touches my fingertips. I open my eyes to find morning light pressing through the window and Adam's journal lying open on my chest. Lucius peeks over the edge of the bed, licking my hand.

"Oh no, it's light already?" I bolt upright, shoving aside my blankets. "You should have woken me hours ago, Lucius! We need to search the woods today, remember?"

I stumble into my favorite blue linen jumpsuit, hurrying to fetch some breakfast for myself and Lucius. I run up to the lantern room to check on the light and examine the sky. Foggy mist hugs the shoreline, and to the west I spot a smudge of dark clouds gathering on the horizon. I watch them for several minutes but can't tell where they are headed. Perhaps out to sea. In any case, there is always a chance of rain in Washington. I can't let it stop me from searching the woods.

I fly back down the spiral staircase and into the backyard—heading straight for the chicken coop behind the house. When I swing open the door, they all squawk cheerfully and scatter in every direction to begin foraging freely in the grass.

"Lucius, come!"

The mongrel flies out the back door and zips to my side. We've trained him to leave the chickens alone, and he now regards them as family.

"Ready to search the woods? We have to be very observant this time. And stay on *one* path so we don't confuse ourselves."

I reach into my pocket and take out Adam's journal, letting Lucius sniff the pages.

"Lucius, find."

He sets off with vigor—leading with his nose, paws vanishing beneath the ferns and undergrowth. I follow his trail, the tall pines dwarfing me as I venture into the forest.

The silence thickens with the trees and ground cover. Young yellow saplings shoot up playfully at the feet of their weather-worn ancestors, and the scent of pine rolls up from the forest floor, mingling with morning dew. Golden fingers of sunlight cascade through clearings to drink up the moisture last night left behind. Songbirds chatter in every direction, warbling and mimicking each other—delighting in their secret language.

Lucius wades through the ferns, his head submerged, hard at work with his excellent nose. I trek forward slowly, putting my own faculties to use. I search for even the slightest disturbance, which is considerably more difficult in the forest than on the beach. I scan the ground for footprints, but I also check the spaces between trees where spiderwebs glisten in the sun, pearls of water sparkling on their threads spun so perfectly from one tree to the next—

This one is broken.

I step closer to examine the web better. It was once large and elaborate, but now the translucent strands hang listlessly in the soft breeze. It's about a foot over my head—the height of a man.

My heartbeat quickens as I stoop to scour the forest floor and notice a scuffle of golden pine needles.

Footprints.

"Lucius!"

His head emerges from the undergrowth.

"Come!"

He hops over, porpoising through the ferns and skidding to a stop at my side. I tap the disturbed pine needles.

"Find."

He sniffs the area and picks up a scent. Moving carefully, he begins tracking it—forward, through the trees, over a log, and veering off to the left. I follow a few paces behind him, searching for more clues.

My heart pounds, hope reawakening in my chest. We're onto something. I can feel it. We're going to find him.

Lucius's head snaps up. He looks to the right as if he's heard something.

I scan the woods around me but see nothing.

Only trees behind trees behind trees.

"What is it, Lucius?"

He sniffs the air delicately, as if pulling apart the layers of scents in his mind. I wait, listening and scanning for anything out of the ordinary, my heart hammering in my chest.

Without warning, Lucius bolts forward with reckless abandon, sending up a cloud of pollen in his wake.

That's when I see a squirrel ahead, flying over the ground in a gray blur of panic.

"Ugh, Lucius, no! We're supposed to be—" I let out a furious growl, chasing after him. My feet race over the soft earth as I dart around trees in pursuit of my dog. But no matter how loudly I shout his name, he doesn't listen. Squirrels are the only creatures that usurp me on Lucius's scale of loyalty.

At last, the offending squirrel chooses a tree to escape into. I see the frantic animal claw its way up the trunk and disappear into the canopy, leaving a small explosion of leaves in its wake.

Lucius skids to a halt, jumping against the tree and barking viciously as if the squirrel will take this as a friendly invitation to come down.

"Lucius!" I'm using my scolding voice now, and he knows it.

He gives me a mischievous side-eye and dares to bark a few more times before I grab him by the scruff of his neck.

"Bad boy," I mutter, dragging him away from the tree. "We were doing so well before you saw that squirrel. We were onto something! Now we're going to have to find those footprints again…"

But that's the thing about the forest—everything looks the same. I should have taken note of some landmarks near the broken spiderwebs and the footprints.

Lucius lopes beside me, panting with his pink tongue out, trying to win back my affection. Futile—I'm focused on the woods around me, scanning every space between the trees for broken cobwebs. But alas, the sun has vanished behind the clouds, bathing the forest in shadow and making the spiderwebs disappear.

After wandering for another ten minutes to no avail, I accept that I've lost the small but promising trace of Adam.

Or was it Adam?

Perhaps I imagined the footprints. Perhaps the spiderwebs had snapped some other way. Perhaps Lucius was tracking that silly squirrel the whole time.

Still, we carry on. I occasionally open Adam's journal and tell Lucius to "find." I check the compass to be sure I'm not going in circles. And I walk. Ever onward, I walk.

As the hours pass, the clouds above grow denser and dim the forest to a grayish-blue gloaming. It looks like rain. I draw the hood of my cloak over my head and continue scouting as best I can in the low light.

When my stomach burns with hunger, we stop for a short break under a tree. Lucius rolls around like a puppy in the grass while I unwrap a small pouch of almonds and two hard-boiled eggs. I devour most of the food but give Lucius one of the eggs because I forgive him for chasing the squirrel.

That's when it starts to rain—big, cold drops falling hard on my shoulders. The canopy shields me from the elements, but it also makes it difficult to tell how heavily it is raining outside the forest. If the wind picks up, I'll have to turn back.

I stand up and brush the stray pine needles off my hands.

"All right, Lucius, let's—"

Blood.

My heart thuds when I see a streak of dark red smeared on my right hand.

I look down at the place I was sitting moments ago. At the base of the tree trunk, I see a scuffle of pine needles among my footprints. When I take a closer look, I find a few oak leaves curiously stuck together, smudged with blood.

I straighten up, my fingertips going ice cold as the rain falls faster. The birds have stopped singing, and a thin layer of fog is beginning to lift from the forest floor, shrouding the world in an eerie mist. Lucius gets a fat raindrop right in the eye and sneezes, then looks at me as if to say, *Let's go home.*

"But he's hurt," I whisper, turning in a slow circle to reexamine the woods around me. "He's out here somewhere, and he's hurt…"

I glance back down at the smear of blood on my skin. A raindrop lands in my palm, sending a thin trickle of watercolor red dripping down my arm.

I haven't been able to get a good look at the sky since I entered the forest—I have no idea how bad this rain will be. And the chickens are still out. The last thing I want to be is stranded in the woods during a thunderstorm.

But what about Adam?

He's injured. He's bleeding. And I can't find him. I can't find him…

Conflicting emotions grapple inside me, pulling me in two different directions. I would stay out here all night if it were up to me. I would scour every inch of the forest, leaving no stone unturned.

But I promised Papa I would take care of the lighthouse. I can't break my promise.

Lucius starts heading north, his tail drooping down between his legs. I know his animal instincts are more sensible than mine. I know it's time to head back home. So I follow him, wordless.

I was so foolish not to tell Papa about Adam Stevenson. He would have known a better way to search—he would have had maps, landmarks, and a firmer command to keep Lucius at heel. With two people searching, we might have found Adam yesterday.

But I didn't tell Papa. Stupidly—so stupidly—I thought I could handle this myself. I was so enamored of the idea that I could rescue Adam, help Jack, *and* impress my father in one fell swoop. But all I've done is cause more harm. What if Adam dies out here? What if it's all my fault?

My eyes are stinging with frustrated tears when I finally reach the forest's edge. Lucius bolts across the lawn, making a beeline for the back door—his tail still between his legs.

What on earth?

I frown, stepping out of the forest just as a fierce wind blows off the sea, flattening the long grass and tugging my cloak hood off my head. That's when I look up and see the monstrous storm in the sky.

GONE, GONE, GONE

jack

The sky looks pissed off.

I roll up the sleeves of my flannel shirt and grab the ax leaning against the barn.

That makes two of us.

Half a cord of wood is still piled at the side of our driveway under a gray tarp. Dad had chopped some of it, and Adam promised he would do the rest. I should have offered to help, but I hate chopping wood. Now the idea of slamming an ax into something over and over again sounds kind of satisfying.

I get to work, forgoing gloves (Adam never wears them) and wrapping my bruised knuckles around the ax handle. I steady a log on the chopping block.

SLAM.

Mom's been crying all day. Dad took the day off work to be with her. She's been cleaning things that don't need to be cleaned, cooking food none of us wants to eat. Just trying to keep herself busy.

I grab another piece of wood, lift the ax over my shoulder, and swing it down.

SLAM.

The first neighbor came this morning. Mrs. Dubois from down the road. The silver-haired lady who used to yell at Adam and me for stealing cherries from her tree back when she didn't have silver hair. This morning she brought my mother a casserole and her "condolences." She saw me for two seconds when I walked through the room. *Hey, Mrs. Dubois.* She smiled, sad eyes. *Hello, Jack. I'm so sorry about your brother.* I didn't reply. I just walked out.

The ax goes up, down—

SLAM.

Orca hasn't called me yet. She's searching the island again today, the woods this time. But no word yet. If this damn fog would lift, I could fly out there and look with her. Now there's a storm coming, and I'm worried that Orca might not know about it. Her dad must have a weather radio, right? Or maybe she can *sense* when a storm is coming. ESP.

I bend down to scoop up the armload of chopped wood, stacking it beside the barn. That's when I hear the screen door whine open, slam shut. I turn around and see Dad walking down the steps. He locks eyes with me, and I know right away I'm his target.

Shit.

I keep working like I never saw him—grabbing the next log, steadying it. I hoist the ax up over my shoulder.

"Jack."

SLAM.

"What?"

"I need to talk to you."

"I'm busy."

"Jack."

It's a warning this time.

I clench my jaw, grab another hunk of wood.

Dad takes a big breath and lets it all out again like the grief is suffocating him too. All that time in the house with Mom crying.

"Jack, do you want to talk about it?"

It.

"About what?" I bite out, not because I don't know what "it" is, but because I want to hear someone say his name. I can't believe nobody has the guts to say his name.

Not even Dad. He shrugs his shoulders and goes, "How you feel."

"How I feel?" My fingers go white around the handle of the ax. "This is how I feel—" I slam it clean through—the log splits with a shredding *CRACK.* "And since when did you become a therapist?"

Dad stares at me, unflinching. "I know you're going through a lot right now, Jack."

"A lot?"

"*Hell.*" Dad clasps a hand on my shoulder and looks me in the face. "You're going through hell right now. But so is your mother, and so am I. We still have each other, son. We need each other… to get through it."

I stare at him, into those eyes that used to be so alive. Those eyes so dark with agony and resignation.

"You're allowed to grieve, Jack."

Grieve.

Just the word makes his voice choke up.

"No," I rasp. "I will *not* grieve. Because Adam… is alive."

I yank my shoulder away from his hand and grab the split logs, hauling them over to the stack. Dad stands by the chopping block, watching me like I'm a stranger.

"Jack, your mother can't take this."

"Take what?"

"You being so stubborn, so unwilling to accept it."

I bark a sarcastic laugh. "And you're *willing* to accept it? You make me sick. Both of you—"

"Son."

"No! I won't accept it!" I grab the ax, getting right in Dad's face to yell, "I won't accept it until I see his dead body lying in front of me!"

Now my eyes are filling up, damn it. I slam another log onto the chopping block. Splinters bite into my fingers. Don't care.

I swing the ax up, my vision blurring—

SLAM.

I miss and get my blade stuck in the block instead. The log topples over, pissing me off more than it should.

"You need to pull yourself together," Dad says. "You need to think about your mother, what she's going through right now. If you refuse to let go of him, you're only going to make it harder on her—and on yourself."

Bullshit, bullshit, *bullshit.*

I steady the log again, my hands shaking. A low growl of thunder rolls through the sky.

"Your mother shouldn't have to be worrying about you right now," Dad railroads on. "She needs to be allowed to grieve and make sense of all this without *you* causing trouble."

"Causing trouble?" I roar, whirling to face him. "I'm chopping your goddamn wood!"

"And when you're done with that, you can repair the damage you did to the barn wall!" Dad bellows, stepping up to dwarf me by three inches. "I know you're angry, son, but so am I. Do you see me losing my temper? No! Because I *can't.* I have to be strong for my family."

"Well, sorry I'm not as *perfect* as you, Dad—"

"Jack!" Mom calls from the porch.

Dad snaps, "Don't you talk to me like that," as Mom yells my name again, leaning out the screen door.

"Yeah? What?" I holler across the driveway.

"It's going to rain! Put the windows up in your car—"

"'Kay, doing it—"

"And come inside!"

I shake my head. Like hell I'm going inside.

"Jack—"

"Yeah? What, Dad? You done lecturing me yet?"

"This is not a lecture. This is a conversation, which I was hoping would be man to man, but now I can see that's not possible since you're still a *boy*—"

Rage grips me like an iron fist around my chest. "You think you know what I'm going through, Dad? You think you know what it feels like? Well, you don't. You've never had a brother." My voice cracks, choking me up. "I know Adam isn't dead. He. Isn't. Dead. I—I have, like, extra… extra-sensory perception about it, okay? I know because I feel it, and I would *feel* it if he was dead. I would *know*, okay? I just—I would just know!" My words smash together like a train wreck, and now Dad is looking at me like I'm out of my mind.

Another rumble of thunder, louder this time. I feel it in the ground, and then Mom's at the screen door again, yelling my name.

"Jack!… Jack!"

I spin around. "What do you want?"

"Don't talk to your mother like that—"

"Stop *lecturing* me!"

"Stop back-talking—"

"JOHN." Mom puts her foot down. "This isn't helping. Come inside, both of you. There's lightning out there."

"Just a sec," I grumble, throwing the ax down. "Gotta put the stupid windows up." I shoot Dad a glare as I turn away. Out of the corner of my eye, I see him pull the tarp over the rest of the wood and return to the house.

Rain starts pelting down in hard, angry tears as I open my car door and turn the key halfway, putting up the windows.

You're allowed to grieve.

I'm so sorry about your brother.

You're on your own, Superman.

The screen door slams behind me when I walk inside. Mom and Dad are right there in the kitchen—her at the table, *grieving*, him shooting daggers at me like slamming the door is a felony. I start to leave the room, but Mom's voice stops me.

"Jackie."

A tired voice. Like a bus ran it over, then reversed and ran it over again.

I stop at the edge of the hallway but don't turn around. "What?"

"Look at your mother when she's talking to you."

Leave me alone, Dad.

I turn to look at them. "What?"

Mom smooths her hands over the table, and Dad's rubbing his forehead, and that's when I realize—

Some kind of conversation happened while I was putting my stupid windows up.

"What?" I say for the third time.

Finally, Mom answers. "We all have intuition, sweetheart. We all have feelings about things… that we can just *sense*." She looks at me, shaking her head, tears welling up. "But this isn't one of those things, Jack. We have no proof—nothing that even *indicates* he could have survived."

"That's not true," I blurt, pulling my phone out of my pocket. I didn't want to do this, but I can see that I have to. I'm grasping at straws, and this is my only chance to make them see. "Someone found his stuff. His backpack and his phone—they washed up on a beach, and this girl found them, and I've been talking to her, and she's been searching for him."

Mom gapes at me, tears standing in her eyes. Dad stares, too, like he did in the driveway. Like I'm out of my mind. The stoic, blank way you stare at a senile coot who's rambling on about people who don't exist.

"I didn't want to tell you guys because I didn't want to get your hopes up if it's nothing, but she's looking. She's searching the island—"

"What island?" Dad says.

"I… I don't know. She didn't tell me the name of it; I don't know if it even has a name—"

"And does this girl have a name?"

"Orca."

Dad blinks. "Like the whale?"

"Yeah, I know, it's weird. But that's not the point—"

"Jack." He reels in a steady breath. "You saw the plane. They found the wreck *seventeen* nautical miles off the coast. There is no way his backpack washed up on a beach anywhere."

I stare at him. "You think I'm making this up?"

"I think—" Dad sighs, looking at me with sympathy in his eyes. "I think this whole thing has been extremely hard on you, Jack. I think your mind… might be creating hope where there is none. *Evidence* where there is none."

"You think I'm nuts? Mom, do you think I'm nuts?"

"Sweetheart, I don't know—"

"You don't know?" I mutter a sarcastic laugh, pulling out my phone and dialing Adam. "Okay, fine, then—don't believe me. Talk to her yourself."

"Jack, I don't—"

"No, I'm gonna call Orca right now, and you can talk to her if you want *evidence*."

I hand the phone to Mom, but Dad's the one who grabs it with a big annoyed sigh like he just wants to get this charade over with. He puts the phone to his ear, and I wait for the look of astonishment to dawn on his face when Orca's voice says hello.

The kitchen is so silent, I can hear the *ring, ring, ring, ring…*

My heart drops.

"No answer," Dad declares, unsurprised.

Thunder rumbles outside.

I lunge forward and grab the phone. "She must be outside or up in the lighthouse or something—"

"She lives in a lighthouse?"

I nod. "Yeah. She lives there with her father, and he keeps the light. But he's gone to the mainland, so she's all by herself right now."

Dad looks at Mom, and I know what he's thinking. But he's wrong.

He has to be wrong.

My fingers tremble uncontrollably as I redial Adam and hold the phone to my ear. My heart hammers as I wait and listen to it ring…

And ring…

And ring…

And ring.

And all the while, Dad stares at me like I'm the one he's lost, not Adam. Like I'm behind a glass wall, and he can't communicate with me anymore, he doesn't know me anymore. I'm gone, gone, *gone*—

"She's real!" I yell, staggering backward and almost tripping over a chair. "I swear on my *life* she is real, and I talked to her—I talked to her just last night!"

"Jack." Mom stands up. "Stop this. We want to help you. Maybe you should let me hold onto your phone for a little while." She opens her hand, looking at me with those gentle eyes full of tears.

I shake my head. "No. No, I know what this is—"

"Sweetheart—"

"No! You think I'm out of my mind, and I'm not. YOU are. Both of you are!"

I turn and run down the hallway into my room—slamming the door. I twist the lock with my shaking fingers and collapse, sliding to the floor. I press my hands to my face, digging my fingertips in. They smell like pine and feel like splinters, but the pain is nothing compared to the knife in my chest.

I'm not crazy.

Orca is real. She *has* to be real.

Right?

Thunder booms through the sky, vibrating in the walls. I sit crumpled on the floor with my head in my hands as the rain starts pouring down in buckets.

Could it really all be in my mind?

I bury my face in my hands and lose it. Silently, so Mom and Dad don't hear, but the sobs still rattle my body like the thunder shuddering through the sky.

THE STORM

orca

A bolt of white lightning flashes across the western sky, followed by a deep bellow of thunder. I glance up from the pile of seasoned firewood to check the storm's whereabouts.

I don't have much time.

My heart has been racing since I returned from the woods and saw a great mob of angry black clouds charging across the water to the lighthouse. Based on the intensity of the wind, I can predict the worst of it will be upon us in ten minutes or less.

I rush to batten down the hatches, first by rounding up the last few chickens and shutting them in their indoor coop. I count seven little clucking hens before bolting the door. Next, I circle the house and secure the shutters, then scramble to haul in the chopped wood that has been stacked outside.

Lucius barks from the doorway—his warning bark, as if he thinks I can't see the storm approaching.

"Oh, Lucius, sometimes I wish you had two hands and could help me!"

I rush past him, dumping the wood on the kitchen floor before flying out the door for another armload.

That's when it *truly* starts to rain.

With another roar of thunder, the sky opens up. Gray sheets of rain roll through the troposphere, blurring the world beyond as it approaches, closer and closer—

I scoop up the last awkward load of wood and run into the house, slamming the door shut just in time.

Rain pours down, pounding against the shutters that block out the view and cocoon the house in darkness. I turn on a few lamps and get to work lighting a fire. The stove has been cold for two days now, choked with ash and smelling of creosote. I kneel on the floor and battle with the sooty beast—scooping ashes out into a bucket and stacking tinder in their place. I strike a match against the edge of the stove and carefully escort the tiny flame inside.

It catches within moments, but Lucius is still shivering. I sit on the floor and wrap my arms around him, sharing my body heat while simultaneously enjoying his. We're both damp and dirty from our romp in the woods, but I have much to do before I can shower.

First, I should call Jack. I inwardly recoil from the idea of disappointing him again, but it cannot be avoided. He'll be waiting to hear from me, and false hope is crueler than the awful truth.

So I fetch the phone from my room and flip it open to make a call.

Nothing happens.

The screen remains black, unresponsive to my touch. I turn it over in my hands, a curious sense of déjà vu washing over me.

"No, no, no," I murmur, jabbing random buttons in attempt to revive it. "What's the matter? Is the battery dead?"

Cold, looming loneliness overshadows me as I realize I no longer have a connection to Jack Stevenson. And with the satellite phone reserved only for emergencies, I am truly all alone.

As the rain continues pounding and the thunder keeps rumbling, I move on to my neglected indoor chores. Unorganized is too kind a word to describe the state of the kitchen. Trays of drying flowers and herbs lie in disarray across the table beside spools of thread and a half-sewn shirt; my harvesting basket sits open on a chair, still stuffed with tomatoes and peas and peppers and strawberries from yesterday morning. The firewood has been not so much piled as flung, and the dishes haven't been washed in two days.

So many responsibilities I've neglected while searching for Adam Stevenson.

And what do I have to show for it? Nothing. I have failed him and his poor brother, Jack. On top of that, I've also failed Papa. I promised him that I would watch the lighthouse—and what have I done instead? Scoured the island from beaches to woods, looking for an injured man who is still out there and probably catching his death—

All because of my incompetence.

Maybe Papa is right.

The weight of that notion crushes me as my bold words return to me like an echo. *I'm eighteen now. I am strong enough for the Otherworld.*

What on earth was I thinking?

I'm not even strong enough for *my* world.

THE STORM GOES FROM bad to worse. Deafening cracks of thunder rattle through bouts of whooshing rain, making Lucius whine like a baby and cower underneath the coffee table. He's never outgrown his fear of thunderstorms, unlike me—but this storm is the first in a long time, which has unsettled me.

From the lantern room, I have a panoramic view of the tempest outside. Billows of navy clouds eclipse the light of evening. Rods of silver lightning slash the sky and illuminate the swaying world for a split second. Bursts of light against huge, rough waves. Then darkness.

I wish Papa were here.

Somehow, even the warm, lamp-lit house feels lonely and frightening without him. The rumbling thunder sets my nerves on edge, and Lucius's panting and pacing doesn't help. I scold myself that I shouldn't be afraid—

not when I'm shut up safely in the house and no danger could possibly befall me.

But I can't stop thinking about Adam. Every time I shut my eyes, I see that smear of blood on my hand—his blood.

To distract myself, I bake. I wash my face and hands with hot water, tie up my unruly mane, and take out the mixing bowls. There is something therapeutic about measuring flour, swirling yeast, and kneading dough. It doesn't put all my anxieties to rest, but it helps to calm the storm in my mind.

I sing all of Papa's songs again as Lucius whines himself to sleep on the kitchen floor. Thunder rolls outside. Waves crash. The rain floods down.

A few hours later, the whole house swells with the scent of freshly baked bread, and the kitchen is spotless once again. Half a loaf of bread is hardly a nutritious dinner, but comfort food is all I can manage tonight. Afterwards, I take a warm shower and change into my linen nightgown and shawl.

I build up the fire in the living room and cuddle Lucius on the floor, my stockinged feet crossed on the hearth and Adam's journal spread open in my lap. Perhaps it's invasive to indulge myself in his private thoughts and deepest feelings. Journals aren't meant to be read by total strangers. But as I page through the book and look at Adam's handwriting, his scribbled-over mistakes, his doodles in the margins… he doesn't feel like a stranger to me. In fact, I feel like I've already met him, in another life.

Riffling back to the beginning of the journal, I find an entry dated the first day of this year.

01/01/97

For the first time in my life, I feel old. Maybe that's foolish, because 28 is not considered "old." But still, it's scary. Where did the last ten years go? Today Mom asked me if there's something I want in life. Something more than what I already have. I think she's fishing to know if I'll ever get married, but to be honest, I can't see that happening anytime soon.

Is it wrong not to have any grand ambitions for my life? I've worked my ass off to get to the place I'm at today, to have a job I love and be my own boss—and to help support my family so Dad doesn't have to work so hard. I think about all those years when I wasn't able to do anything to help my parents. Now at least I can make things easier for them. It's so rewarding just to pay some of the bills, to buy the groceries or get Mom flowers every week. To not hear Dad say, "We can't afford this. We can't afford that." That's all I've ever wanted. To give back to them after all they've given me.

Maybe it's high time I move out and get a place of my own, but I don't really see the point in doing that. Mom says she likes having me around, and unless I get married someday, there's no real reason to spend all that money on a house to live in by myself.

When I do eventually get my own place, I want to build it from scratch. I want to take a pile of bricks and mortar and lumber and turn it into a home. Something about that has always appealed to me. But only if I had someone to build it for—someone to dream with, someone to argue with over things like furniture and paint colors. Anyone can build a house. But it means something more when you're building a home.

The next few pages are filled with that strange foreign language I can't read—scribbles and arrows in the margins, little bits of English crammed in with the rest as if to explain the glorious disaster of it all.

The longer I explore the journal, the more it comes alive with a personality of its own. There is a kind of rough-edged magic in the chaos: jots of ancient languages trapped between lists of mechanical parts and scribbled philosophical rants. Even the torn-out pages, coffee stains, and smudges of black grease add character and history to the little book— proving it's been more places than I ever have.

Further in, I find another entry filled with Adam Stevenson's heart.

03/13/97

I can't stop feeling like I'm missing something. Like there is something beyond the things we all care about and keep busy with—society, work, politics, culture, even religion and philosophy, the "deeper" things that seem to give fulfillment and comfort to some people... Are they just distractions or (at best) reflections of something else, something we're all missing as a species?

What if it's like this: life as we know it is a river, rushing and moving, never stopping. Constantly busy. But there's something at the bottom of the river that's genuinely worth having... and nobody knows it's there because we're so caught up in the river itself. We can't even see what's at the bottom.

I don't know. Maybe this doesn't make sense. It's not really something I can put into words; it's just a feeling I get sometimes. If I talk about ideas like this with Jack, he just tells me I'm overthinking and I need a drink. Maybe he's right. Usually Jack's solutions have less to do with solving a problem and more to do with enthusiastically ignoring it.

I hope I've been a good influence on him. Sometimes I wonder. Jack is smart and more talented than he thinks, but he's also the stubbornest person I've ever met. I'm afraid if he ever takes the wrong path, there will be no getting him back. He's all or nothing with everything he does, hell-bent on getting what he wants. And he always knows what he wants. I guess that can be a good thing... better than living in stagnation and indecision. But sometimes I think even escapism can be stagnation, in a way. A frantic need to feel something (the river?) so you don't stop long enough to think about how frustrated and empty you really are.

But maybe I can't blame Jack for being a thrill-seeker. Maybe we all have our own ways of escaping ourselves.

God, I think I really do need a drink.

BOOM, BOOM, BOOM—

My eyes fly open.

Darkness sways around me as sleep releases its hold. Outside noises push into my awareness: the crashing waves, the howling wind, the rain beating against the shutters, and—

BOOM, BOOM, BOOM.

I jolt upright and find myself on the living room floor, my neck sore from leaning back against the couch. I must have dozed off while reading Adam's journal. Lucius jumps to attention beside me, a low, threatening growl building in his throat.

My first assumption is that a shutter has come loose, and the wind is banging it against the house. But still, a shadow of fear looms over me, holding my heart in its ice-cold grip.

BOOM, BOOM, BOOM, BOOM, BOOM—

Lucius barks, loud and fearsome, scaring me out of my skin.

It's not a shutter.

It's coming from the back door.

My heart is pounding harder than the rain outside as I climb to my feet. Lucius prowls through the living room, his head lowered, growling eerily at the dark and making chill bumps race across my skin.

Crisp thunder cracks the sky, vibrating through the floorboards. Lucius hesitates, staring at the back door.

Just when I think the banging has stopped—

BOOM, BOOM, BOOM.

Lucius barks, startling me again. My heart hammers louder, louder, louder as I step closer, closer, closer to the door.

I hang back, anxiety gripping me tight. But this moment won't become any easier by waiting on it. With one sharp breath of courage, I twist the knob and swing the door open.

No one is there.

A gust of wind blows cold rain inside just as a flash of lightning illuminates the doorstep.

The doorstep where no one stands.

I stare at the black void for a moment, watching the sheets of rain pour down. A burst of thunder echoes after the flash.

I slam the door shut and feverishly lock it—wet fingers slipping, trembling around the bolt. I brace my back against the door and gasp for breath, feeling choked. Lucius stands in the living room, watching me with questioning eyes.

What was that?

It sounded so much like fists pounding against the door. Could it have been… Adam? What if it was? What if he stumbled upon the lighthouse and knocked at the door, and I took too long to answer it?

I need to go outside and look.

Though the hands of terror clench my heart, I know I must find out.

But before I can grab my cloak from the rack—

BOOM, BOOM, BOOM… BOOM.

The front door.

Lucius jumps a mile and erupts into alarming barks punctuated by throaty growls. My heart leaps into my throat, but I don't hesitate this time. I rush across the living room, through the kitchen, and to the front door.

Lucius yelps, scrambling behind me as if warning me not to open the door—

I open it anyway.

Sheets of rain come slashing in at me. At first, I don't see anyone, then a bolt of lightning rips across the sky as I look down… and that's when I see him collapsed on the doorstep.

Adam Stevenson.

FLESH AND BLOOD

orca

I stare at the slumped-over man for a stunned moment before springing into action. Dropping to my knees, I take hold of his arm and try to help him to his feet, but he doesn't budge.

He's unconscious.

Swaths of rain blow relentlessly through the door as I struggle to pull him inside. But he's bigger than Papa and soaking wet. I roll him onto his back and hook my hands under his arms, hoisting him backward into the house with all my might. After some struggle and grunting, I manage to drag him in and shut the door, leaning back against it with a breathless gasp.

For a moment all I can do is stand frozen in place, breathing heavily as I stare at him lying in the dark. Lucius sniffs him curiously like something that washed ashore on the beach, then looks up at me with droopy eyes as if to ask, "Now what?"

I step around Adam and hurry into the living room to turn on a few lights. When I return to the kitchen, I take hold of his underarms and pull him the short distance to the living room, stopping in front of the fireplace.

Now in the lamplight, I can make out his face. It is a tattered replica of the striking man in the photo, but his most distinctive features are unchanged: his eyebrows, his nose, the sharp line of his jaw, which is now covered in stubble and smudged with dirt and blood. A painful-looking scratch runs down his cheek from the outside corner of his eye, like a fallen tear scarring his face.

I place a hand on his shoulder and gently shake him, repeating his name—but he gives no response.

Flesh and blood.

A real person.

From the Otherworld.

Is he breathing?

I tip his chin up slightly and lower my ear to his nose, listening carefully. Soft puffs of breath move in and out of him, tickling my hairline.

He *is* breathing.

He's alive.

A sigh rushes from my lungs as my anxiety unravels into pure relief.

"Oh, thank God," I whisper, blinking away the tears that spring to my eyes. "Thank God…"

He's alive, but he's far from all right. He's bleeding.

As my gaze sweeps over his body, I find blotches of red everywhere, staining his clothes. I spread a hand over his forehead—cold.

I need to get him out of these wet things. I need to see where he's bleeding.

Lucius sniffs Adam cautiously as I unbutton his flannel overshirt and begin pulling the sleeves off his muscular arms. That's when I see a dark red bloodstain near his lower ribs.

My pulse quickens as I reach for the hem of his T-shirt and pull it up, revealing his abdomen. Sure enough, a sticky open wound slashes across his lower ribs, leaving a cloud of dark bruises in its wake. I don't try to peel off his wet T-shirt—instead, I run into the kitchen and fetch a pair of scissors, then carefully slip the blades under his shirt and slice it to the collar and sleeves.

The shirt peels away in two halves, and I cast the scraps of bloody fabric away to better examine his bare chest and stomach. His skin is clammy and cold. The light of the fire casts flickering shadows over the hard, chiseled planes of his chest as I inspect his injuries.

Aside from scratches and bruises, the gash on his side seems to be the worst of it. I run my fingertips over the wound again, feeling for any broken bones. One spot on his lower ribs feels knotted and swollen, but I'm not sure if it's a fracture or just a deep bruise.

All things considered, his injuries don't seem too serious. I'll need to take off his pants to complete the examination.

I crawl down to his feet and unlace his boots, sliding them off and tossing them aside. Lucius stares at me, head tilted, as I reach for the clasp of his pants. They're made from a heavy cotton canvas material, thoroughly soaked, and freezing cold. I pull down the zipper, tugging gently to ease the pants off his body. His underwear slides off with them, and suddenly there is a naked man lying on my floor.

I've never seen Papa even *half-naked*, so the exposed anatomy of a male human is a bizarre sight. I try to direct my attention solely to examining him for wounds, but I can't stop my curious gaze from roaming every inch of his body, every etch and angle that constructs his arms, his legs, and all the strangeness in between.

More dark bruises wrap his shins and knees, and his left ankle is swollen to twice its size. I gently feel the bones and don't find anything too alarming—but how can I know how much pain he feels until he wakes up?

I rush to the bathroom to grab a roll of clean bandage, a wet cloth, a jar of aloe vera, and a bottle of witch hazel. In my bedroom, I pull the blanket and the quilt off my bed, then hurry back to the living room, where Lucius is keeping watch over Adam.

Once I've covered him up to the waist with the blanket and quilt, I get to work cleaning his wounds. I cut a strip of bandage and soak it in the witch hazel before gently washing away the blood from his abdomen. The bruise is worse than the cut itself, discoloring half his side with a shade of angry, throbbing purple.

He's still unconscious, eyes shut, shallow breaths, short dark hair a mess. The waning fire casts honey-colored light across his unshaven face, the sharp line of his cheekbones, the smooth skin of his neck. Even in such a state, Adam Stevenson is a thing of beauty.

I clean his wounds, apply aloe vera, and wrap them in fresh bandages. When I'm finished, I pull the blankets up to his neck and gently wash the dirt off his face using a damp cloth.

"Adam," I murmur close to his ear. "Adam, can you hear me?"

Evidently not. He lies as still as ever, his breath shallow but steady.

I want to call Jack and tell him that I found his brother and he's alive—but that's when I remember: the cell phone is no longer working. Should I use the satellite phone? Should I call the coast guard?

It would probably be the right thing to do.

But it's the very last thing I *want* to do.

Adam is here, and he's alive, and I *have* helped him… even if *he* was the one who found *me*. I don't need the coast guard to come and get him—I can take care of him just as well. When he wakes up, he can tell me the severity of his symptoms, and then we can alert the coast guard.

Besides, it's too stormy to take a boat or a plane out to the island. They will have to wait until the weather clears, so why bother them about it now?

I will call if Adam doesn't wake up in a few hours. But for now, I can manage.

I am capable.

I am strong.

I need to be.

For Adam.

For Jack.

For Papa.

So I wait. I slide a pillow under his head and lug his wet clothes into the kitchen, draping them over the backs of the chairs to dry. I throw more wood into the stove and put on some water to boil for tea—because there will be no going back to sleep tonight.

The rain and wind bellow outside the window, thunder rolling through the floor. Somehow, I have a sense this storm is far from over.

THE LIGHTKEEPER'S DAUGHTER

adam

I wake up feeling like there's a knife in my ribs.

I try to open my eyes—useless. My head pounds with a dull, unrelenting ache. I want to sleep for a lifetime. But now stabs of pain are awakening all over my body: my left ankle, my back, my arms, and my legs. Every part of me feels like it's been crushed.

I drag myself from the comforting void of unconsciousness to find that I'm lying on the floor of a small living room, warm and lamp-lit. Wood paneling on the walls. A soft rug underneath me. My eyes fall shut again as I remember what happened before I collapsed.

A lighthouse. I found a lighthouse on this deserted island after days of searching for civilization. The storm was raging as I banged on the door. No one answered, so I found another door. *Bang, bang, bang,* my fists pounded against the slippery wood. That's the last thing I remember.

The lightkeeper must've dragged me inside when I collapsed. God bless him. The warmth of the fire feels so good, it takes a moment for me to realize that my clothes are gone. I reach underneath the blankets with one hand and find myself butt-naked.

He must have stripped off my wet clothes. I've been shivering in them since the crash—the damp fabric started to feel like it was growing into my skin.

I take a deeper breath, and the knife stabs again—*damn*. My ribs. I touch the place where blood once seeped through my shirt and find a soft bandage wrapped around my middle, the cool sensation of ointment underneath.

That's when I hear a noise in the next room. Dishes clinking. Water pouring.

Water.

I've been so thirsty for so long, the deprivation is impossible even to describe. I was unable to collect any decent rainwater in the forest, and now that powerful thirst reaches past my pain to force the word out of my mouth.

"Water."

Even my voice is weak—the knife pushing up against my ribs, threatening me with another stab if I inhale too deeply.

I wait for the kitchen noises to fall silent, then I try again.

"Water."

Footsteps vibrate through the floor as someone comes rushing into the living room.

It's a girl, not the weather-worn man I was expecting. A *beautiful* girl with long, sandy brown hair and a look of surprised joy on her face. She's wearing a white nightgown, and she says my name like she's known me forever.

"Adam! You're awake!" She rushes over and kneels on the floor beside me. "How do you feel?" She smells like wildflowers, and her suntanned skin glows in the soft lamplight, messy hair crowning her angelic face.

I've forgotten her question.

"I need water," I say, my voice a gravelly rasp.

"Oh! Yes, of course." She jumps up and runs back to the kitchen.

Thump, thump, thump. Her footsteps vibrate through the floor under my head. I shut my eyes for a moment, and there she is again, gently lifting my head and bringing a ceramic mug to my lips. It's the sweetest water I've ever tasted.

She watches me carefully, her sea-green eyes reflecting the firelight. I don't know her—at least, I don't remember her. So how does she know me?

"Is your father the lightkeeper?"

She nods, sitting back on her heels.

"I want to thank him… for helping me."

"Oh, he's not here. He went to the mainland a couple of days ago. I'm the one who dragged you inside and bandaged you up. Your clothes are in the kitchen, drying."

Slowly, I realize what she just said.

She's the one who found me collapsed on the doorstep and dragged me inside. (Apparently, she is much stronger than she looks.) Not only did she bandage my wounds, but she took all my clothes off. Literally, *all* my clothes. They're drying in the kitchen. And I'm lying here naked under a quilt on her living room floor.

I stare at her, dumbstruck. "Oh. Well, uh… Thank you."

"Of course. I've been looking for you for days! First, I searched the beaches, but I didn't find anything. And then I was out in the woods yesterday, and I thought I found a trace of you, but then it started to storm, so I had to come back, and I'm so sorry I didn't get to the door in time. I heard you knocking. I just—"

"Wait," I interrupt; the frantic rush of her voice is hurting my head. "Why were you looking for me? How did you know—"

"Jack asked me to look for you."

"Jack… God, have they all been looking? Has the coast guard? Do they think I'm…"

The girl presses her lips together, nodding slowly. "The coast guard has given up, Jack said. Your parents, they assume you're dead."

The thought of it is enough to gut me. "Poor Mom. Poor Dad, poor Jack—"

"Jack doesn't believe it. He said he refused to accept it even though everyone wants him to."

This feels more like a knife than my broken ribs—it grips me with a kind of pain that brings tears to my eyes. My little brother, Jack, who never gives up.

"Where is he? How did you talk to him?"

"Through your phone," she explains, pointing to something I can't see on the other side of the room. "I found your backpack washed up on the beach. And I was able to communicate with your brother through the mobile phone. Only now it's not working, and I'm not sure why."

"Battery's probably dead," I murmur, shutting my eyes. "I'm surprised it lasted this long. You're going to have to plug it in."

"Oh, you mean to charge it? I didn't know how to do that. Would you like to use the satellite phone? Papa says it's only for emergencies, but I think this would be considered an emergency. You never answered me before. I need to know how you feel—does your head hurt? What's your last name? How many fingers am I holding up?" She spreads one hand in front of my face.

"Five. Stevenson. And yes, my head hurts but not that bad. I can see fine. I just…" I shift slightly and wince at the pain. "I got kind of banged up in the crash. My ankle—I think it's sprained. And my ribs—ow. Damn it."

The girl watches my suffering with worried eyes. "Yeah, your ribs looked pretty bad. I thought I felt something. Let me see."

Next thing I know, she's pulling the quilt off my chest and leaning closer to the bandage wrapping my ribs. A strand of hair slips from her shoulder and tickles my skin. I'm a little surprised by her boldness as she gently slides her soft fingertips over my ribs. Ugly purple bruises cover my abs where the yoke buried itself in me when I crashed.

"Tell me if this hurts," she whispers, and I want to tell her that *breathing* hurts, but I can't make myself speak or even comprehend anything beyond the feeling of her warm hand on my side.

Then the knife digs in.

I roar in pain, jerking away from her touch and gritting my teeth.

"I'm sorry, I'm sorry!" She shrieks a mortar round of apologies. "I'm sorry!"

"It's okay," I say through a grimace. "It's fine. It's just… they're definitely broken. I'll be fine."

"But your lung could be punctured."

"I don't think so. I've been wandering through the woods for days. It hasn't gotten any worse since the crash. It just… hasn't gotten any better."

A moment of quiet slips between us, thunder rumbling outside the window.

"Can't get the coast guard out here in this storm, anyway," I mutter with a sigh. "You can call when the storm's over. I just want my family to know I'm all right. There should be a… ow. An extra power cord. In the front pocket."

She stares at me.

"In my backpack."

"Oh!" she chirps and hops to her feet. *Thump, thump, thump*, into the other room.

I drag a hand over my unshaven face and flinch at the cut sliced down my cheekbone. I can't even remember where that happened, but I remember how the saltwater stung when I swam like mad to shore, leaving my wrecked Beaver behind.

Thump, thump, thump. She returns with my backpack in hand. I realize that I should probably ask her name, since it seems odd how much she knows about me and how little I know about her.

So I say, "What's your name?" but she doesn't hear because she's talking about the backpack, shoving her hands into the compartments.

"I'm not sure what you mean by the front pocket. I looked through all the pockets, and I didn't see anything." She kneels on the floor and offers me the backpack. I can't help but notice that it's empty. She must have taken everything out. Somehow, this feels more invasive than being stripped naked while unconscious.

"It's right here," I say, reaching into the inner flap of the front pocket. Out comes the charge cord for my phone. I look up into her face and try again. "What's your name?"

"Me?"

That makes me smile.

She laughs timidly, looking down. "Of course me. Orca. My name is Orca." For some reason, I feel like I already knew that. I feel like I've met her before. Like I'm not meeting her for the first time but rather remembering who she is.

"Well, thank you, Orca," I whisper, clasping her hand for a moment as I give her the cord. "Thank you for saving my life."

WORMHOLES AND COFFEE

Adam Stevenson is everything I imagined he would be. Jack described him as a god, and he certainly seems like an otherworldly being to me—a real, flesh-and-blood *person* right here in my house! I try to conceal my delight over the fact, since broken ribs and a sprained ankle seem too misfortunate to delight in.

"How did you crash, anyway?" I ask.

"Damn fog snuck up on me," Adam explains through a weary sigh. "I was coming back from Port Angeles, and visibility was fine, at first. But you know how the weather here changes in the blink of an eye. There was a front moving in, and I thought I was ahead of it, but then drizzle turned to rain, and the whole cloud base just… dropped. It was a nightmare. I felt myself descending, but I couldn't see the water. Until I hit it." He shuts his eyes, shaking his head slowly.

I frown. "I thought pilots have instruments to navigate that sort of thing."

"IFR pilots do."

When Adam sees my puzzled expression, he explains.

"IFR means instrument flight rules, which is what the pilots of jets and bigger planes use. It's a whole different game when you're flying a single-engine, like I do. Jets have instruments and equipment to fly through clouds for miles; no big deal. But when you're a bush pilot, it's all up to visuals. As in, what you can *see*. As a rule, I never push the weather, never fly below the minimums… but I don't think any pilot could have foreseen the situation."

"Well, everyone makes mistakes."

Adam grunts. "A mistake like that could cost me my license, my career… everything."

"So you do this for a living?"

He nods. "I guess you could call it an air taxi service, sort of. I mostly fly between the islands, sometimes up to Seattle. It took me a long time to build my business. *And* my reputation."

"Well, you survived. That has to be a point in your favor, surely."

Adam manages a tired grin. "I'm not sure I *would* have survived if it weren't for you."

"That's true, I suppose. But you could always leave out the part about an eighteen-year-old girl rescuing you."

The suggestion makes him laugh, which makes his ribs hurt, which makes him ask me for ibuprofen.

"Ibu-what?"

Adam regards me with a confused frown. "You know, like Advil."

I shake my head, still lost.

"Any kind of painkiller?" Adam's voice is bordering on desperation now, and I can see that he is suffering.

"I have some belladonna."

"Isn't that poisonous?"

"Not in small doses. It will make you tired, though."

Adam shuts his eyes. "I can't imagine being more tired than I already am."

I dash into the kitchen to fetch the belladonna, then scoop out the dose I usually take for migraines. I probably should consider that Adam is twice my size, but I would rather relieve less of his pain than poison him. Imagine my explanation to Jack: *I found your brother but accidentally killed him with belladonna.*

I pour more water and return to the living room, finding Adam half asleep already.

"I'm sorry, would you be more comfortable on the couch? I can help you up."

"No, that's okay," Adam replies quickly. "I'm fine where I am."

"All right. I'll stop bothering you now and let you get some rest. I'm going to leave you some of Papa's clothes. He won't mind you borrowing them."

Adam nods but doesn't seem to care what I'm saying. He takes the belladonna and lays his head back down, a wrinkle of pain still etched between his brows.

I hurry off again to Papa's room. When I open his dresser drawer, the familiar scent of him wafts out. It makes my heart ache all over again, but I remind myself of how proud he'll be of me when he comes back.

Adam has more muscle than Papa, but his clothes should fit well enough. I pull out a pair of worn jeans, a T-shirt, clean underwear, and socks, fold everything into a neat pile, and return to the living room.

Adam is asleep. I leave the set of clothes on the arm of the couch and turn down the lights, keeping the softest lamp lit. Finally, I kneel down and carefully lean over Adam, lowering my ear to his mouth—listening.

"What are you doing?" he whispers, breath against my ear.

I bolt upright. "Sorry—I was just making sure I didn't kill you with the belladonna."

He hums a laugh, opening his tired eyes to look up at me.

My face flushes warm. "Sorry. Go back to sleep."

He does, within moments. I fetch another blanket from my bed and decide to sleep on the couch for the remainder of the night in case he needs anything. Lucius curls up on the floor between us, and I snuggle under the blanket, watching Adam Stevenson sleep until my eyes grow too weary to stay open a moment longer.

1 AWAKEN TO THE PATTER of rain and find the house not much brighter than it was when I dozed off. Dawn has come; I can tell by the soft gray glow seeping through the cracks of the shutters.

It's still raining?

I draw in a deep breath, rolling over and stretching. At first, I'm surprised to find myself on the couch—but then the memories of last night flood back to me.

Adam.

I look to my left, where he had been sleeping on the floor. He's gone now, leaving no evidence that he was ever there to begin with—save the neatly folded blanket and quilt, which proves it wasn't all a strange dream conjured up by my overactive imagination. I had left a fresh set of Papa's clothes on the arm of the couch, but those have vanished, too. Lucius sits beside the coffee table, thumping his tail on the floor and watching me expectantly.

Pushing back the blanket, I stand and wrap my shawl closer around me.

That's when I hear Adam's voice mutter, "Damn it," from the kitchen. He's standing by the window, his back to me, the phone to his ear.

"Is something wrong?" I ask, stepping into the room.

Adam turns around at the sound of my voice, his frustrated gaze softening when he sees me. It's so strange to have an unfamiliar man in my house—and stranger still to see him wearing Papa's clothes. The T-shirt fits snugly enough that I can see the outlines of his muscles and the bandage around his ribs.

"I was trying to call Jack," he explains, nodding to the phone. "But he's not picking up. I thought maybe it's because of the storm…"

"Is it still storming?" I peer out the kitchen window through the swinging shutter, which must have blown open during the night. Rain pours down, and tidewater crashes on the rocks, sending up billows of white mist.

"Doesn't look like it's going to stop anytime soon," Adam says. "Does your dad have a weather radio?"

I shake my head. "We've always predicted the weather from reading the sky."

Adam stares at me, bewilderment in his eyes. They're blue. I hadn't noticed that before.

"How do you predict the weather in the Otherworld?" I ask, but before Adam can formulate a reply, the satellite phone explodes into shrill ringing.

At first, I don't recognize the sound—we seldom receive calls from anyone, so it startles me out of my skin whenever the phone starts ringing out of the blue. Papa has always been the one to answer calls, but today it's my responsibility. I rush into the living room, pluck the phone off its charging station, and press the green button.

"Hello?"

A rush of static. Then, through the fog, Papa's voice.

"Orca? Orca, can you hear me?"

"Yes," I shout into the receiver, trying to be heard over the whoosh of white noise. "Yes, Papa. Can you hear *me*?"

"Oh, thank God," he says with a sigh of relief. "I tried to reach you, but the storm—the connection was too weak. Are you all right?"

"Yes, I'm fine, Papa. Don't worry about me."

"I won't be able to get back to you as soon as I'd hoped. This storm… they're saying… days." Papa's words are choked and garbled by waves of static, but I hear enough to make out what he's trying to say. "Will you be okay… don't get back for a few…"

"I'm fine, Papa," I assure him. "Everything's under control. Don't worry about me."

"You take… of yourself, all right? Don't go doing… dangerous. I hate to leave you… all alone."

My gaze slides to Adam, and for a split second, I consider telling Papa that I'm *not* all alone—that I've met a strange and beautiful man from the Otherworld and even helped save his life. I could tell Papa all about this unexpected, miraculous turn of events. But would it cause more harm than good? Would it make him worry for my safety even more, knowing a stranger is here at the lighthouse with me?

What he doesn't know can't hurt him.

"I'm perfectly safe, Papa. Truly. If anything was wrong, I would tell you; but it's not. Don't hurry back until it's safe to travel—I don't want you getting hurt in the storm."

The waves of static are building now, crashing and whooshing like an angry tide. Through the noise, I can barely make out Papa's reply. "I love you, my girl."

"I love you, Papa… See you soon."

I hang up the phone and return to the kitchen.

"Was that your father?" Adam asks, leaning against the edge of the counter.

I nod. "He was worried about me. It seems the storm is bad enough that he won't be able to come home right away. But I told him it's all right, and not to hurry back. Did you have any luck with calling Jack?"

Adam shakes his head. "It rings and rings, but he never picks up."

"Mmm. I'd offer you the satellite phone, but the connection isn't very good on that one, either. Perhaps once the weather clears, it will improve." I turn to the stove, pushing open the valve and stabbing at the coals with a poker. There's still enough heat in them to get the fire going with a bit of kindling.

Adam sweeps his gaze around the room, taking in every detail. "Do you have… coffee?"

I grin. "Yes."

He seems relieved that I know what coffee is. I cross the kitchen and open one of the cupboards, reaching for the glass jar of fine black powder.

"Coffee is one of those strange treasures from the Otherworld that the supply man brings. But Papa usually makes it, so I can't promise mine will be very good."

I spot the silver percolator sitting on the highest shelf of the cupboard and stretch up for it, standing on my tiptoes—but I can't reach. My fingertips brush hopelessly against the edge of the shelf. Adam limps over to help me, reaching the top shelf with ease and handing me the percolator.

"Thanks," I say, blushing. "Papa forgets that I'm short."

Adam regards me with a glint of amusement and curiosity in his eyes. "What else do you get from the supply man?"

"Pretty much anything we can't make or grow ourselves," I explain, twisting the lid off the coffee jar. A rich, nutty aroma wafts into the air, reminding me of Papa. I begin scooping coffee into the basket of the percolator. "Soap, knives, fresh rope… sacks of flour and rice. And coffee."

I'm about to put the jar away when Adam grabs it and shakes more coffee grounds into the basket. He grins and says, "Weak coffee is a sin, Orca."

I laugh. "Told you I didn't know how to make it." I pour fresh water into the pot and secure the lid on top. While I place the percolator on the stove, Adam keeps glancing around like he's never seen a kitchen before.

"What is it?"

"Nothing." He shakes his head as if dazed. "I just… I feel like I've fallen through a wormhole or something."

"A wormhole?"

"A hypothetical doorway to another region of space-time," Adam clarifies, offering no clarity whatsoever. He pulls out a chair at the table and sits down, wincing from the pain. "Have you lived here your whole life?"

I nod, returning to the counter to fix Lucius's breakfast. "I was born on the mainland, but this island has been my only home. Papa remembers the Otherworld, but he doesn't like to talk about it."

"What is 'the Otherworld,' anyway?"

I turn around to look at him, realizing how peculiar I must sound. "Oh. It's, um, the mainland. Where *you* come from. It's everything that isn't… my world."

Adam stares at me with the same fascinated expression I'm sure I wore last night upon my first encounter with him. It's how you stare at something mysterious and unfamiliar, yet holy in its strangeness.

"And you've never seen it?" he asks. "The Otherworld, I mean?"

I shake my head.

"Wow."

"I want to. More than anything."

"But your father won't take you?"

"He doesn't ever go. Except he had to this time because the coast guard wants to modernize our lighthouse. It's a business trip. He would never go just for pleasure." I swing open the icebox and take out some cooked fish and sweet potatoes for Lucius, who whines on the floor in anticipation of his breakfast.

The stove has heated up now, radiating warmth through the kitchen and boiling the water in the coffee percolator.

"So you live self-sustainably," Adam says from the table, watching me peel a hard-boiled egg for Lucius. "I mean, you don't *need* the rest of the world."

"True… But I'd like to at least *see* it. To know what it's like. I've spent my whole life watching from the lantern room, looking out at that land in the distance and imagining what it must be like to live there." I cast a glance over my shoulder at Adam. "What *is* it like?"

He thinks for a moment, as if carefully considering the differences. I set the bowl of food on the floor for Lucius, who happily scrabbles over to devour it.

At last, Adam says, "It's noisy."

"Noisy? What makes noise?"

"Everything. Even the things that don't make noise make noise."

I don't understand. But I try to. I sit at the table across from Adam and think of him as a different kind of spyglass—a magic, manly spyglass who can tell me things about the Otherworld that Papa would never breathe a word of.

"Well, go on," I prompt when he doesn't continue. "Besides the noise, what is it like? Do you grow your own food?"

Adam smiles a little and shakes his head.

"Where does it come from, then?"

"Farms grow our food, usually someplace far away. We have to buy it with… money?"

"I know what money is."

Adam stifles a laugh. "Wasn't sure."

"Papa pays the supply man. For the coffee and such." I glance at the stove, where the coffee is now percolating, filling the room with a rich aroma.

That's when Adam's phone starts ringing on the counter.

"That will be Jack," I guess as Adam rises from the table and limps over to the phone. "Hopefully he's sitting down."

A grin curves onto Adam's face as he answers the call.

BACK FROM THE GRAVE

jack

I leave my phone on, waiting for Orca's call.

The battery drains, drains, drains. And then it's gone. My room goes dark as night falls, and the storm rages outside.

She doesn't call.

I wonder if I imagined the whole thing—Orca, the lighthouse, the hope that Adam could still be alive.

Mom knocks on my locked door at midnight. *Can I come in, Jackie?* I don't answer her, and she eventually leaves me alone.

Sleep comes in blurry, shifting waves, exhausting me more than anything. It sucks me into dark, unconscious bouts of oblivion, then smashes me against the rocks of brutal reality over and over again.

When morning comes, I lie staring at the ceiling—haunted by my brave words from the past week. All the times I stubbornly back-talked Mom and Dad, insisting that Adam was still alive. Refusing to grieve. Pissing Dad off. Making Mom cry. Holding out that flicker of hope like a burning match in a hurricane, desperately cupping my hands around it, bending my reality around it, losing my mind because of it.

Dad accused me of causing trouble by not accepting that Adam is gone.

But he doesn't understand.

Even if I did what he wanted, "accepting it" wouldn't be a onetime decision.

My brother is dead.

I couldn't accept it once and move on.

I would have to accept it over and over again every morning when I woke up and remembered that he's not here anymore.

Every morning for the rest of my life.

And I don't think I can do that.

I don't think I can go to bed each night remembering and wake up each morning forgetting—just for reality to hit me again like a kick in the balls. I don't think I can get through the next week, the next month, the next year—

Remembering.

Accidentally calling him. No answer.

Wanting to tell him something, even if it's just a stupid joke, something only he understands.

Understood.

Changing him to past tense over and over again.

Accepting it

over

and over

and over again.

I can't.

I just can't.

Feeling numb, I walk across the room and pick up my phone. I untangle my charge cord and plug it into the wall. I watch the battery icon flash on the screen, waiting for it to get enough power to turn on.

I don't know how long I stand there watching it. Everything around me fades into a blur of *I don't give a shit.* Blips of insignificant moments passing, silent and senseless.

I wonder if that's how the rest of my life will feel.

At last, my phone powers on, and I decide to find out what is real—

once and for all. I call Adam one last time and bring the phone to my ear to listen to it ring…

And ring…

And—

Someone picks up.

"Orca?" I say, my heart thudding. "Are you all right? I tried calling you last night, but you didn't answer."

A long moment of silence, then:

"Yeah, Orca's fine. She's right here. Do you want to talk to her?"

No way.

No.

Damn.

Way.

My heart does a backflip and drops through the bottom of my stomach. "Adam?"

"Hey, little brother."

My knees buckle, and I crash to the floor, dropping my phone. I scramble to pick it up again, barely breathing. The room is spinning. Am I dreaming? I'm dreaming… I have to be dreaming—

"Adam!" I scream into the phone, my hands shaking uncontrollably. "You're alive!? You're alive!?"

He laughs like a superhero. "Yes. I'm alive, Jack."

I lose it. I crumple into the fetal position and let myself sob, pressing my forehead to the floor. My body convulsing, I cry harder than I've ever cried in my life.

Before I know it, I'm gasping for air like a drowning man, and Adam is saying, "Hey. Hey, *breathe*, Jack. Breathe. It's okay. Breathe."

He makes it sound so easy. But I haven't been able to breathe for a week.

He's alive.

He's *alive*.

"I thought I frickin' lost you," I gasp, my voice thick and gravelly with tears. "They told us you were dead…"

"I'm not dead," Adam says. "I'm alive."

A sob catches in my throat. "Say it again."

"I'm alive."

"Louder."

"I'm alive! Ow, damn—I have broken ribs, man. I can't yell."

I burst out laughing, tears still running down my face as I climb to my feet. The room is swaying, and my body is shaking, but I know this is real. And I'm going to prove it. I'm going to pull Mom and Dad out of that abyss right now.

"Where the hell is everyone?" I yell through the empty house, feeling possessed as I run around shirtless, covered in tears, Adam laughing on the phone in my hand.

"Jack?" Mom calls through the screen door. She's out on the deck.

"MOM!" I bolt for the door and plow through it, my hands shaking as I hold out the phone. Dad's sitting on the railing, staring at me like I've truly lost it this time—but he's the one who's about to lose it.

"Jack," Mom says, "what on earth is—"

I feverishly shove the phone into Mom's hands, and I hear Adam on the other end, saying, "Hi, Mom."

"Adam?!" Mom screams his name, tears springing to her eyes.

Dad rushes over and kneels on the deck beside her chair, leaning in close to hear through the phone. They're both shouting over each other, desperate to hear Adam's voice again but not letting him get a word in edgewise. My heart is pounding out of my chest, and the tears are still coming, making me feel like a wuss—but I don't care.

He's *alive*.

I watch my parents weep and hug each other and talk to my brother, the one they had boxed up and buried. The one I refused to let go of.

The rush of emotion suddenly comes back like a tsunami wave and hits me so hard I feel sick to my stomach—but in a good way. Like my upside-down world just got shaken right side up again. I leave Mom and Dad on the deck, talking to Adam, and stagger across the yard to the split-rail fence, feeling drunk and disoriented.

Breathe, Jack.

I swipe away the leftover tears with my forearm. Inhaling. Exhaling.

He's alive.

For a few minutes, I just stand here, holding onto the fence.

Eyes shut.

Breathing.

Footsteps come up behind me, Dad's footsteps. A second later, I feel his big, warm hand clasp firmly on my bare shoulder. It says a hundred things, that hand. And so does mine, as I clap it over top of his and hold on tight.

"I'm sorry, Jack."

I nod because I have a lump in my throat and can't even whisper a reply. But I think he knows what I want to say, as I turn and drive my face into his chest, throwing my arms around him—as I break down crying again.

I'm sorry, too.

THE REAL WORLD

adam

It takes a ten-minute phone conversation with my parents before I convince them that it's really me and that I'm truly alive. That's when I realize just how much anguish my family has been through. They all thought I was gone, and who could blame them? They found my wrecked Beaver; they knew I went down over the water. No one in their right mind would assume I survived.

Except for Jack.

"He never gave up hope," Mom says after she recovers from the shock, her voice still wobbly with tears. "He refused to believe that you were gone. In fact, your father and I… were starting to worry about him."

"What do you mean?"

"Well, it was kind of hard to believe that he'd met this mysterious girl called Orca living in a lighthouse on an uninhabited island somewhere…"

Orca is sitting right across from me, sipping her mug of coffee in her colonial-style kitchen.

"He was telling the truth," I say, holding back a grin.

"I can see that now," Mom continues, between a laugh and a sob. "And she has my gratitude for the rest of my life. Oh god, Adam…" She trails off, crying.

"Hey. It's okay, Mom. I'm okay."

"I know," she whispers.

Orca gets a far-off look in her eyes as she listens to me trying to comfort my mother. I wonder what lies behind that look.

"We're going to tell the coast guard right away." Mom sniffles. "We're going to get you home as soon as possible."

"No need to send the coast guard out here. Tell them I'm okay, and Jack can fly out and get me when the storm has passed. Visibility is crap right now, and there's more to this system. Wouldn't be surprised if it lasts a few days."

"Days? Adam—"

"I'm fine. Really. Bruises and scratches, that's it. Maybe a broken rib."

Mom gasps.

"Mom, I'm fine. It's madness to try to fly out to this island. The weather is a nightmare."

While I'm talking, Orca slips out of the kitchen and returns a minute later, wearing a gray jumpsuit and a hooded cloak. "I'll be right back," she says, slinging a huge woven basket over her shoulder before vanishing again with the dog at her heels.

"Are you sure?" Mom persists. "You might have a concussion—"

"I don't think so. Orca's taking good care of me," I add that because Mom will be far less concerned about the situation if she knows a woman is involved.

"C'mon, Mom, leave him alone. Can I have my phone back now?" Jack's voice drifts back onto the line. "Shit, man, I still can't believe it."

I grin. "What do you mean? Mom said you were the only one who believed I was still alive."

"Yeah, I was, for a long time. But last night was rough, Adam. And this morning, I was… I was at the end of my rope."

"I'm so sorry I put you all through that."

"What the hell happened out there, anyway?"

"My worst nightmare. It was partially my fault. I should have paid more attention to the forecast. I wasn't pushing the weather when I took off, but halfway across the straits, the wind shifted, and… the sky fell."

Jack curses under his breath. "You were flying blind?"

"Until I hit the water."

"Damn, that *is* a nightmare. It's a miracle you lived through it."

"Thank God for Orca," I add. "I don't know what would have happened if she hadn't been here to help me."

"Where did she find you?" Jack asks.

"I actually found her. I found the lighthouse, that is. Last night when the storm was really bad, I stumbled upon the place just in time. I figured there would be some rugged old lightkeeper living here—but no, just the opposite."

Jack laughs. I've missed the sound of his laughter.

"I banged on the door, but I was so exhausted I just… collapsed. And when I woke up, I was on the floor of her living room, with, uh… no clothes on."

"What?" he sputters.

"She undressed me, man."

"You serious?"

"I was soaking wet. Freezing. I probably would have died if I'd stayed out in that storm." My gaze drifts to the empty chair where Orca had been sitting. "I owe her my life."

"Pfft, don't be all noble about it. I'm sure she enjoyed stripping your ass."

I roll my eyes, grinning.

"She's something, isn't she?" Jack says. "Her father's some kind of crazy recluse who keeps her prisoner there. Did she tell you that?"

"Yeah, but… I don't think he's *crazy*. He just wants to live a solitary life. What's wrong with that?"

"Um, everything? The girl has never even seen a *movie*. They don't have TV or video games or… anything."

"There's more to life than video games, Jack."

"I know. But it's weird. You have to admit."

I shrug because I can't necessarily admit that. I haven't seen much of

Orca's world yet, but what I have seen could be considered far more "real" than *my* world.

"So you're staying there till the storm passes?" I can't help but notice a hint of worry in Jack's voice.

"Yeah. And don't get started on my broken ribs—I'm fine."

"I wasn't going to. I'm not Mom. I'm just… I can't wait to have you back."

"And I can't wait to *be* back."

We talk for a while until thunder starts rumbling outside, and my connection goes from bad to worse. Jack's voice breaks up between bursts of static until I finally lose him. I sigh, dragging a hand over my face and draining the rest of my coffee.

Where did Orca go?

I carefully stand up, wincing at the sharp pain in my ribs. I limp through the doorway and back into the living room, which is silent and empty. The dog is gone, too.

"Orca?"

The house really does look like something from another century—no frills, no modern conveniences. Everything serves a purpose. I cross the living room, still limping, and glance through an open door into a small bedroom. It's extremely minimal—a bed with gray linen sheets and a quilt. A dresser against one wall. A window, shuttered. Driftwood carvings are scattered across the dresser.

The next room is Orca's. I can tell by the papers covering the walls— illustrations of whales and other marine life, charts of the Pacific, and old maps of the world. Strings of seashells hang like garlands from the ceiling, some trailing down in long strands, clinking softly in the draft. She has wood carvings, too—a whole pod of orca whales lined up on her dresser.

That's when I notice my journal sitting on her nightstand. She must have found it in my backpack. The sight of it lying there startles me. Was she reading it? No. Why would she? There's nothing interesting in there, anyway. Just philosophical rants and scribbles of very bad Latin.

I hope she didn't read it.

Limping back out of the room, I call her name again. "Orca?"

No answer.

Where the hell is she?

I peer through the last door on the opposite side of the living room. It leads to a tiny, dark room that I almost mistake for a closet—until I see the spiral staircase that circles up, up, up, into a tall cylindrical stairwell.

The lighthouse. Of course. She has a job to do, keeping this place running.

As long as she's not outside…

No sooner does the thought cross my mind than the back door is flung open behind me—a sudden *whoosh* of rain catching my attention. I turn and see Orca coming through the door, her cloak dripping with water, her dog bounding in after her.

"Wow," she huffs, flipping her hood down. "Wet out there."

"Where did you go?"

Orca looks up, surprised. "The greenhouse. I had to harvest some vegetables and water the plants. The basin was practically overflowing, it's been raining so hard."

I stare at her as she slides off her basket and hangs up her wet cloak. She looks like something straight out of a Brothers Grimm story.

"But it's storming." I state the obvious, gesturing toward the shuttered window.

"I know," Orca says. "But it had to be done. How was the coffee?"

Here she is, harvesting vegetables in the middle of a monsoon, running a lighthouse by herself, saving me from certain death, and now asking me *How was the coffee?*

I can't help but let out a laugh of amazement. "Uh, the coffee was great. Thank you."

"You shouldn't be walking on that ankle," she says, nodding toward the foot I'm babying.

"I know. But I'm not used to sitting still."

"Are you hungry?"

"That's an understatement."

Orca laughs, lugging the basket into the kitchen. "Come in here. Tell me more about the Otherworld."

I wince as I limp my way back to the kitchen. Damn my stupid ankle.

"What is this obsession with the Otherworld anyway?" I lean against the doorjamb as Orca starts unloading brightly colored vegetables from her basket. "It's not half as interesting as your life here."

Orca casts a dubious glance over her shoulder. "Would you say that if you grew up here and had never left?" Her sea-green eyes reflect the soft light coming through the window. The rain is drying in her sandy-brown hair now, curling the wispy strands into ringlets of gold around her ears and neck. "Would you?"

I refocus. "Would I what?" I sit down at the table, feeling dizzy all of a sudden.

Orca sighs and turns back to the counter. "It's just that I've spent my whole life here. And it's not that I'm tired of it… But I want to know what else is out there. I want to prove to Papa that I'm not weak and incapable."

"Is that really what he thinks of you?"

"He says the Otherworld is full of dangers and darkness. Things that will hurt me."

My gaze drifts down to the dog, Lucius, who is sniffing me like I don't belong in his master's clothes.

"Is that true?" Orca casts me a quizzical look, her hands full of strawberries.

"Sometimes," I admit. "But experience teaches you how to deal with those things."

"Exactly, and experience is what I don't have—because I have never experienced anything. And I'm afraid I never will."

I can't help but smile at her forlorn tone of voice. "You're only eighteen, Orca. Your life is just starting; you have plenty of time."

She sighs. "I know. But sometimes, I don't feel like it. Sometimes I feel like my life is… slipping away. And I'm powerless to stop it."

"Now you sound like Jack."

"Do I?" She grins, tying her acres of hair into a loose bun on top of her head. "How so?"

"He's young and restless. Can't stand the thought of being stuck in one place. Can't even stand the thought of having a job that ties him down. I swear he's said the same thing to me before—about his life slipping away. And he's lived in, uh, the *Otherworld* all his life. It hasn't exactly cured his restlessness."

Orca seems to turn this over in her mind as she scrubs a few purple potatoes under the faucet. I watch the water flow over her small, delicate hands.

"And what about you?" she says, casting me a look over her shoulder. "Do you ever feel trapped?"

I shake my head slowly. "No."

She seems disappointed by this answer, turning back to the sink. She grabs a frighteningly large butcher knife and a cutting board and starts julienning the potatoes like a master chef.

I watch as she slices up a bunch of vegetables and tosses them all into a bowl, cracking eggs, throwing wood on the fire, heating a pan, flitting around the kitchen—strands of hair slipping out of her bun and brushing against her face.

I find it hard to believe that her father thinks she's "weak and incapable." My god, the girl seems capable of literally anything—except maybe reaching the top shelf.

She's totally unaware of the true nature of this situation, but I can see it clearly—being an outsider who is ten years older. It's not that Orca is weak; it's that she's pure. She's innocent. She's grown up isolated from the muck and mire of the "real" world, and I can see why her father doesn't want her anywhere near it.

"Well, Adam," she says after a silence, "I know you wonder about different paths you might take in life."

"Oh?" I raise an eyebrow, crossing my arms over my chest. "And how did you uncover this dark secret about me?"

Orca grins. "What you wrote about the multiverse. The idea that we might exist in another universe, having made a completely different assortment of decisions that have set us on a completely different path in life."

I feel color blaze over my ears as I realize what she's saying—what she's *quoting*.

My journal.

"Uh… yes." I clear my throat, rubbing the back of my neck. "The… uh, the multiverse."

"I find that so fascinating. Can you explain it to me?"

This is a first—a question no girl has ever asked me.

"Sure, yeah. Um." My brain is still caught on the first thing—the fact that she *did* read my journal. What else did I write in there? I can't remember, damn it. "The multiverse is just a theory. It hasn't been proven. But it hasn't been *disproven*, either. Like pretty much everything else in science."

"Like the emotional bonds between orcas in a pod," she chimes in, dropping scoops of the mixture into the sizzling pan on the stove. "They're some of the most intelligent creatures in the ocean—their emotional capacity is more highly developed than a human's."

"Really? I didn't know that."

"Yeah. Something Papa taught me. Sorry, continue. The multiverse."

"Right. So… it's the idea that parallel universes exist. Which, of course, means parallel earths. And parallel lives. So we all exist in these other universes, but we've made so many divergent decisions that even a replica of ourselves looks completely different."

Orca tilts her head, considering this, as a delicious aroma fills the kitchen. I still haven't deciphered what she's making—some kind of potato pancakes?

At last, she says, "So there could be another me, in another universe, who grew up on the mainland. A me who has a completely different life."

I nod. "That's the theory."

It's a concept I've thought about for years but never actually spoken of. Writing down my ideas in a journal is the closest I've ever come to sharing them—and even then, I had no intention of ever letting anyone read it. The journal is only a means of untangling my thoughts, the ones that wrap around my mind during long workdays, after hours of building an engine or rewiring instruments into a dash.

I never thought anyone would read my philosophical rants. But now, Orca has. She didn't know it was private; how could she know? Still, it feels invasive—like my mind has been laid bare in front of her. Is this going to be a pattern with us?

I stifle a smile as Orca continues musing about what her "multiverse me" might be doing right now. "Certainly not cooking breakfast in this lighthouse," she says, sliding a plate of amazing-looking food in front of me. There is freshly baked bread and piles of strawberries, and that's when I realize that I haven't eaten in a week—no wonder I'm starving.

"Probably not," I reply, "but this version of me is grateful you are."

Orca laughs and sits down with her own plate of food. "And this version of me is glad I'm not alone anymore."

IRREVERSIBLE

orca

I don't understand how anyone could find my life here more interesting than the Otherworld. Yet this seems to be the case with Adam Stevenson. For all the questions I ask about the way he lives, he's even more curious about the way *I* live. Self-sustainability may be an unusual concept where he comes from, but it's all I've ever known. It's ordinary and dull compared to the mysterious mainland.

Secretly, I'm glad the storm is severe enough to keep Adam here for a couple of days. If I can't go to the Otherworld, I intend to relish the fact that a small piece of the Otherworld has come to me. I would have been disappointed had the weather been fine enough for the coast guard to come and fetch Adam straight away. Perhaps this is selfish of me since I'm not the one with broken ribs or a sprained ankle—but I cannot control the weather, can I?

Adam keeps me company while I go about my daily chores—most of which involve food preparation in the kitchen. I'm chopping, mixing, soaking, peeling, and scrubbing for the greater part of the day, chattering away and probably driving Adam to the brink of madness with all my questions.

"If you don't grow your own food in the Otherworld, you must make your own clothes."

"No," he says. "We buy those too."

"Do you have to buy *everything* in the Otherworld? With money?"

"Pretty much."

"Where do you get all the money?"

"Working a job."

"Goodness. People must have to spend a lot of time working."

"Yeah. Pretty much their whole lives. Two weeks' vacation every year for most people."

"So when do you have time for other things? Like gardening and fishing and… oh. You don't do that. You work instead."

"Right."

"That seems like a monotonous way to live."

"It is, for a lot of people. I'm lucky to be able to do something I actually like for work."

"Flying planes. And occasionally crashing them."

"Don't even start—"

I burst out laughing, making him laugh too.

He offers to help me with my chores, but I won't allow it. There's nothing I can't handle on my own, and I want to show Papa just how strong I am by shouldering every burden—big or small. I need to impress him, to prove that his worries are unfounded.

I explain this to Adam later that afternoon in the living room. He's lying on the couch at my insistence (despite his repeated declarations of "I'm not tired"), and I'm sewing the hem of a shirt I've been meaning to finish.

"Do you think maybe your father has another reason?" he asks. "For… not wanting you to go to the mainland?"

I frown, glancing up from the needle and thread. "What do you mean? What other reason could he possibly have?"

Adam shrugs. "You tell me."

"Well, I know he would miss me. He does rely upon me for certain things, like tending the greenhouse and the chickens. Besides, it's lonely here, with no one to talk to." Lucius gives me mopey eyes, feeling excluded. "No one who can talk *back*, that is."

Adam frowns thoughtfully at the mongrel before saying, "So even if he *did* give you permission to go, you would feel bad leaving him. Your father, I mean. Not Lucius."

I submit to a little smile. "I would feel bad leaving Lucius, too. But I would come back. It's not as if I would run off and be gone forever."

"No?"

"No. I would just experience life in the Otherworld and then come back home."

"What if you didn't *want* to come back home?" Adam says. "What if you went to the mainland, and… it changed you? Changed the way you see life? What if nothing was ever the same again?"

"In a good way or a bad way?"

Adam ponders for a moment. "Both."

My gaze lowers to the half-sewn hem. "I think I would still want to go, no matter what. I'd still want to experience something beyond… this." I gesture at the room around us. "Do you think that's wrong?"

"No, I don't think it's *wrong*. I just think…" His tired gaze sweeps the walls, then locks back on mine. "Experience is irreversible."

I turn this over in my mind like an elaborate seashell, trying to comprehend it—but the true meaning of it seems too complex for my simple mind to grasp. I continue stitching the hem of the shirt while the rain falls outside.

"I'm sure Papa has all sorts of reasons for not wanting me to go to the Otherworld. When he told me of the dangers and darkness, I didn't want to go—I was a child. I didn't understand. I still don't understand much of it because I've never seen it with my own eyes, of course… but it frightened me. Not so much the way he spoke about it—the thunderstorm people and whatnot—but the way it seemed to disturb him. Haunt him, even. And perhaps you're right; perhaps it would change the way I see life. Perhaps it would make me see life the way Papa sees life. But would that be so very bad? Can it be? Would I not be able to help him better if I understood what he understood? Experienced the things he's experienced? I mean, surely there is benefit in that…"

I glance up from my sewing and bite my tongue.

Adam is asleep.

The poor man is still suffering, and here I am, blabbering about myself. I purse my lips and stitch the rest of the hem, resolved to keep quiet so that he can rest.

The flickering orange light from the fireplace casts graceful, dancing shadows over him as he sleeps. Purple bruises bloom across his skin, darkening his golden, muscular arms and shadowing his face along with the swath of thick stubble growing along his jaw. The cut sliced down his face will leave a scar for a while, but somehow it becomes him—defining his rugged features in an ironically beautiful way.

He seems a more subdued version of the confident man I studied in the photo in his wallet. Or perhaps he's always this quiet and serious. Perhaps I merely took liberties to craft my own idea of his personality based on that photograph. Perhaps true confidence is not found in sparkling charisma, but in quiet strength and steadiness, like the unwavering glow of a lighthouse on a distant shore.

When I have finished my sewing, I silently make my way up to the lantern room, taking Adam's cell phone with me. Through the panoramic windows, I can see for miles. Storm clouds overshadow surging dark waves, ad infinitum. I sit at Papa's desk and smooth my hands over the old maps unfurled there—tracing my fingertip over the lines of the straits, the shapes of islands. I find Whidbey and think of Jack and our first conversation the night I discovered the phone. I was so clueless; he was so desperate.

How things have changed.

I flip open Adam's phone and decide to call him. Adam said the connection was lost earlier, but I have a hunch the signal may be stronger up here at the top of the lighthouse. After three long, droning rings, the call is answered.

"Adam?"

"No, sorry. It's just me, Orca."

"Oh. Hey, Orca." Jack's laugh is surprised, but not disappointed. "How's Adam?"

"He's fine. Sleeping. He wouldn't admit that he was tired until he fell asleep while I was talking." I bite on a smile. "I'm afraid I'm an annoying person to be stuck here with."

Jack grunts. "Don't take it personally; he's always like that. He falls asleep on me all the time when we're talking at night. Ever since I was little, that's how it'd be. I'd be bouncing off the walls at nine o'clock, and he'd be *passed out*. I mean, what kind of teenager goes to bed at nine o'clock? He never went to parties, never kept a girl out past her curfew, just… strait-laced mama's boy to the core."

"He seems to think you and I are similar," I say, still tracing the shape of Whidbey Island.

"Oh yeah? How so?"

"We're both restless."

Jack murmurs a laugh. "Yeah, you could say that."

"But *he's* not," I observe, frowning at the gloomy sky beyond the windows. "He can't relate to this awful feeling of being… trapped. And the fear of never being free."

Jack sighs. "Well, I can relate to it. Adam's an old man stuck in his ways. He's content with his life the way it is. You know? I'm not. I don't know if I ever *will* be. I can't imagine settling for just *one* thing and sticking with that. Like, even aviation—yeah, I love it now. But what if I get sick of it eventually?"

I bunch my lips to the side. "You could do something else, then. I suppose."

"Adam thinks that's weakness. Immaturity or something. He likes to think he's older and wiser."

"He *is* older." I refrain from admitting that he is also wiser, lest Jack take offense.

"But he's different. He's always been different. Kind of a lone wolf. Reserved, you know?"

"Mmm. He's certainly not as talkative as you."

Jack laughs.

"But it's nice to have someone here with me. Papa will be stuck on the mainland for another day or so."

"And Adam will be stuck there until I can fly out and pick him up."

"It would seem so."

"You sound really glad about it."

"Do I?" A nervous laugh escapes me, a blush warming my cheeks. "I just… like having someone around. Only I'm sorry he's in so much pain. And that you'll have to wait to see him. And that he has to endure my endless talking."

Jack groans. "Would you stop putting yourself down? I would trade places with him in a minute."

"What? Why?"

"Because you're…"

I wait, listening. My fingertip freezes over the map.

DAMN THE RULES

jack

You're special and brilliant and strong and sweet and funny.

I want to say all those things. But it feels too… I don't know. Weird.

Sudden.

Like, how can I say that? I don't really know her.

But at the same time, I feel like I know her better than any of the girls I've ever dated. Sure, I've never seen her face. But faces don't matter when we're talking about the girl who *saved my brother's life.*

"Jack?" Her soft voice comes through the phone speaker, reminding me that I still haven't finished my sentence.

"You're so cool," I say, deciding this is a general enough compliment to give anybody—even though she's way cooler than just *anybody.* "If my brother can't see that, he's a dummy."

I'm driving back from the port, one hand on the wheel of my Mustang. It's dusk, still raining. I wanted to fly out to Orca's island today and get my brother, but this crappy weather won't let up. I wanted to thank Orca in person—to tell her that I owe her my life. Over the phone will have to be good enough for now.

"Seriously, Orca, I can never thank you enough. For helping Adam. For searching the island."

"It was nothing."

"It was not *nothing*. It's more than most people do for anyone else in their entire lives. Do you even realize that? It's incredible. I'd be bragging about it forever if I were you."

Orca laughs. The cutest, sunniest laugh I've ever heard.

"I mean it. I was going out of my mind when you called me that night. I don't know what I would have done if it weren't for you. I mean, Adam would still have found the lighthouse, and you still would have helped him. But I wouldn't have known about any of it, and my parents would have convinced me that he was gone, and it just… it would have destroyed me. It *was* destroying me." I pull into the driveway and slow the car to a stop. "What I'm trying to say is… you helped me through the darkest time of my life. You believed when no one else did. And I can never thank you enough for that."

I kill the engine and sit in the dark for a minute, watching the rain slide down the windshield.

"You're welcome, Jack," she answers softly. "I'm glad I was able to help you. I'm… glad I happened to find that backpack."

I smile. "Yeah. So am I."

MOM IS ALIVE AGAIN. Her bed is made, the house is freakishly clean, and she's not wearing black. She's singing when I walk in the door.

Singing.

We eat the stupid casserole Mrs. Dubois gave us, and it's actually really good because my brother isn't dead and because I've hardly eaten in a week. I joke that nobody should tell Mrs. Dubois that Adam is alive, and when he returns, he can show up on her doorstep to bring her casserole dish back. Mom says, "That's awful," but she's grinning. Dad thinks it's a great idea.

For the rest of the night, I keep thinking about what Orca said. How she's so restless, so desperate to see the world. How she feels trapped, afraid that she'll never be free.

I may not have grown up in a lighthouse with a crazy hermit for a dad, but man, do I feel her pain.

Adam doesn't get it; she's right about that. He's so stable. So okay with everything staying exactly the way it is. *He's certainly not as talkative as you,* she said. But she didn't seem to mind. In fact, I detected a hint of admiration in her voice.

I wonder what they *have* been talking about. Orca must be asking him thousands of questions about the "Otherworld" or whatever she calls it—and knowing my brother, he'll be dutifully giving her one-word answers.

I'm kind of jealous of him.

Not for the broken ribs—that sucks. But to be stranded on an island with Orca Monroe, all alone? That doesn't sound like too bad a time.

It's ridiculous, but part of me feels strangely possessive of her. Maybe it's because I "met her" first. Or maybe it's because she stopped me from falling into the abyss of grief—she gave me hope when all hope seemed lost.

I remember what she told me the first night I talked to her on the phone. How her father wants to keep her on that island: no friends, no movies, no pizza. She can't live her whole life like that—it would be crazy. It would be a tragedy.

I won't let it happen.

I meant what I said: I owe her my life. A trip to the Otherworld would be nothing compared to what she's done for Adam and me. As soon as this storm passes, I'm going to fly out to Recluse Island and meet this girl. I'm going to pay her back—to show her the world she's always dreamed of.

Damn the rules.

BUTTERFLIES AND HURRICANES

adam

"*O you take the high road, and I'll take the low road, and I'll be in Scotland afore ye…*"

An angelic voice coaxes me awake like a breath of summer wind. For a moment, I don't know whose voice it is or where I am. Fatigue holds me under the waters of semiconsciousness.

"*… but me and my true love will never meet again on the bonnie, bonnie banks of Loch Lomond…*"

At last, I force my eyes open, taking in the room around me—Orca's living room. Flames crackle in the fireplace, hissing over the split logs. Lucius is sprawled in front of the hearth like an ancient sacrifice. Orca's singing drifts from the kitchen.

How long have I been asleep?

The last thing I remember is Orca sitting in the chair across from me, sewing something, rambling on about how her father won't let her go to the mainland. I must have fallen asleep on her. Now a gray wash of light filters through the windows, brighter than it was before I dozed off. The steady *shhhhh* of rain murmurs against the roof, but the thunder and wind seem to have subsided.

I must have slept through the whole night. My stomach is growling, and my ribs still hurt like hell, but at least I feel human again. My headache has faded completely, and the swelling in my ankle has gone down. When I stand, I can almost put my full weight on it.

What I desperately need is a shower.

I cautiously make my way to the kitchen, where Orca is singing "Loch Lomond." When I reach the doorway, I find her at the counter, mixing a bowl of dough. She's wearing a white blouse tucked into a sage-green linen skirt that falls just below her knees. Her wild hair is woven into a thick braid that tumbles down her back and ends in a ribbon at her waist.

"*But me and my true love*—Adam!" She smiles when she sees me. "You're awake. At last."

I exhale a dry laugh. "Yeah. How long was I sleeping?"

"Oh, years. I've lost track."

I give her a smirk like *That's not funny*. "Hey, do you have a shower here?" I'm half-expecting her to say no, and that she has to heat water in pots on the stove to fill some vintage bathtub.

But to my relief, she nods. "Yes. Through that door across from Papa's room. You might have to run the water for a few minutes before it gets hot."

I nod. "Thanks. Can I borrow a clean shirt from your dad?"

"Of course. Take whatever you need. Papa won't mind."

I limp into his room and open the dresser drawers, taking a clean shirt and a pair of underwear. When I reach into the top drawer, my fingertips brush against something cool and metallic.

Orca is still singing in the kitchen, so I take the opportunity to pull out the metal object and turn it over in my hands.

It's a small silver picture frame containing a wedding photo from the late seventies. Orca's mother and father, I presume. She looks about Orca's age, and Mr. Monroe must be at least ten years older than her. They're standing arm in arm outside an old stone church—her in a white dress, him in a suit and tie. There's something familiar about that stone archway behind them. I've seen it in downtown Anacortes, across from the bank.

Feeling intrusive, I tuck the photo frame back into the sock drawer and leave the room.

I'M NOT SURE I'D call it "hot water," but it feels good after being out in the woods for so long—a fact I keep forgetting but am starkly reminded of when I see myself in the mirror.

I look like hell. My face is discolored with bruises, slashed with a long cut from my eye to my jawbone, and swathed in the beginnings of a beard. I can't remember the last time I went this long without shaving.

I grab her father's razor and get to work. Apparently, shaving cream is not one of those "strange treasures" the supply man brings, so I do my best with soap and try not to add to the collection of cuts on my face. When I'm finished, my bruises stand out more, but it feels much better to be clean again.

Thanks to Orca's homemade ointment, my wounds are beginning to heal, but my ribs are going to need rewrapping.

I find Orca still in the kitchen, working away. Whatever is baking in the oven makes the whole house smell like a childhood memory.

"Storm looks like it's starting to clear up," I say, leaning against the back of a chair.

"Mm-hmm." Orca peers out the window as she scrubs the dishes. "It's still raining, but it seems the wind has subsided. You can see the fog beginning to settle." She sighs and dries her hands on a dishcloth, turning to face me. "Breakfast is almost—" She stops short, smiling as if noticing something new about me.

"What?"

"Your face."

"Oh." I shrug, feeling the edge of my jaw. "Yeah, it's been a while since I shaved."

Orca sidles up to me, a glint of wonder in her eyes. "Papa never shaves all his off," she says, lifting her hand to touch my cheek.

I freeze up, stunned, because it's such an intimate thing to do—but she doesn't know it. Her fingertips are soft and warm, still damp from the dishwater, as she caresses the line of my jaw to my chin. She studies me with innocence in her eyes, like a child stroking the wing of a wounded songbird. Her touch turns my thoughts to gibberish.

"How are your ribs this morning?" she asks, letting her hand fall away.

"Uh… they still hurt pretty bad."

"We should rewrap them. That's what Papa's medical books say to do. Here, take your shirt off. I'll be right back."

While I start unbuttoning my shirt, Orca runs to the bathroom and returns a moment later with a fresh roll of cotton bandage.

"I can probably manage this myself," I say, but Orca casually sweeps my shirt off with a dismissive shake of her head.

"Nonsense! You're injured. Let me help you." She winces when she sees the wound on my side, covered in purple bruises. "It doesn't look as bad as it did before," she admits. "But it still looks painful."

She dips her fingertips into a jar of ointment and smooths it over the wound, making me grimace. I grip the back of the nearest chair, swallowing the fire radiating through my side.

"Sorry—am I pressing too hard?" Orca glances up with concern.

I shake my head. "No, you're fine. What's in that stuff, anyway?"

"A blend of aloe and eucalyptus, along with some other plants that fight infection. We grow them in the herb garden."

"You grow your own medicine?"

Orca nods, tearing off a fresh length of bandage. "Papa has taught me a lot about healing yourself with plants. I have teas to treat just about any ailment. Headaches, fevers, cramps, rashes… Here, hold this end." She smooths the clean bandage over my wounded side, and I hold it in place while she begins wrapping—leaning in close to reach around my torso. I try to ignore the warmth of her breath on my bare chest, the brush of her fingers tracing my back.

"You, uh… you read a lot of medical books?"

Orca shrugs one shoulder. "I read a lot of books. Not all of them are medical. Some are about the ocean and outer space and different exotic places in the Otherworld."

"Any fiction?"

"What's fiction?"

"Well, it's… not true stories, but made-up ones. And nonfiction is anything factual."

Orca frowns, reaching the end of the bandage. "Well, in that case, shouldn't it be… fact and non-fact?"

I laugh, killing my ribs.

"What?"

"Nothing. That's… that's a good point."

She smiles softly, tying off the end of the bandage so it won't slip. Somehow, I don't notice the pain when she's this close; her featherlight touch moves over my abdomen as she checks to make sure the bandage is secure. She looks so beautiful in this light, whispers of hair slipping out of her braid to tickle her rosy cheeks.

I force myself to look away. "What kind of nonfiction books do you have? Philosophy?"

"No… science, mostly. Marine biology. Astronomy."

"History?"

"A few."

"Biographies?"

She shakes her head. "Papa… doesn't like people."

A grin pulls at the corner of my mouth. "Neither do I." Carefully pulling my shirt back on, I add, "Except for you. I kinda like you."

Orca blushes, a smile blooming across her face. "And I kinda like *you*, Adam Stevenson."

AFTER BREAKFAST, Orca takes me to the greenhouse to help her with the harvesting.

"Follow me," she says, smiling from under the hood of her cloak. Lucius trots beside her through the soggy grass, and I follow the pair of them across the backyard. Raw damp enshrouds everything in sight—milky white fog nestling into the trees as if to shield them from the drizzle. One glance at the sky tells me all I need to know about visibility. It's going to be at least another day before we have decent flying conditions.

The greenhouse sits on an open stretch of lawn at the end of a flagstone path. Orca walks ahead, her basket bouncing on her shoulders, ferns splashing the hem of her skirt with rainwater. She pulls open the door, and Lucius bounds inside, vigorously shaking himself off.

The greenhouse is filled to bursting with every kind of plant imaginable—most of which I can't identify. It's all a chaos of fruits, vegetables, ferns, and vines springing up in every direction.

Dozens of butterflies flutter back and forth like lost letters in a windstorm—yellow swallowtails and bright orange monarchs drift from the morning glories to the orchids hanging from the center of the room, where rainwater flows in, filling up a stone basin built in the floor.

"Good morning, my friends," Orca singsongs, reaching up to stroke the blossom of a bright blue morning glory. Viny arms of plant life reach out from every direction like adoring fans bracing at the edge of a crowd, eager to touch Orca as she walks down the row. She plucks a few tiny pink flowers from a hanging basket and slips them into her braid.

"What do you think of it?" she asks, kneeling beside the basin and scooping out water with a clay pot.

I shake my head, lost for words. "It's… otherworldly."

"No, no, *you're* otherworldly." She tucks the water pot against her side and starts walking down the row, watering plants. A tiny pale-blue butterfly dances around her head as if attracted by the scent of a new flower.

"What's with the butterflies?" I ask as Orca moves on to the next plant. The little blue wings go with her.

"Oh, they help to pollinate the plants. We have bees, too."

I stiffen. "Where?"

"Don't worry; they're very shy." She giggles, returning to the basin to refill her pot. "They like Papa best. He's the one who coaxed them here in the first place. Kindly bees, he always calls them. They have plenty of flowers to drink from and protection from the bad weather—what more could they wish for? We try to give them the most delicious nectar. And they give us the most delicious honey in return."

A swallowtail flutters over and lands on a morning glory hanging near my head. I watch as it drinks from the flower's center.

"So… this is where you grow all your food."

Orca shakes her head. "Not all of it. We have a garden in the yard for the hardier vegetables, like potatoes and squashes—but they won't be ready until September, at least."

"And how do you get through the winter?"

"We preserve all we need for the coldest months," Orca says, watering the tomato plants. "The potatoes keep well in the cellar. We never run out of food."

I watch the little blue butterfly do a few touch-and-goes above Orca's head before finally landing in her golden-brown hair.

"They like you," I say with a smile.

Orca looks up. "Who?"

I reach over and gently lift the butterfly out, feeling the brush of her hair against my fingers.

"An Acmon blue," she whispers, admiring the paper-thin wings folding open and shut. "That reminds me… What is the butterfly effect?"

Another entry she read in my journal, no doubt.

"It's the idea that something small and seemingly insignificant can spur a sequence of events that lead to a massive disaster. Chaos." I study the Acmon blue on my fingertip. "The theory is that a butterfly flapping its wings could cause the first breath of wind that eventually turns into a hurricane."

As if feeling personally attacked, the tiny blue butterfly takes off again, fluttering away to find more flowers.

Orca looks up at me, eyes wide. "Does that really happen?"

I shrug. "Who knows? Can't prove it, I guess."

"But you can't *disprove* it, either." She grins and turns back to the tomatoes, reaching in to twist red fruits off the vine. "And you think it happens with more than just hurricanes?"

I step in to help her harvest the tomatoes. "It's in everything. Not just the big catastrophes people try to avoid, but the little things, too. The everyday stuff we don't think about. The way we talk to each other or don't. What we do for others… or fail to do. We always want to blame things on chance, like the universe is just messed up and we're powerless to stop it—to prevent disasters from happening. But what if we can? What if we're all butterflies, and we think we have nothing to do with the hurricane, but really it all started because of us?"

Orca frowns as she pieces it together in her mind. "So chaos… isn't chaos, then."

I bite back a grin. "More like unintentional consequences of intentional actions."

"Which we don't realize are intentional when we do them."

"Exactly. That's *my* theory, anyway." I twist the last ripe tomato off the vine and hand it to her. "I mean, nothing 'just happens.' It can't. Right?"

Orca moves on to the pepper plants, which are overflowing with fruit—orange, red and yellow.

"Even the word *chaos*," I add. "It means nothing—it's Latin, from the Greek *khaos*, meaning a vast chasm or void. So, nothingness. But nothing comes from nothing."

"*Khaos*," Orca murmurs, pulling the peppers out of their leafy beds. "Do you know a lot of Latin?"

"No, not a lot. I'm still learning."

"What does *tenens infinitum* mean?"

A ghost of a smile brushes across my face. "Holding the infinite."

Orca's gaze drifts down to the golden peppers in her hands. "The infinite," she whispers. "That's like the void, isn't it? Nothingness. But at the same time… it could be everythingness."

I smile.

Everythingness.

"If we're the butterflies," Orca muses, "then we decide what the void will be, right? Maybe it's not nothing. Maybe it's just… infinite possibilities."

Listening to her is more captivating than any lecture I've ever heard. I could volley ideas at her for hours just to listen to her analysis on them. For a moment, I forget where we are and what we're doing—I'm so awed by the fact that I'm discussing chaos theory and Latin root words with this incredibly beautiful girl.

"You wrote something about quantum physics," Orca continues, "and how it makes the multiverse possible. But you also said that the butterfly couldn't turn back time. Why not?"

I ponder her question for a moment before turning and squinting at her. "Are you trying to poke holes in my theories, Orca?"

She laughs. "No, I'm just curious. About the time thing. The extra dimensions of time, how it's all invented and not so much a progression as… a repetition. So is there a way for the butterfly to actually turn back time, then?"

I think for a moment, my gaze trailing over the snap pea vines, which Orca is now gently untangling. "I guess there *is* S equals K log W."

She frowns. "What does that mean?"

"It's the equation to reverse entropy, which is physics' version of chaos. Science actually allows disorder to switch direction. To return to order."

Orca stares at me, wonder glinting in her sea-green eyes. "So the hurricane can go back to the butterfly's wings."

I grin, wishing professors would say it like that. "Exactly."

She dwells on this idea for a moment, her gaze softening as she studies my face. For the first time, I notice the freckles scattered across her cheeks. She smiles, looking up at something just above my head.

"What is it?"

She nods to the thing I can't see and says, "They like you, too."

TO FILL THE VOID

orca

Adam smiles when I point out the tiny yellow butterflies landing on his head. He looks younger with no facial hair, and his eyes are the same heavenly blue as the morning glories blooming acrobatically above us.

That's when a light-headed, joyful feeling floods me, making everything else lose its luster and fascination, everything but him. It's impossible to describe this floating, dreamy rush of happiness stirring inside me. I have to force myself to focus on the job at hand: harvesting the vegetables.

With Adam's help, the task takes half the time it usually does. Our hands brush against each other behind curtains of green leaves. Every time I feel the warmth of his skin against mine, little flashes of excitement spark through me—like bursts of sunlight between clouds when they move fast through the sky on a windy day. A glimpse of warm, golden glow; there for a moment, then trapped by a shadow.

As we unload the freshly harvested produce in the kitchen, I notice how low I am on firewood. Papa warned me to always keep the indoor supply well stocked in case of a sudden turn in the weather. He didn't want me to be chopping wood in a storm.

"I'll be right back," I tell Adam, pulling up the hood of my cloak and vanishing outside before he can question where I'm going.

Whistling gusts of ocean wind chase me around the corner of the lighthouse, rain blowing sideways as I yank the tarp off the woodpile. My shoulders sag when I realize that I forgot to split the logs ahead of time. Digging through the stack, I find a few pieces cut from narrow branches—but it's not enough to keep the fire going for the rest of the day.

I'm just going to have to split them now.

With a groan of frustration, I haul an armload of logs over to the chopping block, where Papa's ax is stuck. It's not my favorite chore, especially in this weather, but it must be done.

I steady a log on the block and slam the ax down, splitting it into pieces with a *CRACK!* I toss the wood aside and start on the next log just as a gust of wind blows my hood off. I carry on splitting logs, unfazed by the temperamental weather. Papa wouldn't mind it, and neither shall I.

"Orca?"

I glance over my shoulder and find Adam standing a few yards behind me, bewilderment in his eyes.

"What are you doing?"

"Chopping wood! We need more." I drive the ax into the next log, but it takes a few tries to split the wood in two. "Go back inside. There's no sense in both of us getting wet."

"I can't let you do this yourself," Adam insists. "Chopping wood is a man's job."

"Excuse me, I've chopped wood *many* times, and I'm good at it, too!"

Though I'm not providing much of an example right now, as I wrestle with the log, which is locked around my ax like the jaws of a hungry shark.

"I need to do this, Adam! Go back inside." Gathering my armload of newly split firewood, I start marching back to the door. Adam steps forward to take the burden off my hands, but I dart out of his reach—immediately tripping on a root and falling on my face.

I hiss in pain as I crash to the ground, skinning my arms when I land on the scattered firewood.

"Orca!" Adam is at my side in seconds, only intensifying my embarrassment when he asks me if I'm all right.

"I'm fine. I just tripped—Adam!" I scoff as he grasps my arm and begins pulling me back to the lighthouse. "Adam, let me go this minute."

"You are the most stubborn girl in the world. Has anyone ever told you that?"

"I'm my father's daughter," I snap, frustrated and comforted in equal measure by how quick he is to swoop in and protect me.

He pulls me through the front door and into the kitchen, insisting that I sit on the table and not move. I'm a breathless, soggy mess, grass stains on my knees, wet hair sticking to my neck.

"You're so funny—I keep asking you what I can do to help, and you don't tell me. Instead, you sneak outside to chop wood in the rain."

"I couldn't ask you to chop the wood, Adam. You're hurt."

"And now *you're* hurt."

"It's nothing. Just a scratch."

"Let me see." He gently turns my arms over to assess the damage. "You're bleeding, Orca."

"Not much. Not nearly as much as *you* were bleeding when I first found you." I'm not sure why I feel the need to point this out—it's not as if we're competing to see who is more equipped to look after themselves.

"Well, then," Adam says softly, his gaze roaming over my face, "allow me to return the favor."

My heart gives a fluttery thud when he says that; his thumb lightly skims the inside of my arm. I don't notice how close he is until he steps away, but he returns moments later with a warm, wet cloth and the jar of ointment I used on his ribs just this morning.

"Adam, you really don't need to—"

"And you didn't need to chop that wood," he says, carefully lifting my forearm and washing my wound with the wet cloth. "So why did you?"

I glance down, biting my lip at the sting of pain that races up my inner arm. Somehow, it doesn't burn as much as it should. Not with Adam's warm, strong hand cupping my elbow. Not with him standing this close to me, our legs nearly touching—the soft gray light cresting the lines of his beautiful, bruised face.

"I went out to fetch the wood because I promised Papa I would manage everything on my own," I confess quietly. "I need to prove myself to him. It's the only way he'll change his mind about letting me go to the Otherworld."

Adam remains silent as he finishes washing my other forearm. He sets the cloth aside and dips his fingertip into the ointment, then spreads a thin layer over my pinked skin.

"*Do* you need to prove it to him, Orca? Or do you need to prove it to yourself?"

Adam's question takes me by surprise. I stare up into his deep blue eyes—the eyes of a man who is at peace with life because he knows he cannot control it. I both admire and envy that quiet, unshakable strength.

"I don't know," I whisper, feeling small and feeble under his gaze. "I suppose part of me wonders if I'm doing something wrong… if I have some weakness, some failing that I don't even see, and—"

"Orca." Adam leans forward, his hands on the table's edge, his eyes level with mine. "Your only failing is that you don't think highly enough of yourself. You don't know how experienced and wise and strong you already are." He shakes his head, his gaze darting over my face. "Did you ever think maybe it's not *you*, but your father? Did you ever think maybe he just wants to keep you safe from all of it? All the bad things in the world, all the dangers he spoke of—it's not that they would hurt only *you*. They hurt everyone."

I tilt my head to the side, studying him. "Even you?"

"Even me."

"So you think Papa's right to keep me here?"

"No, I'm not saying he's right. I just want you to know that it's not some failing on your part. It's not your lack of courage or strength… just the opposite." Adam smiles a little as he looks at me. "You're the strongest, most courageous woman I've ever met."

His words kindle a glow of warmth in my chest. "Woman?" I echo the word with a blush. "I still feel like a child most of the time."

"But you're not a child. You're capable of anything, Orca. I hope you'll always remember that."

I am struck speechless for a moment, my eyes blurring with the beginnings of tears.

Papa has never told me this. No one has ever told me this.

"Thank you," I say, my voice a whisper as I let my hand slide out of my lap and fold over his. "Thank you, Adam."

He freezes at my touch, looking a bit surprised—just like he did this morning when I caressed his freshly shaven face. I wonder if it's considered bad etiquette in the Otherworld to touch someone whenever you feel the urge to. But it can't be helped. Something in me hungers to feel his skin on mine—to learn every etch and detail that makes him one of a kind.

"I find it hard to believe you're not married," I say. "You seem like the sort of man every woman would want. Patient, kind, wise, strong… And you're very handsome, on top of it all."

Adam looks taken aback. "Uh, thank you," he replies with a quizzical little frown, like that's not really what he wanted to say. "Marriage is something I've… never gotten around to."

"Because you're too busy working? Or because you've never been in love?"

I can tell by the surprised glint in his eyes that it's a question he's not used to being asked. There's a trace of a smile on his lips as he lets his guard down.

"Never been in love," he admits in a whisper.

"Neither have I."

That makes him laugh. And only then do I realize how silly I must sound—of course I've never been in love. I've never had anyone *to* love except my father.

"You will be," Adam assures me, straightening up but keeping my hand enveloped in his. He looks down at our entwined fingers, gently tracing his thumb over my knuckles. "And whoever you end up falling in love with… he'll be the luckiest man in the world." With that, he releases my hand and steps back. "Now I'm going to go get that firewood. You stay here."

THAT EVENING, Adam helps me prepare dinner. We stand side by side at the counter, slicing peppers and mushrooms in companionable silence while Lucius snores on the floor under the table.

I love stealing glances at Adam when he's not paying attention—taking note of all his little quirks and mindless habits. The way he always clears his throat before bringing up a new topic. The way he takes off his shoes—left foot first, then right. The way he pauses to think before answering a meaningful question. Even the way his hands move the knife gracefully over the cutting board. Slice, slice, slice, through the golden peppers.

"Orca."

"Hmm?"

"I don't… want to pry or anything," Adam begins, his voice soft and tentative. "But I was just wondering…"

"Yes?"

He clears his throat, pausing to slide the chopped peppers into a bowl. "What happened to your mother?"

"She… died," I answer softly.

Adam doesn't seem surprised to learn this. "I'm so sorry."

"It was a long time ago. I was too young to remember anything about her. Sometimes I wish I did, though—even if it meant missing her more. Papa doesn't like to talk about her. I suppose it hurts him too much. He doesn't even have any pictures of her, so I have no idea what she looked like."

"Oh. I thought the photo in his sock drawer was of him and your mother."

I frown. "What photo?"

Adam looks down, a flicker of regret crossing his face. "Sorry, I… just happened to see it when I was borrowing clothes from your dad. You didn't know about it?"

"No… I didn't."

I drop everything and rush out of the kitchen, heading for Papa's room. Sure enough, I find a small silver picture frame in the top drawer of his dresser.

My heart swells as I turn it over.

Mama looks young in the photograph. She's standing on the steps of an old stone church, wearing a high-necked gown of white silk, beaming up at Papa with a smile bright enough to outshine the sun. Papa must be at least thirty years old, with dark, curly hair and a glint of adventure in his eyes.

It was their wedding day. September 29, 1977.

Why did he never share it with me? Does it hurt him too much to see Mama's face? Is that why he prefers to keep her hidden in a drawer like this?

A sudden wave of anger wells up in me. That wasn't fair of him. I deserve to see this picture. I deserve to have at least one small memory of my mother—even if Papa wishes to block it all out.

Adam looks up as I return to the kitchen, the photo frame still clasped in my hands. "Why would Papa hide this from me?"

There is a long silence before Adam speaks, his voice cautious and reflective. "Maybe he was hiding it from *himself.* Maybe it was too difficult… It must have been painful for him to lose his wife like that."

"But at least he *had* her. At least they shared some happy times and made some memories. He doesn't have to think of Mama and only remember what he's lost—he can remember all the good things. All the happy moments they shared. He must remember *some* good things."

Adam steps closer, looking down at the photo in my hands. "Everyone has a different way of dealing with grief, Orca. Sometimes happy memories hurt even more than sad ones."

"How can that be?"

Adam shrugs. "You miss someone the most when you remember what your life was like when you had them. The kind of person you were because of them. And that's what tears you apart—because you feel like you lost part of yourself, too."

"Like if the sun went down and never came back up again," I muse quietly, tilting my head as I take in the details of the wedding photo. "I wonder if she was Papa's sun. I wonder if she was his soulmate."

I prop the picture frame against a jar of fresh lilacs on the kitchen table, then return to chopping vegetables. "I read what you wrote about soulmates in your journal, but your entry was unfinished. You started to write, 'people want to believe in soulmates because…' and that's where you stopped writing."

Adam lifts his gaze to the window, a distant look in his eyes.

"Because…?" I prompt, waiting for the rest of that ever-unfinished sentence.

"Because that way, we can't make a mistake," he says. "We can't choose the wrong person if the right person is already destined for us. And if we find them, this 'other half,' we think they'll magically complete us—they'll fill that void in us, and we won't need to take responsibility or strive to fill the emptiness ourselves."

I ponder this while slicing the last of the mushrooms. "The *khaos*?"

"Exactly. I think the idea of soulmates can be problematic because it makes you believe you need someone else to complete you. Like you can never be whole without that person."

I turn his words over in my mind, studying the undertones like grooves in a branch of coral. "Maybe it's not someone who's preordained," I murmur, thinking aloud. "Maybe some people just *make* soulmates. They find someone and love them so much that they sort of… become part of that person. And it's not that they were one being before, but they are *now*, and that's why it hurts when one of them goes away. Because it only hurts when one of you goes away, right? Not before you ever meet them."

"That's true," Adam says, his eyes reading mine back and forth like jots of Latin. "I never saw it like that before."

An indescribable feeling comes alive in me again, dancing and fluttering like the butterflies in the greenhouse. We're standing only a few feet apart, but it's not close enough. My body hungers to feel him. More of him. All of him.

Without thinking twice, I wrap my arms around him and pull him close—my face against his chest, breathing in his fresh, clean scent. Soap and pine. I avoid his broken ribs, letting one hand catch on the belt loop of his pants, and spreading my other hand over his back.

Why am I hugging him?

I have no idea. I just need to.

After a stunned moment, I feel Adam's arms circle around me. His warm hands settle on my hips as he hugs me in response, not saying anything, just holding me. There is a wordless conversation in our embrace. And somehow, it communicates more than any language could hope to express.

LOGIC V. EMOTION

adam

I don't believe in soulmates. I never have. In my youth, I toyed with the idea of fate and destiny—questioning every impossible thing that laughed in the face of logic and turned our neat-and-tidy theories into chaos. I wondered about fate, studied it like a crystal casting prisms around me. *Is this real, or just a trick of the light?* Maybe love is like that. A glance into the fourth dimension, something intangible yet beautiful—darting away from you the moment you try to hold onto it.

Tenens infinitum.

Impossible.

The infinite cannot be held.

Yet when Orca wrapped her arms around me, I couldn't stop myself from embracing her. I couldn't help wondering if the infinite *could* be held, and this was it—this unexplainable magnetism between us.

I've never felt anything like it before.

It defies all logic, it tramples my preconceived ideas of what love should feel like, it shakes the very ground I stand on, and yet—

I'm not afraid of it.

I'm hungry for it.

There used to be no person in the world I would talk about the multiverse or the butterfly effect with. No person in the world I would feel comfortable discussing the idea of soulmates with. No person in the world until now.

Orca, the girl who saved my life.

Orca, the girl who wears flowers and butterflies in her hair.

Orca, the girl I feel myself slipping, slipping, *falling* for.

If I were a man who acted upon the impulse of his feelings, I would have kissed her right then and there. I would have told her she was beautiful when she looked into my eyes and told me I was handsome. Instead, I said *thank you.*

Thank you? Honestly?

I should have told her the truth—that she is the most beautiful woman I've ever met. Not just on the outside. Not just the way the light sparkles in her eyes like turquoise and gilds the soft folds of her hair, not just the lilt of her voice or the music of her laughter, not just the elegant shape of her body, like a marble sculpture straight out of Michelangelo's proficient hands.

She is beautiful because she is one of a kind—a single, glorious star lighting up her own solar system. Beautiful because she lives in this hidden utopia, far from the madness of the world she desperately, foolishly yearns for.

These thoughts keep me awake late into the night as I lie on her father's bed and listen to the waves crashing outside the window.

There's a reason Orca's father has gone to such great lengths to keep his daughter safe from the harsh realities of the "other world." There's a reason why he doesn't allow trips to the mainland.

Orca's life is a radical, carefully executed plan of protection.

It may not be what she *wants* now, but she doesn't understand how experience can ruin someone. She doesn't understand the value of what she's been given. How could she? When she's never known anything but this?

In a day or so, I'm returning to the mainland, to my home. I'm leaving Orca behind. And I'll likely never see her again.

What good can come of encouraging feelings between us?

She may not be able to intellectualize the concept of romance or love, but she possesses something more admirable than intellect: a heart brimming with purity of emotion.

She's honesty. She's grace. She's even more of a mystery to me than I am to her. She is a forest so perfectly serene and untouched, I am torn between the desire to explore this new wonder of the world and the fear of polluting its holiness by so much as *breathing* on it.

My flesh pushes me one way; my conscience pulls me back. Alone in her father's bedroom, failing miserably at sleeping, I find myself caught in a desperate tug-of-war between logic and emotion.

I can't disrupt her life. I can't upset the delicate equilibrium of her world. I won't be the one to drive a wedge between her and her father. Not to mention, I'm way too old for her. She's still a teenager, and I'm staring thirty in the face.

We can't be destined for each other because everything is standing between us.

If fate is responsible for bringing us together, fate has miscalculated badly.

Still, I can't deny my feelings. I can't pretend the whole world doesn't fall away when she looks into my eyes—and me with it, falling, falling, falling for her.

I can't speak of it.

But I can't hide it, either.

Too restless to hope for sleep, I push back my blankets and switch on the bedside lamp. My journal waits on the nightstand in a ring of tungsten light. Orca was reading it aloud after dinner, which would normally turn me into a mess of nerves and embarrassment. Yet, when she read my deepest thoughts aloud, her voice enshrouded the room in heavenly peace. Everything else ceased to exist, and I felt like I was being seen, truly *seen*, for the first time in my life.

Afterward, she passed the journal to me and begged me to read some Latin bits aloud. Her gaze made the pronunciation tangle stupidly over my tongue, and it didn't come out the way I wanted, but she listened as though it was the best recitation of Latin she ever heard.

Now in the golden lamplight, I part the softened pages of my journal. The latest entry is not an entry at all, but two of the tiny pink flowers that fell out of Orca's braid earlier. I found them on the floor and tucked them into my pocket. Now they lie pressed between the pages of the book, forever reminding me of the way she looked in the greenhouse this morning, talking to the orchids as a little blue butterfly danced around her head.

I press my eyes shut, drawing in a steady breath.

No.

Yes.

"Damn it," I mutter, reaching for a pen on the nightstand. Before I know it, the tip is scrawling across a clean page, lines of ink flowing straight from my heart.

Untouchable beauty
Are you real or fantasy?
Lost to the world, yet found
by that which truly matters

Not a word passes your lips that isn't
Honesty
Yet all I feel in the presence of your wild soul is
Mystery
All I feel is my own soul coming undone

What is the butterfly effect,
You ask me
I tell you what is true
But all I want to say is
You

You are the butterfly
who so innocently flutters her wings
And stirs winds
Strong enough
To destroy me

Untouchable beauty
I wish
In a way
That you were a fantasy

IT'S NOT RAINING when I wake up. The looming quiet is the first thing I notice when I open my eyes. Hazy gray light filters through the cracks in the shutters, indicating another overcast dawn.

I limp into my now-dry Carhartt pants, which Orca managed to wash all the blood out of, but I don't bother with a shirt since she isn't awake yet. As I pass her bedroom door, I glimpse her petite figure sleeping peacefully under a pile of blankets—rivers of golden-brown hair flowing over her pillow. Even now, in the stillness of the morning, I feel that magnetism stirring through the air. It's like a lift in altitude, a change in atmospheric pressure. Something I can only detect when I'm near her.

Shaking myself out of my daze, I silently pull her bedroom door shut and move on to my mission:

Checking the weather.

Without access to a television or radio, it's difficult to gauge the shifts in Washington's erratic weather patterns—but I don't need a meteorologist to tell me visibility is going to be crap today. I don't even need to venture beyond the doorstep to make that discovery.

Cotton-thick fog surrounds the lighthouse in every direction, so dense I can barely see five feet in front of me.

It's a strange feeling, knowing I'm trapped here on this island with Orca and there's nothing anyone can do about it. Strange because only a few days ago, I was struggling to survive in the woods with a sprained ankle and broken ribs, and all I wanted was to be home. But now, it's almost a relief to know that I can't leave yet.

That I can stay here, with Orca. If only for one more day.

No sooner do I step back inside the house than my phone starts ringing from the kitchen table. I flip it open, answering the call.

"How many miles you got on the viz, Captain?" Jack's voice brings a smile to my face.

"Big fat zero," I answer with a sigh. "You?"

"Mmm, about three hundred feet if I close one eye and squint."

"I'm surprised you're up this early."

Jack grunts. "Haven't been sleeping too good. I keep having this recurring nightmare where ceiling and visibility are unlimited, but I can never get to the port no matter how hard I try."

"Sounds like a dream with a deeper meaning."

"Deeper meaning, my ass," Jack fires back. "It means I'm sick of not having you around. I want to fly out there and bring you back just as soon as this damn overcast clears."

I shrug my cell phone between my shoulder and ear as I stoop to toss more firewood into the stove. "Well, it looks like there's no chance of that happening today. Fog's really holding on. But don't worry, there's no rush. I'm doing fine. You can let Mom know that everything is fine."

My brother falls silent for a moment. "You having a good time with Orca?"

"Yeah, I mean… I've been enjoying her company."

"Enjoying her company?" Jack volleys my words back with a laugh. "And what exactly do you guys do together to *enjoy* each other's company?"

"We've just been talking."

"About what?"

"Philosophy and stuff."

"And stuff."

"Jack."

He bursts out laughing. "I'm just trying to piss you off, man."

"Thanks a lot." I run a hand over my hair. "Orca is actually very philosophical. She… has an interesting way of looking at life."

"Mm. Philosophical? Did you tell her that's your biggest turn-on?"

"Very funny."

I change the subject, giving Jack a list of things to manage for my business until I get back. I know he's only pulling my leg about Orca, but even the mention of her is enough to reawaken all the feelings I wrestled with last night.

The poem I wrote at midnight while she slept in the other room.

The way she looked in the greenhouse yesterday, butterflies in her hair.

The ticking clock counting down the hours, minutes, *seconds* we have left together.

What's the use of talking about it? What's the use in telling Jack about my ridiculous inner struggle? No good can come from brooding over these feelings and prolonging the inevitable.

Tomorrow morning, I will leave this place, and Orca will stay.

And that will be the end of it.

ONE FAILING

orca

Will I ever see him again?

I don't know. And I can't ask him. I can't make him feel obliged to return for my sake. Just because Adam Stevenson is the most fascinating person I've ever met doesn't mean he feels the same way about me. In fact, I'm sure he doesn't. How could he? He's met so many people, seen so many places, and done so many things.

I, on the other hand, have been nowhere and done nothing. I can't offer the slightest fascination for him.

So when he tells me of the clear skies forecast for tomorrow, I force an unruffled smile onto my face and make my best effort to seem pleased for him. "Tomorrow?" The word struggles out of me, small and timid.

"Yeah," Adam says. "It looks like a dense fog for the rest of today. But according to Jack, this system should be moving out by nightfall. He says it's going to be clear tomorrow, believe it or not. Jack's going to fly out here first thing in the morning."

I nod, saying nothing in reply. We're back in the greenhouse, and I use the plants to my advantage—hiding my face from Adam lest he catch sight of my disappointment.

I fight to hold back the words: *Don't go, don't leave, don't leave me, Adam Stevenson...*

As I mindlessly water the plants, my thoughts drift to the conversation Adam and I had last night about soulmates. *It's not that they were one being before,* I said, *but they are now, and that's why it hurts when one of them goes away.*

I didn't speak as a mere spectator—I spoke from experience.

Adam Stevenson has become a part of me. Like the Greek myth he wrote about, I feel as though we are not two separate beings but one being. He explained that Zeus was the "god of the sky." Was it not the sky—the violent storm—that brought us together? That has kept us together all this time? Is it not the sky that will tear us apart when he flies away tomorrow morning?

The aching pull in my heart at the thought of him leaving cannot be described as anything other than the feeling of my soul being split in two and tossed asunder.

"IT SEEMS ALL YOUR weather predictions are correct," I muse, peering out the kitchen window at the opaque white world beyond. "This fog's settling in to stay."

From the table, Adam murmurs a laugh. "They're not *my* predictions. Meteorologists forecast the weather."

I sit at the table and lean forward on my elbows, studying the chaos of clock parts strewn in front of him. He noticed the broken timepiece on the fireplace mantel and asked me when it had stopped working.

"Clearly, at half past seven," I said, which made him laugh and clarify what he meant—when did it last tell the correct time? I couldn't remember. Years ago. Papa had opened it up several times in attempts to fix it but called the clock's inner workings "fathomless" and decreed that we had no need for more than one clock.

"He has a point," I told Adam. "I mean, he has a pocket watch, and I never need to know the time. If it's daylight and good weather, I'm outside doing my chores. If it's dark or bad weather, I'm inside."

Adam seemed intrigued by this way of looking at time. I watch as he mends the misbehaving clock, attempting to commit every part of him to memory. His big hands move delicately over the clock's innards; his brow is furrowed with concentration as he works, soft gray light etching the features of his face.

"It's funny, isn't it," Adam says quietly, "how a clock can just stop. And time stands still. At least, our concept of time…" He carefully fixes a tiny gear into place. "I'm sure you read some of my ramblings about it in my journal."

A smile crosses my lips. "Yes. Although I must admit, most of it went over my head."

Adam nods. "Mine too."

"But you wrote it."

"I don't understand everything I write. If I did, I wouldn't write it down."

"Hm. It seems just the opposite for most people. Don't they write books about the things they're sure of?"

"Things they *think* they're sure of," Adam corrects me.

"But… what about science? Biology…"

"Observable data. Most of it is probably true." He looks up from the clockwork and catches my gaze. "But what if the things we're the most sure of are the things we're the most wrong about?"

"Like time," I offer.

"Exactly. Because 'time' is just our measurement of something im-measurable… Otherwise, everything *would* stand still when the clock stops."

"I wish it would. I wish time would stand still right now."

"Why?"

"Because tomorrow… you'll be gone."

The light in his eyes dims when I say that, which makes me wonder: *Does he feel the same way about leaving?*

I can't ask him.

"Your father will be back tomorrow," Adam assures me. "You won't be all alone."

"I know. It's not about being alone; it's just about… it's…" My heart swells inside me as Adam holds me in his gaze. "I'll miss you," I say at last.

Three words too small and simple to describe the enormity of pain I feel when I imagine him gone.

And just for a heartbeat, I see that same ache reflected in his eyes.

"I'll miss you, too," he admits.

The threat of tears blurs my vision as I tug my gaze away from his. The only way to avoid crying is to push the sadness away as quickly as possible and replace it with something joyful.

Gathering up my courage, I rise from the table. "You know what we should do?"

Adam glances at me questioningly.

"Make cookies."

Nothing gladdens an overcast day like baking—a *scientific fact* that I try to convince Adam to believe as I twirl around the kitchen and gather ingredients. He continues working on the clock while I measure the oil and honey, the latter of which I make Adam sample. He agrees that our bees make the best honey in the world. I explain the process of harvesting honey as I crack eggs into a bowl at the counter, whisking and whipping ingredients together from memory. Lucius sleeps under the table, a lazy pile of sandy fur, paws twitching as he dreams of chasing seagulls. It seems that time could be standing still right now—would we know if it was?

I stop mixing to swipe a bite of dough and pop it into my mouth.

Mmm… perfection.

I sigh with satisfaction, closing my eyes. When I open them again, I find Adam's hand in the bowl, stealing cookie dough.

I smack him away. "Adam!"

He laughs, hand retreating. "What? It's not fair if you're the only one who gets to try it."

"All right, fine." I swipe a fingertip of cookie dough and shove it past his smiling lips. They feel as lovely as they look, though I only touch them for a second before sticking my sugary fingertip back in my own mouth.

Adam smirks, his gaze shifting to my lips.

"Why are you smiling?"

He shakes his head. "Nothing. You, uh… you have flour on your face." He reaches up and gently strokes his thumb over my left temple. All my senses seem to intensify within a single breath. The warmth of his skin on mine is *everything*. My heart flutters in my chest as his fingers trail slowly down the side of my cheek, brushing softly against my lower lip.

As if suddenly awakening from a sleepwalk, he withdraws his hand and takes a step back. Just like that, the moment has passed.

Adam turns away to put another log on the stove, and I refocus on my cookie-baking, nervous energy buzzing under my skin. To distract myself, I start singing a song Papa taught me, which Adam recognizes. He says it's called "Wild Mountain Thyme." By the time the cookies are done and the house is sweet with the aroma of cinnamon and sugar, I've taught Adam all the lyrics to the song—and I force him to sing it with me. I perch on the edge of the table, scratching Lucius's head as the water boils for tea, and Adam smiles bashfully because he doesn't know how good his singing voice is.

When the cookies come out of the oven, we settle on the floor in front of the fireplace with ceramic mugs of tea fresh from our flower garden. Lucius lies between us, whining over the cookies he can't have.

I fall into a pensive silence, watching Adam in the firelight and noticing how different he looks now compared to that night I dragged him in from the storm.

"You must be looking forward to your father coming back," he says.

"Yes and no," I admit, gazing down at the steam curling from my mug. "I'll be glad to have Papa home again, but… I'll be sad to lose *you*."

I pause, searching his face for a sign—a hint of regret or pain or dread. *Anything* that could reveal his true feelings without him saying it in so many words. But if he feels anything, he keeps it under lock and key. I glimpse only the barest twitch of his jaw, the slightest flex of his hand in the firelight.

"I can't stay, Orca," he says, his voice a mahogany whisper. "I need to go back home."

"But we can still be friends, can't we?"

"Of course we can be friends." Adam submits to a weak smile. "If you come to the mainland someday, you can look me up."

"And you can come back to the island whenever you want."

He looks down. "I don't know if that will be possible."

"Of course it's possible. You're a pilot. You can fly!"

Adam's smile is like the flicker of a single match struggling against a cold front. A wave of embarrassment hits me, coloring my cheeks with a blush.

"Or don't you *want* to come back and see me? I'm sorry. That wasn't fair. Of course, you have your own life and your own people, and you're very busy—"

"No, I *do* want to come back. I…" He falters, his gaze roaming over my face until his voice returns, softer now. "That's not how I feel about it, Orca. That's not how I feel about… you."

"How *do* you feel about me?"

For a breathless moment, Adam only stares at me—a quiet conflict raging in his eyes. "How I feel doesn't matter." He reaches for a log on the hearth and tosses it into the fireplace, sending a whoosh of golden sparks swirling up the chimney.

Quiet fills the space between us. Adam watches the fire. I watch Adam.

His response might puzzle me if I didn't know him. If I hadn't read his journal and familiarized myself with the way his beautiful, brilliant mind works.

"Do you know *your* one failing, Adam Stevenson?"

He tilts his head to look at me, eyebrows quirked in surprise. "Just one?"

I nod.

"What is it?"

I can tell by the way he asks that he's genuinely curious to hear my answer. There's a strange sort of power in having his full attention—in seeing him eager, waiting, keen to know what I'm going to say.

"You're always putting yourself last."

He peers at me with a puzzled frown. "What makes you say that?"

"Well, when I was reading your journal, it just seemed so obvious. You're always thinking of others before yourself. Jack, your parents… You're always doing things to help them, and at the same time, you feel like you're not doing enough. You wrote about wanting to build a home but not having anyone to build it for. And how if you're not building it *for* someone… it's not really a home; it's just a house. And I thought that was beautiful."

Adam looks down, his ears flushing red. "You really did read the whole thing, didn't you?"

I bite on a mischievous smile. "Sorry."

He only needs to glance at my expression for the truth. "No, you're not."

"No, I'm not."

We both laugh unexpectedly, then fall silent, like two joyful waves crashing on the shore and dissolving in a line of foam.

"I didn't know putting yourself last was a failing," Adam murmurs.

"Well, I suppose it's a virtue," I concede. "But it can also be a vice if it stops you from having the kind of life you want. If you deny yourself because you're afraid you'll be letting someone else down…"

Adam gazes into the fire. Flickering gold light outlines his profile, igniting the scar on his cheek and sharpening the square edge of his jaw. "My dad has always been a hard worker," he begins, his voice low and reflective. "When I was a kid, he worked three jobs. He had a lot of debt and wouldn't sit still until it was paid off and he was free. I wanted to help out, so I started working when I was still in school. My first job was a paper route when I was twelve. Jack was just a baby then, so Mom had her hands full. I'd take care of him when she couldn't—bathe him, change his diapers, read him bedtime stories."

I smile, cradling my tea mug beneath my chin. "Jack said you were like a second father to him."

Adam nods thoughtfully, toying with a bit of tinder that has strayed from the hearth. "Kids at school used to pick on me. Say I was a mama's boy. Maybe I *was* a mama's boy. I didn't care. I saw how hard my parents worked. I saw that I could do something to help them, and I wish I could have done more. But I did what I could." He tosses the kindling into the fire, watching it wither into flame. "When I was fifteen, I got a job working at the airport. Grunt work, really—cleaning bathrooms, taking out the trash, washing the windows. But I loved just being around those planes, watching them land and take off…"

"And that's when you started flying?"

"I started flying because a very generous pilot was nice enough to take a starry-eyed kid for a spin over the islands." A smile forms on his lips at the recollection. "That's when I knew: I wanted to fly for the rest of my life. I didn't care how much time and hard work it would take to get there."

"And Jack followed in your footsteps," I add. "Like father, like son."

Adam grunts a laugh, absentmindedly petting Lucius, who has fallen asleep between us. "Jack has always been the opposite of me."

"Yet he wants to be like you," I point out. "He worships you."

Adam looks unconvinced. "What makes you think that?"

"It's as plain as the nose on your face."

He narrows his eyes at me, as though I'm written in a foreign language he can't translate. "How did you learn so much about us in just a few days?"

I shrug, sipping my tea. "Papa calls it 'reading between the lines.' It means seeing things that are hidden in plain sight. Getting to know someone by the things they *don't* say."

"And what is your conclusion?"

I reach down to stroke Lucius's fuzzy head, letting my hand ebb and flow toward Adam's, hoping for an accidental touch. "My conclusion… is that you're too good to be true, Adam Stevenson."

He gives a modest laugh, shaking his head.

"My conclusion is that you shouldn't always put yourself last. You would be a kind, giving person even if you never tried to be. It's just who you are. And what you feel *does* matter. It matters to me."

Adam looks down, his hand drifting over Lucius's back and brushing softly against mine. I try to ignore the way it makes my heart race double time.

"And my conclusion," he whispers, "is that you are wiser than anyone I've ever met."

I almost laugh. "How can that be? When I know so little of the world?"

"Knowledge is not wisdom, Orca. You could see the whole world, learn everything there is to learn, read every book written by every philosopher… and still go to your grave not a fraction wiser than the day you were born. Most people follow the compass of the world. But you have a different compass." He spreads his free hand over his heart. "Here. And it always points true north. Doesn't it?"

I nod slowly.

Adam watches me, his magnetic gaze wandering over my face, my neck, my lips. He seems to fall into a state of quiet hypnosis—and I fall with him, locked in his gaze, unable to look away. Then, without warning, the spell is broken. He withdraws his hand from Lucius and turns his attention back to the fire.

"Follow it," he says softly. "It will never fail you."

AD ASTRA

adam

A hand gently grasps my shoulder. "Adam. Adam, wake up."

I reluctantly drag myself from the oblivion of sleep, moaning curses under my breath as I roll onto my back. I squint into the darkness, disoriented, until I see Orca standing beside my bed. She's wearing the nightgown and shawl I first saw her in, wild hair tumbling over her shoulders, eyes sparkling in the semi-dark.

"What's the matter?" My voice comes out groggy.

"Nothing," she says. "I just want to show you something."

"Show me what?"

A secretive smile twitches onto her lips. "Something that can't be described with words."

"All right," I relent, climbing out of bed.

I follow Orca through the living room to a narrow door on the opposite side of the house—the door that leads to the lighthouse tower. A spiral staircase soars above us, bathed in navy blue afterglow from a narrow window on the upper wall. Orca skips ahead of me, her bare feet noiseless on the wrought-iron steps. My ankle still hurts when I put my full weight on it, so I use the railing for support and take the stairs one at a time.

When we reach the top, Orca leads me through what looks like a submarine door and into the lantern room. I shield my eyes from the blind-ingly bright light, which stands five feet tall in the center of the circular room—rotating slowly as it pierces the endless black night in every direction.

"Is that an airport beacon?" I ask, recognizing the distinct shape of the light.

Orca nods. "It's visible up to twenty-two miles at sea. Papa says it's been here since he started keeping the light."

"I was expecting something different. One of those lamps that look like a giant lightbulb sliced into pieces."

"A Fresnel lens?" Orca grins. "No, those went out of style a long time ago. But I still love the way they look. This one doesn't need as much maintenance as the Fresnel—it even has an automatic bulb-changing mechanism in case one of them burns out." She kneels beside the base of the lamp and snaps a lever. The light dies, submerging the room in darkness.

"Wait, can you do that?"

Orca stands and brushes off her knees. "For a few minutes. No one will know. Come on."

She grabs my hand and pulls me through another door, which swings open on whining hinges and lets in a gust of cool, salty wind from the sea. We step out onto the narrow catwalk that circles the lantern room.

Orca leans closer to me, her fingers interlaced with mine. "Adam, look up."

The sky is overflowing with millions of stars shimmering like diamonds scattered across an ocean of black silk. The Milky Way spreads her blue and purple wings above us, layers upon layers of stars crowded so close together it's hard to find dark space in between.

"Isn't it beautiful?" Orca's voice pulls me back down to earth. I realize I'm still holding her hand—or maybe she's holding mine. Either way, it's my favorite part of this moment.

"Very beautiful," I say, unable to take my eyes off her. "Indescribably beautiful."

"I knew you'd appreciate it. Papa says we have the darkest sky in the world because there's no light pollution out here."

I tilt my head back, tracing the endless patterns in the night sky. "Do you know any constellations?"

"Some. Do you?"

"Some."

Orca laughs, a snatch of music on the wind. "Ursa Minor," she says, pointing up at the sky. "And the North Star."

"Oh, come on. That's the easiest one."

"Then *you* find one."

It takes some searching before I find the constellation I'm looking for.

"Lupus. The wolf." I point to the edge of the Milky Way with my fingertip, drawing imaginary lines between the stars.

"I see it!" Orca whispers excitedly. "And Scorpius, just there." She reaches up to draw the shape of the constellation, and our two hands become one silhouette in the sky as I align our index fingertips and help her trace the lines of Scorpius.

When I look down, I find her staring into my eyes—as if searching for constellations in me.

I'm close enough to hear every shivering breath leave her lungs. I'm close enough to feel the warmth of her body against mine. I'm close enough to kiss her.

I know I shouldn't. I *can't.*

But she's here, in my arms, and tomorrow she won't be. She's here, standing beside me at the top of the world, the edge of the universe. Starlight illuminates the curves of her neck, the wind tangles softly in her hair, and she's looking at me like she wants me to kiss her.

Does she want me to kiss her?

It doesn't matter what she wants. It doesn't matter what *I* want.

Don't do it, Adam.

Desire grips me from the inside, pulling me under like an inescapable current. Should I say something? Should I tell her how beautiful she is? Should I tell her that I'm falling in love with her? I don't have the words.

"Adam?"

I snap out of my thoughts. "Yes?"

Orca glances from my eyes to my mouth. "I… I have a very strange feeling when I'm near you. It's like the whole world is tipping, and I feel like I'm losing my balance. And my heart starts pounding like I just ran up and down the stairs three times, and I want… I want…"

Her gaze slips down my body, sending a blaze of warmth coursing through me. I wait for the rest of her sentence, fighting hard against the current.

"I want you," she whispers.

I can't have heard right.

"Me?" I echo in disbelief.

She nods, spreading her free hand over my heart. "You."

Her description of this "strange feeling" is so simple and innocent, but I know exactly what she means. I know exactly what it is.

I feel it burning inside me with the violence of a forest fire. Destroying me.

This butterfly setting off a hurricane.

Have I done the same to her?

I can't believe it.

All I can do is stare at her, my control slipping.

"I feel that way, too," I confess at last, tucking a strand of hair behind her ear and tracing my fingertips down the curve of her neck.

Orca's glinting eyes dart back and forth between mine. "Do Otherworlders have a word for it?"

The overwhelming desire for her builds in me like a cresting wave and dwarfs my willpower. I can't fight it back any longer. All I can do is lean close to her face and whisper, "Yes. We do."

And I kiss her.

LOVE

orca

Time stands still as Adam's lips part to softly take mine captive. I feel his fingertips brush against my cheek, sliding into my hair and curling at the nape of my neck. His other hand cradles my waist, sending a rush of fever through my whole body.

My lips soften and open for him, and he kisses me so gently, so deeply—I feel like my heart is falling away from me. Everything is falling away from me.

For a moment, we are two stars floating in the infinity of the universe.

Then Adam eases back. I look into his face, searching for a clue as to what comes next. His eyes burn with a thousand unspoken words, but he only leans his forehead against mine and whispers, "We'd better go back inside."

"Must we?" I rasp, my lips so close to his yet so far away. I want to kiss him again, to move in the same smooth, experienced way he does; to run my fingers through *his* hair so he knows how good it feels. The longing for him squeezes me so tight inside, I can hardly breathe.

I catch the reflection of that same desire in his eyes, but he steps back, taking his hands off me. Only then do I notice the cold wind blowing off the ocean.

"Yes," he says. "We must."

I follow him through the door to the lantern room, snapping the light back on before we descend the stairs into the house. We part ways in the hallway between our respective bedrooms.

"Goodnight, Orca," Adam says, vanishing into my father's room.

"Goodnight, Adam."

I have no idea what just happened, but I loved it. Every part of it.

I love *him*. Every part of him.

That's the word he was going to tell me before he kissed me.

Love.

I think about that word as I lie awake in the dark, listening to the crashing surf outside my window.

Love.

I've used it to describe many other precious things in my life. Papa, Lucius, the ocean, the greenhouse, the orchids, and the driftwood carvings on my dresser. All of those things kindle such different sorts of love in my heart. My love for Papa has always been the deepest of all.

Until Adam Stevenson showed up.

Looking at everything else in my life, I can't find a comparison to the immensity of love I feel for him.

It frightens me because tomorrow he will be gone—yet my feelings for him will remain. I will be torn in two, and I fear I will bleed inwardly. I will be forever cursed with an invisible wound that I have no remedy for.

Will he feel the same way when he leaves me behind?

At the top of the lighthouse, he said he *did* feel the same way about me. And then he kissed me. Not on the forehead, as Papa has always done, but on the lips. A kiss so soft and gentle, yet so overwhelming and dizzying. A kiss I shall never forget as long as I live.

How will I bear it when he leaves tomorrow? How will I say goodbye? How will I watch him fly away, far away from me?

How will I live with my soul torn in two?

ODYSSEUS AND THE SIREN

adam

What was I thinking?

That's the question I ask myself when I'm back in bed.

What was I thinking, kissing her like that? Am I out of my mind?

There is no logical way we can be together. I've told myself that a hundred times. I've accepted it. We are going to part ways tomorrow. I'm leaving for Whidbey Island, and she's staying here, and I *refuse* to disrupt her life. I already feel like I've polluted her purity with that kiss.

I curse myself for it, kick myself for it. I wish I could go back and force myself not to do it. But if I hadn't, I might be regretting *that* decision instead.

I lie awake in the dark, listening to the pounding waves outside.

Maybe I'm just overthinking all of this.

We kissed. So what?

It changes nothing.

No, it changes everything.

I AWAKEN AT SUNRISE. For the first time in what feels like an eternity, patches of blue sky peek through the slats of the window shutters.

Orca's bedroom door is still shut, so I try to be as quiet as possible as I limp into the kitchen and get the fire going to start some coffee. Lucius follows me around, sniffing for his breakfast. I scratch his ears and tell him that he'll have to wait until Orca wakes up.

When I open the front door, a gust of salty morning breeze rushes inside, carrying the cries of seagulls as they swoop and dive in the sunshine. It's a perfect morning—ceiling and visibility unlimited. Jack will be thrilled.

As I descend the front steps, I take in the view that's been hiding behind fog for days.

Breathtaking is an understatement.

Miles and miles of ocean unfurl in every direction, an endless vista painted every shade of blue—the waves, the sky, the distant islands bathed in morning haze. The lighthouse stands perched on the edge of it all, like a fortress guarding the ends of the earth.

Now I can understand why Orca calls it the Otherworld. The neighboring islands seem far away out here. There are no signs of civilization except the boats and planes she must occasionally see passing by. Everything is so out of reach.

A hand touches my back, making me jump.

"Sorry," Orca apologizes with a little amused smirk. "I didn't mean to startle you."

"It's fine. I just didn't hear you coming."

She looks even more beautiful in the sunlight, her hair crowned by a halo of gold. I wish I could run my fingers through it.

"Did you sleep well?" she asks, eyes sparkling as she looks up at me.

I shake my head. "Not particularly. You?"

"Not particularly." A blush colors her cheeks as she looks down, trailing one fingertip over my forearm until her hand slides into mine. The gesture is easy and comfortable, like we're an old married couple who have done this a hundred times.

Damn.

"It's a beautiful morning," I force myself to say, turning back to face the view.

"Mm, it certainly is. The sun feels good." Orca leans her head on my arm, and I feel the warmth of her cheek against my bicep.

I clench my jaw, staring at the horizon with the concentration of a sailor trying not to get seasick. The water is as calm as a lake this morning, calm enough to hear the telltale *PSSSHHHH* of a blowhole somewhere close by, sending up a plume of white mist in the sunshine. The unmistakable exhale of a whale coming to the surface.

Orca gasps, squeezing my hand, when she sees a swirl of movement in the water below us. Just beyond the rocks, a pod of killer whales porpoise gracefully through the swaying kelp, their dorsal fins piercing the surface of the water as they come up for air.

Orca drops my hand and takes off running down the slope of grass to the rocky shore.

"Hey, where are you going?"

"To say hello, of course!" She laughs over her shoulder. "Come on!" She skips down the flagstone path, her hair rippling in the wind.

I follow her down to the shore, cautious of where I step with my bad ankle. The rocks are staggered like natural steps, leading down to the tidal pools below. Sea mist splashes the hem of Orca's nightgown as she hops from stone to stone, featherlight and barefoot, finally stopping on one massive rock surrounded by whales.

Geysers of mist spray up everywhere, punctuated by the sound of massive lungs exhaling, inhaling.

PSSSHHHH, WOSHHH...

Orca laughs from where she stands on the barnacled rock, looking like a siren with legs—a divine, mythical creature born from sea and stardust. No sooner does the thought cross my mind than she cups her hands around her mouth and cries out a siren-like vocalization so authentic, I wonder for a second if it came from one of the whales. I can only hear the difference when one of them calls back to her.

She reaches down as an orca swims by, her fingertips gliding across its shimmering black skin before it vanishes beneath the water.

I watch in amazement, enchanted by the beauty of her soul. A wild beauty unlike anyone else I've ever known.

Perhaps she *is* a siren, and I am Odysseus, wrestling with temptation, fighting to ignore the seductive music of her song. Perhaps this is my challenge: to resist the spell that draws me towards her, to keep my willpower stronger than my emotions, to remember that one moment of weakness will end in shipwreck and tragedy.

When the whales move on, Orca skips back over the rocks and meets me on the shore. I ask her how she learned to vocalize like a killer whale, and she only giggles and says she picked it up by listening to the pod. She takes my hand, leading me back up the slippery rock steps to the lighthouse. That's when she stops and looks up into my eyes, an expectant smile curling onto her lips.

There's a strand of hair hanging in her face, and everything in me wants to brush it away, to feel the wind-flushed skin of her cheek, the curve of her neck, her shoulders. I want to kiss all those places, too; I want to pick her up and carry her inside and kiss her, kiss her everywhere—

"I should, uh… go get my stuff together," I say, releasing her hand and taking a step back.

Orca nods solemnly, the light flickering out of her eyes.

I don't have much stuff to "get together." I just need to distance myself from her before I do something I shouldn't. So I take my time making her father's bed, leaving it as creaseless and shipshape as a military bunk. When I finish, I pick up my journal and open it to the last page I wrote on—the poem for Orca, stained by the pink flowers that slipped out of her hair.

> You are the butterfly
> who so innocently flutters her wings
> And stirs winds
> Strong enough
> To destroy me

The logical part of me still regrets writing those words, because they can never be unwritten. But deep down, I know: it couldn't be helped. I had to either write it down or tell her face-to-face—and the latter was not an option. It would disrupt everything.

But didn't I tell her last night? Didn't she describe the feeling of falling in love, and didn't I say, "I feel the same way?"

Then I kissed her.

For God's sake, Adam. You've already disrupted everything.

I might as well tell her how I feel. Not in person, but in written words—so that I will be long gone by the time she reads them and discovers the truth.

I put my pen to the page and begin to write.

AFTER BREAKFAST, Orca and I watch for planes from the lantern room. On a sunny morning like this, you can see for miles in every direction. It takes some discipline to not look at Orca; instead, I keep my gaze fixed on the sky, watching for a sign of my red-and-white Beaver. Part of me can't wait to see it—can't wait to see Jack. But another part of me is dreading it. Because I know what it means: saying goodbye to Orca. These could be our last minutes alone together.

I can see the pain in her eyes, too. The same longing, desperate look she wore yesterday when we sat by the fire and she asked me how I felt about her.

How I feel doesn't matter.

Maybe, in another universe, we are together.

But not in this one.

Suddenly, Orca gasps behind me. I turn to find her peering through a spyglass at something on the horizon.

"What is it?" I ask, squinting in the direction her spyglass is pointed.

"I can't tell yet… A boat. I think it's coming this way."

Moments later, I see what she is describing: a small ocean vessel slicing a white curtain of wake through the water.

Orca's eyes light up with joy as she jumps to her feet. "It's Papa!"

Hellos

orca

I fly down the spiral staircase and through the living room, Lucius barking at my heels. He doesn't know what he's excited about, but he can sense my excitement, and it's enough to make him giddy. My heart races as I swing open the front door and run to the ledge overlooking the beach.

As the boat draws closer, I make out two figures on board—a bearded man behind the steering wheel and Papa closer to the bow. He waves when he sees me racing down the beach, Lucius bounding after me.

"Papa!" I shout through cupped hands. "Welcome home!"

He smiles, slinging his messenger bag over his shoulder as he climbs off the boat. He thanks the mariner, then rushes to meet me, his boots splashing through the shallow water. I laugh as I crash into him, wrapping him in a hug.

"Oh, my dear girl, I missed you so much," Papa says, holding me at arm's length. "Let me look at you. Are you all right? I was so worried when the storm hit. It was raining for days on the mainland. Was everything—"

"Everything was *fine*," I assure him with a confident smile. "I'm fine! It was a little rainy, but I had plenty of firewood, and I took care of the chickens and the light, and I had no troubles whatsoever."

The worry subsides in Papa's eyes as he sees that all is well. Lucius whines for attention, and Papa finally grants him a scratch on the head.

"I'm so sorry the storm kept me away," Papa says. "I was going out of my mind knowing you were here all alone."

"I wasn't alone."

He frowns. "Lucius doesn't count for much company, Orca."

"No, not Lucius. There's someone else here."

"What?"

I loop my arm through Papa's and start up the bank. "It's ever such a long story. But in short, I found some things washed up on the beach, and as it turns out, they belonged to a pilot who crashed his plane off the coast of the island. Nobody had found him, so I searched the island—first the beaches and then the forest—but I didn't find him. But then he showed up at the lighthouse, and he was badly hurt, so I helped him, and he's so nice, Papa, you'll love him—"

"Whoa, whoa, slow down a minute." Papa stops in his tracks, looking shocked and bewildered.

"It's all right, Papa. He's a very nice man. His name is Adam Stevenson, and his brother is flying out to pick him up this morning. You should come and meet him before he leaves."

I can see a thousand questions spinning through Papa's mind. As we approach the lighthouse, Adam steps out the front door, squinting in the sunlight.

"Papa, this is Adam Stevenson. Adam, this is my father."

"Lawrence," Papa says, shaking his hand firmly.

"Good to meet you, sir," Adam greets him. "I know you weren't expecting to find a stranger here, in your home."

"No," Papa says, "I certainly was not."

I frown, detecting a hint of hostility in his voice. I'm about to remind him that Adam was seriously injured from his accident and that he needed help—but Adam speaks for himself.

"The truth is, sir, I owe your daughter my life. She took me in without a second thought. She helped me when I was unable to help myself." Adam's gaze slides to me for a second. My heart squeezes. "I'm very grateful to her. And to you, of course."

"Well, I'm glad you're safe, son," Papa says with some reluctance. "It's your good fortune Orca stayed behind after all; otherwise, nobody would have been here to help you."

That's a good point, I decide, upon reflection. My not going with Papa to the Otherworld has worked out for the best in this case.

"You have a remarkable daughter, sir," Adam adds. "You should be very proud of her."

This appears to cause Papa more trepidation than reassurance. His polite smile falters, and the light changes in his eyes. But he says only, "I am. I am proud of her." He puts an arm around my shoulders and kisses the top of my head. "Orca said your brother is coming to pick you up."

"Yes. He should be here any time now." Adam's bright blue eyes scan the clear sky. I hope my memories of him will remain as vivid as the image of him before me now.

"Come inside, Papa. We made coffee. Did you have a fair crossing? The sea is so calm today. I think it's finally resting after making a fuss all week." I laugh, dancing up the steps, through the kitchen and over to the stove, where the percolator sits on the back burner to stay warm.

"Orca."

I twirl around to discover that Adam has not followed us inside. Through the window, I glimpse him standing on the ledge overlooking the sea. Papa lays his messenger bag on the table and repeats my name, his voice low and serious.

"What is it, Papa? You look so worried."

"I need to know what happened… while I was gone."

"I told you. Adam told you."

Papa shakes his head. "I don't mean how he came to be here. I mean…" He rubs his forehead with his weathered fingertips. "What I'm trying to say is… did anything happen *between* you?"

"Between us? What do you mean?"

Papa looks at me, anxiety haunting his gray eyes. He searches for words the way Adam searched for the English translation to describe his Latin phrases to me—something I would know and understand. It takes Papa a long moment to find the right words.

"Did he touch you?"

My heart stutters as I remember our kiss at the top of the lighthouse last night. Adam's hands against my waist and on my cheek, his fingers gently combing through my hair, his lips on my lips—

It was beautiful. Indescribably beautiful. But the look on Papa's face suggests otherwise. Is "touching" something bad? Reproachable, even? The last thing I want is for Papa to disapprove of me. If he thinks me irresponsible for any reason, I may lose his trust—and with it, any hope of seeing the Otherworld.

"Orca," he says, "tell me the truth."

I can't.

I shake my head. "No, Papa. He didn't touch me."

Relief dawns in Papa's eyes, washing away the fear. "Good… Good. He seems like a respectful young man."

"He is," I agree. "He's wonderful. I'll be sorry to see him go."

That's when I hear a familiar sound: the telltale buzz of an engine not far away.

An *airplane* engine.

Seconds later, Adam reappears in the doorway, smiling.

My heart jumps when I see his expression. "Is that a plane I hear?"

Adam nods.

"Superman?"

He laughs. "Superman."

RECLUSE ISLAND

jack

"Jackie… wake up."

Those words bring me back to my middle school days—Mom's hand nudging my shoulder, her voice sweetly reminding me that if I don't get my ass out of bed soon, Adam won't give me a ride in his truck, and I'll have to take my bike to school.

"Five more minutes," I grumble, rolling onto my stomach and pulling the blankets over my head.

"It's a beautiful morning," Mom singsongs, swishing the curtains open. "Thought you'd be a little more excited about that clear sky out there."

My heart does a backflip as I realize what she's talking about.

Adam.

I bolt upright, tossing off my blankets and springing out of bed like a kid on Christmas morning. "Clear sky? For real?" I vault over Adam's bed to get to the window, grinning from ear to ear as I look up at that unlimited visibility.

It's not a dream this time.

"Why didn't you wake me up earlier?"

Mom raises her eyebrows. "I tried to, several times. You sleep like a bear in hibernation."

I grab yesterday's clothes from the floor and throw them on, snatching my aviator shades from the nightstand.

"Do you want some breakfast first?"

"No time." I give Mom a quick kiss on the cheek. "I'll be back soon."

"Be careful, Jack. Pay attention to your flying."

"Yep, will do!"

I rush out the door before she can badger me any more.

My heart is pounding the whole drive to the port. I rap my fingertips on the steering wheel and ignore the speed limit completely, running stop signs with no shame. When I arrive at the port, I park my Mustang outside Adam's hangar and jump out, sprinting to the docks like I'm competing in a one-man decathlon.

I complete the preflight inspection, then cast off the moorings and push away from the dock. Scrambling up the ladder and into the cockpit, I slam the door shut behind me. Shades down, headphones on. Propeller spinning, spinning. *Come on, warm the hell up.* My eyes dart over my checklist as I go through the pre-takeoff motions.

Once the engine is warmed up and purring like a kitten, I power out to the broadest part of the harbor and crank up the volume on my Walkman cassette player, blasting an AC/DC tape as I reach for the throttle. Sunlit waves blur underneath me as the floats skid over the water, faster and faster and—

Takeoff.

The world shrinks below me as I climb up, up, up into the vast blue sky. My heart is hammering harder than the day of my first solo.

Only *minutes* until I see Adam again.

Until I see Orca, too.

As the mainland shrinks behind my wings, I glance down at my compass and check the hand-drawn map I sketched last night. Based on Adam's coordinates, Recluse Island isn't super far away. An easy seventeen nautical miles, lying dead center of Victoria, Port Angeles, and Whidbey.

I start dropping altitude as soon as I spot the tiny island, scouting the coastline for a good landing spot. There's a nice-looking cove on the east side, but it's too far away from the lighthouse, which clings to the rocky northern tip of the island like a ship's figurehead.

No docks in sight. I should have expected that—the dad's a hermit. I guess that's *one* way to keep visitors away.

Luckily for me, the water is about as calm as it gets. I push the yoke out and glide down to make a landing. Not as graceful as Adam, but I don't care as long as I keep my floats, well, *floating*. My adrenaline is still rocketing as I ease the throttle down and coast over the skin of the water, slowing to a stop parallel to the beach.

I power up to the sand and kill the engine in the shallows, then hop out and grab my rope. The water is colder than it looks, but I barely notice it—too busy trying to rein the Beaver in like a lassoed mustang. The tide is high enough for my line to reach a convenient log of driftwood half-buried in the sand. I wind the rope around the log several times and tie a knot.

"Jack!"

I spin around to face the lighthouse. Adam is standing about fifty yards away at the top of a grassy slope, his arms crossed over his chest. Grinning in the sunlight.

I run to him. Slipping on wet rocks and springing over gnarled limbs of driftwood, I race across the beach and up the hill—crashing straight into him.

He laughs and lets out a roar of pain, and that's when I remember his broken ribs.

"Oh, shit! I'm sorry—"

Adam shakes his head, still grinning. "I'm fine." He grabs my shoulders and pulls me into a hug.

He's alive.

God, it hits me so hard—a rush of emotion barrels into me with the force of a tidal wave. I start crying like a wuss, clenching fistfuls of his shirt and burying my face in his neck. I'm half afraid he'll disappear if I let go.

"I missed you, little brother," Adam says, and I can tell by the way his voice cracks—he's fighting tears too.

"You asshole," I sob into his neck. "Don't you ever put me through hell like that again, got it?"

Adam slaps my shoulder. "Got it."

I step back to look at him, taking in the nasty bruises all over his face and arms. That resolute calm is still there in his eyes. Same old Adam.

"You look like hell," I joke with a laugh—but he doesn't look as bad as he could for someone who survived a plane crash. Damn superhero.

"I know," he says. "You can thank Orca for taping me up."

The mention of her name makes my heart rate skyrocket. I almost forgot she was here. I turn around, and there she is, standing ten feet away, smiling at me.

"Hello, Jack," she says.

Wow.

She's even prettier than I imagined. Long, wavy hair that looks brown until the sunlight turns it to gold. Eyes like crystals, blue or green—I can't tell which. She's wearing a white dress, which makes her look like an angel. I can't believe I'm looking at her. I can't believe she's looking at *me*.

She's real.

She's *beautiful.*

I don't know how to thank her. Words don't cut it. All I can do is walk up to her, walk *into* her, and hug her. She laughs her adorable little laugh and wraps her arms around me, pressing her face to my chest.

"Thank you," I rasp, all choked up. Her hair smells amazing, and it feels like silk between my fingers. For a moment, we just hold each other, and I can't help noticing how good, how *right* she feels in my arms.

GOODBYES

orca

Jack Stevenson is like a wild gust of wind off a restless sea. He's not quite as tall or as muscular as his brother, but they share similar features, the same pronounced jawline and the same handsome smile.

"I can hardly believe you're real." I laugh.

Jack steps back to look into my eyes. "And so are you! My parents almost convinced me that you were just a figment of my imagination."

"At first, I feared you were a figment of *mine*."

Jack is about to reply when Papa appears beside us, apprehension creasing his brow. He looks Jack up and down, then extends a hand for him to shake.

"I'm Lawrence. Orca's father."

I catch a glint of irritation in Jack's eyes as he shakes Papa's hand. "Hi. I'm Jack. Orca's told me a lot about you."

Papa frowns, puzzled, and turns to me. I know what he's thinking—how on earth did I tell Jack a lot about anything?

"Oh, I forgot to mention—I talked to Jack over the phone. That's how I learned about Adam going missing in the first place."

This new piece of information makes Papa stiffen and look at Jack differently. He says nothing else—only nods and strides back over to Adam.

"Anyway, Orca," Jack huffs, shaking his head. "This is your island, huh? It's… got a nice view." He casts a glance over the expanse of glittering water.

"Yes. A very nice view," I agree, still looking at him.

"But no pizza."

"No."

"And no video games."

"No—"

"And no friends."

"*You're* my friend. And Adam's my friend, too." I glance at the ledge, where he is still talking with my father, silhouetted by the morning sun.

What is Papa saying to him?

I tug my gaze back to Jack. "So, there. I have friends."

His smile fades. "It's not the same when we're on two different islands. Plus, you don't even have a phone. I won't be able to talk to you."

"Perhaps Papa will let me use the satellite phone," I offer hopefully. "I can ask him. I'm sure once I explain the situation, he'll let me use the phone to talk with you and Adam… occasionally."

Jack mutters an indignant laugh. "Occasionally."

"Well, it's better than nothing."

"You're right. It is. I just… I want to get to know you better."

"I'd like that, too," I admit quietly.

In Jack's hazel eyes, I see my own thirst for more: for life, for freedom, for everything I've never known. It's like he can see right through me, see me in a way Adam can't. He knows how I feel. He knows the ache of the invisible, indestructible chains around me. And he knows something I don't: how to break those chains.

"Orca." Papa's voice cuts into our conversation. "I think it's time to say goodbye."

"Already? But Jack only just—"

"Tide's going out," Papa says, nodding to the beach. "Any longer, and Jack's plane might be stranded here."

I follow his gaze to where Jack tied down the red-and-white float-plane. Papa is right. The line is pulled taut, leaving no slack for extra time with the Stevenson brothers.

Jack casts Papa an irked glance, a muscle twitching in his jaw. "Is Adam ready to go?"

My heart squeezes as I glance around, looking for him. I turn just in time to see him disappearing into the house.

"He's collecting his things now," Papa says, then goes on to ask Jack something about the flight conditions, the weather, I don't know. Their words fade away behind me as I rush back into the house.

I find Adam in Papa's room, zipping his backpack shut. He glances up when I appear in the doorway, an unreadable conflict in his eyes.

"What's wrong, Adam? What did Papa say to you out there?"

Adam stares at me for a long moment as if trying to decide how much to tell me. Or if he ought to tell me anything at all.

"Adam, please tell me."

"I want you to have this," he says, holding out his journal for me to take. "Write down your ideas about life. About philosophy and the universe."

I glance up at him. "You mean the multiverse?"

"Yeah," he says with a weary laugh. "The multiverse."

The sadness in his voice makes my vision blur with tears. "Thank you," I whisper, my throat tight. "I will cherish it, Adam Stevenson."

I reach out and entwine my fingers with his. Rays of golden sunlight spill through the window and glow against our skin, shadowing the delicate lines of his veins and highlighting the blonde hairs on my forearm.

"I have to go," Adam rasps so softly it's as if he's talking to himself. "I have to go back to the mainland, and I don't know when I'll see you again. Or... *if* I'll be able to see you again."

I had no idea such a small word could cut so deep into my heart.

If.

"Adam, please tell me what Papa—"

"No," he says, shaking his head. "Don't make me tell you, Orca. I don't want to cause any hard feelings between you and your father. He's a good man. I respect him, and I respect his wishes."

The look in Adam's eyes is unshakable. Resolute. Final.

This *is* goodbye.

Forever.

"No, Adam, I *will* see you again—I'm sure of it. Papa will let me go to the mainland once he comes to see that I can take care of myself out there. Once he realizes how well I've handled everything this past week… he'll see that I *am* strong enough for the Otherworld. I know Papa. I know he'll listen to me. I know he'll be reasonable." I manage a forced smile. "And you've encouraged me, Adam. You've given me confidence in myself. I can never thank you enough for that."

Adam squeezes my hand. "I can never thank you enough for saving my life."

A tether pulls taut between our hearts; I can almost feel the threads snapping. How can love be so beautiful and so agonizing at the same time? I may never fathom the depths of its meaning. But I know one thing for sure—I can't let him leave without kissing him.

There's just one small problem: I can't reach his lips.

"Can you sit?" I ask softly, my heart racing as I gesture toward Papa's bed.

Adam frowns. "What?"

"Can you just… sit down? For a moment?"

"Okay…" He follows my request and sits on the edge of the bed, looking puzzled.

I take one step closer to him and lay my trembling hands on his shoulders, a rush of nervous warmth coursing through my whole body.

Slowly and carefully, I lean in close to his face and gently kiss him. The rest of the world vanishes in a single breath. All that remains is the soft warmth of his lips moving under mine, the weight of his hands on my hips, my fingers relaxing their hold on his shoulders as I unravel inside.

For a moment, time stands still.

The clocks stop, and the earth ceases to turn.

I ease back from Adam's lips, my heart pounding furiously as my eyes flutter open to meet his gaze.

"Did I do that right?" I whisper against his mouth.

He smiles and touches his forehead to mine. "Perfectly."

I WALK DOWN TO THE BEACH with Adam and Jack to where the plane is tied down. Jack climbs inside to start the engine while I say goodbye to Adam.

I wrap my arms around his torso and press my face to his chest—breathing in his scent, wishing I could bottle it up and keep it with me, along with the encompassing comfort of his strong arms around me.

"Goodbye, Orca."

I have no voice to reply.

He rubs one hand over my upper back, then lets go.

The tether between us snaps.

I stand frozen in place, staring as he walks away—every step carrying him farther away from me until he climbs up the plane's ladder and disappears inside.

"Orca!" Jack's lively voice jolts me out of my heartbroken daze. He leaps down from the plane's starboard float and jogs up to me, still grinning. "Don't be sad. This isn't goodbye forever." He pulls me into his arms, hugging me tightly. "Okay?"

When he steps back and looks at me, I see wild determination sparkling in his hazel eyes. He glances toward the lighthouse, where Papa stands watching on the ledge.

"I'll see you again," Jack says, fierce confidence in his voice. "Soon."

With that, he runs off to the shallows—*splash, splash*—and jumps up onto the portside float of the seaplane, climbing back in and closing the door behind him. I try to catch one last glimpse of Adam through the windshield, but the propeller is spinning too fast.

I feel hollowed out, unable to move, as I watch the plane pull away from the beach and glide out to open water.

BRRRRRAAAAAAAM!

The engine roars as the plane picks up speed, skidding fast over the tops of the waves, finally tilting upward and taking off. Slowly but surely, it climbs into the cloudless sky and soars away, sunlight flashing on its wings. I watch the aircraft shrink smaller and smaller as it draws closer to the Otherworld and farther away from me.

I watch until it disappears.

MENDACIUM

adam

It rips my heart out to leave Orca. The whole flight back to Whidbey Island, I'm at war with myself. Logic and Emotion altercate in my conscience—out of the courtroom and onto the battlefield, swearing they'll fight to the death.

Logic will win. He always does.

He's the voice that spoke back there on the island when Mr. Monroe pulled me aside and said, "You understand that Orca has no dealings with the outside world."

I nodded.

"Which, of course, precludes relationships with people from the outside world." His gray eyes shifted to mine. "Including you."

Guilt tightened in my chest. "I understand that, sir."

I *did* understand. I understood days ago when Orca first explained the situation to me. I pieced together in an hour what Orca has been trying to demystify her whole life. I saw the fear on Mr. Monroe's face when he first set eyes on me—the question he wouldn't come out and ask: *What did you do to my daughter when I wasn't here?*

If I hadn't done anything, I'd be able to look him in the eyes. But he was right to suspect me of overstepping the mark.

I had.

I fell in love with his daughter—kissed her, touched her, literally had to force myself to walk away before I did anything more with her.

And I feel terrible about it.

I let my selfish emotions rule me, seduce me, and smother my reasoning. Yet, standing there before Mr. Monroe, I couldn't bring myself to admit any of it. I told myself it would make matters worse for Orca and held my tongue. But now I wonder, was that the real reason? Or am I simply a coward?

Mr. Monroe is a good man. I presumed that before I even met him, but I confirmed it when he spoke with such honesty about his daughter.

"I've endeavored to make a comfortable life for us here," he said. "It hasn't been easy without Orca's mother… but I've tried to make her happy. I know the kind of life we live is unusual. Strange to most. But it suits us. And I intend for it to continue." Mr. Monroe looked off across the water to the hazy shapes of islands in the distance. "It's not that I have something against you, son. I would just appreciate it if you would respect my wishes and not contact my daughter again."

"I understand, sir. I'll make no attempts to contact Orca. I don't want to disturb her life here. Or yours."

Mr. Monroe nodded. "Well, then. We'll say no more about it."

Emotion fought hard, but Logic wrestled him to the ground. I decided to make a clean break with Orca. No touching, no kissing, no tearful farewells.

I failed.

Orca cornered me in her father's bedroom—irony of all ironies—and asked me what I'd been talking to him about. I almost told her, but decided it would only create more turbulence in the storm I'd set off, a ripple effect I wouldn't be around to witness, but one that would weigh on my conscience like a crime.

So instead, I gave her my journal, with my letter to her inside. Because I *do* want her to know how I feel—but only after I'm gone. Out of reach. Unable to do more damage.

Logic made a compelling opening statement. But once Emotion took the stand, I knew I was a goner. Orca slid her beautiful hand into mine and asked me to sit on the bed. I immediately knew what she meant—that she wanted to kiss me. Logic yelled, *Objection!* But then her lips pressed against mine, and the judge in my heart whispered, *Overruled.* I kissed her back.

It was her first time initiating a kiss, and I could tell she was nervous. Her hands were trembling, warm on my shoulders. Afterward, she asked me if she had done it right. I didn't know it was possible to fall even more in love with her, but at that moment, I did.

And now it's over.

She's on her island, and I'm on my way back to mine.

Worlds apart.

WHEN WE LAND at the port, Mom and Dad are waiting.

Mom cries me a river and hugs me tighter than she ever has, kissing me a thousand times. She fusses over my bruises, my scars, and my broken ribs, which I insist are feeling much better. She looks years older, and I know it's all my fault. I hold her for a while and let her cry, kissing the top of her head and reminding her that I'm okay, it's okay, and I'm so damn sorry for putting her through hell. Dad cries too. He hugs me, slaps my shoulder, and welcomes me home.

Jack, on the other hand, can't stop grinning, laughing, rambling about the island and Orca and how good it is to have me back, and I look like hell, did I know that? I shove him, he shoves me, and Mom tells us to *stop, don't get so close to the edge of the dock*, like we're still children.

While they head home in Dad's truck, Jack shows me the remains of my poor Beaver, which the coast guard transported to my hangar last week.

I run my hand over the white-and-blue fuselage as I examine the damage. "She's gonna need a lot of work before I can get her flying again."

"Well," Jack says, "if anyone can do it, you can."

I smack his shoulder and nod to the door. "Come on. Let's go home."

As soon as we get back to the house, Mom tells me I have a doctor's appointment in thirty minutes. Jack whines about how I "just got home," but Mom is already putting her shoes back on. I shrug and remind my brother, "She's the boss," following her out the door again.

The doctor tells me what I already know: two broken ribs that are on the mend, one sprained ankle, which is also on the mend, and countless bruises and scratches that won't even leave scars. The cut on my face is what bothers Mom the most—she winces every time she looks at it, despite how many times I tell her *It doesn't hurt.*

By the time we get back home, it's late. Mom starts dinner while I bring my stuff to my and Jack's room. I find him lying on his bed, listening to his vinyl of *Dark Side of the Moon*, which is spinning on the record player.

Nothing has changed.

Yet everything has changed.

I stretch out on my bed, shutting my eyes and breathing in the smell of home. "God, I feel like I've been gone for a year."

"Felt that way to me, too," Jack says, glancing over at me. "Orca seemed sad to see you leave."

His words take me back to the beach this morning—the feeling of her in my arms for the last time. Her tears shimmering in the sunlight.

"Yeah." I sigh.

"Were *you* sad to leave?"

"No. Not sad, exactly. I was… I don't know. It was complicated."

"What do you mean?"

I reel in a deep breath, rubbing my forehead. "Her father talked to me before we left. He basically told me never to contact Orca again. That she doesn't have dealings with the outside world… or people in that world."

"Christ," Jack scoffs, sitting upright, irritation flashing in his eyes. "I hope you told him no frickin' way."

"No. I told him that I understood, and I—"

"What the—"

"*And* I respect his wishes."

"His *wishes?*" Jack scrunches his face in disgust. "He 'wishes' Orca to never have a life, for crying out loud. He 'wishes' to keep her prisoner on that dumb island. You respect that?"

I have a thousand arguments for this, but I'm too tired to fight with Jack about it. He doesn't see the whole picture as I see it, and I'm not convinced that a rhetorical monologue would change his perspective. So instead, I shrug and state the most obvious fact: "She's *his* daughter."

"Yeah, I know," Jack grumbles, flopping back on the bed. "But did you see the way he came up and was like, 'Oh, gotta say goodbye, Jack's plane's floating away' or whatever—"

"He didn't say it was floating away; he said the tide was going out."

"Whatever. He didn't want me talking to her. He was, like, all weird and paranoid about it."

"I think he just didn't want my plane to get stuck on the beach."

Jack sighs. "*Whatever.* I only got to talk to her for, like, five minutes. And now she doesn't even have a phone, which means I can't call her anymore, and… I miss her, okay?"

Oh no.

I should have seen this coming. I should have heard it in his voice before. I should have seen it in the way he looked at her this morning when he met her face-to-face. The way I've seen him look at other girls in the past.

I know that look.

I know that voice.

I know the feeling of *I miss her.*

I'm feeling it now—so intensely that the words "So do I" slip out of my mouth before I know what I'm saying.

Jack props himself up on his elbow. "Yeah?"

My brain scrambles to put together a decent fib. "Yeah, I mean… she was interesting. We had some good conversations."

"About philosophy."

I shut my eyes. "Yes. Philosophy."

"Nothing else?"

He's fishing.

If I trip up now, I'm busted.

"Nothing else," I say, adding an irritated sigh for good measure. "Now, come on, stop."

"Okay, okay. Just checking." Jack grins. "She *is* hot, you know. Like, way hotter than I thought she'd be."

I cut him a disapproving look.

"What? Don't say you didn't *notice*."

"Of course I noticed."

"But… nothing happened. Between you guys. Right?"

"Jack, I already told you nothing happened. Now would you stop?"

He laughs and throws a pillow at me. "Okay, fine. I'll stop. I believe you."

"Good." I throw the pillow back at him and stand up. "I'm going to go help Mom with dinner. I suggest you get off your ass and do likewise."

Jack mutters some childish complaints, but I leave the room before I hear most of them. In the hallway, I stop and think about what I just told him.

It was a lie.

Not the half-hearted denial he can see right through, but a serious, deliberate lie.

I'm not sure why I did it. Maybe because it's strange for us both to like the same girl—for me to like a girl Jack's age.

Or maybe because a lie is less complicated than the truth.

Either way, it doesn't matter.

I promised Orca's father it was over and done. I gave him my word that I wouldn't try to contact his daughter. That I would leave them both alone.

And I will.

She's so young; she'll get over me. Jack might fantasize about her for a while, but it won't be long before his head turns for another exciting girl with fewer dating restrictions.

It's better that he doesn't know what happened between Orca and me.

It's better for all of us.

THE LETTER

orca

How many days did you say that young man was here?"

"Three, Papa."

"Including today?"

"No. He was only here for a few hours today."

Papa nods, picking up a gnarled branch of driftwood. We're walking down the beach, collecting shells and driftwood while Lucius enjoys a romp through the shallows.

"And was he badly injured?" Papa asks.

"Not badly, no. He had a broken rib, and his ankle was sprained. Besides that, just some cuts and bruises. I cleaned the wounds right away and treated them with witch hazel and aloe."

"Could he not clean his own wounds?"

"No, he was unconscious when I found him. It was the first night of the storm, and he showed up at the door. But by the time I got to the door, he had collapsed. Poor man. I had to drag him inside."

Papa seems surprised—and, dare I hope, impressed?

"He was soaking wet," I continue, reminding myself to include every commendable detail of the situation. "So I had to take off his clothes and get him dry and warm again."

At this, Papa stops walking and stares at me, taken aback.

"That *was* the right thing to do, wasn't it, Papa? I was trying to follow what you taught me. About exposure."

Papa shakes himself out of his daze and nods. "Yes, Orca. It was the right thing to do. I'm glad you didn't panic, and you relied upon your knowledge. That's not easy to do under stress."

"Well, I was only remembering what you taught me. Adam was unconscious for a little while, but he woke up on his own. If he hadn't, I would have called the coast guard. But I thought, with the weather so bad, the coast guard wouldn't have been able to help, and…" I fidget with a broken shell, glancing back up at Papa. "To be honest, I wanted to help Adam myself. I wanted to prove that I was capable of it."

Papa squints at me through the sunlight. "And did you?"

"I don't know. Did I?"

"Of course you did, Orca." Papa steps over a driftwood log to come up beside me, placing a hand on my shoulder. "I am very proud of you, my girl. I knew the island would be safe in your hands."

Happy tears sting my eyes as a smile blossoms on my lips. "Thank you, Papa."

His words rekindle the hope in my heart and ease some of my sorrow at losing Adam. I know it won't be forever. Papa *is* proud of me—and finally convinced of my strength and capability. Just as I had hoped.

"HOW WAS THE OTHERWORLD?" I ask Papa at dinner, watching as he divides roasted vegetables and fresh seared fish among two plates. I'm sitting at the table with the wedding photo nestled discreetly in my lap. Mama's smile gives me the confidence I need to face this conversation.

"It was just as I remembered it," Papa says.

"And when is the coast guard coming out to install the new light?"

He sets the plates on the table and takes a seat in his chair. "The end of next month."

I nod slowly, picking at my food with a fork. "You know, at first, I thought it would be strange to have this modern automation. But perhaps it's better this way. I mean, if no one needs to be here to keep the light… then maybe I can go with you to the mainland. Next time."

"There won't be a next time."

"Oh?"

Papa nods, not looking up. "Yes, thankfully, I'll be spared any more meetings for the foreseeable future."

"Well, it doesn't have to be a business trip," I remind him. "It could be just for fun—"

"No." Papa glances up into my eyes, his expression resolute and un-flinching. "No, Orca."

"What do you mean, no? Papa, I… I thought you were proud of me. For everything I did here while you were gone."

He looks at me as though I've changed the topic. "I am. Very proud of you."

"You said I proved myself strong, capable. Didn't you?"

"Orca—"

"Didn't you say that earlier, on the beach?"

"Yes."

"But you didn't mean it."

"I did mean it," Papa says, holding my gaze firmly. "I've always known you to be extremely bright and capable, Orca. That's why I trusted you to stay here and manage things."

"But you don't trust me enough to go to the Otherworld."

"It's not about trust."

"Then what *is* it about?" I sit back in my chair, crossing my arms over my chest.

Papa draws a weary breath, then lets it all out again. "Orca, I know you feel like there's so much more out there. Like your life is passing you by. But the mainland isn't as wonderful as you imagine it to be. It's—"

"Full of dangers and darkness, I know," I finish for him, a sharp edge to my voice. "But if you really think I'm as strong as you say, then surely I can handle it."

"I can handle it, too," Papa says, "but I choose not to. I chose this life because it is far superior in many ways to what the so-called 'real world' has to offer."

Adam would agree with him there. I recall him saying something about my world being far more *real* than his.

"Yes, you chose that," I fire back. "But when have I ever had the chance to choose what *I* want?"

"I'm not trying to deprive you of anything, Orca," Papa says, his voice low and somber. "I only wanted to keep you—to *protect* you from it."

To keep me here. That's what he was going to say. That's what his real motive is. To keep me here, forever—not for my sake, but for his. All the while watching me yearn for the Otherworld. All the while, watching me stare through the spyglass at the pinpricks of light on the horizon, hoping to catch a glimpse of the place I long to see.

Anger bubbles up inside me, squeezing tighter, tighter, tighter around my heart—crushing my tender bruises and extinguishing my last flicker of hope.

Adam's gone. And it *is* forever.

I think of the way he hugged me, the way he said goodbye. A sadness in his eyes so final, a sadness I saw only after Papa spoke to him.

"Papa… What did you tell Adam? Before he left?"

Papa looks like he would give anything not to answer that question. "I told him of our situation here."

"He knows. *I* told him of it."

"Yes, but I needed to be sure he understood."

"Understood what?" Frustrated tears quiver in my eyes as I wait for the answer, already knowing what it will be.

"That we don't have dealings with the outside world. And that future communication with you would be impossible."

"Impossible," I rasp, trying to blink away my tears but only succeeding in making a few of them fall—right onto the picture frame sitting on my lap.

"He understood," Papa says. "He agreed."

Agreed.

That word pierces my heart, making it ache even more. I look down at the photograph of Mama on her wedding day. My fallen tear rolls down the glass, blurring her smile.

"Adam found this in your dresser drawer." I place the frame on the table between us.

Papa's face goes pale.

"Why did you hide it from me?"

His gaze remains fixed on the photograph for a long moment. "Orca, I… I never intended to—"

"Yes, you did!" The words burst out of me. "You told me all these years that you didn't have any photographs of her. Every time I ask you about her, you avoid answering my questions. I don't even know how she died, just that she got sick! I don't know a single thing about her because *you* refused to tell me. You want to forget her. Why? Because the memories hurt you too much? Did you ever think that maybe *I* needed some of those memories?"

Papa stares into my tear-streaked face, his eyes wide, his expression unreadable.

"Since the day I was born, you've been controlling who will be a part of my life." My voice wobbles, my breath hitches—but I can't stop. "First it was Mama. Now it's Adam."

"Your mother…" Papa looks down, bracing himself to say the words. "Your mother *died*. I didn't take her away from you; she was taken away from both of us."

"But you're taking *Adam* away from me."

"He left of his own volition—"

"And you made him promise to never return!"

"Orca, it's for the best—"

"I love him."

Silence slashes the room. Papa stares at me as though I just struck him across the face.

"I love him more than I've ever loved anyone. And he loves me, too."

Confusion and fear tangle in Papa's eyes as he stares at me. "You told me nothing happened between you and that young man."

"I lied." It stings to say those words, but it is a rewarding pain. Like ripping off a bandage. "I lied when I said he didn't touch me. He *did* touch me. He held me in his arms, and he kissed me. And I kissed him back, and I would give anything to do it again. To love him again, to feel him hold me again—"

Papa slams his hand on the table, making me startle. "How dare you!" There is a fire blazing in his eyes, a desperate, hopeless fury I've never seen before. "Have I taught you *nothing*, Orca? I thought you were smarter than that! I told you, those people over there aren't like us. I taught you not to trust them, didn't I?"

"Yes, but they're not all bad—"

"That young man took advantage of your innocence," Papa argues, his voice like thunder. "He filled your head with nonsense about life on the mainland. He invaded our privacy, made it his business to rifle through my things and find this picture and give it to you! He made you believe he cared for you, and made *me* believe nothing inappropriate happened while I was gone. Filthy, ungrateful scoundrel—"

"Adam is not a scoundrel!" I shout, jumping to my feet. "And he didn't invade your privacy. I let him borrow some clothes, and he accidentally found that picture. He thought I knew about it already. You misjudge him. You misjudge *everyone*! You're so narrow-minded, so controlling—"

"Orca."

"You don't want me to love anyone but *you*. Why? What are you so afraid of?"

Papa stands abruptly, his voice stone-cold as he looks down at me. "Orca, that's enough. I never want to hear you mention that young man's name again, do you understand? You will never see him again."

My heart wrenches inside me, a sob spilling past my lips. "Papa, please…"

"This is exactly what I was afraid of." Papa lowers his voice, a glint of tears in his eyes as he slowly shakes his head. "This is exactly what I warned you about so many times. If only you had listened."

BACK IN MY ROOM, I lean against the sill of my open window and look out at the velvety blue fallout of the sunset. Stars glimmer overhead, and a cool breeze runs its fingers through my hair.

No replacement for Adam.

You will never see him again.

I close my eyes and remember the way his fingers felt, woven through mine—the way he helped me trace constellations in the starry night sky.

Now all I have left of him is his journal. The worn covers part softly in my hands as I sit on my bed and swish through the pages. His wondrous, beautiful ideas. His scribbles of Latin, that strange and slippery language. I've already read every entry (in English), but that doesn't stop my fingers from journeying through the ink-stained pages.

This time, something new slips out and falls into my lap.

Pressed flowers. Tiny pink ones from the greenhouse. I remember sliding a few of them into my hair that day Adam and I harvested the vegetables together. They had fallen out of my braid at some point, and he must have found them.

A soft smile brushes over my lips at the thought of it. Adam's handwriting fills the page, black ink speckled by the rosy pigment of the flowers.

Untouchable beauty
Are you real or fantasy?
Lost to the world, yet found
to that which truly matters

Not a word passes your lips that isn't
Honesty
Yet all I feel in the presence of your wild soul is
Mystery
All I feel is my own soul coming undone

What is the butterfly effect,
You ask me
I tell you what is true
But all I really want to say is
You

You are the butterfly
who so innocently flutters her wings
And stirs winds
Strong enough
To destroy me

Untouchable beauty
I wish
In a way
That you were a fantasy

My heart swells in my chest, and fresh tears blur my vision. I can almost hear his rich voice speaking these words. I remember the brush of his hand as he lifted a butterfly out of my hair and explained chaos theory, blue wings fluttering on his fingertip, matching the color of his eyes. In my memory, I hear no words—I just see the shape of his lips moving. Lips I kissed before he left, lips that moved in a dance with mine for a moment so perfect I can hardly believe it happened at all. *Did I do that right?* I whispered. *Perfectly*, he replied, his forehead touching mine.

"Oh, Adam," I rasp, my voice caught in the tears. "I miss you so much."

I turn the page to find one last entry in the book.

Orca,

I wish a world existed (in another universe, maybe) where only we two lived. It would be a world with nothing but ocean and this one little island. I wish the "Otherworld" didn't exist, not so that you didn't long to see it—but so that I didn't have to belong there. I don't belong there. I belong with you. And you don't belong there, either. We're not made for this world, you and I. We're made for each other.

Orca, I've fallen in love with you. I can't remember when I started to feel this way about you. I was in over my head before I knew it had begun. And now, I never want to leave you. I want to wake each morning to the sound of your voice; I want to hear every idea you have about philosophy and science and life. I want to be with you every day, every hour, every minute.

I know we can't. I know there's the matter of your father and your life on the island. The last thing I want to do is ruin that. But I have to tell you the truth. I have to tell you what a beautiful and unique person you are. Your innocence inspires me to make this world a better place... if only a small corner of it, just for you. I almost don't want you to see the Otherworld, because it is so flawed and polluted, and you deserve a perfect world. Because you are perfection itself.

I, on the other hand, am so far from perfect. It's probably a good thing that we can't be together. If we were, I would feel so unworthy of your goodness, your grace, your purity of spirit. I cherish those things about you—and so, like the moral scientist, I must leave you wild and free, where you belong... however much I may want to bring you into my world and make you my own.

I love you, Orca Monroe.

And that's why I'm letting you go.

By the time I've finished reading, hot tears have slipped off my cheeks and dropped onto the page, smudging some of the words.

This is why he gave me his journal.

This is his last goodbye.

"No," I gasp, a broken whisper. I touch my fingertips to the final line he wrote.

Don't let me go, Adam.

Don't go, Adam.

Don't.

The pain in my chest has spread everywhere, like an infection in my bones. From my fingertips to my toes, I miss him. I want him. I *need* him.

Why does love have to hurt so much? When it seems so simple, it's actually the most complicated. I can't choose between him and Papa.

Love is impossible.

A minefield of roses.

Leaving the journal spread open on my bed, I return to the window, squinting past my tears and the darkness to the flickers of light in the distance.

Adam is out there, somewhere in the Otherworld.

And I'm stuck here, in my world.

Infinity between us, forever.

That's what Adam knew when he left this morning. He agreed to Papa's wishes. He promised never to communicate with me again.

I know my papa, I said so foolishly. *I know he'll be reasonable.*

Adam had only looked at me, tormented sorrow in his beautiful eyes because he already knew: Papa wouldn't be reasonable.

He already knew that he would never see me again.

As tears slide down my face and drip off my chin, the stars sparkle overhead, undisturbed. It's the same sky Adam and I gazed up at last night, our hands laced together, tracing the shape of the constellations.

He was my strangest and most beautiful treasure from the Otherworld.

But now, he's gone.

And I am left with nothing but the memory of him.

And the ache in my heart.

And his journal, full of wondrous ideas.

And the pinpricks of light on the horizon.

part two

WORLDS APART

June 22, 1997

A PROTECTED PRISONER

jack

Sunlight.

That's the first thing I see when I open my eyes—rays of light pouring through the window and landing on Adam's bed.

On Adam.

For a second, I think it's only a dream. But then I realize I'm awake and it *is* Adam lying there, breathing deeply, the morning light glowing on his bedhead.

He's back.

Alive.

I get up and pull a T-shirt over my head, following the smell of coffee to the kitchen. Mom is humming at the counter, mixing a bowl of something. I don't know what it is, but I stick my finger in it as I walk by.

"Jack—!"

"Good morning." I lick the batter off my finger and narrowly escape a slap. "Adam's in a friggin' coma."

"You let your brother sleep," Mom says, giving me a warning look over her shoulder. "He's been through a lot and needs his rest."

I pour myself a coffee and lean against the counter, watching Mom heat a cast-iron skillet on the stove. Adam must have heard me get up because a few minutes later, I hear the shower running in the bathroom down the hall. Having him back makes home feel like home again.

"Did Adam say anything to you about Orca's father?"

Mom shakes her head. "He said they met briefly yesterday before you flew out to pick him up."

"That's all he said?"

"Mm-hmm. Why? Did something happen?"

"Well, kind of. I guess it didn't matter much to Adam, since he didn't even mention it." I grunt into my coffee. "Long story short, Orca's dad has forbidden me or Adam from ever contacting his daughter again. He's just as crazy as I imagined."

Mom pulls a carton of eggs out of the fridge, swings the door shut with her hip. "He sounds very protective of his daughter. I don't know if I'd call him *crazy*."

"You would if you met him. The guy's, like, the strictest parent of all time." I sigh, sitting down at the table and propping my feet up on the seat of another chair. "He doesn't want Orca to have any friends. Which is ridiculous, because technically she's an adult. She should be allowed to make her own decisions."

Mom shrugs, swirling butter in the skillet. "I'm sure she does."

"No, she doesn't. That's my point. I've talked to her, and I know the kind of crap she has to put up with from her dad. He's a dick."

Mom clicks her tongue disapprovingly just as Adam walks into the kitchen, his hair damp from the shower. "Who's a dick?" he asks.

"Please," Mom says.

"Orca's dad—and *don't* take his side."

"I don't take sides, first of all," Adam argues, stopping to kiss Mom on the cheek.

She drops everything to wrap her arms around him and hug him tight. "I'm so happy you're home, sweetheart."

He rubs her back and murmurs to the top of her head, "It's good to *be* home, Mom." When the homecoming hugfest is over, Adam crosses the room to pour himself a cup of coffee. "Jack, I'm not trying to defend Orca's father. I'm trying to objectively observe the facts and come to an unbiased conclusion."

I roll my eyes. "Here are the *facts*: Orca's father has brainwashed her into thinking she's some frail little girl who can't handle the real world. Did she tell you that?"

Adam takes a seat across from me. "Yes, and I told her that wasn't true. She's way tougher than she looks."

"Yeah, see? You agree, then—her dad's mental."

"He's not mental."

"What do you call locking your daughter away on an island and forbidding her from having friends—totally normal behavior?"

Adam sighs and sips his coffee, a comeback on its way. I turn to Mom before he can answer.

"Mom, you think that's normal behavior?"

Mom chuckles under her breath, ladling pancake batter onto the skillet. "No, it's obviously not something you see every day—"

"But that doesn't make it wrong," Adam interjects, taking the lunatic's side. "He just wants a different kind of lifestyle."

"Yeah, well, Orca *doesn't* want that lifestyle."

"I know. I've talked to her, too." Adam's voice gets a defensive edge, like he knows Orca better than I do. Maybe he does. He's spent days with her, while I've only talked to her over the phone.

"And what did she tell you?" I challenge, crossing my arms over my chest.

"Probably the same thing she told you. Her father doesn't want her to go to the mainland, and he's always told her it's because the world is… a scary place, more or less."

"Yeah, which is bullshit—"

"Not necessarily. He has a point. And he wants to protect her."

"Prisons also protect people," I point out, at which Adam gives me an unamused scowl. "See? You're annoyed 'cause I'm right. She's a prisoner on that island for her own 'protection.'"

"I think there's more to it than that."

"Like *what?*"

Adam falls silent, staring into his coffee mug while Mom flips the pancakes, and the whole kitchen fills with the scent of childhood.

"You're about to run out of time to state a reasonable reason," I say, pointing to the clock.

At last, Adam says, "Orca's mother died when she was very young."

I shut up at this new piece of information. Orca never mentioned her mom to me… but she discussed it with Adam? It makes me wonder what else they talked about. Clearly, it wasn't all *philosophy*.

"How did she die?"

"I don't know. I didn't ask for details. And Orca didn't seem to know much about it, herself. She said her dad never really talks about it. I got the impression that her mother's death really broke her father's heart. There weren't even any pictures of her in the house—except for one, in his sock drawer."

I raise an eyebrow. "What were you doing in his sock drawer?"

"Borrowing clothes. And you're missing the point."

"Which is…?"

"That maybe Mr. Monroe's obsession with protecting his daughter has less to do with 'keeping her prisoner' and more to do with the fear of losing her. Like he lost his wife."

"That makes sense," Mom adds. "I wouldn't be surprised if that's his reason for trying to keep Orca out of harm's way."

Adam gives me a look that I translate as, *See? Mom agrees with me.* He stands and goes to the stove to help cook breakfast while I consider this theory.

I guess he has a point, which I may have overlooked. If the guy lost his wife unexpectedly, he might be holding the "dangers" of the world responsible.

"Okay, fine. There are fewer things to kill Orca on Recluse Island," I admit, stating the obvious. "But it's not like he can protect her from *every-thing*, even in his own little world. She could get struck by lightning. She could accidentally fall into the ocean and drown. She could slip on a piece of driftwood and hit her head and die."

Mom grunts. "I think the chances of that are very low."

"You're missing *my* point, now. You can't protect someone from *everything.* Orca probably does a lot of dangerous stuff all the time on the island. Just because it's not the mainland, it's A-okay? That's stupid. It doesn't make *sense.*" I rub my eyes, leaning against my elbows on the table.

"It's not about what she *does,*" Adam says, cracking eggs into another pan. "It's about where she is, who she's around."

"Nobody."

"Exactly. So she's safe from emotional pain."

"Ugh. Don't get all philosophical."

Adam turns to Mom. "You know what I mean, right?"

"Yes—"

"I *know* what you *mean,*" I cut in. "I just think it's a dumb argument. What about the 'emotional pain' her dad is causing by keeping her—"

"If you say 'prisoner' one more time…" Adam points a warning finger at me.

"Safe from harm," I quote Mom, kind of mockingly but whatever. "I mean, you were hanging out with her for days, Adam. Didn't she seem unhappy?"

Adam hesitates. "I would say… dissatisfied—"

"Okay, fine. Dissatisfied. And all she wants is to see the mainland. Right?"

"Yes."

"So, why not? I mean, what harm could it possibly do? She doesn't want to move out permanently. She just wants to see what life is like in our world."

Adam gets all quiet and contemplative, stirring the eggs with a spatula while Mom divides the pancakes among plates. I'm about to consider myself the winner of this debate when Mom says, "It could do *some* harm. If her father doesn't want her to go, and she goes anyway… it could drive a wedge between them."

I wonder if that would be such a bad thing. I still stand by my opinion that the guy is an unreasonable dick. I could tell just by the way he looked at me, like I was some punk intruding on his life and violating his daughter by having a simple conversation with her.

"There's no point talking about this," Adam says, sitting down with his breakfast. "There's nothing we can do about it."

I tilt my head to the side. "I don't know about *that*."

He shoots me a no-nonsense look. "Stay out of it, Jack. I mean it."

"Is that a threat?"

Mom sighs. "Boys."

"No, seriously, I want to know. Why are you so defensive about this? The guy's a *lunatic*—"

"Jack, let's talk about something else." Mom sets a heavenly-smelling plate of pancakes and eggs in front of me.

For her sake, I drop the topic. Adam and I aren't going to see eye to eye on it, and that pisses me off. He may have spent more combined hours with Orca, but he doesn't understand her like I do—he doesn't see how unhappy she is, deep down.

Maybe I'm the only one who *can* see it.

Maybe I'm the only one who can rescue her.

THE RIVER LETHE

adam

Time off is the last thing I need right now, but according to the doctor, it would be "extremely unwise" to do any professional piloting until my ribs are fully healed. That means four weeks of no income, which is arguably more painful than the fracture itself.

But it's not just the money I'm worried about.

It's Orca.

All rest and no work means too much time to think about her—and everything that happened between us on the island. Too much time to regret every word, every look, every touch—simultaneously wishing I could turn back time and be with her all over again. Wishing what I wrote in that letter were true, that she and I lived in a world with just the two of us. No place to belong except in each other's arms.

Damn it.

I'm supposed to be getting *over* her. I told myself I would. I told myself the memory of her would fade. But so far, it's only grown more vivid. No matter how hard I try, I can't get her out of my head. I start seeing her in my dreams—lucid visions of her standing on the rocks, singing with the orcas, or leaning against the railing at the top of the lighthouse, wind tangling in her wild hair.

Even when I'm up to my elbows in restoration work on my Beaver, I can't stop wondering: what is she doing right now? Has she found the letter I left for her in my journal? What did she feel when she read it?

Sometimes, I catch myself smiling for no reason and realize I'm thinking about Orca. The way she looked in the greenhouse, butterflies all over her; or what she said about *infinity* and *chaos*; or the sweet music of her voice singing ballads from the kitchen while I slept on the couch; or the way she touched my face after I shaved that morning, her soft fingertips moving across my skin.

It's over. She's gone.

I tell myself that again and again whenever a memory comes back to haunt me. And each time, it feels like sticking a knife in my chest.

Sometimes I wish I could tell Jack, but then I think about how betrayed he would feel, knowing I lied to him before. It would only cause more trouble. So I keep my mouth shut.

I DRIVE MOM HOME from work on Wednesday afternoon because her car is at the shop, and Dad is at the marina. It's raining, as usual. I don't say much on the drive; I just listen to the rain pattering the windshield and feel like I'm not here—like I'm dreaming, sleepwalking. Like part of me is still somewhere else.

With someone else.

"Adam?"

I snap out of it, turning to look at Mom. "Yeah? Sorry, what did you say?"

"Nothing. You just seem preoccupied."

I rap my fingers on the steering wheel, slowing down for a red light. "I was just thinking about the parts I need to order for my Beaver."

Mom glances over, watching my fingers. *Tap, tap, tap.*

"You were never much good at lying, you know. Jack, on the other hand—he's an expert con man. He must get it from his father."

A laugh stumbles out of me despite the heat blazing over my ears.

"I don't mean just now," Mom clarifies. "You've been preoccupied since you came back from that island."

"It's just the pain medication; it makes me tired. I'm fine, Mom. Really."

"Not distracted at all?"

"No."

BEEP! A car blares its horn right behind me. I startle at the sound, glancing up—

The light is green.

Mom smirks. "You might want to step on it."

I curse under my breath, driving through the intersection and getting back up to speed.

"Would you like me to drive?"

"*No,*" I bite out.

Mom falls silent. For a few minutes, it's nothing but rain and the quiet rumble of the engine. I feel a sense of relief when Mom brings up a different topic.

"Dad's going to get Jack some work at the marina this summer."

"Oh? And does Jack know about this yet?"

"Mm-hmm. I told him this morning. Wasn't too thrilled, but you know Jack."

I grunt in agreement, knowing exactly what she means.

"I think it will be good for him," Mom adds. "He's already made it clear he's not interested in college, which is fine, but... I'd like to see him go after *something*. He's not self-motivated like you."

"No."

"But maybe a job would help him gain some discipline."

"Maybe."

"At least it'll keep him out of trouble."

"*Maybe,*" I say with a half-smile. "Jack has a remarkable talent for getting himself *into* trouble—despite everyone's best efforts to keep him out of it."

My knuckles whiten around the steering wheel as I remember the debate we had a few mornings ago—a debate that has resurrected itself many times since, with no end in sight as long as I disagree with him on the topic. Our quarrels usually bother him much more than they bother me—and he won't let me see the end of an argument until I've assured him that he is correct, in at least some small capacity.

"I hope he doesn't try to interfere with Orca and her father."

Mom turns to give me a puzzled frown. "You really think he would?"

"I don't know. He keeps talking about her, saying he wants to get her out of there. He thinks her father is some villain. Not to mention, I can tell he has a crush on her."

"Jack has a crush on every girl."

"Yeah, I know, but this is different. *She's* different. She lives in another world, which might make her sheltered, but it also makes her pure and unpolluted. Special. Beautiful, yes. But she's off-limits, and he can't be with her. He needs to accept that. And move on."

Mom's gaze burns against the side of my face. I sense her seeing right through me, reading my mind.

"Can he accept it?" she asks softly. "Can he move on?"

I brake at a stop sign and look over at her.

She knows.

I know she knows.

So I drop the act.

"No," I confess, my voice a cracked whisper. "I don't think he can."

A look of sympathy softens Mom's eyes as it all clicks into place. I'm ashamed to watch the realization hit, so I turn my attention back to the road.

"I suspected you were hiding something," Mom says. "I could see it in your eyes. I thought you might have talked about it with Jack, but he said you told him nothing happened between you and Orca."

"I lied. And apparently, I'm a good enough con man to convince *him*."

There's a long pause, filled with the sound of rain on the truck roof.

"So… what *did* happen between you and Orca?"

I shake my head because I don't know how to put the answer into one coherent sentence.

Everything, and *nothing.*

Chaos.

"I don't know, Mom. I thought I was going to die, and then there she was, like a godsend. She saved my life, but it wasn't just gratitude I felt. It's unexplainable, something I've never experienced before. Yes, she's sheltered, like Jack said… but there's something so beautiful about that. She knows more about *real* life than most people in the world. She talks to orcas. Literally." I smile at the recollection of her skipping over the rocks, singing whale songs. "She's just so different from anyone I've ever met before. I know that sounds cliché, but—"

"It doesn't sound cliché," Mom says. "It sounds like you're in love."

My heart stumbles over itself, leaving me feeling weak and senseless for a moment. I shake my head, trying to get a grip.

"Did you tell her?"

I shrug one shoulder. "Sort of. Not in so many words, but… She got the point."

"And how did she reply?"

A memory flashes back to me—the night I kissed her at the top of the lighthouse, ran my fingers through her silky hair, and felt the warmth of her hand on my chest.

"She said she felt the same way," I admit. Before Mom has a chance to make a statement, I add, "But we can't be together."

"Why not?"

"Well, first, because I'm too old for her."

Mom gives me a dubious look. "I'm five years older than your father."

"And I'm *ten* years older than Orca. She's still a teenager, for Christ's sake. She's Jack's age. Second, her father is very protective of her. He made me promise not to contact her, and I respect that. I don't want to come between them. I don't want Orca to have to choose between her father and me, and have a broken heart either way. I know how important family is." I sigh, rubbing my forehead with one hand. "And like I said, Jack seems to be interested in Orca himself. I already told him nothing had happened between us. If the truth came out now, he'd be angry with me for keeping it from him. Trust me, it's better for everyone if I leave it alone."

Mom thinks about this as I tap on the directional and turn down our dirt road. I can practically hear the gears spinning in her mind as she descends into the thoughtful silence of her mental war room. She's trying to find a solution that makes everyone happy—but it doesn't exist. Not this time.

"Mom. Seriously. At this point, the best thing to do is just… not talk about her. Please. And don't tell Jack anything I said, either."

"Of course. But, Adam… there must be a way—"

"No." I shake my head decidedly. "There is no way for this to work. Now, I'd rather not talk about it anymore. Jack will forget about Orca soon enough. I'm sure he'll meet plenty of hot girls in bikinis at the marina this summer."

Mom huffs disapprovingly.

"And Orca will live with her father, undisturbed. Happily ever after."

I pull into the driveway and park the truck. For a moment, we sit there, watching the raindrops race down the windshield.

"And you? What will you do?"

I stare straight ahead, an ache spreading through my chest as the rain intensifies. I swallow, my jaw tight, my voice steeled with resolve when I answer.

"I'll move on. I have no other choice."

LONELINESS

orca

The days following Adam's departure are some of the loneliest I've
ever lived.

When I'm in the greenhouse, I think of him, and my heart aches
that he's not harvesting vegetables with me and telling me about his
theories. When I'm in the kitchen, I think of him, and my heart aches that
he's not cooking supper with me while I sing. When I'm at the top of the
lighthouse, I think of him, and my heart aches that he's not watching the
stars with me, holding my hand, kissing me.

It's not just the fact that he is gone, and I miss him so desperately—
it's the animosity smoldering between me and Papa that has filled our
house with a heavy silence neither of us can break. We feel like strangers.
Ghosts of who we once were. A chasm has split open between us—a divide
that may never be mended.

Papa of all people should understand what it's like to love someone
and then lose them. So how can he drive Adam away like this, when he
knows how much it hurts me?

A senseless storm of feelings rages inside me, every unanswerable question crashing against my mind like tidewater onto the rocks. How can I

carry on as if nothing ever happened? How can I go on living without Adam? We are two halves of the same soul.

I read his letter every night. In the soft golden light of my bedside lamp, I smooth my fingers over the pages, tracing the shapes of his words; I close my eyes and imagine that I'm feeling his skin.

Orca, I've fallen in love with you.

And I with you, Adam Stevenson.

And now, I never want to leave you.

Then why did you leave me?

I want to wake each morning to the sound of your voice.

I want to wake each morning to yours.

I want to be with you every day, every hour, every minute.

Then why did you leave me?

Every night, as I'm carried off to sleep, I imagine him coming back to the lighthouse. I imagine spotting his plane in the sky. Running down the beach to meet him. Feeling his arms around me. Kissing him. Hearing the smooth, deep timbre of his voice telling me that he loves me, that he won't give me up, that he *can't.*

But I know this will never happen.

It's impossible.

Papa has *made* it impossible.

TIME DOES NOT PASS in our world—instead, days repeat themselves. Night dissolves into a gray wash of morning. Rain comes and goes. Afternoon slips mournfully into the black robes of twilight. And the cycle repeats all over again.

I awaken one morning to a drizzling rain. The clouds hover low over our island, wisps of cotton fog reaching like fingers through the evergreen treetops. Seagulls cry, and waves crash. Our world turns, ever the same.

Despite the dreary weather, I go for a walk, Lucius trotting by my side, panting giddily and spraying sand underfoot. I pull my cloak hood up over my head as I inhale the scent of wet green earth. The spicy aroma of pine, the salty tang of kelp washed ashore, the sweetness of the rain as it falls, darkening the trees and blooming new patches of moss in its wake.

I walk because I can't bear to be in the house any longer. I can't bear the effort it takes to be around Papa. To talk about the weather and the crops and all the things we used to talk about before Adam.

Now, everything is different.

I'm afraid of what I might say to Papa if I let my heart control my mouth. And though the words may be true, where will they lead me? I have no option but to carry on and live my life. I have no choice but to obey my father.

"Come on, Lucius!" I call to the damp mongrel, who is burrowing his nose into the sand in search of something. He glances up at the sound of his name and romps over, following me up the rocky slope and into the forest.

I let my fingertips brush over tree branches as I pass them, cool raindrops splashing on my skin. It feels like only yesterday I was out searching these woods for Adam. Scouting the ground for footprints, examining every broken spider's web. Looking for evidence that I was not alone in my world.

Now, I need no evidence. I am very, very much alone. The cold, encompassing weight of loneliness surrounds me like a starless night.

I continue through the forest, the dripping pines thinning out as I near the cove where Papa likes to fish. I know every tree, every bush, and every rock like the back of my hand. That's why today, I stop short when I glimpse something unfamiliar ahead.

A streak of red through the woods.

My breath catches. Lucius stands at attention, glancing around.

"It can't be…"

I rush forward, weaving through the trees and dodging gnarled roots as I race toward the cove. Flashes of bright red beckon me onward until I finally stumble out of the forest and onto the sandy shore of the cove.

And there, parked on the water, is Adam's plane.

MISSION IMPOSSIBLE

Enough of this shit.

I'm done listening to Adam's baseless arguments about Orca. I'm done hearing him defend her father like he's some hero for shielding his daughter from the big, bad world. I'm done debating because no matter how I say it, Adam doesn't get it.

He can't put himself in Orca's shoes. He's too old and complacent. He'll leave the whole thing alone and gallantly step out of Orca's life—to "respect her father's wishes."

But if he thinks I'm going to do the same, he's got another think coming.

I drop the subject for a couple of days, and Adam seems relieved, as if he thinks I've forgotten about Orca, just like that.

Not a chance, bro.

I let Adam believe that because I don't want him to know what I'm planning. I don't want him to try to stop me. If no one else is going to step up and help Orca, I'm going to have to do it myself. Without anyone's say-so.

I wait for the right moment. Aka: a moment when Adam isn't around. He's off pilot duty for the next three weeks, which means he'll be spending all his time in his hangar at the port, restoring his disaster of a de Havilland Beaver. If I'm going to sneak off in his other plane, I'll have to wait for a day when he's not around. So I bide my time, impatient and restless.

Meanwhile, Mom gets annoyed with me hanging around the house—annoyed enough for Dad to find me a summer job at the marina, which he says will be a good "learning opportunity" for me. The only upside is that it's part-time, so he can always pull strings if I *really* don't want to be there. (One of the perks of living in a small town.)

Every night, I fall asleep thinking about Orca—wishing she had a phone so I could talk to her about all the things I want to show her, all the places she's always dreamed of seeing. But I don't just want to tell her about those things—I want to bring them to life. I want to see her face as she takes it all in.

I want to give her the world.

On Friday, the opportunity comes. I overhear Adam grumbling about some doctor's appointment he doesn't want to go to at three o'clock.

"You have to go back to the doctor's?" I ask, pretending to be only half-interested.

"Yeah," Adam says. "Some routine thing. They need to check on my ribs. Waste of time."

Mom starts arguing that it's *not* a waste of time and he *needs* to go, then offers to drive him, which he firmly refuses—but by this point, I'm not paying attention.

Adam will be gone for hours. Away from the port. Away from his plane.

Now's my chance.

I watch the clock, waiting for him to leave. At last, he does—and before his truck even pulls out of the driveway, I make my move.

"Dad called and said he could use me at the marina," I tell Mom, totally lying but whatever. She won't double-check this with Dad. I can tell just by her laid-back tone when she replies with a distracted, "Okay, sweetie. Drive safe."

I grab my bomber jacket and my keys, rushing out the door. It's an overcast day, but visibility isn't too bad. Muscle memory gets me to the port without thinking about where I'm driving—and it's a good thing because all I can think about is Orca.

Her face is all I see in my mind as I park my Mustang outside the hangar and dash across the parking lot to the docks. Adam's red-and-white Beaver waits for me, already fueled up for this mission.

If my brother knew what I was doing right now, he would regret ever teaching me how to fly.

I feel like a carjacker (planejacker?) as I skulk through the preflight inspection, constantly checking over my shoulder to make sure I'm not being watched. Once I'm inside the cockpit, I can breathe easily and focus on my engine-start sequence. While the Beaver warms up, I slide on my headset and go through my checklist—concentrating just enough to get myself into the sky without a hitch. The weather is decent enough to fly in but lousy enough to weed out any joyriders.

Visibility is good compared to that foggy morning when I flew out to look for Adam. I was totally out of my mind back then—it feels like a lifetime ago. Yet that was the first day I talked to Orca.

I catch myself smiling, thinking about her again.

Imagining how surprised she'll be to see me.

Okay, focus, Jack.

I glance down at my altimeter, pushing the yoke forward to descend a few hundred feet. Recluse Island is already coming into view—a clump of evergreens huddled over the glassy gray water. I remember seeing a hidden cove on the island's east side, so I fly in that direction—banking hard left as I watch my compass. 240...220...

A spray of whitewater rushes around my floats as I come down for a landing. My free hand works the throttle as momentum carries me over the tops of the waves toward the mouth of the cove. It's wide enough to allow for my wingspan, but I still take it slow—watching for any rocks that could eat my floats. Adam will kill me if I wreck his only working aircraft.

Once I've comfortably docked the Beaver in the cove, I hop out and descend the ladder, rope in hand. I'm close enough to jump to the shore and keep my feet dry. After I knot the end of the rope around a tree trunk, I step back to examine my docking job.

Damn good, if I do say so myself. Adam would be impressed.

Though I'm confident that the Beaver is well hidden from the lighthouse, I can't guarantee no one will find it. A big red floatplane isn't exactly easy to keep out of sight. If Orca's dad comes down to this cove, I'm dead meat.

The clock is ticking, but at least the hard part is over.

I'm here. Orca's here.

Now all I need to do is convince her to run away with me.

NOW OR NEVER

orca

I stand frozen on the shore of the cove, my mouth hanging open in shock as I stare at Adam's red-and-white floatplane.

He's come back.

My racing heart leaps into my throat, all my dreams flashing back to me—visions of Adam returning to the island to tell me that he loves me, that he will never leave me again.

I approach to get a better look and find the plane's cockpit empty. The rope has been knotted securely around a tree trunk, but there's no trace of Adam—aside from smudges of footprints in the wet sand.

I turn in a slow circle, peering through the forest.

"Adam?" I call out. "Adam, can you hear me?"

No response but the sound of chirping birds and dripping rain. Deeper in the woods, I hear the crisp drilling of a woodpecker.

Where would he have gone? Towards the lighthouse, no doubt. He would have followed the coastline to avoid getting lost in the woods.

"Come on, Lucius. Let's go this way."

Side by side, we trek onward—staying close to the shore so I can scan the forest for him. The anticipation is enough to awaken a storm of butter-flies in my stomach.

He's here. He's come back for me.

"Adam!" I shout through cupped hands. "Adam, are you there?"

I stop and listen carefully, untangling the layers of sounds around me. Lucius hesitates, looking quite annoyed with how damp he has become. I glance over my shoulder to confirm that I did see the plane and that it wasn't my imagination fooling me. That I wasn't dreaming it all up because I wanted it to be true.

"Adam?" I call again, raising my voice louder.

A heartbeat of silence, and then—

"Orca?"

The voice is distant, and for a moment, I don't know where it comes from.

I spin in circles, my gaze sweeping the forest.

"Yes!" I call back. "I'm here!"

A rustle of brush up ahead catches my attention, and my heart thrusts against my ribs. I'm prepared to run to Adam—jump into his arms and kiss him and tell him how many times I dreamed of this moment.

That's when Jack Stevenson steps out from behind the trees. His bright hazel eyes lock on mine, and the shape of my name brings a smile to his lips.

"Orca!"

"Jack!" I gasp, reeling to an abrupt halt. A peculiar pang of disappointment jolts through me. "What are you doing here? Where's Adam?"

"Adam's not here."

"But his plane—"

"I borrowed it," Jack explains with a cheeky grin. "Well, I guess you could say I *stole* it. But he won't mind."

Lucius yips joyfully, bounding over to Jack, thwacking his tail and demanding attention until Jack bends down to slather him with hugs and affection. I stare at him in astonishment, my mind racing.

"Wait, do you mean Adam has no idea you're here?"

Jack straightens up. "That's right. I didn't tell anyone about it. I didn't want them stopping me."

"Stopping you from doing what?"

"Rescuing you." He smiles, a bold spark of adventure igniting his eyes as he watches my reaction. "I want you to come back with me. To the mainland. I want to show you the world, everything we talked about—everything you've always dreamed of."

My heart thuds in my chest. "What?"

"It's the least I can do," Jack says, grasping my hands. "After what you did for Adam and me… Let me give you this, Orca. Let me bring you to the Otherworld."

This is all happening so fast—I can't think. My head is spinning, a million thoughts swirling through my mind.

Papa will never let me go…

But if I don't go, I will never see Adam again.

Jack seems delighted by my speechless shock. He glances over his shoulder at the plane, lowering his voice to a hasty whisper. "Don't say anything to your father. Just grab some clothes and come with me—"

"Run away, you mean?"

"Not forever."

"How long, then?"

"I don't know, a week?"

"A week?"

My pulse races at the idea: *A whole week in the Otherworld. A whole week with Adam.*

"*Two* weeks. However long you want." Jack's gaze darts back and forth between my eyes. "Come on, Orca; I know you want this. You want it so bad, you're *starving* for it. And it's like the hunger is part of you—it *is* you. There's nowhere you can go that you don't feel it."

"Yes… I know." My voice cracks under the weight of longing, tears blurring my vision. He's just put into words exactly what I've felt all my life.

"Orca," he rasps, cupping my face in his hands, "I feel the same way about so many things. Adam doesn't get it; your dad doesn't get it. They don't know what it feels like… but I do. I know how much you want this, how much you *need* this." Jack's gaze softens, roaming over my face and hesitating on my lips. As if suddenly realizing how close we are, he drops his hands and draws a step back. "It's time to make your own decisions, Orca. You have to choose your *own* path in life. You can't just sit back and let your father decide it for you—"

"But I can't run away. It would break Papa's heart."

"And what about him breaking *your* heart? Breaking your trust? How can you even *trust* the guy? That's what I want to know—"

"Because I love him," I argue. "And he loves me, too… in his own way."

Jack stares at me, shaking his head. "If he loved you, he'd want you to be happy. You know that."

I do. And the injustice of it all drives a splinter of pain through my heart.

"Orca, you don't have to be so strong all the time. Not for me. I know you're tough and independent and badass, but you're *lonely*, too. And that's okay. It's okay to need other people. This life might be enough for your dad, but it's not enough for you. And it's wrong of him to force it down your throat. To keep you prisoner here—"

"I'm not a prisoner—"

"Yes," Jack insists, "you *are*. Don't you see? He's gonna keep you here forever if you don't make a move. He's always going to come up with some excuse to make you stay, and you'll spend your whole frickin' life wondering what the world is like and never seeing it—is that what you want?"

"No! Of course not."

"Then *come with me*. Just for a week." Jack lays one hand on my shoulder, reckless hope burning in his eyes. "Orca, it's now or never."

When I think about climbing into that plane and flying off to the Otherworld—when I think about seeing Adam again, *my Adam*—the thought is enough to ignite my heart with a thrill of dizzy excitement.

I want to shout *yes!* at the top of my voice and follow him wherever he may lead, but the jaws of guilt clamp hard around my conscience, unwilling to let go.

"I can't run away, Jack. I can't sneak off without telling Papa. He'll be so worried, so confused—he'll think something bad has happened to me."

"But, Orca—"

"You know how much it hurts when someone you care about goes missing!"

The ghost of a painful memory crosses Jack's face. He nods understandingly.

"Not to mention, Papa will probably call the coast guard when he can't find me."

"I hadn't thought of that." Jack huffs a frustrated sigh, forking one hand through his chestnut brown hair as he glances out to the ocean. He falls silent for a moment. "What if your father gave you *permission* to go with me... would you?"

"Of course. But he won't."

Jack's gaze snaps to mine, a challenge sparking like a match in his eyes. "Well, you never know until you try." He turns abruptly and starts striding toward the lighthouse.

"Wait, Jack!" I catch up to him, grabbing his arm. "What are you doing?"

"I'm gonna talk to your father."

"I don't think that is a good idea."

"Why? Does he not like me?"

"He... barely knows you. But that's not my point. I've been asking him for this for *years*—don't you understand? He won't change his mind. He's the most stubborn person in the world."

Jack glances down at my hand clasped on his arm, then back up to my face. A self-assured grin twitches onto his lips. "The second most stubborn," he says. "Right after me."

LOVE CONQUERS ALL

orca

On the way back to the lighthouse, I try to convince Jack to let me go in first so that I can gently break the news to Papa.

"What's the point of that?" Jack counters. "I'm not afraid of him." He marches on with renewed determination, and I hurry to keep up. Lucius trots beside us, his ears perked at the sense that something is out of the ordinary.

At last, we reach the lighthouse. The chickens are pecking around the yard, and the back door is open, but I don't see Papa outside. I cut in front of Jack to enter the house first, but he follows right on my heels. We find Papa in the kitchen, lugging an armload of firewood through the front door.

His name bursts past my lips as I stop in the doorway of the kitchen. He has his back to me as he sets down the pile of wood. "Orca, I was wondering where you went. I didn't see…"

That's when he turns—his gaze landing on Jack, who stands just behind me. I brace my arm across the doorway, barring him in the living room.

"What are *you* doing here?" Papa growls, his expression darkening.

My heart hammers in the back of my throat. "Jack was just—"

"Jack can speak for himself," Papa interrupts, motioning for me to release the boy from the doorway.

When I don't move, Jack pushes my arm aside and strides into the kitchen. "I've come to ask your permission to bring your daughter to the mainland. It'll only be for a week, and she'll be staying with my family, so you don't have to worry. My mom and dad really appreciate everything Orca did for my brother, Adam, and we'd like to return the favor. I know how much Orca wants to see the mainland."

For a breathless moment, there is nothing but silence. Papa stares at Jack, a flare of outrage and panic in his eyes.

"That is out of the question," he says, his voice deceptively calm. "Now, please leave my house and do not come back."

I rush forward. "Papa—"

"No," Jack snaps. "I won't. Now, I don't want to fight with you, sir— but I want you to hear me out. Orca will be fine; she'll be with my family. We'll take good care of her. I think she deserves this chance, don't you?"

Papa's jaw sets as he sizes up Jack in one glance.

"Your daughter has *begged* you, for years, to take her to the mainland. Just to see it. And you've denied her again and again."

"Don't presume to tell me how to raise my daughter—"

"She's not a child anymore! She's an adult, and she deserves to be a part of the world, even if it's too awful and scary for *you* to handle."

A flash of rage sparks in Papa's eyes.

I jump in, lifting a hand to silence them both. "Papa, I think what Jack is trying to say—"

"I know *exactly* what Jack is trying to say. And my final answer is no."

"But, Papa—"

"No!" he roars, turning to face me fully. "Now, I told you the subject is not open for debate. You belong *here*. And you never thought any different until *his* brother came along and filled your head with all this nonsense!"

"That's not true. I've always wanted to go to the Otherworld, and you've always made me feel like I couldn't handle it, like I wasn't strong enough. All Adam did was tell me that I *am* strong—something you never bothered to do!"

"Don't you go there—"

"She's right," Jack interrupts, narrowing his eyes indignantly at Papa. "*You're* the one who's filling her head with bullshit, telling her she can't handle the world. Maybe *you* can't handle the world, sir—but that doesn't mean your daughter should be a prisoner here."

"She is not a prisoner."

"She is!" Jack yells, his eyes wild. "And *you're* her prison guard."

It's the last straw. Papa's expression hardens with an anger like I've never seen before. His voice is no louder than a whisper when he speaks.

"Get out."

When Jack doesn't move, Papa's knuckles whiten around the back of the chair he's gripping—fury blazing in his eyes.

"I said *get out*, boy."

"Fine." Jack gives a stiff nod. "I will. But I'm taking Orca with me."

"You leave my daughter alone!" Papa bellows, startling me back a step. "Get off my property and don't come back, you hear me?"

"Papa—"

"Orca isn't a child! It's *her* choice whether she decides to stay here with you…" Jack's gaze slides to me, a thread of hope still holding on. "Or come with me."

My heart pounds in my throat as I look at Papa. I feel like my soul is splitting in two all over again.

"So why don't you ask her what *she* wants?" Jack challenges. "For once in your life."

Papa's jaw twitches in irritation, but his gaze remains fixed on mine, something weak and desperate behind the storm clouds of anger raging in his eyes. "Orca," he says softly, "tell him that this *is* what you want. That you don't want to go with him."

I am speechless. I am frozen. I am standing on the precipice of everything I've ever longed for. Some part of me doubted this moment would ever come—I certainly never expected it to come like this.

But now, here I stand, facing an impossible choice.

The Otherworld and Adam… or my father.

Perhaps two weeks ago, I would have chosen my father.

But that was before I fell in love and learned what it is to have my heart broken. Now, part of me is lost in the Otherworld with Adam—and I will never be the same again. I will never be complete without his love.

I can't go back to the way things were before.

The hurricane cannot return to the butterfly's wings.

A great divide has split open between Papa and me. The childlike admiration and trust I once held for him now withers like a dying flower, scorched by his bitter words.

"I want to go with Jack," I whisper, my voice shaking almost as much as my heart. "I can't live like this anymore."

Papa stares at me, looking like I just struck him across the face. Pain and fury stir in his eyes. "Fine," he replies, his voice as cold as ice. "Go."

I can hardly believe my ears at first. I don't think Jack can, either. We both stand there, frozen with shock.

"Go!" Papa barks, gesturing sharply toward the door. "Get out! Both of you."

I recoil back a step and feel the warmth of Jack's hand slide into mine, but my gaze remains fixed on Papa until he storms out of the house. I stare at the empty doorway, a deep ache splitting my heart.

Jack's voice shakes me out of my daze. "Orca."

"Yes?"

"Grab some clothes. Let's go."

I nod and obey his command, going to my room and sliding open drawers, lingering only as long as it takes to shove several sets of clothes into a linen bag. The last thing I slip into the bag is Adam's journal. Then I rejoin Jack in the living room, where he stands guard as if ready to defend me with fists against my father.

Lucius hides by the sofa, cowering from the conflict and watching me with droopy eyes. I kiss his head and whisper, "Goodbye, Lucius. I'll be back, I promise. Be good for Papa, okay?"

"Come on, Orca," Jack says. "We have to go."

I pull myself away, and Lucius whines—making me want to cry. But I *will* be back. I loop the bag over my shoulder and follow Jack outside.

A little voice in the back of my mind tells me to wait, to think, to be sure I'm doing the right thing.

No, I tell myself. *I am doing the right thing.*

I'm following my heart, and following one's heart can never be wrong.

JACK HELPS ME ONTO the starboard float of the red-and-white seaplane, reaching up to open the door for me. I carefully scale the short ladder and climb into the cabin.

While Jack unties the mooring lines, my curious gaze wanders over the wall of instruments: meters and knobs and dials and levers. It's all a fathomless chaos of information, somehow beautiful in its complexity. The cabin is small and cozy, but spacious enough to seat six passengers. Windows line the aircraft on either side, promising an unforgettable view once we take off.

Jack grins as he climbs into the pilot's seat, unclipping his sunglasses from his bomber jacket.

"Do you know what all those things do?" I ask, gesturing toward the instruments.

"I *have* to know in order to fly this thing."

"That's amazing. It must have taken an age to learn everything."

Jack shrugs one shoulder. "I had a good teacher."

"Adam?"

He nods, passing me a strange device with an arched band connecting two padded circles. "Here, put these on."

"What is it?"

Jack looks at me like I'm crazy. "Headphones. They go over your ears like this." He slides a pair onto his head, and now I see how they work.

"Oh!" I fix them over my ears and marvel at how muffled everything sounds. "But how will I hear you?"

Jack turns one of the knobs, and a *whoosh* fills my ears, along with the sound of his voice as if he is *inside* the headphones.

"They have built-in mics," he explains. "And this is a radio, so I can communicate with other pilots, let them know where I'm flying." He winks at me, his hands darting over levers and knobs until the engine is humming smoothly. I watch in silent fascination as Jack maneuvers out of the cove and onto open water.

I still can't believe I'm inside a plane, about to take flight. So many times, I've spotted aircraft like this from the lighthouse, but I never dared to hope I would ride in one someday.

That day is today.

Jack turns to me with a smirk and says, "Ready to fly?"

My heart squeezes. I nod.

Jack focuses on the ocean ahead of him, reaching up to grab one of the levers. As he slowly pushes it forward, the plane picks up speed—moving faster and faster until we are rocketing over the surface of the waves. I look out my window at the whitewater spraying around the floats, a blur of deep blue Pacific underneath the rush of everything else.

Then, suddenly, gravity vanishes.

My heart plummets as we lift up, up, up—leaving the earth behind. At first, it's a bit terrifying to watch the world shrink beneath me as we tilt and soar into the sky like a bird. I'm not sure I could ever get used to the wobbly, floating sensation of being airborne. My stomach is doing somersaults until Jack levels out the plane, easing back the throttle to a gentle cruising speed.

"You okay?" Jack's voice crackles through my headphones. "Not too scared?"

"Not at all," I assure him with a laugh. "I'm just… lost for words. It's so beautiful. It's Otherworldly!"

Jack grins. White teeth and sunglasses. "Want to go higher?"

I grip my seatbelt. "Is it safe to?"

He laughs and flexes his suntanned fingers around the steering controls. "Trust me."

Gravity forces me back in my seat as the plane tips her nose to the clouds and ascends, weightless in a sea of space. My heart is racing, and my nerves are buzzing with adrenaline. I've never felt so exhilarated, so *captured* in a moment. Everything is so big and blue and overwhelming, impossible to describe.

We're on top of the world.

I begin to spot houses far below us, hugging the coastline of the islands—the Otherworld. My heart swells with wonder and awe at the sight of civilization.

"Is that Whidbey Island?" I ask, pointing out the windshield.

Jack squints ahead, then nods. "Sure is. How did you know?"

"I recognize the shape of the coast from one of Papa's maps."

"You sound like a seasoned pilot, Orca."

I laugh, turning my gaze back to my window and taking in the wondrous beauty sprawling below me. I want to fully absorb every detail, to enjoy this surreal moment for all it's worth—but that's a difficult thing to do when my mind is full of Adam.

Only a little while until I see him again.

I've taken the leap; I've made my own choice, for the first time in my life.

I've chosen Adam Stevenson.

And now, I can't stop imagining our reunion. How surprised he'll be to see me. How much I will kiss him and delight in the feeling of being held in his arms once more. My coming will be a confirmation—proof that we *can* be together, that our love is not as impossible as he believed it to be.

There's a Latin phrase he taught me from his journal: *omnia vincit amor.*

It means "love conquers all."

I don't think I've ever heard a more beautiful combination of words put together. And today, I am giving new meaning to that ancient proverb—I am going to show Adam that it's true of us.

Our love can conquer anything.

GUESS WHO'S COMING TO DINNER?

jack

I can't decide which is more fun: watching Orca's reaction to flying or watching how much she likes my Mustang. Ironically, she finds the car more fascinating. I thought it would be the other way around, but then I remember: she's seen planes before. She's never been in a car.

"What do you use them for?" she asks.

I try not to laugh too much at her question. "Uh, for getting around?"

"But you have a plane. You can fly places."

"I can't fly to my house."

Orca frowns. "Why not just walk?"

"It's… too far to walk." I pull open the passenger-side door for her. "Here—get in." I stand there for a whole minute while Orca carefully studies the interior of the car before climbing in.

"How does it work?" she asks when I drop into the driver's seat. Her blue-green eyes are wide with curiosity as she takes it all in.

"Uh, well, it's pretty simple," I explain, reaching over to pull the seatbelt out for her. "Cars have engines like planes do, but they're, um… smaller. And they don't have wings. Obviously."

Orca smiles, buckling up as I start the engine. "And fewer instruments," she says, pointing to the dash clock.

"Yeah, that's the radio, actually."

"Oh. Is that how you talk to… *land* traffic control?"

I laugh.

She's serious.

"Uh, no. No, there's no land traffic control. That's just for planes."

"That… doesn't seem very safe."

"Don't worry. I'll see if a car is going to hit us."

As I navigate out of the parking lot and head toward home, Orca investigates the car. "What does this button do?" she asks about every button in sight. It's like she's a time traveler from the eighteenth century, amazed by the sheer wonder of air conditioning and visor mirrors.

I'm half in love with her already.

"Will something bad happen if I press this?" she says, pointing to the handle of her door.

"No, that opens your window."

"Oh wow, the windows open?"

I nod, grinning.

Orca braces herself, carefully pushing the button and watching in amazement as the window slides down.

"That's incredible!"

I stealthily reach over to my driver's switch and put her window back up, just to freak her out.

She gasps, springing back in surprise. "Did you do that?"

"Do what?" I smirk, putting the window back down.

"That! You're doing that, aren't you?"

I burst out laughing and put all the windows down, all the way. Fresh air whips through the Mustang, blowing Orca's hair around her beaming face. Next, she discovers the radio—and you can imagine how that goes. She spins, spins, spins the dial, going through all the stations at least three times, her mouth hanging open in astonishment.

"This is amazing!" she screams over the rush of the wind.

She stops at an Oasis song—"Hey Now!"—and I crank up the volume while Orca sits back, sticking her face out the window like a dog. The wind tangles her hair into a beautiful mess as she watches the new sights fly past.

That's when I realize: it was worth it. Just to see that look of wild joy on her face.

The conversation with her dad might not have been too great, but he backed down eventually. All's well that ends well, right? Not that it ended *well*, exactly… But Orca has forgotten about it. She's so distracted by the newness of everything, she hasn't had a moment to regret what happened back on the island. And I'm sure as hell not bringing it up again.

As far as I'm concerned, it's all water under the bridge.

But there's something I haven't considered: Mom and Dad are going to ask me about it. I can imagine Mom's disapproving frown when she finds out what I did behind everyone's backs. Dad will be disappointed in me, too—double demerits for lying to Mom about going to the marina when I wasn't.

We need a plan.

I reach over to the radio and turn the volume down. "Hey, Orca?"

"Yes?" She pulls herself away from the window, her cheeks rosy from the wind.

"I was just thinking… we should probably figure out what we're going to tell my parents."

"What do you mean?"

"Well, we can't let them know how your father was so against you leaving."

"Why not?"

Because I'll get my ass whooped. In front of you.

"Because they'll want you to go back," I say, not untruthfully. "They'll side with your dad and make me take you back right away."

Orca thinks about it, pinching her lip between her fingers. "Well, he *did* tell me to go. At the end…"

"Yeah, so let's just tell them about that part," I suggest, nodding convincingly. "Let's say we asked his permission, and he was okay with it. And you're going to stay with us for a week or so, then go back home."

Orca narrows her eyes. "Isn't that lying, though?"

"It's just a white lie."

"What's a white lie?"

"Harmless. For their own good. For *your* own good. It's better that they don't know, right? You want to stay here and explore the Otherworld with me, right?"

Orca nods. "Of course I do."

"Well, then. That's what we'll tell them."

ADAM'S TRUCK IS STILL GONE when we pull into the driveway and park. He must have gotten stuck in rush-hour traffic or something. Orca looks bummed out to hear it, but I assure her that Adam will be back soon.

Our conversation ends as soon as I step through the front door, and Mom cries, "Jack Stevenson, where in the world have you been?" She looks ready to read me the riot act until she spots Orca hovering behind me. "Who is this? I didn't know we'd be having company this evening."

I grin, introducing her with a flourish. "This is the one and only Orca Monroe."

Mom blinks in disbelief, looking her over. "But you… your father…" She cuts me a sharp look. "You flew out there, didn't you? That's what you were doing. You weren't at the marina—"

The door swings open behind us, and Dad steps in with a stern frown. He doesn't even see Orca at first. "Jack, where the hell have you been? Your mother was getting worried."

"I was—"

"John," Mom cuts in, tugging his sleeve and nodding to Orca.

Dad gives her an irritated smile and says, "Hello," before driving his attention back to me. "You told your mother you were working at the marina. That wasn't true, was it?"

"No."

"So where were you? Obviously, out with this young lady, whom you've yet to introduce us to—"

"I'm Orca," she says.

Silence.

The realization seems to hit Dad even harder than it hit Mom.

I clear my throat. "I can explain."

"Please do." Mom plants her hands on her hips and raises her eyebrows expectantly.

"I flew out to the island and asked Orca's dad for permission to let her come to the mainland for a week," I explain, keeping my voice steady and confident.

"And your father granted you permission?" Mom asks, glancing at Orca as if she expects a more honest answer from her.

I keep my mouth shut and let her have the floor.

Remember the white lie, Orca.

"Yes," she answers haltingly, wringing her hands behind her back. "Yes, he was perfectly fine with it."

"Really."

"Yeah, perfectly fine," I insist. "We discussed it for a little while, and then Mr. Monroe decided that Orca deserved a little vacation."

She nods quickly. "He told me to go. Actually."

It's true, in a way. Mom usually has a nose for sniffing out bullshit, but Orca and I are an impressive double act—smooth enough to convince both my parents.

Dad still holds my feet to the fire. "And why did you feel the need to *lie* to your mother about this excursion?"

"Because I knew she'd try to stop me. Right, Mom? You would have stopped me."

Mom crosses her arms stubbornly. "I would have told you to wait and ask Adam's permission before taking his plane."

"See? That's why I didn't say anything—"

"You should *never* go flying without telling someone."

"Yeah, I know. Sorry." I sigh. "Can we just... agree that the ends justify the means?"

Mom looks like she wants to argue, but she only shakes her head and steps in to hug Orca.

"It's lovely to meet you, sweet thing."

Orca smiles and hugs her back. "It's lovely to meet *you*, Mrs. Stevenson."

"I can never thank you enough for helping my Adam," she says into Orca's hair. "You don't know what a gift you've been—to all of us."

Now Dad gives in, too, welcoming Orca and thanking her for helping Adam. She's my lucky charm, I guess. If I didn't have her sweet smile to soften the blow, Dad would be tongue-lashing me into the middle of next week.

"Where *is* Adam?" Orca asks, glancing around the living room.

"He had a doctor's appointment," Mom says, "but he called a few minutes ago to say he was running late. Traffic is always crazy at this time of day. Are you hungry, sweetheart? Dinner will be ready soon. Jack, why don't you offer Orca something to drink? I need to go see if the guest room is ready."

"I'll give you a hand," Dad offers, which can only mean one thing: my parents want to have a private conversation about this turn of events.

With that, they both disappear down the hallway and leave me alone with Orca, who doesn't look remotely interested in dinner or drinks. She wanders through the living room, gazing at everything like she's in a museum—the wood-paneled walls, the plaid couch, the coffee table scattered with books, newspapers, and an abandoned coffee mug. Mom has pine-scented candles burning, which makes the whole place smell like Christmas.

I can't help but notice that Orca is fidgeting—pulling tangles out of her hair and blushing as she glances at the clock.

"I thought he'd be here already," she murmurs, more to herself than to me. "I didn't think I'd be the one waiting for *him* to show up."

I grunt a laugh. "You nervous?"

"A little," she confesses. "But not in a bad way. I just miss him."

I shouldn't feel a sting of jealousy when she says that. I shouldn't. It's nothing. It's stupid to feel jealous over *nothing*. Adam told me they were just friends, that's it. He said they talked about philosophy and boring stuff like that.

"Has he missed *me*?" Orca asks suddenly, turning to look up at me with hopeful eyes. "Has he talked about me at all?"

I brush aside the irritated prickle at the back of my neck. "Uh, I mean, we've talked about you. A few times. About the whole… situation. With your father." I shrug, sticking my hands in the pockets of my bomber jacket. "We haven't really seen eye to eye on it."

Orca frowns. "Did he not want you to come to the island? Is that why you waited till he was gone to take his plane?"

I can tell the truth will hurt, so I sugarcoat my answer a little. "You know Adam—he hates to cause trouble. Me, I don't mind. I'm always causing trouble. People expect it of me at this point."

That gets her to laugh.

"No joke—this is my lot in life. Troublemaker Jack can't leave well enough alone." I shake my head. "But leaving you stuck on that island wasn't 'well enough' for me. It was torture."

Orca squints at me, smiling like she isn't sure if that was a compliment or a joke or me flirting with her. Third one, definitely. To make it more obvious, I step closer and catch a strand of her hair, gently working out one of the tangles.

"Adam is always playing by the rules," I say, focusing on her knotted hair and trying not to think about how badly I want to kiss her. "He's obsessed with doing the right thing."

Orca's cheeks go even pinker. "There's nothing wrong with trying to do the right thing."

"No," I whisper, lost in her eyes. "But I'm glad I broke the rules this time."

ENTROPY

adam

As I predicted, the checkup is a waste of time—then I get stuck in traffic on the way home, which is yet another waste of time. All I have to show for it is a bottle of pain medication and another large medical bill.

It's after seven by the time I pull into the driveway. The lights are on inside the house, and as I approach, I hear my family's laughter and voices drifting through the half-open windows.

They're in the middle of eating dinner when I walk in.

"There he is!" Mom says, and I reply with a murmured, "Sorry I'm late." I cross the kitchen to wash my hands at the sink, catching a glimpse of a girl sitting at the table next to Jack. I figure it must be some new girl he's met, and I immediately feel a sense of relief.

It's exactly as I expected. He's getting over Orca.

I wish I could say the same.

As I finish washing my hands, I notice the conversation at the table has died upon my entrance. Jack starts laughing like he does when he's pulling a prank on someone.

"Uh, hey, Adam?" he says. "Notice anything different?"

I frown, grabbing a dishcloth and turning to face him. "What do you…"

My heart stops.

Orca.

Orca is the girl sitting beside him.

Orca is here, in my house, having dinner with my family.

Impossible.

Her gaze locks on mine, and a smile blooms over her face, lighting up her eyes. "Hello, Adam," she says. That's when I realize I'm not hallucinating.

"Orca," I whisper, stunned. "What… What are you doing here?"

Jack speaks up, answering for her. "Orca's come to spend some time on the mainland."

My gaze switches to him, and the rest of the story clicks into place.

Jack went and got her.

While I was gone, he must have snuck out in my plane, flown to the island, and brought her back here.

I know without even asking. I know from the glint of rebellious triumph in my little brother's eyes when he looks at me. I know from the smug, self-satisfied grin that hasn't left his face since I walked in the door.

Damn it.

This is exactly what I was afraid of.

"Does your father know you're here, Orca?"

She hesitates, her smile faltering. "Yes… He's fine with it. He gave me permission to come."

I can tell she's lying by the look on her face. I know her. I know Jack.

Mom clears her throat to break the silence. "We're very happy to have Orca with us," she says, casting me an unsure look out of the corner of her eye. "You're welcome for as long as your father can spare you, dear."

Dad murmurs his agreement, Orca thanks my parents for their kindness, and Jack keeps looking at me, that unapologetic spark in his eyes.

My mother starts to say something else, but I interrupt her.

"Jack, I want to talk to you for a minute. Outside."

I don't mean for it to sound like a death threat, but apparently, that's how Mom hears it. She passes me a look that says *Don't fight with your brother*, but I'm already walking away. I push through the screen door and stride into the cool night, crossing the driveway and stopping at the edge of our woods, well out of earshot.

Jack takes his sweet time following me. Eventually, I hear the screen door whine open and slam shut. Footsteps approach, but I don't turn to face him yet. I stand my ground, staring at the darkened forest, my nerves thrumming.

"What the *hell* were you thinking?"

Jack remains silent for a long moment, then says, "I don't know what you're talking—"

"You know *exactly* what I'm talking about." I whirl on him, my blood boiling. "Her father gave her permission? Bullshit. Who do you think you're fooling? Mom and Dad, maybe. But not me."

Jack looks away, crossing his arms over his chest.

"I might not have known him for more than ten minutes, Jack, but that man would *die* before he let his daughter fly off with some eighteen-year-old guy—"

"I'm an adult now—"

"I don't care. The point is, Orca's father wouldn't allow it."

Jack glares at me, jaw twitching. I'm getting closer to the truth.

"So what *really* happened, Jack? Did you kidnap her?"

"No! First of all, she's not a *kid.*"

I scoff.

"And second, I *did* ask her old man's permission. I made him listen to what I had to say—"

"Oh, you *made* him listen?"

"And he was a total jerk about it. He kept threatening to kick me off his dumb island like I was some criminal—"

"For trespassing, you mean?"

"For questioning his authority." Jack spits the words indignantly. "For daring to say that his daughter might be happier if she wasn't locked up like some prisoner. I called him out, and he just… bit my head off. He wouldn't even *listen*—"

"So he forbade Orca from leaving, then."

Jack stares at me. Busted.

"And you took her anyway."

"I didn't *take* her," he argues. "Her father told her to get out. You should have seen the way he yelled at her. I thought she was gonna start crying." Jack sighs in disgust, shaking his head. "There's no way I could have left her alone with that monster."

I fall silent, pressing my fingertips to the ache in my forehead. Mr. Monroe isn't a monster. No, I wasn't there to see him blow up at Jack, but I can imagine it was only the result of shock and fear, his carefully protected daughter being torn away from him without warning.

"Don't act like you wouldn't have done the same," Jack adds.

My head snaps up to look at him. "I *wouldn't* have done the same."

"Oh, right. Because you don't give a crap—"

"No, because I *do* care. More than you could possibly imagine! You're so selfish, you don't even see what you've done. You have meddled and disrupted someone else's family when you had no right to. It was childish. And it was wrong."

Jack takes a step closer, lowering his voice. "You think *I'm* selfish? You're the one who walked away and left Orca on that island after all she did for you. She saved your fricking life, and you left her there. But I, on the other hand, happen to care about her. I want her to be happy. She's a remarkable girl… and she *deserves* the world. I'm sorry you disagree."

On that final word, he turns and storms back to the house. The screen door slams behind him. My hands curl into fists, a bomb of frustration detonating in my chest. I want to punch something—or some*one*.

I thought I had it all planned out—I thought Jack would leave it alone, Orca would stay with her father, and one day I would get over the loss of her. I thought the pieces were settling into place, maybe not as I'd have liked them to, but exactly as they needed to be.

Then Jack had to go and flip everything upside down.

I told him nothing had happened between Orca and me during my time at the lighthouse. I lied and said that I had no feelings for her—that we were just friends who talked about philosophy.

Nothing could be further from the truth.

But I can't tell him the truth now. It's too late.

The screen door whines open again and shuts—softly, this time. Quiet footsteps approach, and for a moment I assume it must be Mom coming to make sure I didn't snap my brother's head off.

"Adam?"

My pulse quickens at the sound of Orca's voice. I turn and find her standing a few feet away, watching me. For a moment, neither of us says a word. Her eyes glimmer in the moonlight, her wild hair tumbling around her shoulders.

"I'm sorry if I've caused trouble between you and your brother," she says, quiet and solemn.

I shake my head. "You haven't."

Orca looks at me the way she did the day I left her, so pure and sweet and hopeful. The silent tension between us is like an extra law of physics, some force of attraction beyond our control. She bends to its will before I do, reaching out to touch my hand.

I pull away.

It's one of the hardest things I've ever done, but I can't let her touch me. I can't let this continue.

Orca's hand retreats to her side, her voice returning timidly. "Aren't you glad to see me?"

The hurt in her eyes makes me want to kick myself.

"Of course I am, but—"

"I found your letter. The one you left for me in your journal."

My mind drifts back to the day I wrote it—the day I left the island. I thought it would be the final word. The last goodbye. The half of my soul I left behind.

"I cherish it," Orca says, her voice a thread about to break, her eyes glossing with tears. "And I wanted to tell you that… I feel the same way about you. I want to spend every day, every hour, every minute with *you*."

"Orca—"

"I love you, Adam Stevenson." Her lips tremble as a single tear escapes, leaving a shimmer of wet moonlight on her cheek. "Have you stopped loving *me*?"

Those words pierce my armor and stab right through to my heart. "No, Orca. I could never stop loving you. But it's not as simple as that."

"Why not?" She steps closer, taking my hand. Her skin feels like silk on my calloused palms, so warm and innocent. "It *was* that simple at the lighthouse. Nothing has changed."

God, how many times have I imagined this moment, waking and dreaming? How often have I caught myself wishing I could see her again, hold her again, kiss her again?

She wants me to kiss her. I can tell by the way she looks at me, her soft gaze roaming over my face, her fingers tracing my knuckles. The magnetism builds between us like electricity, reaching for me, reaching for her—

I close my eyes, smothering the fire inside me. "I think I should fly you back home tomorrow."

Orca's hopeful expression melts into shock. "What?"

"You need to make things right with your father. You'll always regret it if you don't."

"No, Adam. I'm not going back. I've already made my decision."

"In haste. In anger. Jack told me what happened, and I understand how you must be feeling right now. But don't you see? Your father was only afraid of losing you. That's why he was so upset—"

"You don't know the half of it," Orca snaps, pulling her hand away from mine. "Papa and I were at odds for days, long before Jack showed up. We had a fight the night you left the island." She shakes her head, eyes dimming with sadness at the memory. "He wasn't cruel. He just... he was so angry. When I told him that I loved you, he accused you of all sorts of horrible things, and he forbade me from ever seeing you again. He will never change his mind—about the Otherworld, about you, about me...

And I'm afraid of going back. I'm afraid if my world shrinks that small again, I won't be able to breathe." Orca looks up at me through cresting tears. "I can't go back to that same empty existence. I love Papa, but I can't love only him."

"Orca, I understand how hard it must be—"

"No, you don't!" she bursts out. "How could you understand? You have a mother. And she's…" Her voice cracks, wobbling and weak. "She's wonderful. Your family is whole and together and *wonderful.* For so long, I wondered what that must be like." She glances back towards the house, at its open windows glowing in the dark, the still night air carrying the voices of my mother and father and brother talking at the dinner table.

"That?" I point at the house. "*That* is what you're throwing away right now, and you don't even see it."

She backsteps, shaking her head stubbornly.

"No, listen to me, Orca. Your father *loves* you. You're his whole world. And you might be upset at him right now, but I know how you really feel about him, deep down. You can't let this drive a wedge between you."

"It's already driven a wedge between us."

"Then it's even more important for you to make things right with him now."

Orca stares at me, the look in her eyes so shattered and betrayed. "You were never going to come back, were you?"

The question hits me like an uppercut to the ribs. I don't know what to say.

"*Were* you?" she repeats, battling back a sob.

"I don't know, Orca. I never wanted to leave you in the first place, you know that. But… I didn't want to make you choose between your father and me. I promised him I would respect his wishes, and—" I break off with a sigh, rubbing my forehead. "The truth is, I'm too old for you."

"No, you're not—"

"Yes, I am. You're only eighteen, Orca, and I'm the first man you've ever met, for god's sake. You have so much life to live. So much to learn and experience. Leaving you was one of the hardest things I've ever done, but I knew it was the right thing. I knew you would forget me in time."

Orca shakes her head. "You think I'm that feeble, I would give my heart to you and then *forget* about you? We must have very different definitions of the word love."

"I do love you, Orca—"

"No! If you loved me, you wouldn't want to take me back to the lighthouse."

"It's *because* I love you that I want to take you back. Because I know you'll regret this decision one day, and by then, it may be too late to mend this bridge between you and your father."

"Well, maybe it's *his* job to mend it!" Orca argues. "I've done everything I can to make him happy, and all he's ever done is tell me what I *can't* do. And you're no better—you sound just like him. Telling me that I'm too young, too much of a child to make my own decisions."

I reach for her hand. "Orca—"

"No." She pulls away, her cheeks flushed with righteous anger. "Jack understands me. He's the only one who truly cares about what *I* want."

It's just her anger talking; I know that. But it still feels like a knife in the back.

With that, she turns away from me, hurrying across the driveway and up the porch steps. She hesitates at the door and glances back for the briefest moment—a beautiful silhouette against an orange rectangle of light. Then she vanishes inside, leaving me alone in the darkness.

THE LIST

orca

"Orca? Are you okay?" Jack looks worried when I return to the kitchen, my face hot and my heart pounding.

No, I want to say, *I'm not okay.* But I manage another white lie—rubbing my temples and sighing. "The truth is, my head is splitting. It's been a long day. I hope you won't mind if I go to bed early."

"Course I don't mind," Jack says, getting to his feet to look at me, something honest and searching in his eyes. "You sure you're all right?"

I nod stiffly, fighting back the tears. "I'll be fine if I can just lie down."

Mrs. Stevenson shows me to the guest room and encourages me to holler if I need anything. I manage to smile gratefully and thank her for her hospitality—but as soon as she leaves the room, I collapse into tears.

Oh, Adam.

I imagined our reunion a hundred times, and none of my dreams looked like this. Adam was supposed to run to me, embrace me, and tell me how much he missed me. He was supposed to sweep me off my feet and kiss me. He was supposed to say, *I'm never going to leave you again.*

But he has done the opposite—insisting that he fly me back home tomorrow, that I make things right with Papa. Insisting that we can't be together because he's too old and I'm too young, too inexperienced to make my own decisions.

Within the span of a few minutes, he crushed all my dreams to dust.

Tears rush down my cheeks as I change into my nightgown and crawl into bed. I lie in the dark for a long time, replaying our conversation over and over again in my mind.

Adam may be ten years older than me, but that doesn't make him smarter in every way. He may be more experienced, but that doesn't mean he knows what's best for me. How could he? He doesn't know what it's like to be me. Nobody but Jack seems to understand.

He's the only one who truly cares about what I *want.*

I threw those words in Adam's face tonight and watched him flinch. Some part of me regretted saying it, but another part of me enjoyed the feeling. I wanted him to know what it's like to be pushed away.

Sleep comes to me eventually in blurry waves of dreams and darkness. I see Papa shouting at me to leave, then begging me to stay. I see Adam's face in the moonlight, hear his voice encompassing me like steady thunder: *I could never stop loving you… but it's not as simple as that.* The night seems endless—a black hole of self-doubt and heartache swallowing me up.

I awaken to a rapid knocking on my door. When I open my eyes, I find morning sunlight pouring through the window and scattering across my strange new bed. The clock on the nightstand reads nine thirty.

I've slept the morning away.

The knock comes again. I push aside my sheets and climb out of bed, shuffling across the room to open the door.

"Good morning, Orca." Jack leans against the doorjamb, smirking at me. His hazel eyes glint with both the thirst for adventure and the promise of it. "I hope you slept well because today we explore the Otherworld."

A flame of half-remembered hope sparks to life in my chest. "Oh. I nearly forgot."

"Forgot?" Jack laughs. "Come on, you've been dreaming about this your whole life! Thought you'd be a little more excited."

"I *am* excited…" I look down at the floor, rubbing my bare arms.

Somehow, I expected it to feel different. When Jack flew me to the mainland yesterday, my heart was dancing with giddy joy and anticipation. Now I feel nothing but a heavy disappointment weighing on my chest like an anchor.

"Orca?" Jack's soft voice draws my gaze back up. "What did Adam say to you last night?"

"What makes you think he said anything to me?"

"Because you were so happy before he showed up. And then, after you talked to him outside… well, I could tell you were upset. I hope he didn't say anything out of line."

I shake my head. "Not exactly. He just… He thinks I should go back home and apologize to my father."

Jack sighs, rolling his eyes heavenward. "What the hell. Don't listen to him, Orca. You belong here. You *deserve* this. Stop feeling guilty and just enjoy yourself for once in your life." He grins in that unapologetic Jack Stevenson way of his. "We've got plenty of time to be responsible grown-ups—trust me. Let's enjoy being young while we can still get away with it."

Though the conflict of last night still weighs on my mind, I can't help feeling a bit lighter when Jack looks at me like that—his eyes sparkling with possibility.

"Go get dressed," he says. "I'm taking you out for breakfast."

"*Out* for breakfast? What does that mean?"

"You'll see." He winks, pulling the door shut. "Meet you in the driveway!"

Perhaps Jack is right—I've come this far. Why should I have regrets? I should enjoy my time in the Otherworld without looking over my shoulder and feeling guilty for things I didn't do. I've longed for this adventure my whole life. I've wanted it since before I can remember.

So why am I not more excited? Why do I find myself standing at the threshold of my dream, hesitation clutching my heart?

Perhaps because, more than the Otherworld and all its glory, I want Adam Stevenson to love me again.

IT'S CALLED A "DINER," according to Jack, and I've never seen anything like it before. The whole building is one big open room crowded with tables and chairs where people sit, talking and eating breakfast. The atmosphere is a chaos of voices and clacking dishes and delicious aromas. Music plays from a radio in the ceiling, barely audible over the noise of everything else. Jack takes my hand and leads me to an empty booth by a window, where we sit across from each other.

"Why would people come here to eat instead of cooking for themselves?"

"Because it's easier," Jack says, grinning as he watches me take in the otherworldly sights around us. "And who wants to cook, anyway?"

"But who makes the food?"

"Uh, the people working here."

"Why would they do that?"

"To get paid?"

"Oh, so it's one of those 'jobs' Adam was talking about."

"Yeah. Most people have one," Jack says. "Some people have two. Or three."

"I still can't believe how many people live in one place!"

"This is a really small town, Orca. Like, everyone knows each other."

"Really? Wait, how is that possible?"

Before Jack can answer this question, a middle-aged woman with deep brown skin stops beside our table and says, "Good morning, Jack. Who's this pretty young lady?" She's wearing an apron and a little pin over her heart that says *Celine*.

Jack grins and gestures across the table to me. "This is Orca. She's new here."

I give a smile and a tiny wave. "Good to meet you."

"Honey, you look too sweet to be hanging around with this *wild* boy." Celine ruffles Jack's hair, which makes him laugh, his ears flushing red.

"Oh, he's not so bad," I say with an indulgent smile.

Celine nods slowly. "Mm-hmm. You say that now. But just be warned… this one's a heartbreaker."

Jack looks up at Celine with the most innocent smile, batting his eyelashes. "I haven't broken *your* heart, have I, Celine?"

She rolls her eyes and gives him a playful shove. "Oh, stop it. Coffee?"

"Coffee would be great. Thank you."

Celine continues down the row of tables while Jack shakes his head, looking like a little boy whose mother just embarrassed him.

"So…" I smirk, leaning forward on my elbows. "You've broken hearts, have you, Jack Stevenson?"

He blushes, tipping his head back. "No."

I twitch an eyebrow, waiting for the truth.

"Well, maybe a few."

"Ah. And who were they?"

Jack shrugs, making a face like he just swallowed something unpleasant. "Just some girls I've gone out with."

"Gone out with?"

"Like… dated."

"Is dating like flirting?"

"The two usually go hand in hand, yeah."

"So you've dated a lot of girls," I surmise, leaning back in the booth.

"I guess," Jack admits. "Not more than the average guy my age—"

"What about Adam?"

Jack tilts his head, thinking about it. "Adam's weird. Like, he's the guy who has to have a million of these 'just a friend' dates before he works himself up to ask the girl on a *real* date… and by then, he's decided she's not really 'the one' or whatever. He takes everything too seriously. Doesn't know how to have fun."

"And *you* do?"

He gives me a smirk. "I invented fun."

That's when Celine returns, two mugs of coffee in hand. Jack and I both say "thank you" in unison, and then Celine asks what she can get us.

I'm not sure what she means, but Jack understands all this Otherworldly etiquette. He tells her something about waffles and chocolate chip pancakes, and she laughs at him for being predictable. Moments later, she is walking away, and I'm raising an eyebrow at Jack.

"Did you just decide what I'm going to eat?"

"Yep." Jack winks. "So what do you want to do after breakfast? You've been dreaming about coming to the Otherworld for so long, you must have a list of things you want to see and do, right?"

"I want to see everything," I say with a laugh. "Where do you suggest we start?"

A new idea sparks in Jack's eyes. "I'll be right back." He slides out of the booth and vanishes outside. I watch through the window blinds as he dashes through the parking lot to his car. Moments later, he drops back into the seat across from me, a small notebook in hand.

"What's that for?" I ask, cradling my coffee under my chin.

"A list. So we can keep track of everything." Jack opens the notebook to a clean page and clicks his pen against the table. "Okay, so I know we talked about some things on the phone, right? All the stuff your dad's forbidden?"

"Yes…"

"Remind me. I know you've never seen a movie." Jack shakes his head with dismay, writing something at the top of the page. "Insanity. Oh, and video games! I have to show you video games."

"Mm, the elusive video games…"

"You're going to be *so* into it," Jack assures me. "Mark my words."

I watch him write a few more items on the list; then he looks back up at me, tapping the pen against the paper. "What else?"

"Ummm… pizza?"

"Oh god, yes. I can't believe I forgot that." Jack writes "PIZZA" in all capital letters on the paper. "And all the good food in general that you've been deprived of."

"Like what?"

"Like ice cream and soda and fries and cheeseburgers…"

That's when Celine reappears with two sweet-smelling plates of food. She slides them onto the table, and I can't help staring. I've never seen anything quite like this before.

"… and waffles," Jack finishes with a grin. "Thank you, Celine."

"Sure thing, baby."

I tilt my head, studying the strange symmetrical shapes of the waffles, which are piled with strawberries and blueberries and dusted with a white powdery substance. The other plate is stacked with pancakes the size of my head, speckled with chocolate pieces. When I look back up at Jack, he is trying not to laugh at me.

"What? I've never seen food like this before." I pluck one of the strawberries from the pile. "Except this. I grow these on my island."

"Okay, but here's the ultimate question," Jack says. "Pancakes or waffles?"

"The ultimate question, huh?"

"The *ultimate*. Like, we can't even hang out anymore if you don't pass this test."

I try both the pancakes and the waffles before determining that they taste the same. Jack argues that they are most definitely *not* the same, and I can tell he prefers the pancakes since they are already half gone. Upon further reflection, I decide the waffles are superior. Jack takes it as a personal insult.

"Okay, if this is a *small* town," I say at last, "what does a *big* town look like?"

"They're called cities. You want to see one? I'll take you to see one." He grabs the notebook and pen, writing something down. "We can go to Seattle."

"Isn't that far from here?"

"No, it's not too far. If you're amazed by how many people live *here*, your mind will be blown by Seattle."

"Okay, well, maybe we should stick around here to start."

"But it's boring here."

"Nonsense! It's where you grew up. I want to know everything about it! It's your *world*."

Jack sighs. "Yeah, exactly. It's all I've ever known. Just like you, stuck on your island. That's why I can't wait to get out."

"Well, Seattle can't be that much better."

"I don't want to go to Seattle," Jack says with a dry laugh. "I want to go everywhere. I want to see the world."

"The *whole* world?"

"The whole world." He nods emphatically, eyes brightening at the idea. "I want to take a boat and sail across the Pacific Ocean, visit Tahiti and Bora Bora, and then I'll get to Australia eventually—pet some kangaroos, learn how to surf. Then I'll go to India and Nepal and maybe stop to see Mount Everest. Not to hike it, just to take pictures. But I'm *definitely* going to hike the Swiss Alps—"

"You've got it all planned out, haven't you?"

Jack laughs, shaking his head. "More of a dream than a plan."

"Well, sometimes dreams come true. If you wait for them long enough."

He leans forward with his elbows on the table, his eyes softening as he studies me. "I want to make *your* dreams come true, Orca."

A twinge of bittersweet pain stirs in my heart. If only Adam had said those words to me last night. If only he understood the way Jack understands. If only I could make him want me as desperately as I want him.

I manage a smile and say, "Well, since we only have a week, I think Mount Everest is off the table."

"Scratch Bora Bora, too, huh?"

I nod with a laugh. "I just want to see *your* world, Jack Stevenson."

"All right," he relents, tearing the list out of his notebook and folding it like a sacred document. "But I have to warn you, my world is nothing special."

CAN'T HELP FALLING IN LOVE

jack

I'm used to girls riding shotgun—girls who complain about the heat or the cold or the rain or their hair or the dirt on my car, all the while asking me where we're going, what we're doing, and expecting me to start every conversation. Girls I need to work hard to impress while making it look like I'm not working hard at all.

Orca, on the other hand, is the easiest girl to impress. I literally don't have to do anything. We just drive around my little hometown, and she thinks it's the greatest thing ever. It's funny, but also kind of refreshing. It's easy to be with her, because she's not expecting anything from me. She's spontaneous and happy, okay with everything. No restrictions on what she can eat or where she can walk in those shoes or any of the usual crap girls whine about.

I love that about her. She's so real, so down to earth. She points to things out the window and laughs at all my jokes and plays with the car radio and can't stop marveling at "how wondrous it is." She's not worried about time or work or school or politics or any of the dumb stuff that everyone is always hung up on. Orca says she's visiting the Otherworld, but in a way I feel transported to another world, too—just by being with her.

"Is that a library?" she asks, pointing out the window to the sign planted on the side of the road. "I've always wanted to roam around a library and look at all the books."

"That's boring."

"So far you've said that about everything."

"Well, it's true! This stuff might be all new to you, but it's old hat to me. Oh, hey, this is where I went to school." I tap on the directional and swerve into the empty parking lot.

Orca shifts forward in her seat to study the sprawling brick building—the sight of it apparently as odd to her as it is familiar to me. Those ugly windows I stared out of for the last four years, those concrete steps where I got in my first real fistfight, that corner of the parking lot where Adam always used to pick me up before I was old enough to drive.

"What do you do here?" Orca says, still frowning at the school with a clueless expression on her face.

"Uh, nothing anymore. I graduated this year, so I'm done. Thank God."

"Graduated what?"

"High school."

"And what is… high school? Is it like a school of fish?"

I laugh, because that was actually kind of funny. But then I notice that Orca is not laughing; she looks completely serious. She *is* completely serious.

"Uh, no. No, like school. Y'know, where kids go to learn stuff."

"What kind of stuff?"

"I don't know. How to read and write and do math?"

"You mean your parents didn't teach you that?"

"No." I almost laugh, just imagining how chaotic that would have been. "I mean, I guess they could have. But most parents don't homeschool their kids."

"Why not?"

I shrug. "They're just… busy, I guess. A lot of parents work at jobs all day, so there's that. Plus, teachers are more educated. That's why we go to school, to learn from them."

It takes Orca a few moments to fully absorb this. "So you're telling me this happens *everywhere*?"

"Yep."

"That's... so odd." She shakes her head. "You people are so odd."

"Well, most people would think *you're* odd."

Orca sputters a laugh. "Living on my own island and growing my own food is not nearly as bizarre as going to some communal building to learn how to read and write."

"Well, how did *you* learn? Your dad teach you?"

Orca nods as I pull out of the parking lot and back onto the street. "Papa taught me everything. He has all sorts of books, about science mostly. About the ocean and all the creatures who live there... but we didn't just read about it—we studied it up close. He always said it's better to learn that way. To let the ocean tell you what it wants you to know." She traces patterns in the fog on her window, falling into a thoughtful silence.

I sense her reminiscing about her dad and getting all morose, so I quickly change the topic.

"Well, school isn't just where you learn how to read. You also meet people there. Make friends."

"Ah, yes. *Friends.* I've yet to see any of yours."

"I don't hang out with them a lot anymore. We used to see each other all the time at school, but now everyone's busy with their own lives. Most of them are going off to college." I see another question forming in Orca's eyes and answer it before she can ask. "College is also school. It's, like, more in-depth study on a certain topic. So you can be more qualified to do your job or whatever."

Orca nods slowly, going back to her fog. "Does Adam have a lot of friends?"

"Nah. He's a lone wolf. I mean, I never went to school with him 'cause he's so much older than me... but I heard stories." I slide her a meaningful smirk. "Couldn't small talk beyond 'how are you?' He's still like that."

Orca smiles, fingertip squeaking on the glass. "He just likes talking about deeper things."

Her voice gets all gooey and soft when she says that, and she has this look on her face—a look I've seen on other girls. The girls Adam never even noticed were totally crazy about him. The ones who looked at me like I was a little kid and looked at him like he was James Dean. I know what a girl looks like when she has a crush on my brother. And Orca has that Look.

But after the way Adam upset her last night, I can't imagine why she would have any feelings for him now. Besides, she's clearly more interested in hanging out with me. There's no sense in me worrying about some silly unrequited crush.

Mark my words: I'll get her to fall in love with me by the end of the week.

ORCA WANTS TO SEE "my world," so I show her. I drive down streets I know better than the back of my hand while she asks me a million questions about what Adam and I used to do growing up. I give her a million stories in reply, stories that aren't very interesting, but she hangs on every word like it's the best entertainment she's ever had.

We drive to the old downtown of Anacortes and walk around, because the sun is shining and that's something to take advantage of. I give Orca my aviator shades, and she looks stunning in them. I want to kiss her, but hold off. Too soon, right? Yeah. Way too soon. I never overthink timing on kissing, but Orca is different—she's never been kissed before, and I don't want to freak her out or move too fast.

So instead we walk around town, looking in shop windows. Orca's hand catches on my arm whenever she sees something she wants to ask me about. Her laughter is my new favorite sound, snatched up by the wind and street noise. Bursts of music and air conditioning spill from the open doors of shops, which I pull Orca into just to see her reaction. Stores, art galleries, coffee shops—she's never seen anything so "magnificent and otherworldly" in her life.

But I've never seen anything as magnificent as *her*—sunlight flashing off the waves, lighting up her long, messy hair. We're standing at the edge of the harbor now, looking out at the deep blue water and all the glossy white boats bobbing gently on the tide.

"Let's go sneak onto the yachts," I whisper into her ear.

"What's a yacht?" she says.

"I'll show you."

I grew up in marinas, running the docks and sneaking onto empty boats. It's not new to me, and it's not the first time I've done this with a girl either—but I don't want to remember the other times. Orca makes all my memories feel like black-and-white photographs of someone else's life.

"This seems wrong," she says, giggling, as I whisk her aboard a shiny yacht called the *Aphrodite*.

"It's not, I swear. I know the owner."

"Really?"

"I mean… I know he's a millionaire."

Orca snort-laughs, and I decide *that's* my new favorite sound. She leads the way to the bow, her skirt rippling in the wind, her sunlit fingers skimming over the rail. When she reaches the front of the boat, she stands facing the wind, taking in the view.

"Can you imagine sailing around the world in one of these?"

Orca shakes her head. "No, I can't imagine."

"Wouldn't it be awesome, though? To be out there all on your own, nothing to hold you back… To sleep under the stars every night and do absolutely nothing all day?"

She laughs. "You have a way of making everything sound so fun and romantic."

"It *would* be. Fun and romantic. We should go together."

"All right," she says, turning to grin up at me. "When do we sail, Captain Stevenson?" The sunglasses are off now, folded in her hand—and god, those eyes. They flick back and forth between mine, blue and sparkling like everything around us. Her face is so close, it would only take a split second to get my lips on hers.

Damn it. I can't wait any longer.

I decide to just kiss her, right now. What's the worst that could happen? When I see her gaze shift to my lips, I know it's okay to move in. My hand drifts to her waist, and the space between us slowly shrinks to a few inches, and we're *so* close to actually doing it when—

THUD.

The boat rocks.

Footsteps.

I freeze, and Orca gasps, looking up at me.

"We should probably get out of here," I whisper, holding back a laugh.

We run, leaving the kiss-that-didn't-happen behind us. I take Orca's hand and lead her down the starboard deck, narrowly escaping in the nick of time. Orca's eyes widen as I vault over the side of the boat and land on the dock below. She sits on the edge but looks too scared to jump, so I reach up and grab her waist. She gasps my name as I lift her down, her fingers gripping my shoulders and sliding down my chest. It feels way too good.

"Thanks," she whispers, looking up at me.

"You're welcome," I whisper back, my hands still on her hips.

That's when voices from the yacht catch my attention and snap me out of it.

"Come on," I say, and we run like fugitives all the way back to shore, dodging tourists and mariners on the docks.

We're both laughing and out of breath by the time we get back to the street. I'm starving, and I'm sure Orca is too, so we grab pizza at the best place in town and sit on a bench, facing each other with the box between us.

"Oh my goodness," Orca says, taking her first life-changing bite. Her eyes roll up into her head, and for a moment she has no words.

"Told you."

She devours the pizza, speechless. I love how she eats like a normal person, not like these girls who are so obsessed with their "diet" or the way they look when they're eating. I actually don't know what their problem is, but whatever it is, Orca doesn't have it. She eats half the pizza, and I eat the other half while watching her watch everything around her—sensory overload.

"What are fireworks?" she asks, out of the blue.

"What?"

"Fireworks. That sign over there says, 'Fireworks over the harbor Saturday night.' What does that mean?"

Instead of explaining it to her, I smile and say, "That's tonight. I'll take you to see them."

"But what are they?"

"You'll see."

When the sun gets close to setting, we drive to the top of Cap Sante and climb out on the rocks. The views are great, especially now; everything is lit up pastel, and Orca looks like she's part of a painting.

Cap Sante is the official makeout spot of Anacortes, but there are way too many tourists up here right now. Besides, I've made out with other girls here—and I don't want them in the back of my mind while I'm kissing Orca. So I try to be happy just watching the sunset with her. We sit on the rocks, and I casually let my arm circle around her waist, and she points out the white mountain peaks in the distance, and I don't really notice anything special about them. I'm too busy watching the sunset happen on her face.

THE FIREWORKS USED TO be our summer tradition when I was a kid. We'd pile blankets and pillows into the bed of Dad's truck and drive down to the harbor and lie on our backs and watch the sky blow up with color, sparks shimmering off the waves below. I want to do that again, but with Orca. Just Orca.

The only snag is that I have to borrow Adam's truck.

When we get back home, I find him in the kitchen, helping Mom clean up after dinner. Orca hovers in the doorway behind me, shy and hesitant all of a sudden.

"Hey, Adam, can we borrow your truck for a couple of hours?"

"Why do you need it?" he asks, taking a handful of glasses to the kitchen sink. Orca's gaze follows him, and I could swear she's checking him out.

A coil of jealousy tightens in the pit of my stomach.

"I'm going to take Orca to see the fireworks," I say, surprised by how rough my voice sounds.

Adam falls silent, and I know he knows why I want the truck. I know he can imagine it all, in a split second: me and Orca, huddled under blankets in the dark, watching the fireworks. Maybe I'll get to hold her hand. Maybe I'll get to kiss her.

Maybe she'll kiss me back.

Would Adam have a problem with that?

Orca watches him, like she's waiting for some sort of reaction. But after a minute he just nods and says, "You can take the truck. Just don't stay out too late."

I narrow my eyes at him. "What's it to *you* how late we stay out?"

"Jackie," Mom says, her voice a soft warning, "Adam's right. Don't keep Orca out too late."

"Yes, Mom."

Adam walks over to give me his keys, and I catch a look between him and Orca that I can't read. Maybe it's nothing. But somehow, it seems like a hundred things, a thousand things, flying between them at the speed of light, there and gone in one glance. When Adam leaves the room, Orca watches him go, a gutted look on her face.

I wish I didn't feel the green-eyed monster sinking its fangs into my chest.

But I do.

THE KISS

orca

Is he jealous?

That question echoes through my mind as I watch Adam, waiting to glimpse a hint of envy in his beautiful blue eyes. But if he feels anything, he doesn't let it show. He needs secret books and ink and sleepless nights to put his feelings into words. Like little birds, they jump away from me when I try to get close. I feel foolish for looking for a sign.

He hasn't changed his mind. He still wants me to go home.

I wish we were back at the lighthouse, where things were simple. I wish I could turn back the clock and freeze time, to live forever in that moment when he loved me. When he wanted me. When I could feel his desire in the air between us, like an electric charge before a storm.

Now I can't find the tether that once connected our hearts. I feel a pull inside me, but when I follow that rope through the darkness, I never reach the other end. I can't tell if his heart is still mine.

It's a deeper pain than the day he left my island. Because even when I'd lost him, I still had his love.

Now, I have lost that too.

And it is the worst sorrow I've ever known.

On the drive to the harbor, his words from last night circle back through my mind. *Leaving you was one of the hardest things I've ever done, but I knew it was the right thing... You have so much life to live.*

Doesn't he realize I don't want to live that life without him?

I *can't* live my life without him.

He may be the first man I've ever met, but I don't care to meet anyone else. He and I are soulmates—destined to be together.

How can I make him see that?

When we arrive at the harbor, the sky is nearly dark. Jack pulls the truck into a parking space so that we are backed up to the water's edge.

"Any closer, and we would be going for a swim," I point out.

He laughs, reaching into the backseat to pull out a pile of blankets and pillows. I watch as he tosses everything into the bed of the truck, then drops the tailgate and helps me climb up.

He sprawls out on his back, leaning against the pillows, his smile a streak of white in the purple dark. I flop down beside him and pull the blanket over us to block out the cold breeze. For a long moment, we lie in silence, staring up at the sky spread over the harbor like great shadowy wings.

"I don't see any fireworks," I say to Jack after a long pause. "Just a lot of indigo."

"Oh, yeah, your favorite color."

"Mm-hmm." I point to the edge of the horizon, where the purple-blue fallout of sunset glows in the gathering dark. "See it?"

Jack nods. "I see it."

That's when a burst of bright gold fills the sky, illuminating Jack's face for a split second before—

BANG!

The explosion is so loud and sudden, I jump a foot into the air.

Jack chuckles at my surprise. "Oh, sorry. I forgot to tell you: it's going to be loud."

I smack him for leaving out that minor detail, but his boyish smile and the wild joy in his eyes make it impossible to be truly angry with him.

"Look," he says, pointing out over the water.

A shimmering streak of light shoots up from the darkness and bursts open in the sky, sending streams of brilliant crimson in every direction with another ear-splitting *BANG!* Three more chase after it—blue, white, and green.

BANG-BANG-BANG!

I gasp, watching in wonder and amazement as the indigo sky erupts with bursts of glittering light that dwarf the stars and drench the world with color. They reflect on the glassy water below, then fade into long, cascading trails of sizzling sparkles and smoke.

"That's fireworks?" I whisper to Jack.

He nods, looping his arm around my shoulders. "That's fireworks."

BANG, BANG, BANG!

Purple, gold, scarlet.

"They look like sea urchins," I say, which makes Jack laugh. It sounds like an insulting laugh, so I return with a sharp "What?" and he answers, "Only you would say that."

When I turn to look at him, I'm only a little surprised to find him not watching the fireworks, but watching me. A flash of reddish gold lights up one side of his face, sparkling in his hazel eyes—and the next thing I know, his lips are pressed against mine.

It happens so suddenly that I don't see it coming. My whole body freezes up, a confusion of emotions stirring inside me as the realization hits in slow motion.

He's... kissing... me.

Just like Adam kissed me at the top of the lighthouse—but so incomparably different. When Jack's lips capture mine, I feel nothing but a small jolt of surprise. No dizzying storm surge of love rushing through me, no butterflies swirling, fluttering, pressing against my ribs—

Nothing but a half-empty ache in my soul.

Kissing Jack feels wrong when my heart is so full of Adam.

I dip my head down, shying away from his lips with a nervous blush. The fireworks go *boom, boom, boom,* then sizzle out to bathe us in darkness once more.

"Sorry," Jack murmurs, easing back to put a bit of space between us. "I, uh… I couldn't resist. You're just so beautiful. Please don't hate me."

I breathe a sheepish laugh, looking down. "I don't hate you, Jack. You just took me by surprise."

"I know. I'm sorry. Sometimes I don't think before I jump."

"Sometimes?"

He smirks, eyes glinting in the dark. "*All* the time." He threads his fingers through mine and gives my hand a little squeeze. "Forgive me?"

I shake my head with a reassuring smile. "Nothing to forgive."

THE CHURCH REGISTER

adam

Jack is sound asleep when I wake up at seven a.m. He stayed out late with Orca last night. I know because I heard them pull into the driveway at quarter to midnight. Jack tried to be quiet coming in, but stealth has never been his forte. I could hear whispers in the hallway. His voice. Orca's soft laugh. That kept me awake long after Jack had crashed into his bed and fallen asleep.

I keep telling myself, *This is better.* Orca needs to experience being with someone other than me. Even if that "someone" is my brother. Even if it kills me to think about her going off with him alone. To think about her and Jack in the bed of my pickup truck, watching the fireworks together.

It's not jealousy I feel. Jealousy is too simple a word to describe it. Too black and white. If Orca was spending time with some other guy I didn't know, maybe *jealous* is exactly what I'd be.

But this is Jack.

My brother.

Jack, who I've been sharing a room with since he was two years old. Jack, who used to have nightmares and climbed into bed with me to feel safe. Jack, who wanted to do everything I did, so I taught him—how to fish, how to fire a gun, how to fly a plane.

He could never be my enemy, my rival. He could never be anything except my little brother. And if Orca had to be with anyone else in the world, I would want it to be him.

We've barely spoken since the night she first arrived, and our conversation in the driveway hasn't stopped replaying in my mind. Every time I close my eyes, I see her angry tears quivering in the moonlight. I hear her voice caught between confusion and heartbreak.

Jack understands me. He's the only one who truly cares about what I want.

To Orca, love is simple—a be-all, end-all that conquers every obstacle. She's too young and inexperienced to understand just how messy and complicated love *really* is.

I tried to tell her that the night she arrived. But no matter what I said, I couldn't make her see.

This morning she's wearing a blue linen jumpsuit, drinking coffee with Mom at the kitchen table. We say nothing beyond "Good morning" and "Did you sleep well?" And god, I have never hated small talk more than I do right now. A thousand unspoken words smolder in Orca's eyes, and I wonder if she can see that I'm battling back a thousand words too.

"Adam, I need a few things from the grocery store, if you don't mind," Mom says, finishing her list and sliding it over to me.

"Sure, no problem." I down the rest of my coffee and rise from the table.

"Why don't you take Orca? I'm sure she would like to go with you."

I hesitate, my gaze sliding to Orca, who watches me with an expectant glint in her eyes.

"Do you want to come with me?"

She nods. "Yes... of course."

Mom passes me a little knowing smile. "Well, go on, then. I'm sure Jack won't be awake for another hour, at least."

On the drive to the grocery store, Orca remains silent in the passenger seat, staring out at the raindrops sliding down the window. For the first time since we met, there seems to be a wall between us. Something holding her back. Something holding *me* back. And with every passing moment of silence, the pressure builds—like floodwaters rising against a dam.

Finally, I can't take it anymore. "So, did you have a good time with Jack last night?"

Orca looks down, twisting the seatbelt around her finger. "Yes. I did. He took me to town and showed me lots of new things; then we went to see the fireworks. They were so beautiful and otherworldly; I'd never seen anything like it before." She pauses to glance over at me, watching for my reaction. "Jack is so fun and sweet and understanding. He seems to want nothing more than to make me happy."

I swallow, my fingers tensing around the steering wheel. "Well, good. I'm glad. You *should* enjoy your time with him. You two seem to have a lot in common."

Orca falls silent. I tap on the directional and turn into the grocery store parking lot, searching for an empty spot close to the entrance. The rain is falling harder now, making people run for their cars, umbrellas up.

"I would rather it was you."

I park my truck, turning to face Orca.

"Jack is wonderful," she says softly. "But the whole time I was with him, I was wishing *you* were the one showing me the Otherworld."

God, if only she knew how much I wish the same thing.

I kill the engine and stare out the windshield for a long moment because I have no idea what to say.

"What did I do wrong?" Orca asks, her voice hesitant. "What did I do to make you stop loving me?"

Those words couldn't hit me harder if they were a punch in the face.

"I haven't stopped loving you, Orca. I spend every day, every night, thinking about you—wanting you. But the truth is, we hardly know each other. We only spent a few days together, and yes, they were incredible. But how do you know we'll feel the same way five years from now? Ten years from now?"

"I'll feel the same way. I know I will."

I press my eyes shut, shaking my head.

"Do you doubt me?"

"Not your intent. But you're too young to know what you truly want—"

"Stop saying that," Orca cuts in, her eyes glossy with tears. "I may be young, Adam, but I'm not a child. I'm not some foolish girl, infatuated with one thing today and another tomorrow. My feelings for you are real. They're not going to fade, no matter how much you push me away. You're the only man I could ever want—"

"I'm the only man you've ever been with. You've been so sheltered…" I sigh, looking down at my hand clenched around the steering wheel. "If you *truly* love someone, you're supposed to let them go. That's what I'm trying to do, Orca. I want you to be free… to discover what you really want. Who you really love."

Her warm hand slides over mine, softening my white knuckles. "I know who I love," she whispers. "It's you. It will always be you."

I look into her eyes as a tear slips down her cheek. That force of attraction reawakens between us as she leans closer; her voice comes as a soft breath against my lips. "Don't push me away, Adam."

She kisses me.

Just like that, all my willpower dissolves, and I am defenseless, a weapon melted down into weakness, *wanting*. Her fingertips slide up my neck and into my hair—sending a surge of desire blazing through me like fire, opening up the floodgates.

I kiss her like I'm dying and her lips are the fountain of youth. My hands cradle the curve of her lower back, drawing her in closer until her knees bump the steering wheel, and she laughs, forcing us to break apart.

"Oh, Adam," she breathes, sliding her hand over my chest. "I missed you."

"I missed *you*," I rasp, "so much it felt like dying a little each day." I lower my face to the curve of her neck, pressing a soft kiss to her hairline.

She shivers, resting her head on my shoulder and gripping a fistful of my T-shirt. For a moment, we stay like that—embracing in the driver's seat.

At last, I find the strength to pull myself out of the floodwater before it carries us away.

"We can't do this, Orca."

She eases back to look at me. "Why not?"

"Because—"

"If you say you're too old one more time, I'm going to smack you."

I manage a weary smile, taking her hand in mine. "Orca, you need to experience being with someone other than me. Someone your own age, someone spontaneous and adventurous like Jack—"

"I don't *love* Jack."

"Maybe you could. Maybe you *would* have if you'd met him first."

Orca stares at me, stunned. "Are you saying that if Jack had crashed his plane and he'd been the one to show up at the lighthouse… I would have fallen in love with *him* instead? Is that what you're saying?"

After a moment's hesitation, I nod.

"Well, you're wrong. I could never feel for Jack what I feel for you. Don't you see? Fate brought *us* together—"

"I don't believe in fate. Remember?" I look down at her hand in mine, running my thumb over her silky knuckles. "The choices we make are what determine the future. Whether those choices are big or small. Emotional… or rational."

"Can't the right choice be emotional *and* rational?"

"It can. Sometimes. But sometimes emotions trip us up. Make us blind to what's right in front of our eyes." I brush a strand of wild hair away from her face, my fingertip tracing the rim of her ear. "Just because we feel this passion for each other right now doesn't mean our lives would fit well together… and I would never forgive myself if later in life you regretted choosing me."

"That would never happen."

"And what about your life on the island? What about your father?"

"I don't want to talk about him—"

"You have to, Orca. He's back at the lighthouse right now, waiting for you to come home. He loves you, and you love him. I know you do."

Orca presses her eyes shut, shaking her head. "It's more complicated than that. The day you left, we argued. I showed him the picture you found of Mama… and he denied hiding it from me. He acted like he didn't mean to keep it a secret, but I know he did. He's *always* kept her a secret. It's like he's afraid that if I learned about her, I might love her. And he doesn't want me to love anyone but him." A pained sob wrenches out of her, and she collapses against me, pressing her face to my chest.

"Shhh, don't cry." I smooth my hand over her hair.

"I only wanted to know what she was like. Who her family was… They would have been *my* family, too. I don't even know if any of them are still alive."

"Did your father ever mention any relatives?"

"No… Nobody has ever come to visit us." She sniffs, tilting her head to look at me. "Do you think it's possible I *do* have relatives?"

I brush a tear off her cheek with the back of my finger. "There are ways to find out. I could help you."

"Really?"

"On one condition."

Orca looks down, as if she already knows my condition. "And what is that?"

"Once we find out about your mother's family, you'll go back to the lighthouse and make things right with your father."

There's a long silence while Orca thinks about it. She finally nods and leans in to press one last kiss to my lips. "I promise."

BY THE TIME WE EXIT the grocery store, it has stopped raining. I load the bags into the backseat of my truck and drive us downtown, finding a place to parallel park on Main Street. Orca keeps asking, "Where are we going?" but I don't breathe a word until we have walked to the little stone church across from the bank.

"Does this place look familiar?"

Orca peers up at the church for a moment before realization dawns on her face. "The picture! Mama and Papa's wedding. They got married here, didn't they?"

I nod. "The church will have a register of all the marriages that took place here. If we can find your mother's maiden name, we might be able to track down her relatives."

Orca beams at me, her whole face lighting up like the first rays of dawn. "Thank you, Adam."

"Don't thank me yet. There's a chance you don't have any living relatives."

She shakes her head. "At least we'll know for sure. Come on."

With her hand in mine, we walk down the flagstone path and through the granite archway into the church.

It doesn't take long to explain our predicament to the pastor, who is tidying up after Sunday service.

"Your parents were married here twenty years ago?" he asks, stroking his silver mustache.

"My father's name is Lawrence Monroe," Orca supplies. "He and my mother were married on September twenty-ninth, nineteen seventy-seven."

The pastor strides over to an old mahogany door and swings it open, revealing a shallow closet. Leather-bound register books are stacked on shelves inside, one for every decade. He slides out one of the books and places it on a nearby table, paging to the correct date.

"Ah, here we are." The pastor taps an entry in the book. "September twenty-ninth. Lawrence Monroe and Miriam Rushbrook."

Orca's eyes light up with curiosity as she steps closer. "Rushbrook," she murmurs under her breath. "Sir, do you know if she had any family? Any relatives who still live nearby?"

The pastor shakes his head. "I'm afraid I don't know any Rushbrooks. But her parents' names are listed there."

Orca frowns, studying the register. "Adam," she says, beckoning me over, "do you think her parents could still be alive?"

"It's possible." I squint to read the scrawly handwriting.

Olivia Rushbrook.

Harrison Rushbrook.

"We can try to track them down. If they're alive and living anywhere in Skagit County, we can probably find their phone number in the public records."

Orca looks up at me, a hopeful smile blossoming on her face.

"But we should get Mom's groceries home first."

SLEEPLESS IN SEATTLE

jack

"I hope you didn't have any fun while I was sleeping."

Orca flashes me a grin from the passenger seat. "Well, actually... I did."

I clutch my chest with one hand dramatically. "Ugh, Orca! You're breaking my heart!"

"I'm sorry. But Adam had to go to the grocery store, and your mom suggested I go along... And, well—afterward, we went to the church where my parents got married and looked in the register book to find her maiden name and the names of her parents. Adam had the notion we should figure out if I have any living relatives in the area—someone who knew my mom when she was alive and could tell me more about her."

I frown. "Don't you know if you have any relatives?"

"Well, Papa always told me that I didn't... But sometimes, I wonder if he was right about that. Maybe he *thinks* they're all dead, and they're actually not. Adam thinks it's worth a try, anyway." She smiles dreamily, resting her head on the passenger window. "We were going to search the public records to see if we could find my grandparents' phone number, but Adam said we had to bring the groceries home, and then you abducted me to go on an adventure with you."

"Hey, you *wanted* to come," I argue. "Besides, where I'm taking you is going to be way more fun than poking through some dusty old record books in a library."

Orca's smile falters. "You sound like you don't approve."

"I just think it's best to leave the past in the past. You know? What's the point in dredging up old memories that are just gonna make you sad?"

"It wouldn't make me sad to know what my mother was like."

"But she's *gone*, Orca. It's awful, I know. But don't you think you should look to the future instead of living in the past?"

She gazes out the window. "Are you just mad because I asked Adam to help me and didn't ask you?"

"What? No." I flex my fingers around the steering wheel, a prickle of annoyance bristling in my chest. "You can do whatever you want with Adam. I don't care."

I *do* care.

I hate the idea of them going out together, searching for her long-lost relatives. I hate it because I've seen the way she looks at him—like he's a celebrity, a god. If he's as smart as I think he is, he wouldn't be leading her on like this.

But I tell myself, *Don't worry about it.* What I have with Orca is so much more than a crush. I could tell by the look in her eyes last night when we watched the fireworks together. That's why it was kind of a bummer when I kissed her and she didn't reciprocate. But I tried not to take it personally because this was Orca, the girl who'd never been on a date until yesterday. The girl who'd never been kissed or even *complimented* by a guy. I predicted it would be a little awkward the first time I made a pass at her— but she didn't give me the friend-zone talk, so that was a good sign.

I still have time to win her over.

"So," she says, propping her chin up on her fist as she watches me drive, "where are we going?"

"The big city."

She gasps. "Seattle?"

"Don't get too excited. It's going to be the most stereotypical date *ever*."

Orca laughs and starts playing with the radio. She looks incredibly hot in that little blue jumpsuit, her long hair woven into a messy braid. I love how she doesn't hide her face behind a ton of makeup. I love how she doesn't even know what makeup is. I love the way she smells, the way she laughs, the way she walks—with her head held high, taking in everything like she can't get enough of it.

We spend the two-hour drive listening to all the cassettes in my glove box, most of which are Nirvana and AC/DC, some of which I supply terrible karaoke for, at Orca's request. Finally, the city skyline rises in the distance, and I point it out to Orca. She can't believe "those things" are buildings until we get closer, and they are towering over us, gleaming in the sunlight and reflecting the thousands of cars flying around us in every direction.

I try to keep my eyes on the road and not Orca's face as she takes it all in, her jaw hanging open.

"Like it?" I laugh over the music.

"I love it! It's amazing… it's otherworldly!"

After five hundred hours of looking for a place to park, I find a tiny lot that only charges half a kidney to ditch your vehicle for six hours. I pay my dues, then grab Orca's hand and start heading downtown. She is speechless, taking it all in—spinning in circles as she stares up at the skyscrapers reaching for the clouds. The look on her face is like the feeling I get thinking about all the unexplored places I want to travel to, and just seeing that smile makes me want to take her with me to those hundreds of Otherworlds.

Maybe I will. Who knows?

For now, it's Seattle.

We get lost a few times, but there's nothing wrong with getting lost as long as you don't get mugged and you still remember where you parked. We avoid anything that looks touristy and instead wander around like truants without a cause—running across the streets when the sign says not to, cutting through markets that smell like everything good in one place, which reminds me that I'm starving.

We grab some fish and chips, and I watch Orca's eyes widen as she experiences the phenomenon of fried food.

"Oh… my goodness."

"Right?"

"Mm."

She steals most of my fries, and I don't even care. That's how I know I am serious about this girl.

"That's a strange one," she says, pointing up at one of the towering buildings a few blocks away.

"Yeah, that's the Space Needle. Wanna go up inside it?"

"Can we?"

"Hell yes."

We hit it at a good time because there's no line. Orca looks like she wants to read all the boring plaques, but I pull her into the elevator before she can get distracted.

"What is this we're in?" she asks me, which makes the elevator operator squint at us.

I laugh awkwardly and pull Orca close, whispering into her ear, "It's an elevator. It'll take us up to the top."

She raises an eyebrow. "No stairs?"

"No stairs."

When the doors open, she looks shocked to find herself six hundred feet in the sky. I pull her out and lead her to the glass wall overlooking the city. Canyons of steel and glass yawn beneath us, rivers of cars and bikes and people flowing down the streets like ants, everyone hurrying to be somewhere else.

"Wow," Orca breathes, her fingertips on the glass.

"What do you think? Better view than your lighthouse? Or… same?"

She tilts her head, considering the answer. "They're both beautiful in different ways."

"That makes sense. Like deserts and mountains. Have you ever seen pictures of Egypt? They've got these dunes—they're like… as tall as that building down there. It's called the 'Great Sand Sea' because there's just *nothing* but sand for hundreds of miles. And then, mountains—god, there's so many. Nepal. Peru. Brazil. They look like they could all be on different planets, but it's crazy to think they're not even that far away."

Orca twirls around to face me. "Jack."

"Yes?"

"You are here." She pokes my chest with one finger.

"What?"

"Seattle. Washington. America."

I laugh at myself. "Right. Sorry. I just… I get so…"

"Restless?"

"Yeah."

"I know," she murmurs, her gaze drifting out over the skyline. "But you'll see all those places someday, Jack. I know you will. And it will be wonderful. Don't be in such a hurry to be gone."

That's when I notice the shimmer of tears in her eyes.

"I want you to come with me. You deserve to see all those places, too." I loop my arm around her shoulders, pulling her close. "You deserve the world, Orca."

She presses her lips into a sad smile. "I don't know if I want the whole world, Jack. I just… I want to be *here*. Right now."

"Fair enough." I kiss the top of her head.

When she's had her fill of the view from the Space Needle, we head back down to the street and decide it's time for ice cream.

"I think this is the fastest I've ever gone through a to-do list in my life," I say, which makes Orca laugh.

Ten minutes later, I am sitting at the bar of an old-fashioned drugstore, watching Orca eat ice cream for the first time in her life. Swiveling on the stool, legs crossed. Eyes shut. Spoon in her mouth.

"Oh… my… goodness."

I grin. "Right?"

"Wow." She shovels more ice cream into her mouth. "Wow."

I will never get tired of watching her try new foods.

"So what do you like better? Ice cream or pizza?"

Orca frowns, like that's the hardest question she's ever been asked. "I don't know! They're both amazing in different ways. Like you and Adam."

I burst out laughing. "Me and Adam? That's... one hell of a metaphor."

"I mean it in a good way!" Orca says, clapping her hand over my knee. "Seriously. It's a compliment."

"Just as long as I'm the pizza in this metaphor."

"Okay. You can be the pizza, Jackie."

"Whoa, whoa, whoa." I point my spoon at her accusingly. "It's Jack."

Orca tilts her head. "But your mom calls you Jackie."

"She's... the only one who's allowed to call me that."

"Because she's your mom?"

"Because she's my mom."

Orca taps her foot against mine. The jukebox is playing Redbone's "Come And Get Your Love." I want to spend every day of my life like this.

"So," she says at last, "what's next on the list?"

I refocus, taking the list out of my pocket and unfolding it on the bar. "You still haven't seen a movie."

So when the ice cream is gone, I whisk her outside and across the street, weaving through a chaos of stopped taxis blaring their horns.

"I would never be able to live in a city." Orca gasps, dodging a speeding cyclist. "There are too many people!"

We walk two more blocks before stumbling upon a cinema playing the first *Star Wars* movie—some special showing to celebrate the twentieth anniversary of its release. Adam and I used to watch it constantly when I was younger. So much that the guy at the Blockbuster let us keep the VHS tape because we'd renewed it twenty times over.

I tell Orca that story as we're standing in the ticket line, and she laughs, twirling her braid around her fingers. I pull her close, letting my hand slide down her back and rest on her hip. She doesn't shy away from my touch.

Progress.

"This is so otherworldly," she whispers excitedly as I lead her down the darkened hallway into the theater. "Don't let go of me; I might lose you."

I don't let go of her the whole time. That's the best part. I barely even watch the movie because I'm fully absorbed by Orca. The light from the screen flashes over her face, reflecting in her wide eyes, reminding me of how beautiful she looked at the fireworks. Eventually, I loop my arm around her back, and she rests her head on my shoulder. Her hair smells so good. My hand finds the curve of her waist again, the perfect place to hold her. I hate this armrest between us.

When the end credits roll up on the screen, I take Orca's hand, and we dash out of the theater together.

"That was so amazing!"

"Right? I knew you'd like it."

The streets are dark now, sidewalks lit up gold by long rows of shop windows. The temperature has dropped about twenty degrees, which makes Orca shiver and rub her arms.

"It's freezing."

I put my arm around her and keep her warm on the walk back to the parking lot. When we finally reach my Mustang, I dive into the backseat and pull out my bomber jacket.

"Here, put this on."

Orca thanks me and slips the jacket on. God, she looks so sexy in it. She nuzzles her face into the collar and says, "It smells like you."

"Hopefully that's a good thing."

She laughs. "A very good thing."

WE DRIVE BACK HOME baptized in the black night, headlights on wet pavement. Orca has discovered a cassette of Bryan Adams in my glove box (a mixtape I stole from Adam forever ago), but it sounds different to me now. When "Heaven" starts playing from the stereo, I realize it is everything I feel for Orca wrapped up in a song.

The house is dark when I pull into the driveway and park. *Is it that late?* I glance at the clock.

11:53

Guess so.

I turn the music down soft and turn to face Orca. "Well? Was it the most stereotypical date ever?"

She bites on a smirk. "I don't know. Was it?"

"It was. But not completely. It's not a *real* stereotypical date until I kiss you in a parked vehicle in my driveway."

Orca exhales a nervous little laugh, easing away from me. "In that case, I think we'd better go inside."

I heave a dramatic sigh and shut off the engine. "You're good at playing hard to get, Orca Monroe."

I don't take it personally. I know she's just sheltered and shy. But it's all right. Good things are worth waiting for—at least, that's what Mom always says.

We sneak into the house, trying to be as silent as possible. Orca stops outside the guest room door and slides off my bomber jacket, handing it back to me. "Thanks for letting me borrow this."

"You can keep it if you want. Looks better on you, anyway."

She giggles and shakes her head. "Goodnight, Superman."

"Goodnight," I murmur, watching her vanish into the dark and shut the door.

I sigh, plowing my hands through my hair and cursing under my breath. Part of me wishes Orca were a little more like other girls—if she were, we'd be back in the driveway right now, making out in my Mustang. She would be curled up in my lap, and I'd be kissing my way down her neck, feeling around for the zipper on her jumpsuit.

Cool your jets, I remind myself. *Good things are worth waiting for.*

I walk down the hallway and quietly slip into my and Adam's room, surprised to find the lights still on. Adam is sitting at his desk, hunched over some papers.

"Wow, you're still up?"

He casts a glance over his shoulder as I shut the door behind me. "You're one to talk."

I grin, tossing my jacket onto the wall hook. "I was out with Orca."

"Mm. I know. You stayed out pretty late."

I kick off my shoes and stretch out on my bed. "Aren't you supposed to be my brother, not my babysitter?"

"Just observing."

"Well, stop *observing*."

Adam drops his pencil onto the desk. "No. I won't. Orca's not going to be here for long. She's going to return to her island soon, and… I don't want to see her get hurt."

"You're one to talk," I deadpan.

He stiffens. "What do you mean?"

"I heard all about your little trip with her this morning. You took her to some church to try to find her long-lost relatives. What's all that about?"

Adam turns in his chair to look at me. "She wants to know more about her mom."

"Her mom's dead, Adam. I don't see what good it's gonna do, dragging up the past."

"You don't understand. Her father has never told her anything about her mother. He doesn't want to relive the pain of it all, I guess… but Orca needs something to hold onto. Something to identify with."

"*I'm* giving her something to hold onto. I'm showing her what her future could be here in the real world."

Adam grunts a dry laugh. "You're having fun with her, Jack. That's it. Don't fool yourself."

"*You're* the one fooling yourself," I fire back, sitting upright. "Helping her on this mission to find her family. You trying to make her fall in love with you?"

"What?"

"You heard."

"Jack, I'm only trying to help her," Adam says. "She saved my life; the least I can do in return is try to help her find her family—if she has any."

What am I supposed to say to that? Irritation and jealousy stir in my chest like a brewing storm. I stand up, pacing to my dresser and pulling off my T-shirt. A tense silence fills the room as Adam turns back to whatever he's writing. I shove my jeans into the nearest drawer and climb into bed, folding my hands behind my head.

"Well, don't worry, Adam. I'm not gonna break her heart. Orca and I are just trying to make the most of what time we have left together."

"I know that's how you see it," Adam replies, "but she's different. Just… be careful with her. Okay?"

"Yeah, yeah, I will. Thanks, *Dad*." I roll my eyes and throw a pillow at the back of his head. It bounces off his shoulders and falls to the floor. He turns around sharply, glaring over his shoulder.

"Go to bed."

"I'm *in* bed."

"Then go to sleep."

"*You* go to sleep."

"Fine." Adam stands and snaps off the desk lamp. "I was only staying up to make sure you got home safe, *son*."

The pillow hits me in the face.

"Hey! You asshole—"

"Shh!" Adam scolds me, micromanaging as always. "You'll wake the whole house."

"Then I'll just fake that I'm sleeping, and they'll blame you."

"You've tried that before," he says, yanking off his T-shirt and getting into bed. "It never works."

I lie awake for a while after Adam falls asleep. His words keep looping through my mind.

You're having fun with her, Jack. That's it. Don't fool yourself.

He's wrong.

I'm not just having fun with Orca. I'm not just giving her a tour of my world out of gratitude. She's not just one of my summer-break crushes. Not just another girl I take to see the fireworks.

She's different.

She's unlike any other girl I've ever met before.

She's wild, restless, beautiful.

She's only here for a little while longer.

And then she'll be gone.

It wouldn't be so hard to think about that if I *were* just having fun with her. But the thought of her leaving forever—

It makes me feel like I'm suffocating.

Time is running out.

Tomorrow means one less day.

I hate it when Adam reminds me that time is running out.

My life is slipping away.

Orca is slipping away.

When I close my eyes, I see a million snapshots in my mind—her braided hair under my fingers, her smile in the movie theater, the way she sniffed my jacket, her laughter over the music on the radio. The way I felt on the drive home, listening to that love song in a whole new light.

Orca has changed everything for me, and I want to be the one to change everything for her. I'll do whatever it takes to prove how much she means to me.

BOATS AND BIKINIS

orca

All the pleasures of the Otherworld do not come without the pang of guilt I feel in the pit of my stomach every time I think about Papa, all alone, at the lighthouse.

His is the face I see in my mind when I awaken on my third morning in the Otherworld. Those kind, gray eyes I know better than my own reflection. To think I'm so far away from him…

I tell myself I shouldn't feel this way. Papa told me to leave. His parting words to me have burned like embers on my conscience since the moment I left with Jack. I chose to comb them under the brighter, stronger fire of new experiences. But still, they burn me, echoes of guilt in a lonely chasm, and I am lost somewhere inside it.

No, I tell myself, pushing away the pang of regret. *Papa told me to leave.*

I did everything I possibly could to gain his blessing. I did everything I could to prove myself to him. But still, he refused to give me what I longed for.

I shouldn't pity him.

I don't.

Today, Adam will help me find my family—help me answer questions I've been asking Papa all my life. And once I've found those answers, I will return home to the lighthouse.

I FIND ADAM IN THE GARAGE, crawling under his truck, doing some mechanical thing. As I approach the open barn doors, all I can see are his legs sticking out from underneath the truck—jeans smudged with dirt and black grease. Sounds of clinking metal echo through the engine.

"Are you hiding from me?" I question the legs, half in jest.

Adam gives a quiet, husky laugh. "No. I'm trying to replace this starter…"

"Will it take long? I was hoping we could continue our search today. I spent a lot of time thinking about it last night. These 'public records' you talked about—can you find other people with the same last name?"

Adam grunts, dropping something on the concrete floor. "Technically."

"Because I was thinking, even if my grandparents *aren't* around anymore, there might be others who are related to my mother."

Adam slides out from under the truck and sits upright to look at me. There's a black smudge on his forehead, and something about it is extremely attractive. "Orca… I don't want to raise your hopes just to dash them. It's very possible there's no one left."

"I know that. But there's a chance." I manage a little smile for him. "And either way, I assure you, my hopes won't be dashed. Besides, it gives me the perfect excuse to be with you."

Adam falls silent, looking down at the wrench in his grease-smudged hands.

"So, when can we go look through the records?"

He rubs his forehead, avoiding my eyes. "I, uh… I don't know. I can't go anywhere until I get this new starter installed." And with that, he dives back under his truck.

I cast a furtive glance at the house before getting down on my knees.

Lying on my back, I slide under the vehicle with Adam, shimmying up beside him. My dress will be covered in dust, but I don't care.

"Show me how it works."

Adam gives me a little quizzical smirk. "You never cease to surprise me, Orca Monroe." He turns back to the task he's been working on, his hands caught up in the truck's undercarriage. "This is the starter right here. I just finished disconnecting these wires, which go to the battery and the ignition. So when you turn the key, the battery supplies power to the solenoid, which makes this motor spin, and that's what turns the crank-shaft—"

I kiss him, interrupting the explanation. It feels like forever since the last time we did this, and I can tell he's missed it as much as I have. When our lips touch, he relaxes into me, shifting onto his side to cup my face with one hand. I could lose myself in the infinity of this moment—his spicy skin, the sandpapery edge of his jaw, the tender push and pull of every kiss.

"You don't even care how it works, do you?" Adam whispers against my lips.

"No, no, I do… You're just…" I trace one finger down the edge of his jaw. "Your lips are very distracting."

"So are yours," he murmurs, drawing me into another soft, languid kiss.

I lean into him, my hands gripping his T-shirt as his lips move over mine. I can't get close enough, even here in the narrow crush of space. Adam's hand curls around my hip, drawing me closer until my leg slides over his waist. We could be in a gold-plated palace or sprawled on a dirty garage floor—it would make no difference to how I feel in his arms.

That's when I hear Jack's voice calling my name from across the driveway. "Orca? You out here?"

I break away from Adam's kiss and look into his face, finding his eyes wide with alarm. "Quick," he urges, shooing me away.

I roll out from under the truck and stand up, brushing the dust off my blue cotton dress. Just in time, too. Jack strides up to the open barn doors as I swivel to give him an unruffled smile.

"Jack, good morning. Were you… looking for me?"

My heart is still racing, warm blood coursing through my whole body. I smooth a hand over my hair, trying my best to look as though I haven't been kissing his brother under the pickup truck just moments ago.

But Jack must have seen me climbing out because now he's peering at me with suspicion. "What are you doing out here? Adam putting you to work?"

A nervous laugh tickles my throat. "No, he was just… I wanted to know how the engine worked. He was showing me."

Jack steps closer and says, "You have a smudge on your cheek." He reaches up to gently swipe it away with the pad of his thumb—the same spot Adam touched moments ago as he kissed me.

I look down at the floor, my cheeks flushing hot. "I… must have brushed against something."

Jack nods slowly, glancing at his brother's feet sticking out from under the truck. "Or something brushed against *you*." It's impossible to miss the undertone of irritation in his voice. "Anyway, I was looking for you because I want to take you to work with me today. At the marina. Sun's out, and there's this boat Dad needs someone to test drive… What do you say?" His hazel eyes search mine for an answer—so hopeful, so sure. As if he has a million ideas for us beyond test-driving the boat.

"Sounds wonderful," I say, "but Adam and I were hoping to go look through the records today to find my relatives—"

"You'll have plenty of time to do that later," Jack cuts in. "Once Adam gets his truck fixed, he can pick you up at the marina. I have to work all afternoon, anyway. That good with you, bro?"

"Sure," Adam replies from under the truck. "No problem."

"Great." Jack snatches my hand. "Let's get out of here."

MUSIC PLAYS SOFTLY on the radio as I watch sunlight flash over the windows dappled by tree shadows. We haven't been driving for ten minutes when Jack says, "Oh, shoot—we have to go back."

I give him a puzzled frown. "Did you forget something?"

"I forgot to tell you to bring your swimsuit. I thought we'd take the boat up to Bricker Cove. If you're not too scared of the cold water."

"I am *not* scared of cold water. But I don't own a swimsuit."

The car slows as Jack turns to look at me. "You're joking."

"No."

"So you swim naked?"

"No!" The suggestion makes me laugh. "What an idea. I swim with my clothes on, of course."

Jack wrinkles his nose in disdain. "That sounds uncomfortable."

"Well, what do Otherworlders swim in?"

"Guys wear shorts—" he indicates the ones he's wearing "—and girls wear bikinis."

"Bik-eenees."

Jack smirks at me. "You'd look fantastic in one."

To prove it, he drives us into town and parks the car at a crowded intersection. Where he leads, I follow—down the sidewalk, around the corner, and through the door of a clothing shop. All around me lies a mesmerizing chaos of clothes and hats and shoes and towels and umbrellas and other things I've never seen in my life. For a moment, all I can do is turn in a slow circle and take it all in—which elicits an amused smirk from Jack.

I laugh and smack his suntanned arm. "Oh, stop. It's overwhelming!"

"I know. Here, I'll help you choose something."

Jack leads me through the maze of clothes racks dripping with colorful fabrics. As he rifles through the clacking hangers, I finally see what a bikini looks like: underwear. Underwear you don't wear anything over. I spot a picture on the wall of a woman wearing a teal blue one—out in public on a sunny beach, her blonde hair flowing behind her.

I'm not sure I will ever understand the strange customs of the Other-world.

"This one," Jack says, picking out a stringy red bikini and handing it to me. "Trust me, you'll look so hot."

I raise one eyebrow. "Hot?"

"Yeah, you know. Sexy. Beautiful. *Otherworldly.*"

He leads me to the dressing room, which is more like a well-lit closet with a tall mirror and hooks on the wall. He instructs me to try on the swimsuit and shuts me inside the tiny room, waiting outside the door.

I unclip the bikini from its hanger and slip it on—but I still feel naked, even after fastening all the proper clasps. I tilt my head at my reflection, concluding that I *do* look pretty. The cut of the fabric accentuates the curves of my body, the scarlet red a sharp contrast to my pale skin.

"Do you have it on yet?" Jack questions through the door.

"Yes."

"Can I see?"

"No!"

He laughs. "Oh, come on, Orca. Don't be so sheltered."

I bite my lip, scrutinizing my reflection in the glass. I *am* sheltered; Jack is right. As I look at myself in this bikini, all I can think is: *Papa would not approve.* But somehow, that makes the idea more exciting.

Jack sighs and jiggles the doorknob, but it's locked. "If you want it, you're gonna have to give me the tag so I can buy it for you."

I find the price tag he's talking about and tear it off—slipping my blue dress on over the bikini before I swing open the door.

Jack's face falls when he sees me fully clothed. I hand him the price tag. "Here you go."

He smirks, leaning close to my ear and whispering, "The suspense is killing me."

THE SKY IS DAZZLING BLUE when we arrive at the marina—sunlight glinting off the crests of waves, boat sails snapping in the wind. Jack leads me into a huge open garage where his father is working on a boat, elbow-deep in the guts of an engine.

"Hey, Dad."

"Jack." He doesn't look up. "You're late."

"Yeah, I know. Sorry."

Mr. Stevenson fires a severe look at his son, which softens when he sees me standing here. "Oh, hello, Orca."

"Hello—"

"I thought I'd start by taking that Regal for a quick test drive… with Orca. That cool with you?"

Jack's lighthearted voice doesn't fool Mr. Stevenson. "Where to?"

"Uh…" Jack hesitates, running his fingers over the back of his neck. "Just up to the cove and back. We won't be long."

I can tell his father has noticed Jack's swim shorts and my red bikini strap peeking out the neckline of my dress. With a relenting smile and a tip of his head, he says, "Key's on the hook. Make sure you're *not* too long."

Jack grins. "Sure. No problem, Dad."

We hurry off before Mr. Stevenson has the chance to change his mind. Jack finds the key in an adjacent room, and then we head back outside into the sunshine. I follow him down the mazelike docks crowded with ocean vessels bobbing up and down on the water.

Jack stops at the end of a dock where a glistening boat awaits us. He extends one hand with a flourish to help me step aboard.

"It's no yacht," he says. "But I'm no millionaire."

I laugh and slide my hand into his, stepping carefully over the watery gap and onto the cushion of the backseat. Jack hops in after me and turns the key. The engine sputters a bit, then rumbles to life. I cast him an unsettled look, and he laughs. White teeth in the sunlight.

"It's fine. Just takes a second for the gas to get to the carburetor."

I have no idea what he's talking about, but he clearly knows what he's doing. I perch on the passenger seat and watch as Jack unties the boat and tosses the ropes onto the dock.

Within minutes, we are flying out of the harbor and across the shimmering blue waves, our wake a long, sharp line of white splitting the deep blue water behind us. The sun is bright, and the wind takes my breath away, tangling my hair, rippling Jack's T-shirt. He drives the boat as he piloted the seaplane—with that easy confidence, that sharp jawline against a robin's-egg sky, that unabashed smile that makes me think he doesn't belong to the world, but the world belongs to him.

Before I know it, the exhilarating ride is over. The boat slows as Jack steers us into a crescent-shaped cove. The rocks jutting out on either side create an ideal swimming area.

"Wow, it got warm," Jack says, reaching back and pulling his shirt off. Sunlight etches his tanned skin, highlighting the muscles in his back as he opens up a compartment in the bow and pulls out an anchor. He tosses it into the water with a splash.

Jack catches me looking at him and says, "I know. I'm sexier than you thought." He lowers his sunglasses to wink at me. "I'm sure you would be, too, if you ever took that dress off." There's a taunting edge to his voice, a playful challenge under his impatient smirk.

"You think I'm not going to?"

Jack shakes his head. "Nope. You'll swim in your clothes because you're too afraid to try something new."

That accusation sparks a flare of determination in my chest. I hastily untie the ribbon, letting my dress fall to the floor. Jack has his back to me, busy shutting off the engine, so I take him by surprise when I ball up my dress and toss it onto the dashboard in front of him.

"You're not the only one with a sense of adventure, Jack Stevenson."

He freezes, staring at my disembodied dress for a second before whirling around. Even through his sunglasses, I can see his gaze sliding down my body. And I *do* feel like I'm standing naked before him. But, to my surprise, it's not awkward.

"Wow," Jack says, slipping off his sunglasses as he walks up to me. "I was wrong. You don't look awesome."

My heart flinches a bit, faltering on the edge of embarrassment.

Jack grins and whispers, "You look *incredible*."

In one swift motion, he sweeps my legs out from underneath me and scoops me up in his arms.

"Jack! What are you doing—"

"Hold your breath!" he hollers, jumping off the back of the boat.

I scream and gasp a sip of air before we crash into the cold water together. It's a shock to my system, at first. When I burst back up to the surface, I splash Jack in the face and call him a selfish beast for throwing me in without warning. He says he *did* warn me. I dunk his head underwater, then swim away, circling the boat while Jack tries to catch me. I'm a good swimmer, but his long arms give him an unfair advantage. He grabs my leg and reels me in, yelling, "Hey, I think I caught a killer whale!"

I laugh, linking hands with him underwater. "I'm the top predator of the ocean."

"Really? Even more than great white sharks?"

I nod. "Some orcas *eat* great white sharks."

"Wow," Jack says. "I didn't know that."

"There—I taught *you* something for once."

"You did."

He dives underwater and tickles the bottoms of my feet, making me burst out laughing. We swim in the cove until our lips turn purple; then we climb back onto the boat and lie on the deck with our faces to the sun— sparkling wet and gasping the sweet, cold air. Jack tells me stories about summers like this one when he was a boy. How Adam taught him to swim in this very same cove.

"Is there anything Adam *hasn't* taught you?"

My question makes him laugh. "Probably not. Adam knows everything."

"He *is* ten years older than you. He's got a head start."

Jack grunts, rolling onto his stomach and folding his arms under his chin. "I'm the one who needs a head start."

"You say that as if you're in competition with him. Trying to get ahead."

Jack falls silent for a moment, his eyes focusing on something far away. "Sometimes I feel like I am. Not trying to outdo him, just trying to… live up to him. I know my parents wish I was more like him."

"I'm sure they don't," I say, propping my head on my fist. "They love you exactly as you are. Adventurous and funny and reckless and daring and… *you*. It would be a shame to change all those things about you just to be more like Adam."

Jack's eyes soften as he looks at me, a drop of seawater trailing down his jaw. "You really think so?"

"Of course."

"You wouldn't like me better if I was more like Adam?"

It's a strange question, one I'm not sure how to answer. I can only say, "I like you just as you are, Jack Stevenson."

He submits to a half-smile, his gaze roaming down the length of my body. "And I like you just as you are, Orca Monroe."

WE RETURN TO THE MARINA far later than we were supposed to, but Jack says it doesn't matter. My hair is still damp, more tangled than ever, and I haven't put my dress back on—because the sunshine feels so good on my bare skin.

"That was fun." I sigh happily as Jack pulls the boat up to the dock.

He laughs a sad little laugh, knotting the rope around the proper cleats. "I hate that phrase."

"'That was fun'?"

"The 'was' part. Because it means the fun is over. But I don't want it to be. I don't want this to end." He turns off the engine, leaving only the gentle splashing of the waves underneath us.

"Well, the day has to end, Jack—"

"I don't mean the day. I mean you. Us." His smooth, cool hands find my waist, pulling me closer. "Orca…"

"Jack…" My hands have nowhere to go except to his bare chest, which is firm with lean muscle, sun-kissed golden. I can feel his heart racing underneath my fingers.

"I was thinking a lot about you last night," he murmurs, tracing his thumb over the curve of my waist. "How much you've changed things for me. How much I'm going to hate it when you leave." He looks down, a shadow passing over his face. "What I'm trying to say is… I've never felt for any girl the way I feel about you."

"Jack—"

"I know you might not feel the same way," he interrupts. "And that's okay. I don't want to rush you. But I want you to know that you're more than just a good time to me. More than just a friend. And if there's even the *smallest* chance that you could feel the same way about me… I would wait for you." His words are raw and honest, the light in his eyes so hopeful it nearly breaks my heart.

"Oh, Jack, I like you so much. I don't want to hurt your feelings—"

"Then don't." He stops me, gently pressing one finger to my lips. "Don't say any more. Let's just… leave it there. We've had such a good day; let's not ruin it." He tucks a damp strand of hair behind my ear, a little smirk quirking at his mouth. "After all, you changed your mind about the swimsuit. Maybe you'll change your mind about me, too."

His gaze darts over my face, resting on my lips. My heart gives an anxious flop as I remember the last time he looked at me like that—at the fireworks, right before he kissed me.

I'm frozen in place as he leans closer to my lips, his warm hands encircling my waist. He's about to kiss me when—

"Jack!"

We break apart at the sound of Adam's voice. I whirl around to find him standing on the dock, looking at me in a way he has never looked at me before.

AEMULUS

adam

"Here's the oil gauge," I say, placing a box on Dad's workbench with a *thunk*.

He glances up from the carburetor in his hands and nods. "Great. Thanks." The storage building around us is loud with echoing voices and idling engines. "You get things done much faster than your brother."

I grunt, leaning back against the workbench. "Unless it's something he *wants* to do."

"Like test-driving that boat, which has been, let's see…" Dad turns his wrist, glancing at his watch. "A *two-hour* test drive, now. If he thinks he's getting paid for that—"

"Two hours? You think something's wrong?"

"Nah, he had Orca with him," Dad says, setting the carb aside to examine the oil pressure gauge I just delivered. "They were going up to the cove…" He gives me a sidelong look. "So you know what that means."

I sure as hell do. The cove doesn't even need a name; it's just "the cove" to locals. The cove where I taught Jack to swim. The cove where he first got drunk with his high school friends, and I had to drive him home at two in the morning, pulling over intermittently to let him puke on the side of the road. The cove where he's taken other girls to "go swimming," which is a code that loosely translates to making out with as few clothes on as possible.

Is that what he's trying to do with Orca?

"Go see if they're back," Dad murmurs, turning the gauge over in his hands. "You know how distracted he gets."

"Yeah. I'll check. Which dock?"

"C-four."

"Got it." I head for the door.

Dad calls over his shoulder, "Remind him that he's here to work!"

I laugh and say, "Will do," but I know as well as Dad does: it's pointless. Jack has never understood the concept of work—he's here out of obligation, the same reason he does anything remotely difficult.

Outside, the sun is blazing bright. As I follow the signs down to dock C, I spot the boat right away, tied up where it should be. I stride down the dock, preparing a fatherly tongue-lashing for my carefree, careless little brother.

I'm about to yell an accusatory, "You're late!" But I stop short when I see him.

When I see *them*—in each other's arms.

Orca has her hands on Jack's bare chest, and she's wearing a skimpy red bikini, and that alone makes my brain stall, like, *Holy crap, she's practically naked.* My gaze shoots down the length of her body, taking in her startlingly bare skin and lighting up an unwelcome blaze of desire inside me.

Jack is about to kiss her—I can tell by the way he slides his hands up her waist, tilting his head and leaning in for her lips. The expression on Orca's face is hesitant, halting, like she wants to step away but can't move.

Jealousy sinks its fangs into my heart. Just like that, I feel possessed—controlled by something primal and irrational. It's beyond reason; it knows no logic, only two words: *She's mine.*

"Jack!" My voice comes out razor-sharp.

The two of them fly apart, whirling around to stare at me. Orca gasps, one hand covering her mouth, while Jack glares at me. "Adam? What the hell are you doing here?"

What the hell are you *doing with your hands all over my—*

I suck back my rage, reeling in a deep breath.

"I had to drop something off for Dad," I explain, keeping my voice steady. "He was wondering if you got lost."

Jack rolls his eyes, but I can't tell who he's more annoyed at: Dad or me. "No, we didn't get *lost.*"

My gaze slides back to Orca. Her cheeks are almost as red as her swimsuit.

"What does Dad want?" Jack grumbles, putting his T-shirt back on. "I was just about to go find him."

Oh, I'm sure you were.

"He's in the storage," I say, not answering his question because he can do that himself. I step forward to help Orca off the boat before Jack can, that primal urge taking over. I offer her my hand, and she gives me a little smile as she slides her smooth, cool palm into mine, hopping over the gap and landing right next to me.

"Thank you," she says softly, embarrassment written all over her face. She looks so different wearing that bikini. Beautiful, yes. But a little too much like every other girl.

The Orca Monroe standing before me right now is not the same Orca Monroe who sings with whales and watches the stars from her lighthouse.

"You can head in," I tell her. "Jack will be there in a minute."

My brother cuts me a questioning look as he secures the knots around the dock cleat. I wait until Orca is out of earshot before saying, "You should be more careful with her."

Jack grunts, grabbing the key and stepping out of the boat. "What do you mean?"

"Exactly what I said. Careful."

He scoffs an incredulous laugh. "You've never told me to be 'careful' with any of my other girlfriends."

I shove down the flare of anger that rises in my chest. "Orca's different. She's not like your…" I can't bring myself to say the word. "She's not like other girls."

"Yeah, I know. That's what I like about her."

I sigh, rubbing my forehead and turning away from him.

God almighty, do I have to spell it out?

"What?" Jack snaps. "What's that face for? What's your problem?"

"My 'problem' is what I just saw happen between you and Orca. I know you, Jack. You like to push your luck. Nothing to lose, right? Well, Orca isn't that kind of girl. Don't think you can have your way with her."

Jack stares at me, a muscle in his jaw twitching. "You don't know what happened between us—"

"Oh yes, I do." I nod slowly, taking a step closer and lowering my voice. "I might not be as cool as you and your friends, Jack. But at least I know how to tell when a woman wants me… and when I should back off."

He narrows his eyes. "And when's the last time *you* were with a woman, huh?"

My mind flashes back to this morning—kissing Orca underneath my truck, her fingertip tracing over my jaw, her breath on my lips.

"You know what I think?" Jack says, a competitive edge to his voice. "I think you're jealous. Because Orca would rather spend time with *me* than you."

"Don't be ridiculous—"

"I'm not being ridiculous. I've seen the way you look at her. If she were just some random girl, would you be standing here reading me the riot act?" He shakes his head, a humorless smile curling onto his face. "I can't help that Orca would rather be with me. We're closer in age, personality, interests. What exactly do *you* have in common with her?"

"Listen, Jack. I don't want to fight with you about this. I just want you to be a little more considerate. You're too used to getting what you want when you want it. If you really cared for Orca the way you say you do, you wouldn't be trying to force yourself on her. You'd let her come running to you on her own."

Jack stares at me, his eyes flashing with a thousand warring emotions. For once in his life, he has no good comeback to throw in my face.

So without another word, I walk away—letting my brother stare after me.

DAD IS NOT HAPPY with Jack slacking on the job, so he sends him off to clean boats for the rest of the afternoon. I offer to give Orca a lift home, much to my little brother's annoyance. Some part of me enjoys irritating him—riding off with Orca in the passenger seat.

We drive downtown and pull into the parking lot of the public library. Orca smiles excitedly when she realizes why we're here: to continue the search for her family. She has that look in her eyes, like I'm the only person she wants to be with.

If only it were that simple.

Her face lights up when we walk into the library. "This is incredible!"

"Shh—we have to be quiet."

"Oh. Sorry." She giggles into my arm, turning away from the librarian, who cuts us a sour glare from behind her desk.

"Come on," I whisper. "This way."

She grabs my hand as we weave through the bookshelves to the reference section at the back of the library. There we find the records I'm looking for: phone books covering Whidbey Island, Fidalgo Island, San Juan Island, and all the others. I pull out every directory that might be useful and spread them out on an empty table.

"So, do you know if your mother was born around here? Or if her parents lived nearby?"

Orca pulls out a chair and sits down. "I have no idea. Like I said, Papa hasn't told me anything."

"Right." I flip open the directory for Anacortes and riffle to the section of last names beginning with *R*. "Let's start here, then."

Orca leans over my shoulder, scanning the page of names. "So many people," she breathes, sounding overwhelmed. "How can they keep track of them all?"

"Well, they can't keep track of them *all*—look at your father. I wouldn't be able to find *his* number in here."

"Because he doesn't have a number." Orca frowns, resting her chin on her fist. "I suppose there's a kind of freedom in that, isn't there? No one knowing that you even exist. You could just… disappear."

"You could."

"I wonder if that's why Papa became a lightkeeper in the first place. Because he wanted to disappear. He didn't want to be a number in a book somewhere. Just another one of the billions of people in the Otherworld."

I turn to look at her. "Sounds like you're starting to like the idea of isolation."

"Pfft. No." She shakes her head decidedly, flipping open the San Juan Island phone book. "Unlike Papa, I'm not afraid of people."

Rushbrook. My gaze catches on the name.

"Orca."

"Hmm?"

"Here's something."

She practically jumps out of her seat to get a closer look. "Rushbrook, Daniel… Rushbrook, Patricia… Rushbrook, Frederick." She frowns, studying the coinciding addresses and phone numbers listed after each name. "Do you think any of them could be related to me?"

"Only one way to find out," I say, reaching across the table to snatch a sheet of paper and a pencil. "Call them."

"But… what if they're *not* related to me? Won't that be awkward?"

"I'm sure they won't mind being asked a simple question," I assure her, jotting down the number for Daniel Rushbrook. "I can call for you if you want."

Orca pinches her lower lip between her fingers. "No, no… I should do it. But I want you to be there. In case I need help. You know, talking to strangers."

"I thought you weren't afraid of people."

She gives me a playful shove and laughs into her hands. I kiss the top of her head as I reach across her to grab the Fidalgo phone book. It takes a few minutes to find every Rushbrook in the vicinity and write down their phone numbers. When we finish, I take the piece of paper, and we head outside to one of the benches along the brick wall of the library.

We go through the list one number at a time, making the calls on my cell phone. Orca has me do the initial "Hello, is this so-and-so Rushbrook?" Then she sandwiches her face to one side of the phone to listen to the voice on the other end.

Daniel has never heard of Orca's mother.

Patricia doesn't answer her phone.

Frederick thinks I'm a telemarketer and hangs up on me.

"Try this one," Orca says, pointing to one of the last numbers on the list. *Harry Rushbrook.* "I'm wondering if it's my grandfather's name, short for Harrison."

I type in the number and wait through six rings before it disconnects. "No answer?"

"No… What was the address?"

"La Conner, Washington."

I flip my cell phone shut and slide it into my pocket. "That's only ten miles from here. Let's go."

LA CONNER IS ABOUT as postcard perfect as small-town Washington gets—a crush of townhouses and waterfront shops built on the edge of a glossy blue harbor, everything buzzing in the peak of tourist season. Orca smiles as we cross the bridge, pointing out my window to the snowy-white ridge of a mountain in the far distance.

Following the address for Harry Rushbrook, we wind up parking in front of an old yellow Victorian house surging with rosebushes and porcelain cat lawn decorations. A sign above the wraparound porch reads North Coast Bed and Breakfast.

Orca squints suspiciously as she matches the house number with the address in her lap. "This can't be the right place, can it?"

I shrug, popping open my door. "Let's go find out."

We walk up the crushed-shell path and come to a stop on the porch. Orca hesitates with her finger hovering over the doorbell, so I go ahead and knock.

She casts me a defensive but grateful look. "I was going to ring the bell."

"Well, what were you waiting for?" I pull her closer, kissing her temple. "Christmas?"

She elbows me in the side.

"Ow, damn it. That's my broken rib—"

"Oh my god, I'm so sorry!" Orca gasps and starts fussing over me just as the front door swings open. A curvy blonde woman in her late fifties steps out onto the porch, wearing an apron covered in rainbow cats.

"Good afternoon, welcome to North Coast Bed and Breakfast! My name is Loretta. How can I help you folks? Are you all right, young man?" She frowns, noticing the way I'm gripping my side and smiling through a grimace.

"He broke his ribs," Orca explains without much context.

"Oh my goodness! Come inside and sit down—do you want me to call a doctor?"

"No, no, it was a while ago. Thank you—I'm fine now." I rush to calm her panic. "I'm still recovering, that's all. My, uh… girlfriend just took exception to something I said and jabbed me in the ribs."

Orca's cheeks flush pink at that word—*girlfriend*—and I have to admit, it feels pleasantly strange and satisfying to hear it roll off my tongue so easily.

Loretta the innkeeper smiles at the two of us. "And I take it you and your girlfriend are looking for a nice, cozy place to spend the night."

"Spend the night?" I repeat the words, momentarily thrown off by the image that flashes through my mind. It doesn't take much imagination— especially after seeing Orca in that sexy little bikini—and now I'm the one whose face is turning red. "Uh, no. No, we're... looking for someone. Harrison Rushbrook. I think he used to live here."

"Yeah, that's right! I knew Harry. Sweet old gentleman. He and his wife used to own this house. I was their neighbor for years; I lived in that little place across the street there. The Rushbrooks were both such lovely people. Olivia passed away in nineteen-ninety, and Harry lived here all on his own until two years ago..." She pauses to make a pouty face. "Poor man. He was never quite the same after losing his wife. Some say he died of a broken heart, and I think they may be right."

The hope in Orca's eyes flickers out as she absorbs this news.

Both her grandparents are dead.

It's exactly what I was afraid of.

She presses her fingers to her lips and turns away, drifting to the other end of the porch and leaning against the rail for support.

Loretta looks worried that she said something wrong. "Is she all right?"

"The Rushbrooks were her grandparents," I explain in a low voice. "She never had the chance to meet them."

"Oh, I am sorry..."

"Do you know if they had any relatives?"

"Yes, they had a daughter," Loretta murmurs thoughtfully. "She came to visit them sometimes, and I met her when we closed on the house. Her name was... Susan? No, no... Sara."

"Do you have her number, by any chance?"

"I might. Let me go check. I'll be right back." With that, Loretta vanishes into the house, and I cross the porch to meet Orca at the railing.

"Hey," I whisper, looping my arm around her shoulders. "You all right?"

She nods stiffly, but I can see the glint of tears cresting in her eyes. "I told myself I'd be prepared for the worst—and I was. But it still hurts."

"I know." I draw her closer, kissing the crown of her head. "It's perfectly natural to be upset. I'm sorry you had to find out like that."

She presses her face to my chest and holds on to me for a few minutes, saying nothing. I rub her back, letting her have a moment to breathe, to cry, to make sense of it all.

Maybe Jack was right. Maybe this whole idea was doomed from the start.

Orca sniffles and takes a step back, drying her eyes. "Perhaps we should stop looking."

"Not yet. There's one more person I think we should call."

She frowns. "Who?"

"I found it!" Loretta singsongs triumphantly, reappearing on the porch with a scrap of paper. "I haven't called her in over a year, but the number should still be good."

Orca looks puzzled, but I waste no time explaining. I take the note and say, "Thank you for your help, ma'am. We really appreciate it."

Loretta beams at me. "Good luck, hon!"

I link hands with Orca and lead her back towards the street, ignoring her persistent demands that I tell her whose number it is and what any of this has to do with her grandparents.

"Her name is Sara Rushbrook," I explain, stopping beside my parked truck to dial the number on my cell phone. "And I think you should be the one to talk to her."

"Why?"

"You'll see why." I pass her the ringing phone, noticing how her hand trembles as she presses it to her ear.

"Wait, I want you to hear, too," she says, tugging my sleeve.

I lower my head against hers, and we share the speaker while waiting for someone to answer the call.

Come on, come on…

"Hello?"

Orca freezes up, speaking only when I nudge her foot. "Hello. My name is Orca Monroe. I'm looking for Sara Rushbrook."

There is a long silence on the other end of the line. "Orca Monroe? You're joking. This… this is Miriam's daughter, Orca?"

She squeezes my hand, like she can't believe what she just heard. "That's me. How do you know my mother?"

"I'm her sister," Sara replies, sounding almost as shocked as Orca looks. "I can't believe it! Little Orca, you were just a baby the last time I saw you."

The smile that breaks over Orca's face is enough to light up a solar system. "You mean… you're my aunt?"

THE VISIT

orca

"So let me get this straight—you have a long-lost aunt you never knew about who lives a stone's throw away on San Juan Island and hasn't seen you for eighteen years?" Jack volleys the question across the dinner table with a skeptical frown.

"Yes. She's my mother's younger sister. Apparently, she met me when I was just a baby, but I don't remember her. Adam and I arranged to meet her tomorrow. She's going to tell me about my mother."

Adam sits next to me at the table, and I can't resist sneaking him a little smile.

"Tomorrow?" Jack says, disappointed. "I had plans for us tomorrow."

"Nothing that can't wait, I'm sure." Mrs. Stevenson gives Jack a meaningful look. "It's not often Orca will have a chance to visit her aunt."

"We can still do something when I get back," I add, attempting to mend his smile. "We're going to set out first thing, but I'm sure we won't be gone long."

Jack shrugs one shoulder. "Doesn't matter. No doubt Adam will make sure it lasts all day." He swerves a glance in his brother's direction, and I can't help but notice the undertone of animosity in his voice.

Adam exchanges a long look with Jack, but says nothing in response.

I wonder if it has anything to do with the conversation they had on the docks this morning. I discreetly reach under the tablecloth and gently take Adam's hand in mine. He stiffens at first, then relaxes as my fingers slide into the spaces between his.

Mrs. Stevenson is the only one who seems to notice that I've switched my fork to my left hand.

TUESDAY DAWNS OVERCAST AND DAMP. The sky is a gray, in-between thing—no rain, no sun. I dress in linen trousers and a green cable-knit cardigan, then eat breakfast with Adam and his mother before heading out. Jack is still sleeping when we leave the house, so I take the opportunity to steal a cassette tape from the glove box of his Mustang. On the drive to the harbor, I slide the tape into the player in Adam's truck.

"What's that?" he asks with a raised eyebrow.

"It's a cassette tape Jack says he stole from you. And now I've stolen it from him. Because one of the songs reminds me of us."

Adam raps his fingers on the steering wheel. "Us as in…?"

"You and me."

A smile quirks at the edge of his mouth. "Oh, my Bryan Adams mix-tape," he says when the music starts playing. "I was wondering where that went."

I'm still new to technology, so it takes a few minutes of fast-forwarding, rewinding, and flipping the cassette tape to find the song I'm looking for. When I finally land in the right place, I turn up the volume and lean back in the passenger seat—holding Adam's hand and watching his profile as he drives. He tells me the song is called "Heaven," and that's exactly how I feel when I'm with him.

We arrive at the harbor right on time to board the next ferry. I've never been on a boat big enough to drive your car right onto it, even though I've seen them through Papa's spyglass—dark shapes slowly skating across the horizon, transporting people and freight to distant islands.

Once Adam parks the truck in the garage area, we venture up to a higher deck, which wraps around the ferry and provides a beautiful but overcast view of the surrounding landscape. The water is calm today, a dark, stormy blue to contrast with the pale cloudy sky. I stand at the railing with Adam as we pass the islands, which look like humped backs of great whales breaching the cold, silky water. Evergreen giants, frozen in time.

"Adam?"

He glances over at me, leaning forward with his elbows on the metal rail. He looks like a rugged adventurer in that brown leather bomber jacket, the ocean wind messing up his hair.

"Have you ever kissed a woman before?" I ask, my voice sounding small. "Before me, I mean."

Adam seems to find the question amusing. "Well… yeah, of course. I mean, I've dated before. But it was nothing to write home about."

"Have you ever made love to a woman?"

There's a flash of surprise, then a twitch of a bashful grin, then a frown, and then a flush of pink colors his ears. He looks down at the waves sloshing below us. "Why are you asking me this, Orca?"

"I'm just curious. Jack said you're the sort who doesn't fool around with girls. You need to be her friend for a long time before you know if she's 'the one.'" I glance down, rubbing my thumb over the worn metal rail. "I think maybe you *do* believe in soulmates."

When I glance back up at Adam, his deep blue eyes are fixed on mine. "Maybe I do."

I embrace him, pressing my face to his chest and breathing in his spicy, manly scent. Any place in the world could feel like home with his arms wrapped around me.

FRIDAY HARBOR. A perfect little coastal town, if ever I saw one. Colorful shops line crooked streets, and every lamppost bears an American flag or a blossoming flower basket—everything splashed in cheerful shades of red, white, and blue.

After disembarking from the ferry, Adam and I track down a map of the island and squint to read the names of squiggly roads, searching for Hemlock Avenue—my aunt Sara's street. The address she supplied us with yesterday is written on the scrap of paper in my hands. I act as a navigator from the passenger seat while Adam drives down the long, winding streets of San Juan Island.

At last, we turn onto Hemlock Avenue, and my heart is racing by the time we pull into the driveway of house number seven and park.

Adam turns to give me one last questioning look. "You ready?"

I nod.

Hand in hand, we approach the front door of the little whitewashed cottage. Wildflowers scatter the front yard, swaying in the breeze as if to wave hello to us—a sea of petals, pink and yellow and violet. We don't even reach the front door before I hear a voice call out my name.

"Orca! Is that you?"

I stop halfway up the flagstone path, whirling around to see a huge straw sunhat pop up from behind a lilac bush. A middle-aged woman with high cheekbones and bright copper eyes steps out from behind the foliage, peeling off her dirty gardening gloves as she approaches. Her nutmeg-brown hair is woven into a long braid that coils down her back.

"Pardon the mess," she says cheerfully, stepping over a fallen rake and a bag of potting soil. "I'm not used to having visitors." She pulls me into a fierce hug, then holds me back at arm's length to get a better look at me. "Goodness, how long it's been—I can hardly believe you're standing here right now! You look so much like Miriam."

"I do?" A flicker of something warm and sad awakens in my chest when she says that. "Thank you for letting us come over, Aunt Sara. Can I call you Aunt Sara?"

She laughs. "Absolutely, my dear. And who is this?"

"Oh, this is Adam," I say, putting my arm around him. "The love of my life."

"Quite an introduction," Aunt Sara says with a grin, making Adam blush.

He shakes her hand. "Pleasure to meet you, ma'am."

Aunt Sara escorts us both inside, offering us some tea and insisting that we make ourselves right at home.

The cottage is small and cozy, swept with a cool breeze from the cove beyond the hemlocks. Everything is tidy and organized—a bookish hideaway filled with potted houseplants and jars of fresh-clipped flowers. It's the sort of place that feels instantly familiar, even if you've never been there before. A sweet old Labrador lopes over to greet us, sniffing our shoes and thwacking her tail in approval.

"This is Daisy," Aunt Sara says, gesturing toward the dog. "She wouldn't hurt a fly."

While she prepares a pot of tea, I notice how quiet the cottage is. Nothing but the whistle of the kettle and the wind chimes on the back porch. "Is your husband at home?" I ask.

Aunt Sara shakes her head. "I'm not married."

"Oh. I'm sorry, I just assumed…"

"It's all right. Most people do." She gives me an easy smile, patting her dog's head. "But I'm quite happy on my own despite what people may think. I have my books and plants to keep me company. And Daisy, of course."

With a contented sigh, the dog lies down on the linoleum floor.

"You have a beautiful spot here," Adam observes, looking out the kitchen window to the backyard, which offers sprawling views of the glittering blue cove beyond the trees.

"Mm, isn't it lovely? I'm a bit of a sentimentalist, so I couldn't bear to sell it when Dad passed. This little cottage has been in our family for a long time. It was built back in San Juan's logging and lime days before the island became a tourist destination." Aunt Sara strides over to a wall covered in framed photographs. She points out a faded black-and-white picture of two little girls playing together on a rocky beach. "This was the summer of sixty-seven… Miriam and I used to have cairn-building competitions down in the cove. Whoever toppled theirs first had to do the other's chores for the rest of the day." She chuckles, remembering it. "I usually lost, but Miriam never let me do her chores all on my own."

I study the photograph: two messy, sandy girls stacking up towers of flat stones on the beach. My mother and my aunt. It's strange to think of my mother as a child, a little girl who grew up swimming in the same waters as I have. Perhaps she watched the same migrating orca pods, too.

"So you used to come here as a kid?" I ask, my gaze roaming over the other old photographs on the wall.

Aunt Sara nods. "Every summer. The island wasn't so built up in those days. We had the cove practically to ourselves."

"What was my mother like back then?"

"Oh, she was such fun. Way more adventurous than I ever was. I remember one time she built a raft and insisted we both sail to British Columbia on it. We got as far as the neighbors' beach before we shipwrecked and had to swim to shore. Dad was so furious, and Mom nearly had a heart attack."

Aunt Sara has many stories to tell, and each one is a brushstroke of color painting the blank canvas that has been waiting with my mother's name on it. Every detail is a new piece of the puzzle, coming together to show me a vivid picture of what my mother was like. We sit in the cozy little living room and drink tea from ceramic cups, passing around photographs from summers long ago.

Eventually, Aunt Sara says, "I'm surprised your father never told you about her."

"I think it makes him too sad to talk about it," I murmur, looking down into my teacup. "He misses her a lot, even still."

Aunt Sara nods slowly. "I miss her, too. I haven't seen her since the funeral."

I frown at her choice of words. "Is that the last time you saw Papa, too?" My heart is heavy as I imagine what a sad, sad day that must have been—for all of them.

Aunt Sara shakes her head. "I haven't seen your papa since you were a baby."

"Yes, I know… That's when Mama died. When I was two years old."

My aunt stares at me for a long, breathless moment—astonishment written all over her face. "Is that what your father told you?"

My heart gives a heavy, anxious thud. "What do you mean?"

Aunt Sara takes a measured breath as if bracing herself for what she is about to say. "Your mother isn't dead, Orca."

The world falls out from underneath me.

"What?" I rasp, my pulse racing as the room tips on its axis. "But… you just said you last saw her at the funeral—"

"Our dad's funeral," Aunt Sara explains. "He passed away two years ago. Miriam was there. We read the will together. He left me this cottage, and he left her the penthouse in Seattle. She's living there now with her husband."

Her husband.

Penthouse in Seattle.

She's living there now.

My hands tremble, threatening to spill my tea all over Aunt Sara's couch. Adam gently takes my cup and sets it on the coffee table, then circles his arm around my back.

"She can't be," I whisper, shaking my head numbly. "She's dead. Papa always told me she was dead."

Aunt Sara opens her mouth to speak, but I can tell she doesn't know what to say. At last, the truth finds its way out.

"Orca… I don't know how to tell you this. Miriam left your father when you were two years old. She divorced him. She said she couldn't stand living like that, isolated from the rest of the world. She was only twenty when she married your father. I think she loved him at the time, but she always had a rebellious streak. She loved the idea of breaking off from the family. Doing something wild and adventurous—marrying a man much older than her and running off to live in a lighthouse on a secluded island. She enjoyed it for a while, but… the fascination soon faded."

This is all too much. I can't believe Papa lied to me all these years. Now I know why he never told me how Mama died.

Because she didn't.

I feel Adam's strong arm around me, the warmth of his finger gently moving over the backs of my knuckles.

"Did Miriam ever attempt to contact Orca?" Adam asks.

Aunt Sara shrugs and shakes her head. "I wouldn't know. We haven't been very close since she divorced Orca's father. She moved to the city and dove headfirst into the rat race. She works at a magazine now, on the board of directors."

My mind is reeling, trying to keep up. When I finally manage to speak, my voice is thick with tears. "Did she… want me? To live with her, I mean?"

Aunt Sara presses her lips into a thin line, looking down at the old photographs scattered across the coffee table. "The divorce was handled quietly. Miriam didn't want to disrupt your life."

"In other words, she didn't want me."

Aunt Sara leans forward to look me straight in the eyes. "Your mother loved you. It was never a question of whether or not she wanted *you*. She just didn't want that kind of life. I didn't support her decision, Orca. I thought she was making a huge mistake, giving up on Lawrence and the life they could have had together. I tried to talk her into giving it another chance, but that's the thing about Miriam. Once she's made up her mind, she has *made it*. And there's no convincing her otherwise."

I swallow hard, a pang of hurt lancing through my heart. "I under-stand."

But I don't.

I never will.

24 Washington Blvd., Suite 103, Seattle, WA.

I watch the address flutter in the wind, caught between my fingers. Aunt Sara wrote it on a scrap of paper before we left. *In case you want to look her up.* She also wrote Mama's phone number beneath the word

"Seattle." Now I stand at the ferry railing, wondering if I should let the paper slip from my fingers and fall into the sea.

Hundreds of emotions whirl through me, a hurricane with no sense of direction or intent—a violent, spinning chaos of pain and unanswered questions.

"I can't believe Papa deceived me like this," I confess to Adam, who stands beside me at the rail. "All this time, Mama was alive—and he kept me from her."

"Don't judge him too harshly, Orca. I'm sure he didn't intend to hurt you by keeping it a secret."

A bitter laugh catches in my throat. "No, of course not. He only wished to 'protect me,' as usual. But I don't need protection from the truth. I could have borne it. Even if he told me that Mama despised me and never wanted to see me again, I could have borne it."

Adam falls silent for a minute, staring out at the distant islands shrouded in white mist. "Maybe *he* couldn't."

"What do you mean?"

"I mean, maybe your father needed to protect *himself* from the pain. Maybe it helped him cope, to rewrite the story of what really happened. To make you believe it and accept that she was gone forever. Maybe that was the only way *he* could accept it."

I turn this over in my mind, trying to see it from Papa's perspective. But it's like peering through the wrong end of a spyglass. Everything is dark and strange and warped.

I can't make sense of this mess, no matter which way I look at it.

"Papa knew she was out there," I murmur, shaking my head. "He can't be so delusional that he convinced himself she *was* dead. Maybe that's the *real* reason he didn't want me to come to Otherworld. He was afraid I might look for her. And find her. And love her."

Adam puts his arm around me and pulls me close, saying in a low voice, "Or maybe he was just afraid of you leaving. Like your mother did. Afraid of losing you, too."

A pang of guilt cuts through me like the snap of a whip. My eyes sting with tears, but a bitter laugh stumbles out on my next breath. "Or maybe he was just afraid of being alone." I fold up my mother's address and tuck it into my pocket. "I might have been able to forgive Papa for everything else… but I don't think I can forgive him for this."

BAD BLOOD BROTHERS

jack

Orca barely says two words to me when she returns from visiting her aunt. I'm in the driveway, repairing the wobbly parts of the deck rail—Mom's idea, not mine. Apparently, coming home from work early means inheriting Dad's unfinished to-do list of chores.

"Hey, Orca," I say as she glides past like a ghost, silent and pale. "How did it go? You get to see your aunt?"

Orca stops halfway up the porch steps, a hollow look in her eyes. "Yes… I saw her. She was wonderful."

"What's wrong? You look sad."

She swallows, glancing down. "I can't talk about it right now." And with that, she turns and disappears into the house. The screen door thwacks shut.

I spin to face Adam, my grip tightening on the hammer in my hand. "What the hell happened?"

Adam sighs. "It's a long story."

"Then give me the short version."

Adam is the kind of guy who takes a full minute to think before he can put together a nutshell version of anything—so while waiting, I drive the last nail into the porch railing.

SLAM, SLAM, SLAM.

"Orca's mother is alive."

I almost drop the hammer on my foot. "What?"

Adam nods slowly, running a hand back over his head. "Turns out she didn't die after all. She divorced Mr. Monroe when Orca was a baby and moved to Seattle."

"And Orca's dad has been telling her that she's dead all this time?"

"Seems so."

Now I understand that gutted look on Orca's face. It's one thing to be hit with the bulldozer that someone you love has died—I know what that feels like. It's the worst kind of pain. The kind you can't put into words.

But how does it feel when you learn someone you spent your whole life believing to be dead is actually alive? And that person is your mom?

"Did you go see her, too?" I ask.

Adam shakes his head. "Orca's aunt gave her an address where she could find her mom if she wants to look her up."

"Don't."

My brother frowns, like *What's gotten into you?* "It's Orca's decision, Jack. I'm not going to stop her from seeing her mom if that's what she wants."

I set the hammer down before I smash something with it, and close the distance between us. "Her mom left her, Adam. *Abandoned* her. Never even contacted her all these years. What kind of person does that? What kind of *mother* does that?"

Adam looks away, sighing heavily through his nose.

"You seriously think it's gonna help Orca to go see this woman?" I challenge, keeping my voice low. "If you ask me, both her parents suck, and she shouldn't have anything to do with them—"

"Well, I *didn't* ask you," Adam snaps, a hostility in his eyes I'm not used to seeing. "Her mother obviously has some… issues. I understand that. But there are two sides to every story, and without all the facts, you can never know the truth. Would you rather keep Orca in the dark? Dominate her life as you accuse her father of doing?"

"Don't compare me to that guy," I growl. "I'm the one who rescued Orca from him. And if it was up to me, I'd never bring her back."

"Turning her against her father won't do her any good, Jack."

"And taking her to see her screwed-up mom won't do her any good either," I fire back. "You think *I'm* the one trying to 'dominate' her life?" I mutter a disgusted laugh. "It's time you take a look in the mirror."

"I'm only trying to help her because—"

"Because she saved your life," I finish for him, my voice seething with mockery. "Yeah, that's what you keep telling me. But I don't think that's the only reason."

Adam stiffens. "What are you saying?"

"I think you see how things are between Orca and me. You saw it yesterday at the marina. She *loves* being with me. I'm the one who's been giving her what she always wanted. So what do you think you're doing? Swooping in to be the hero who reunites her with her family? Are you trying to make her not like me or something?"

Adam scoffs, shaking his head. "Believe it or not, the world doesn't revolve around *you*, Jack."

"Don't give me that crap. I've done nothing but think about Orca since day one. All I've been trying to do is make her happy—"

"Then we both want the same thing. So why are you fighting with me?"

"Because I'm sick of you going off with her alone," I burst out, a blaze of anger flaring through my chest. "I'm sick of sharing her with you."

Adam narrows his eyes, a muscle twitching in his jaw. "You talk about Orca like she's something you own. What about what's best for *her*? What about letting her decide for herself what she really wants? You don't want me to compare you to Orca's father, but you're starting to sound just like him."

With that, Adam turns and climbs back into his truck. He starts the engine, and before I can think of a good reply, he jams the gearshift down and drives off. I stand in the middle of the driveway and watch his truck vanish down the road, a fire of jealous anger still burning in my core.

"ORCA?" I WHISPER THROUGH THE CRACK in the guest room door, knocking softly in case she's asleep. "Can I come in?"

Her murmured response sounds affirmative. I open the door and step inside to find her curled up on the bed, staring at a wrinkled scrap of paper in her hands.

"What's that?" I ask, taking a seat on the edge of the mattress.

"My mother's address. And phone number." She folds it up and places it on the nightstand. "I assume Adam told you what happened."

"Yeah… He did." I glance at the paper, wishing I could rip it up and throw it away, make her forget it ever happened. "You thinking about calling her?"

Orca shrugs. "I don't know. I sort of want to. But at the same time, I don't want to. I'm not sure what to do." She rubs her fingertips over her closed eyelids. "This morning, I thought she was dead. And now, to learn that she's alive, that she's never attempted to visit me or even *contact* me… It's hard to know what to feel."

"That's understandable."

I wish I could say something better. Something that would comfort her without sounding like I'm downplaying the whole thing. But I've never been good with bedside manners.

"You know what I think you need, Orca?"

She looks up at me, so tired and sad. "What?"

"A distraction."

"What sort of distraction?"

"I don't know… Something that would make you smile. Make you laugh."

Orca shuts her eyes. "Nothing could make me laugh right now."

"Is that a challenge?"

I reach over to tickle the bottoms of her bare feet. Her eyes pop open, and a startled little gasp catches in her throat. "Stop! I'm ticklish."

"You are? I didn't know that…"

"No. No, Jack, don't you dare—!"

I dive on top of her, tickling her stomach and making her dissolve into a fit of giggles. She flails around on the bed, laughing and begging me to stop between gasps of air. But I don't stop. I love making her laugh and forget her troubles, even for a few minutes.

That's when Mom swings open the door to the guest room and says, "What's going on in here?"

I roll off Orca, jumping to my feet. "Uh, nothing."

"Well, it looks like something to me." Mom glances from me to Orca, who is still sprawled on the bed, blushing and out of breath. "Better leave this door open, Jackie."

"That's okay, Mom. We were just leaving." I take Orca's hand and pull her to her feet.

"Where are we going?" Orca asks, following me to the front door and slipping her shoes back on.

I give her a wink over my shoulder. "We're going to do the last thing on our list."

Okay, so it's not *exactly* true. The last activity on our Otherworld list is "video games"—but I don't want to stick around the house with Mom's hawk eyes and Adam's accusations following me around. Not to mention that damn address sitting on Orca's nightstand.

I want her to forget about it all—to have a good time and enjoy the world like she always dreamed of doing. Adam might think he's doing her a favor by digging up her past and dragging her all over the islands looking for relatives who are better off dead. Maybe he thinks it makes him some kind of savior. Whatever.

I'm the one who knows how to make Orca laugh, even when she's down in the dumps. I'm the one who understands what she *really* needs.

We drive downtown to the arcade because it's the closest thing we have to video games around here. And this way, I can keep her out—away from Adam—for as long as I want.

"All right, this is definitely the *most* Otherworldly thing I have seen so far," Orca says as soon as we walk into the arcade. The whole place is low-lit by strobing neon lights from all the different games, synthwave music pulsing from the overhead speakers.

I escort Orca over to the ticket line, explaining the whole system of playing to win prizes. I buy her way more tickets than I can afford (because that's just who I am), and then we weave through the arcade, hand in hand, stopping whenever something catches Orca's eye and she drags me to a stop. The whole time she's asking, "What does this one do?" and, "What about this one?" and, "Teach me how to play this."

That's how we spend the afternoon—me leaning over her shoulder, showing her how to win (and cheat) at my favorite arcade games. At first, she insists she's no good at any of it, but soon she's laughing and button-mashing and cheering over her victories. Whenever she starts to lose, I dive in and rescue her from certain death—congratulating her when the machine spits out another reel of tickets.

"No, that was *you*," she argues, objecting to an unfair win.

"All right, fine," I admit, swooping up the tickets. "But I'll give them to you. For a kiss."

She pops up on her tiptoes and kisses my cheek. I tear one ticket off the roll and hand it to her.

"Wait, but…"

"One kiss per ticket."

She laughs, giving me a shove. "That's not fair!"

"Okay, fine. You can pay me back later," I say, looping my arm around her shoulders and steering her to the back of the arcade. "Let's go get your prizes."

I'm expecting Orca to go crazy over all the "otherworldly" things in the prize section, but in the end, she points to a cassette player under the glass and says, "That one."

I raise my eyebrows at her. "You sure?"

She nods. "I can take it back to the lighthouse and listen to your music. It'll be like still being here. Kind of."

"You're already thinking about leaving me? Jeez." I shake my head in dismay, though I'm smiling for her sake. "Cassette player it is, then. You know what that means."

"What?"

"You need music."

After leaving the arcade, I take her to the music store, where we look for all the tapes I've been playing in my Mustang since she first arrived.

"Something tells me your dad wouldn't approve of AC/DC," I say, snatching *Back in Black* off the shelf and handing it to her. "Or Pink Floyd. Or Queen."

Orca grins, giving me a suspicious side-eye. "Something tells me you take pleasure in doing things Papa wouldn't approve of."

"You found me out," I whisper conspiratorially into her ear.

She shoots me a stern look.

"Oh, come on." I drop one more tape into her hands. *Dark Side of the Moon.* "Don't pretend you're not enjoying it, too."

Orca looks down. "Perhaps I am… Only now, it's more complicated than it was before."

It's impossible not to notice the shadow of remorse in her eyes. The betrayal written all over her face.

"Because your dad didn't tell you the truth about your mom?"

She nods slowly. "Adam says he probably did it to protect me and to protect himself… because he didn't want to relive the pain of it all."

"I don't give a shit what his reasons were. It was wrong. And if I were you, I'd never want to go back to him."

Orca frowns. "I don't resent him, Jack. I just… don't understand. I thought I knew him better than any other soul in the world. And then, to learn that he kept such a monumental secret from me… It's just a lot to take in."

"I know. But let's not think about it anymore, okay? You're supposed to be having fun. Letting all your worries fade away."

She manages a half-hearted smile. "You're remarkably good at distracting a girl, Jack Stevenson."

"Baby, you ain't seen nothing yet."

She laughs. I pay for her cassette tapes and notice all the ones she picked out—Adam's favorites. It shouldn't feel like a splinter in my brain, but it does. After the music store, I'm on my last ten bucks—just enough to take her out for burgers, and that's about it. But it's only eight thirty, and I don't want to take her home yet. I don't want to take her home ever.

So instead, we drive to the marina, where I spent the morning cleaning and polishing rich people's yachts. The harbor is mostly abandoned at this time of night—a perfect place to take your girl dancing when you have a cassette player and no money. Sailboats rock gently on the low tide, glistening in the pale light of the full moon overhead.

Orca follows me down the docks, her tape player in hand. "Where are we going?"

"Shh. You'll see."

The docks are no better than a maze in the semi-dark, but I know every boat in this marina like the back of my hand. I stop at the stern of the *Aphrodite* and hold out my hand to Orca.

"Isn't this the one we almost got caught on?" she asks, hopping aboard.

"Well… yeah. But we won't get caught this time. Owner's out of town."

"How do you know?"

"Because I spent the morning shining it up," I explain, leading her up the narrow stairs. "Just for you."

When we reach the upper deck, I twirl her into my arms. "I wanted to take you dancing, but I ran out of money."

Orca breathes a nervous little laugh. "I've never been dancing before. I'm not sure I know how."

"It's simple. Here, put your hand on my shoulder. Wait—first, let's get some music going. What did you put in here? *Back in Black*?"

Orca laughs and shakes her head. "Bryan Adams."

"Better choice for slow-dancing, I guess." I hit the play button and crank up the volume, setting the player on the edge of the deck. "Okay, so here's how it works. I put my hand on your waist, and you put your hand on my shoulder, and it's just *one, two, three…*"

I lead her in slow circles around the deck, careful not to come too close to the edge. She's shy and hesitant at first, but after a few minutes, she falls into step with my rhythm, surprisingly smooth for this being the first time she's ever danced with a guy.

I like being her first. Her only.

Yet, even here, slow-dancing to "Everything I Do" with the hottest girl on top of the fanciest yacht in the harbor, I can't stop hearing Adam's voice in my mind.

What about letting her decide for herself what she really wants? You don't want me to compare you to Orca's father, but you're starting to sound just like him.

Remembering our argument in the driveway is enough to stoke the fire of jealousy still smoldering inside me, every single paper cut of doubt stinging me all over again.

How she snuck off this morning with him.

How she picked out his favorite music in the store.

How she said, *Adam says he probably did it to protect me. Adam says he'll take me to see my mom if I want to. Adam says, Adam says, Adam says…*

I want to stop dancing right now and make her look me in the face and tell me which of us she would choose—him or me. I want to hear her say the words.

I would choose you, Jack.

Only you.

Always you.

But what if she doesn't? I can't ask her. I don't want to know the answer. I'd rather stay in the dark because ignorance is bliss. Orca is bliss, with her hand on my shoulder, her laughter like music, and her eyes sparkling in the moonlight.

A SHINY, PERFECT LIFE

orca

That night, I lie awake in the dark for hours, thinking about Mama and staring at her address on my nightstand.

I remember her face in the wedding photograph. Her smile, bright as the sun. She was happy that day. She loved Papa that day.

When did she stop?

When did she decide he wasn't enough for her?

Aunt Sara said Mama had a rebellious streak—that she loved the idea of breaking with her family, marrying an older man, and running off to a romantic, remote island to live in a lighthouse.

Was their love not enough to keep them together?

Was her love for *me* not enough to keep her on the island?

I dread the idea of finding out. When I think about calling Mama or visiting her, all I can imagine is the worst outcome. A refusal to see me. A door slamming shut in my face. Perhaps she and Papa were both in on the deception. Perhaps she, too, wishes me to believe her dead.

As the moonlight slowly carves a path across my bedroom, I try to conjure up an image of the best-case scenario.

Mama is happy to see me. She has been waiting for me, hoping one day I would come to the Otherworld to find her and make peace with her.

She has pictures of me as a baby, and she cries every time she looks at them. Papa asked her to stay away; that's why she hasn't visited me all these years. She thought I would be happier without her.

If I don't go to see her, I'll never know which story is true.

But do I want to know?

Is it better to leave the question unanswered?

For now, I convince myself that it is. I fall asleep between waves of doubt and reassurance—the dizzy push and pull of unmade decisions blurred by exhaustion.

When I open my eyes to late-morning sunshine, a new question strikes me:

If Mama were dead, and I could bring her back to life to see her just one time, would I do it?

The answer is yes.

Absolutely, unequivocally *yes*.

So I make my bed and get dressed, then wander around the house, looking for Adam. Mrs. Stevenson is the only one I find. She says both her boys are at their respective workplaces, so I call Adam on the Stevensons' phone. He sounds surprised to hear my voice.

"I want to go see my mother. Today."

There is a moment's silence. "Are you sure?"

"Yes."

"Do you want to call her first?"

"No." I press my eyes shut, shaking my head. "I need to do this in person. I need to see her face."

"All right," Adam says. "When do you want to go?"

"As soon as possible if you can spare the time."

"I'll be right there."

THE RIDE TO SEATTLE IS QUIET—the polar opposite of the drive Jack and I took to the city just days ago. That sunny, windswept afternoon was filled with joyful oblivion. I had nothing to worry about. Nothing to fear.

Now I sit wordless in the passenger seat of Adam's truck, watching the road signs counting down the distance between us and Seattle.

Between me and Mama.

"We don't have to go through with this," Adam keeps reminding me. "If you change your mind—"

"No," I cut in every time. "I want to. Truly."

He squeezes my hand. I squeeze back.

The gleaming skyline looks less like a mysterious spectacle to me now and more like another realm—a place so strikingly different from the natural world in every way, shape, and form. A place Papa would hate.

Is that why Mama moved here?

I can't help but ponder that question as we walk down Washington Boulevard, hand in hand. The city is so crowded we had to park the truck a distance away from the building where Mama lives. I keep glancing at the wrinkled address in my palm, but I don't need to. I stared at it enough last night for the numbers and letters to be seared into my mind forever.

24 Washington Blvd., Suite 103, Seattle, WA.

Building 24 is impossibly tall and wrapped in thousands of glass windows—reflecting the gloomy gray sky overhead. A gilt revolving door ushers us into the lobby, which is elegantly furnished with thick carpets and twinkling chandeliers. Adam leads me into the elevator and presses the button for the top floor.

"How do you know that's the right one?" I ask.

"Your aunt said the penthouse. That's always the top floor." He turns to give me a little smirk. "Just think: if you grew up living with your mom, you'd be some fancy, private school penthouse girl. You'd never look twice at a guy like me."

"Oh, yes, I would." I hug his arm, resting my face against his bicep. "I would have looked *three* times. A *hundred* times."

He murmurs a laugh and kisses the top of my head.

That's when the elevator stops with a soft *bing*, and I realize we've reached the top. My heart thuds as the shiny gold doors slide open to reveal a small landing covered in the same plush carpet as the lobby. We find the door marked 103.

Mama's apartment.

Now that I'm finally here, standing in front of the door with my heart racing in my chest, I wonder if this was a mistake. There's still time to turn back. She would never know I had come this far.

But I would know.

I would always wonder.

So I press the doorbell and wait. My breath is unsteady as I glance at Adam, who stands beside me, a quiet fire in his eyes.

"You're strong. You can do this," he says softly. Those words feel like a life raft underneath me—something to hold onto in the midst of a raging ocean.

The door opens.

"Can I help you?"

Her voice is crisp, high, and professional. So unfamiliar to my ears, yet something deep inside me twists with bittersweet heartache when I hear it. Something in me *remembers* that voice.

She looks older than she did in the wedding photo. Her dark blonde hair is short now, cut into a spiky pixie, which seems to sharpen the angles of her face. Her arms and legs are long and graceful; her smile pretty and insincere. The other details come to me in snatches: a gray pencil skirt and a matching suit jacket. A gold wristwatch. Diamond earrings. Snakeskin high heels.

"Well?" she says, crossing her long arms over her chest. "Are you going to tell me who you are? I'm a very busy woman."

Adam clears his throat to speak for me, but I step forward first. My voice trembles as I introduce myself. "It's me, Orca. Your daughter."

She stiffens, surprise washing over her face like a rogue wave—erasing the pinched frown of impatience. Her gaze darts over me, head to toe, taking in the details of my appearance in a new light.

"Orca…" The name rushes out of her like someone just knocked the air from her lungs. She takes a deep breath and squares her shoulders. "I never expected to see you after all this time."

"I never expected to see *you*," I confess, my voice still shaky. "Until yesterday, I thought you were dead."

Mama frowns, squinting at me in disbelief. "What?"

"Papa told me you died when I was a baby. Yesterday I went to see Aunt Sara… and she told me the truth."

Mama stands frozen in place for a long moment, her mouth hanging open as she absorbs this news. I wait breathlessly for her reaction, my heart pounding in my throat.

All last night, I was wondering how this moment would be. I wasn't expecting a tearful, heartfelt welcome. I wasn't expecting her to embrace me or tell me she was happy to see me. Yet still, I feel a pang of disappointment when she takes a step back and holds the door open for me, as you would for a stranger on the street.

"I, uh… I think you'd better come in. Both of you." Her gaze shifts to give Adam an analytical once-over. "Orca's boyfriend, I assume?"

"Adam." He introduces himself. "Pleasure to meet you, ma'am."

But I can tell by the way he holds onto me—his hand tense and his jaw set—that the expression is a mere formality. He looks ready to sweep me up in his arms and carry me out of here at the first sign of trouble. It's impossible to overlook the gentle fierceness in his eyes, just as it's impossible to miss the judgmental curl of my mother's lip as she scrutinizes Adam's rugged good looks.

Mama's apartment is unlike the lighthouse in every way. There is nothing cozy or quaint about the suite of rooms that unfurl around us in a flawless show of sleek, modern efficiency. Everything is sharp and glossy. Marble and stainless steel. Cold and impersonal. Massive glass doors at one end of the living room open up to a sprawling balcony that overlooks the city skyline. I wonder how anyone can feel at home in this place.

"I have a work meeting at two o'clock," Mama says, gliding into the shiny, perfect kitchen to select three shiny, perfect glasses from the counter. "So I'm afraid I only have twenty-five minutes to talk. Would you like something to drink?"

I wasn't expecting a tearful, heartfelt welcome.

But I wasn't expecting *this*, either.

Adam glances at me, trying to read my expression. But I hardly know what to feel. Last night, I pondered the worst- and best-case scenarios, predicting that today's visit would be one extreme or the other. But to my surprise, the mood is neutral. Painfully, startlingly neutral.

Mama snatches a decanter of pale golden liquid from the counter and splashes a small amount into her glass. She fills the other two glasses with water and sets them on the low table in the living room.

"So," she begins briskly, taking a seat on the edge of the stiff-looking chair. "You finally ran away from Lawrence. Everybody runs away from him in the end. It's just a matter of time."

"I didn't run away, exactly," I explain, sitting on the opposite couch beside Adam. "I wanted to see the mainland."

"The mainland? So the mission wasn't to seek *me* out."

I shake my head. "As I said, I didn't know you were alive until yesterday."

"So Lawrence made you believe I was dead," Mama says with indignation, taking a sip of her drink. "The man is more deranged than I thought."

I shift uncomfortably, smoothing my sweaty hands over my linen skirt. "Papa isn't deranged. He just… misses you terribly."

At this, Mama laughs. Not a genuine laugh, but a short, contemptuous sort of bark. "For god's sake, it's been sixteen years. How long is the man going to stew in his own self-imposed misery?"

"You talk about him like he's your enemy."

"Do I?" Mama tips her glass back and swallows the rest of the drink. "I'm sorry. I have no hard feelings against Lawrence anymore. Honest, I don't. He chose his life, and I chose mine. Don't look so horrified, Orca. Surely you know more of the world by now—look, you've gone off on your own and met someone." She gestures at Adam. "Are you two living here in Seattle?"

"What? No."

Adam clears his throat awkwardly. "We're not… living together."

"Oh." She gives an elegant shrug. "Well, in any case, you know what I mean. We all have to be free to make our own choices."

I peer at her, taking in the details all over again. Her wristwatch. Her sparkly earrings. Her ugly high-heeled shoes. It's all beginning to look like a facade to me—a beautiful outer shell meant to disguise something hollow underneath.

"Do you still work at the magazine?" I ask, my voice small and strained.

Mama nods. "Mm, yes. I've recently been promoted to senior creative director. It's my dream job. I'm surrounded by the things I love every day—fashion, art, culture, the life of the city." She gestures around her at the glamorous, empty apartment. "What more could I ask for?"

Papa, I think. *Ocean waves roaring outside your window. Orca pods singing in the distance. The forest, the beach, the cove, the lighthouse. Me.*

Mama watches me for a silent moment before saying, "I know it must be hard for you to understand. You've spent so much of your life on that tiny island. But I couldn't live like that, Orca. If I'd stayed, it would have *killed* me. Your father and I would have ended up hating each other."

"Papa would never hate you. He loves you—even still. He gets so sad every time he thinks about you. I always thought it was because you died."

Mama presses her lips into a prim frown, tipping her chin up. "Lawrence doesn't know how to love. Only how to *possess.*"

The word is a fishhook—sharp and unexpected. It catches on my heart and pierces something tender, something bruised.

Mama swiftly rises to her feet, taking her empty glass back over to the counter and pouring herself another drink. "Something about him was appealing to me when I was young. A handsome, mysterious older man who lived alone on an island. Well, you couldn't get more controversial than that in my family." She hums a discontented laugh, dropping the top back onto the decanter with a *clink!* "I didn't want to follow the path my parents had planned for me. I wanted an adventure. And Lawrence *was* that adventure… for a while." She paces across the room to the big glass sliders, her heels clicking on the tile floor. "But I wasn't prepared for that sort of life. The isolation, the boredom, the same thing day after day after day… I began to see I'd been too hasty in my decision to get married and move away from everything I knew and loved. Lawrence could see that I was unhappy. He could see that he was losing me a little more each day. And do you know what he did?" She cuts me a look over her shoulder. "He decided we should start a family of our own."

The hook pierces deeper this time, not just from her words but from the icy disdain in her voice, the sharp edge of her glance in my direction.

"Lawrence knew that I never wanted children, and we were always careful to take precautions… At first, I thought it was an accident when I got pregnant with you," Mama continues, lifting the glass to her mouth and taking another sip. "But after you were born, I realized that it was all part of his plan—to keep me there, with him. If I had stayed, there would have been more children. I'm sure of it. My life would have spiraled into a never-ending cycle of cooking, cleaning, and taking care of babies. I wasn't prepared to throw away my life like that. I wasn't prepared to be *miserable* so that Lawrence could be happy."

For a moment, I don't know what to say. I sit frozen on the uncomfortable couch, Mama's words twisting inside me like small doses of poison.

I never wanted children.

I wasn't prepared to throw away my life like that.

If Mama had stayed with Papa and me, that's what she would have seen it as: a waste of her life. A never-ending cycle of chores. Boredom. Loneliness. Misery.

I swallow back the ache of tears in my throat, reaching for Adam's hand. A question burns in his eyes. *Do you want to leave?*

I shake my head. Not because I don't want to—every part of me wants to leave this shiny, perfect apartment and go somewhere quiet and secluded where I can cry in Adam's arms.

But I need to stay. I need to face her.

I am strong enough.

I am capable of anything.

"Are you happy here, Mama?"

She turns sharply to face me at that word, *Mama.* I wonder if she ever heard me call her that before. I wonder if she stayed long enough to hear my first words.

"I am," she replies with a diplomatic smile. "I have a wonderful husband who respects me as a businesswoman *and* his wife."

Perhaps that shouldn't feel like a slap across the face. But it does.

"Alexander and I mutually agreed that children didn't suit our lifestyle. No distractions. We focused completely on our careers."

I want to say, *A career can't kiss you goodnight.*

A career can't sing you happy birthday, can't bake you a cake and throw you a surprise party.

A career can't make up stories with you, braid your hair, or dance in the kitchen with you.

A career can't say *I love you.*

"I hope you're happy too, Orca," Mama says at last. "I hope you don't let your father tie you down or stop you from pursuing the life *you* want. Never forget that—it's *your* life, not his."

I nod slowly, looking down at Adam's hand in mine.

"I'm sorry to cut this short, but if I don't leave now, I'll be late for my meeting." Mama taps the face of her watch, striding across the apartment to swing open the door. "It was good to see you're doing so well, Orca. Thank you for stopping by. Perhaps we'll cross paths again someday."

She says it with a lilt in her voice and a pleasant smile on her lips, but somehow it feels like a long, sharp blade sinking through my chest.

It's not the way a mother ought to say goodbye.

Still holding Adam's hand, I make my way to the door where she stands, waiting for us to depart. I stop to face her one last time, whispering through the lump in my throat, "Thank you for your time. I'm glad I got the chance to meet you. I'm glad you're alive."

I turn away before she can see my tears.

HERO AND LEANDER

adam

Orca doesn't speak on the drive home. She's still in shock, and who can blame her?

That meeting was worse than I'd anticipated.

I don't want to make her talk about it, but I also can't talk about anything else. So we spend the drive in contemplative silence—her sniffling and wiping her eyes as she stares out the passenger window, me blaming myself for this whole damn mess.

Jack was right; I should have left it alone. I should have had the sense to stay out of Orca's past. But I loved how her face lit up at the thought of meeting her lost relatives and learning about her mother. I wanted to give her something to take home with her—even just a secondhand memory.

I never predicted the nightmare this would turn into.

Miriam wasn't cruel—but she was cold, and in a way that was almost worse. She said she never wanted a child, and that it would've been a waste of her life to stay at the lighthouse with her daughter. I watched those words sting Orca, and I could do nothing to shield her from the pain.

I'd had half a mind to rip that drink out of Miriam's hand and smash it on her expensive floor, to unleash my anger and tell her to take her high-society city life and stick it—

"Adam?"

I snap out of my thoughts, turning to glance at Orca. "Yes?"

"You're driving kind of fast."

"Oh. Sorry." I ease off the gas, watching my speedometer go from eighty to sixty-five. I flex my fingers around the steering wheel, trying to relax. "You okay, Orca?"

She gives the slightest nod.

"I'm so sorry about all of this."

"It wasn't your fault, Adam."

"Yes, it was. If I hadn't dug up the past—"

"You were only trying to help me," Orca interrupts, her voice quavering and thick with tears. "It was infinitely kind of you. And I'm grateful for it."

But she's wrong. I wasn't *only* trying to help her. I had other motives for inciting this search for her family—I wanted a good excuse to be with her. An excuse so virtuous and benign, it would be impossible to misinterpret as selfish.

I've stirred up secrets that should have stayed buried and forgotten. I've put Orca through an agonizing confrontation with her mother, which only caused her more pain.

I've released a butterfly and set off a hurricane.

If only I could turn back time and do it all differently.

Wʜᴇɴ ᴡᴇ ᴀʀʀɪᴠᴇ ʜᴏᴍᴇ, Orca heads straight to the guest room and shuts herself in, saying she wants to rest for a while. Everyone else is out, and I don't want to leave Orca home alone, so I go outside to chop up an old dead pine that fell behind the barn during the last storm.

I take off my shirt and grab an ax from the chopping block, grateful to have something I can take my anger out on. For the next half hour, I hack branches off the tree, chopping them into pieces and then hauling everything over to the woodpile to be split and seasoned later.

Eventually, Jack pulls into the driveway. I glimpse the flash of his red

Mustang through the trees, but I'm too far away for him to see me. His footsteps echo on the porch steps, and the screen door claps shut.

I keep working, mentally preparing myself for what's coming next: Jack will talk to Orca. She'll tell him about the meeting with her mother. He'll be mad as hell and come find me just to say "I told you so."

Sure enough, that's exactly what happens.

Slam, the screen door.

"Adam?"

I release a heavy sigh, swinging the ax down. "Behind the barn!"

Moments later, Jack storms over, whacking tree branches out of his way. "I need to talk to you—"

"I know. I know exactly what you're going to say, and you're right—okay? But it was Orca's decision, and I couldn't stop her once she'd made up her mind."

"She's in there *crying*," Jack snarls, his eyes ablaze. "I told you yesterday, don't take her to see her mom. I told you it wasn't a good idea—"

"She called me and asked me to take her. What was I supposed to say? No? I won't?"

"You should have let *me* take her."

"Oh, I'm sure that would have helped a lot." I snatch my bowsaw from the ground and slice through the tree trunk. "We both know you can't control your temper, Jack. You would only have made the situation worse."

"Oh yeah? And you've, what—made the situation *better*? Seems to me you've done nothing but cause her more grief. Orca was happier when she thought her mother was dead!"

"Orca wasn't happy," I argue, sawing more violently. "She wanted a sense of belonging, identity—she wanted more than a date to the movies and a bikini and to go see the fireworks. She wanted more than just a vacation." I throw another chunk of wood onto my pile.

Jack stares at me, shaking his head. "You're such a jerk sometimes, you know that?"

"You've told me that a few times, actually."

"I've done *way* more for Orca than you ever have," Jack seethes, lowering his voice as he narrows the distance between us. "You might think you're some kind of hero just because you don't take sides—you want to defend her dad, her mom, look at everyone's side of the story. Well, sometimes, there's only *one* side of the story, Adam. Sometimes you've gotta take the side of the person you care about and have the balls to fight for them, no matter what."

I narrow my eyes at him. "You think I'm not on Orca's side?"

"I think you try so damn hard to be the middleman that you forget that some people are just screwed up. Like Orca's mom. She's a selfish bitch. I could have told you that yesterday. I *did* tell you that, but did you listen to me? No, you had to go put her through hell instead—"

"For the hundredth time, I was only trying to help her."

"But you *haven't* helped her! Have you?"

I step over the log and pick up the ax again, my back to my brother as his words hammer into me like a mortar round.

You haven't helped her.

"No," I admit, defeated. "No, I haven't."

ORCA STAYS IN HER ROOM for the rest of the evening. She doesn't even come out for supper. Jack tries to tempt her with take-out waffles, but she claims she's not hungry, and Mom eventually says, "Leave Orca be. She'll come out when she's ready."

Jack takes this opportunity to shoot daggers at me and add, "I'm not the one you should be telling to leave her alone."

I don't rise to it. Ever since our quarrel earlier, Jack has been in attack mode—locked and loaded, looking for a fight. But I'm not going to give him the satisfaction. He'll cool off in a few hours; he always does. Nothing deflates my little brother's anger like an empty fighting ring, no enemy in sight.

He takes off in his Mustang, and I figure that's the last I'll see of him tonight. He's been known to run off when things aren't going his way—

usually to hang out with his friends. Someone who will listen to him complain. He'll return tomorrow morning with a hangover and a hundred apologies for how angry he was the night before.

Still, Mom waits for him to come home, curled up on the couch with the TV on low. I'm sitting at the kitchen table, going over some business stuff I've been neglecting—specifically, balances that don't balance. But it's hard to concentrate on work when Jack's accusations from earlier keep lashing through my mind.

Seems to me you've done nothing but cause her more grief... Orca was happier when she thought her mother was dead.

He's right, and I resent that. I *did* encourage Orca to search for her family. I *am* the one who blew it.

If only we hadn't called her aunt. If only we hadn't looked for her mother's name in the church register. If only I hadn't seen that damn picture in her father's dresser drawer.

How far back would I have to go to fix the damage I've done?

Would Orca have been better off if I'd never crashed near her island in the first place?

The next time I look at the clock, it's eleven thirty, and Mom is fast asleep on the couch. I spread a blanket over her and turn off the lights, silently making my way down the hallway to the guest room. When I ease open the door, I find Orca curled up on the bed in her nightgown, looking cold and lonely.

At first, I think she's asleep—but when I start to cover her up with a quilt, she whispers my name.

"Adam." Her hand reaches out for mine. "Don't leave."

"I thought you were asleep."

"No... I can't."

I sit on the edge of the bed, gently brushing a strand of hair away from her tired, swollen eyes. "Do you want to talk about it?"

She shakes her head. "Not really. I just... I don't want to be alone tonight. I want to be with you."

I want to be with her just as much. But I don't deserve to be—I don't deserve *her*. I don't deserve her love, her forgiveness, her hand in mine so warm and constant, the look in her eyes so sad and hopeful.

"I'll be right back," I whisper, kissing her forehead and slipping into the hallway. Mom is still sound asleep in the living room, so I take the opportunity to grab a book from my desk and sneak back into Orca's room undetected. I leave the door open a crack so I can hear if Jack comes home.

"What's that?" Orca asks, nodding to the book in my hands. I snap on the bedside lamp and show her the title. "*Gods and Goddesses*," she reads.

"It's a collection of Greek mythology," I explain, stretching out on the bed with her. "Worst case, it'll bore you. Best case, it'll put you to sleep."

Orca snuggles up to me, and I read Greek legends to her while rain patters gently on the roof.

"Hero was a young priestess of Aphrodite who lived on the shores of the narrow straits of the Hellespont. Hero was remarkably beautiful and served the goddess dutifully in her temple, though she herself knew nothing of love. All the men from the nearby villages dreamed of being with Hero, but there was one young man who desired her more than any other. His name was Leander, and he came from a poor family who lived just across the straits. From the moment he first laid eyes on Hero, he longed to be with her."

Orca lays her head on my shoulder and spreads her hand over my heart. I try to concentrate on the words and not get distracted by the feeling of her body nestled against mine.

"At last, Leander found the courage to declare his love for Hero. But when she looked at him, he was struck dumb by her beauty. Hero was moved by the tender shyness of this young man and found herself enchanted by him, as she had never been before. She said to him, 'Is there something you wish to tell me? I am merely a girl, unschooled in the ways of men. And I don't think my father would be pleased to know that such a handsome young man is trying to seduce me.'

"Leander answered, 'I promise you, my intentions are entirely honorable. I have admired you for so long and love you with all my heart. I would never treat you with disrespect. The goddess you serve is dear to me, and I have the highest regard for your father. But how can you serve Aphrodite when you have never known the touch of a man? It's true, I am only a poor boy, but my love for you is pure.'

"As he spoke, Hero was overcome with love for him. But she knew that her father would never consent to her marrying this humble lad from across the straits, so they promised their love to each other and vowed in their hearts to live as husband and wife.

"Every night, Hero hung a lamp from her bedroom window in Sestus, and its light shone across the narrow straits to Abydos. When Leander saw it, he would swim across the channel to meet his true love. He would arrive soaking wet, and Hero would greet him with ardency. The two would make love all night; then as the dawn was breaking, Leander would reluctantly swim back across the channel. They told no one of their secret marriage, for they knew such love was forbidden…"

Orca tips her head back to look at me—a smile softening her lips. I think she's beginning to see why I chose this story.

"Winter came, and tempests blew down the Hellespont. Hero pleaded with Leander to wait until spring to come to her, but he refused to let the storm separate them. One night, as Leander swam across the straits, the lamp blew out, and he was lost in the darkness. With no light to guide his way, he struggled on—but the wind was unrelenting, and the waves swallowed him up.

"When the sun rose the next morning, Hero desperately searched the tidewater, hoping to catch sight of her lover coming to her. But instead, she found the body of her beloved Leander lifeless on the rocks below. Overcome with grief, Hero threw herself out the window and to her death."

Orca jolts back to look at me, her eyes wide with shock. "What?"

I stifle a laugh, a little amused by her reaction to the tragic ending. "She'd rather die than live without him."

"But that's so sad. It can't end like that."

"Well." I flip to the next story. "It does."

"Rewrite it, then."

I raise my eyebrows. "Rewrite a Greek myth?"

"Yes," she says, with all the sweet innocence that made me fall in love with her. "I'll do it if you won't." She pauses to gather her thoughts. "Leander is a *smart* young man, so he does as Hero tells him. He waits for spring and finds that he loves her even more when they meet again. And she loves him so much, she can't remember what her life was before she knew him. But they can't keep their love a secret forever… Hero knows that. So she talks to her father about Leander. She knows that if her father could only see what a brave, kind, wonderful man he is… surely he would let them be together."

"And what if her father says no? What if he forbade Hero from ever seeing Leander again?"

The sparkle in her eyes weakens, but she pushes a half-hearted smile onto her face. "Then I suppose they would have to carry on in secret… without his consent."

"Wouldn't that be wrong?"

Orca shakes her head. "How could love ever be wrong?"

It shouldn't be. It's *not*. But I can't ignore the weight of guilt bearing down on my chest. I can't silence the voice in the back of my mental courtroom, objecting, *This is wrong, this is wrong.*

"So," Orca continues the alternate ending, "Hero and Leander run away together and live in their own cottage by the sea, far away from everyone else… And they get *properly* married and have babies and live happily—" she kisses me fast "—ever—" another kiss "—after." The third kiss stays longer, and *god*, I didn't realize how much I was thirsting for her lips until I taste them again. Like sweet living water I've traversed a desert to find.

We break apart for a second, an inch of breathless space between us, foreheads touching.

"I like your ending much better," I confess softly, tracing my finger over the curve of her neck. She's so beautiful, lying here in my arms—the lamplight gilding her skin, glowing in her wild hair.

I look back up just in time to see a tear slip down her cheek.

"Orca, please don't cry."

She presses her eyes shut, another tear sliding down her face. "I'm not. I just… I just keep thinking."

"About your mom?"

She nods, her voice returning threadbare. "I almost wish Papa's story were true. I almost wish… that she wasn't alive." Orca opens her eyes to look at me with a flinch of shame. "Does that make me a bad person?"

I shake my head, reaching up to brush her tears away. "No, Orca. It makes you *human*."

A tiny, aching sob stumbles out of her, breaking my heart in a single breath. "It was so hard, Adam…"

"I know."

"I feel like I lost something close to me," she rasps. "But I can't have, because I always thought Mama was dead. I couldn't even remember her from before. How can you lose something you never had?"

"Because you loved her. Even though you couldn't remember her, you loved the person you thought she was."

Orca nods, thinking about it while I gently dry her cheeks with the backs of my knuckles. At last, she sniffles and says, "But she didn't love me. I wasn't wanted. I wasn't worth staying for."

"You were," I insist, cupping her face in my hands. "You're worth more than all the riches in the world, Orca. If your mother can't see that, *she's* in the wrong. She's the one who lost something. She lost *you*. And she has no idea how poor she is because of it."

Orca manages a sad, trembling smile. "You're just saying that to make me feel better."

I stare at her, my heart engulfed in so much passion it terrifies me. "Is that what you think? After all this time, do you really not know how beautiful, how priceless you are to me? God, if only you knew how much I've battled with myself to not want you… To let you go and be free to find yourself. I didn't want you to make the same mistake your mother did, marrying an older man, not knowing what you really wanted. I didn't want you to wake up one day and regret your decision. But now I realize… I can't let you go. From the moment I first met you, I never wanted to leave your side. I love you with every breath I take, Orca. You're like a wildfire I can't put out—you've consumed me, body and soul."

Orca's eyes dart back and forth between mine as I lean in close and capture her lips. She relaxes into my kiss, her hands sliding up around my neck as the world falls away. Just like that, there is no guilt for the past or fear of the future. There is nothing but the feeling of her lips moving over mine, her pulse racing under her skin. The rest of the world doesn't exist.

Orca *is* my world.

I run my fingers through her hair, drowning under the spell of her intoxicating beauty as she pushes deeper into my kiss, drags her fingers down my chest, clutches handfuls of my shirt.

Her tears keep coming, falling onto *my* face as she rolls on top of me, her body pressed against mine. She kisses me like she never has, waves of emotion rushing out of her with every breath. I can feel her unraveling in my arms, the pain as sharp and real to me as if her heart is trapped in my chest, and mine is trapped in hers.

It's the most intimate, vulnerable feeling I've ever experienced.

Orca presses her forehead to mine, out of breath. "Adam, I will wake up every day knowing I'm exactly where I should be—right beside you." She spreads her hand over my chest, over my heart. "I promise I will never stop loving you."

"And I'll never stop loving you," I vow, burning inside with the passion I feel for her at this moment, the passion I will feel for her until the day I die. "I promise."

She sinks back onto her side, her fingers resting on my neck as she watches me. "I have to go back home tomorrow," she says. "I have to make things right with Papa. I realize now how much I must have broken his heart when I left. Just as Mama broke his heart all those years ago."

"Don't blame yourself, Orca. You didn't know."

"But now I do. And you were right, Adam. Nothing matters more than the love of your family. I was too foolish to see that, even a week ago.

But I see it now. And as much as I want to stay here, with you…" She smiles sadly, tracing her fingertip over my jaw. "I want to be with my father. He needs me. And I need him more than I ever knew."

I catch her hand in mine, kissing all five of her fingertips. "I'm proud of you, Orca."

She sniffs, wrapping her arm around me and nuzzling her face to my chest. "Will you fly me back home tomorrow morning?"

I nod, holding her close and breathing her in one last time. "Of course I will."

I READ TO ORCA until she falls asleep in my arms, which is precisely what I was hoping for. She needs a good night's rest after the hellish day she had. It takes a lot of self-control not to let myself doze off beside her, but I know how disastrous it would be if someone found us tangled up in bed together come morning. So after some awkward maneuvering, I sneak my arm out from underneath her without waking her up. I turn off the bedside lamp, leave one last kiss in her hair, and return to my own room.

As I predicted, Jack doesn't come home during the night. His bed is empty when I rise at six thirty and get dressed. Orca's door is still shut, so I head to the kitchen to pour myself a coffee before stepping outside to check the sky.

Mom is seated in one of the deck chairs with her coffee mug. "Looks like it's going to be a beautiful day."

I nod, releasing a slow sigh. "Yeah. Couldn't ask for better visibility."

"You need to fly somewhere?"

"I'm taking Orca back to her island," I say, and the words feel like setting a broken bone. I know it's for the best, but it still hurts like hell. "She asked me to take her back last night."

"Last night when you were in her room?"

I freeze, my gaze darting to her. "I thought you were asleep."

"I woke up sometime after midnight. I saw you two together."

"I was, uh… reading to her. I thought it would help her fall asleep."

Mom tilts her head, giving me a look. "You weren't reading when I walked by the door."

Of course, she probably walked by at the worst possible moment—when Orca was on top of me, tangled up in my arms, kissing me more passionately than she ever had before. But there's no point in denying it. By the look in Mom's eyes, I can tell what she saw last night didn't come as a surprise. She's known for a long time.

I finally let myself say it. "I never stopped loving her, Mom. Not for a second. I tried to convince myself I'd get over her eventually, back when I thought I'd never see her again. I was determined to leave her alone, but when Jack brought her here, I just… couldn't. At first, we argued because I wanted her to go back and make things right with her father, but she was still pretty hurt by the way they parted. Now she knows the truth about what happened with her mom, and… well, I guess it's helped her to see things in a different light."

"And she wants to go back home?" Mom asks.

I nod slowly, looking down into my coffee cup.

"So what are you going to do?"

I shrug one shoulder. "I'm going to fly her out there as soon as she wakes up."

"I mean, what are you going to do about the fact that you're in love with her? And she's in love with you?"

I feel my face heat up as I consider my answer. "I don't know, Mom. There are so many obstacles in our way… I almost wonder if it's the universe keeping us apart. Maybe this just isn't meant to be. Maybe she's meant for someone better."

Mom rises to her feet and crosses the deck to stand beside me. "Adam," she says, tipping my chin up to meet her eyes, "there is no one better for her. I don't think you realize what a wonderful man you are. Any woman would be lucky to have you."

"But I'm so much older than her."

"What does that matter? I've seen you with her—she's like the other half of you; she… lights you up. That kind of love doesn't come along often, Adam. It would be a mistake for you to let her go."

"But what about her father? I can't make her choose between him or me. It wouldn't be right."

Mom tilts her head to the side. "Maybe it doesn't have to be a choice."

"You're saying I can get her father's consent? Befriend him, even?" I mutter a lifeless laugh. "I guess stranger things have happened."

"I can't speak for her father," Mom admits quietly. "But if you truly love her, you have to hold on. You have to trust that everything will work out somehow—maybe not right away, but one day."

Those words are like a lifeline in a stormy black ocean. I want to grab hold of them and never let go.

"You haven't told Jack about any of this," Mom says cautiously. "Have you?"

I shake my head, blowing out a sigh. "No. And he's going to hit the roof when I do."

"Probably. But he'll understand. He's not as much of a powder keg as you think."

I grunt. "Have you met my brother?"

"I gave birth to your brother," Mom contends. "And I watched him fall to pieces when we thought we lost you. He loves you more than anything in this world, Adam. He wouldn't hold this against you."

"I feel like I've betrayed him," I whisper, looking down at the ground. "I know how much he likes Orca—"

"He likes her, sure," Mom says. "But he doesn't *love* her. He's been having fun with her this past week. But look—last night, when Orca was upset about her mother, where did he go?"

"Probably to get drunk with his friends."

"And where were you?"

"With Orca."

Mom nods slowly, letting it sink in. "Jack's still a kid. He jumps from one exciting thing to the next. He's not ready to commit to anyone or anything. He'll get over her in a couple of weeks, mark my words."

"I hope you're right."

Mom squeezes my shoulder. "I'm always right."

That's when the screen door whines open, and Orca steps out onto the deck. "Good morning," she greets us with a tired little smile. She's holding her linen bag of belongings.

"Good morning," Mom says. "I hope you slept well. Adam was telling me that you're leaving us this morning."

She nods. "I want to thank you and Mr. Stevenson so much for your hospitality. It was so kind of you to welcome me into your home like this."

Mom pulls her into a hug. "It was a pleasure to have you, sweetheart. I'm sure we'll see each other again soon." She passes me a knowing look, and it feels like a glimpse of sunlight in the middle of a hurricane.

"Adam?" Orca looks at me. "Are you ready to go?"

"Don't you want to wait and say goodbye to Jack?"

She shakes her head. "I left him a note. I know he'll be upset and try to talk me into staying, and… I think it will be better this way."

Mom nods, giving her a half-hearted smile. "Perhaps you're right."

Jack will raise holy hell when he finds out I took Orca back home while he was out. But he could have stuck around last night if he wanted to be here for her.

Orca says goodbye to Mom, asks her to say goodbye to Dad for her, and heads for my truck. I turn to follow her, but Mom stops me with a hand on my arm and a concerned look in her eyes. "I want you to talk to your brother about this."

"I will," I promise. "As soon as I get back."

THE LAST KISS

orca

The sun is glorious on our drive to the port—a cheerful contrast to the weight of sorrow bearing down on my heart.

I'm ready to go back home. To wrap my arms around Papa and tell him how much I love him, how much I missed him. But at the same time, I want to stay here with Adam forever.

I watch him drive, trying to soak in every detail of him. Morning sunlight spills through the windshield to crest his fingers and chisel the cords of muscle in his arms. We both remain silent until we arrive at the port.

Adam parks the truck and says, "My keys are inside."

I've never been in his hangar before. It's strange to see a floatplane parked inside a building, not docked in the water or soaring through the sky.

"Is this the one you crashed?" I ask, peering up at the aircraft as Adam searches his workbench for the keys to his other plane.

"Yeah, I've been working on fixing her up. Pretty soon, she'll be ready to fly again. Just a few last minor adjustments… and I'm thinking of giving her a new paint job."

"What color will you make it?"

"I don't know. What color do *you* think it should be?"

"Hmm…" I ponder my answer, walking over to the workbench. "I think… yellow."

"Yellow?"

"Yes."

Adam laughs under his breath.

"What? Yellow is cheerful."

He cocks his head to the side as he studies the plane, imagining it. "Well, if it would make you smile…"

I don't care what color he chooses. This plane will be my favorite sight no matter what because it will be the vessel that carries Adam back to me when I have returned to my island and there is an ocean between us again.

"I heard you talking to your mom about… the future," I say gently. "I know it's not going to be easy to convince Papa to let me be with you. But I think between the two of us, we *can* change his mind. It may take a while, but I'm willing to wait if you are."

Adam takes my hands in his, looking into my eyes. "I would wait forever for you, Orca. But I don't want to make you choose between your father and me. I don't want you to change your life, everything you know and love—"

"I won't have to. Papa will love you once he gets to know you. I'm sure you'll be great friends one day." I press a hopeful smile onto my lips. "You could come live on the island."

"At the lighthouse?" Adam raises an eyebrow. "I don't think your father will ever like me *that* much."

I laugh, shaking my head. "We can live next door. You can build me a cottage by the sea, like Hero and Leander—in my version of the story. You can lay the stones and whitewash the wood. I can fill the rooms with wildflowers and seashells, and we can argue about paint colors and curtains and silly things like that. You can fly back to the mainland to work… or I can teach you how to live without money."

Adam smiles as he imagines this fairytale future that could be ours.

"We can get married," I whisper, reaching up to spread one hand over his heart. "We can share the same name, the same life. We can live in that world you wrote about—a world built just for the two of us." I smile, tracing my finger over his chest. "Well, maybe *more* than just the two of us… someday."

Adam frowns like he doesn't quite understand. "What do you mean?"

I blush. "I mean I want to make babies with you, Adam Stevenson."

He smiles and draws me closer, his hands curling at my waist. "Oh yeah? How many?"

"As many as you want."

"Hmm. How about two?"

I grin. "A boy and a girl."

"A boy needs a brother."

"Well, a girl needs a sister," I argue. "So I suppose we'll have two girls and two boys. You'll have to make a lot of love with me, Adam."

He murmurs a laugh, leaning in to kiss the top of my head. "God, Orca. I want to spend the rest of my life with you. I'd marry you today if I could."

"Well, technically, you could. I'm eighteen now. I don't need my father's consent. We could get married, and then you could take me back home. That way, Papa would *have* to get used to you."

Adam seems amused by the idea but shakes his head. "I would never marry you without your father's permission. It wouldn't be right."

"I know you wouldn't. If you did, you wouldn't be the man I know you to be. But you *could* talk to Papa, couldn't you? Today?"

"I'm not sure today would be the best time…"

"Oh, please, Adam. He'll be grateful to you for bringing me back. I'm sure he'll listen to what you have to say."

Adam falls silent for a moment, then nods. "All right. I'll speak with him."

"Thank you." I grasp a handful of his shirt and gently pull him down to my level. "Thank you, my love." I take his face in my hands and kiss him.

It's the last time we'll be alone together for a while, and somehow just knowing that makes this last moment more fragile and precious.

Our lips part softly for each other, familiar with the rhythm of this dance. Adam holds me with sweet tenderness, as though I am a mere vapor that could vanish away. I interlace my fingers behind his neck to remind him that I am not going anywhere, not yet. He can take his time; he can love me slowly.

In one effortless motion, Adam lifts me off my feet. I am weightless in his arms—my fingers clutching his shoulders, my legs wrapped around him.

He never stops kissing me; I never stop kissing him. He sets me on the workbench, shoving tools aside with a graceless sweep of his hand. I laugh, surprised by his bold, hot-blooded urgency. I tasted a glimpse of it last night in bed; I felt the warmth of a fire burning under his skin, singing my name. Now that fire is spilling out of him, breaking free in the form of kisses, frantic kisses—racing down my neck and over my collarbone as I run my fingers through his hair, my body curling into him. He whispers my name, his breath trembling and warm against my neck. An indescribable feeling floods me like liquid gold, making my heart swell with love for him.

Suddenly, the door bursts open.

I look up just in time to see Jack storm into the hangar, murder in his eyes.

"What the hell do you think you're doing?!"

WORLD WAR 3

jack

I wake up to a hammer knocking against my head.

BANG, BANG, BANG.

When I open my eyes, I find myself sprawled across the front seat of my Mustang, my head tipped against the driver's window. My neck is sore, and there's an empty bottle of Heineken in my cup holder.

That's when it all comes back to me: how I spent last night at Matt's house with a couple of other guys from school. Would I rather have been out having a hot date with Orca? Hell yes. But thanks to Adam, she was all upset last night. Shut herself inside her room and wouldn't even let me talk to her. Just told me to go away. And then Mom was all, "Leave her alone," and Adam kept glaring at me like I was some kind of villain.

I couldn't take it anymore. If I stuck around the house for a minute longer, I knew I'd explode. So instead, I spent the night getting drunk with my buddies. I must have passed out around two o'clock in the morning, but now I awaken to the sound of Matt knocking on my car door.

I twist around in my seat and put the window down.

"What time is it?" I groan, rubbing a hand over my face.

"Seven."

"What the hell, Matt? I thought you told me to sleep it off."

"Yeah, well, my dad's giving me shit about your car sitting in the middle of the driveway. He needs to go to work." Matt gestures across the driveway. "You can pull over there and go back to sleep, man."

I shake my head, reaching for my keys. "Nah, I need my bed."

"You good to drive?"

I pass him the empty beer bottle through the window. "I am now."

Matt laughs and slaps my shoulder. "Later, Stevenson."

On the drive home, I wonder how Orca is doing. Maybe a good night's sleep was all she needed to put yesterday behind her. Even though my head is splitting, I'm still going to take her out today. I want to make her laugh and forget about her troubles. Maybe I can talk Dad into letting me test-drive another boat, and this time I can bring Orca farther up the coast. We can disappear all day, go whale-watching or swimming, or lie in the sun and imagine we're sailing around the world like we talked about. Maybe we'll stay out all night and watch the stars together, and when the moment is right, I'll kiss her.

Maybe she'll kiss me back this time.

When I pull into the driveway, I notice that Adam's truck is gone. Hopefully he hasn't taken Orca to meet some new not-dead relative she didn't know she had. Inside, the house is quiet—except for the drone of the vacuum cleaner coming from Mom and Dad's room. I wander down the hallway and knock softly on the guest room door.

"Orca? You awake?"

Nothing but silence. I shoulder open the door and step inside. The room is empty, sunlight peeking through the curtains. I'm about to head back to the kitchen when I notice something strangely familiar lying on her bed.

Adam's journal. That black leather one I always used to see him carrying around.

What's Orca doing with it?

I pick it up and take a closer look to see if it's just similar to Adam's. But no, that's definitely his handwriting. Looks like a bunch of scribblings about philosophy and science, with some gibberish mixed in. Wasn't he teaching himself Latin for a while? That must be what it is—Latin. Still doesn't explain why Orca has it on her bed.

I'm about to close the journal when something falls out. A tiny pink flower pressed thin as paper.

That's weird.

I frown, reading what's written on that page. It almost looks like a poem.

> Untouchable beauty
> Are you real or fantasy?
> Lost to the world, yet found
> to that which really matters
>
> Not a word passes your lips that isn't
> Honesty
> Yet all I feel in the presence of your wild soul is
> Mystery
> All I feel is my own soul coming undone

"What the hell?" I murmur under my breath, turning the page to read the rest. That's when I see something even stranger.

A letter to Orca.

From Adam.

Orca,

I wish a world existed (in another universe, maybe) where only we two lived. It would be a world with nothing but ocean and this one little island. I wish the "Otherworld" didn't exist, not so that you didn't long to see it—but so that I didn't have to belong there. I don't belong there. I belong with you. And you don't belong there, either. We're not made for this world, you and I. We're made for each other.

Orca, I've fallen in love with you. I can't remember when I started to feel this way about you. I was in over my head before I knew it had begun. And now, I never want to leave you. I want to wake each morning to the sound of your voice; I want to hear every idea you have about philosophy and science and life. I want to be with you every day, every hour, every minute.

I know we can't. I know there's the matter of your father and your life on the island. The last thing I want to do is ruin that. But I have to tell you the truth. I have to tell you what a beautiful and unique person you are. Your innocence inspires me to make this world a better place... if only a small corner of it, just for you. I almost don't want you to see the Otherworld, because it is so flawed and polluted, and you deserve a perfect world. Because you are perfection itself.

I, on the other hand, am so far from perfect. It's probably a good thing that we can't be together. If we were, I would feel so unworthy of your goodness, your grace, your purity of spirit. I cherish those things about you—and so, like the moral scientist, I must leave you wild and free, where you belong... however much I may want to bring you into my world and make you my own.

I love you, Orca Monroe.

And that's why I'm letting you go.

No way.

No.

Goddamn.

Way.

My stomach plummets as I stare at those words at the bottom of the page, scrawled in my brother's unmistakable handwriting.

I love you, Orca Monroe.

I scan the page for any indication of when it was written. And sure enough, smart-ass Adam was dumb enough to write the date in the top corner of the entry.

06/21/97

That was the morning I flew out to Orca's island to bring Adam back home. The first time I saw her. I remember the sun in her hair. The way Adam hugged her before we left. The way she cried as she watched him go.

It hits me like a kick in the balls.

He's been in love with her this whole time.

He's been lying to me this whole time.

That first night he came back home, I asked him if anything had happened between him and Orca. And he looked at me like I was crazy to think so. He said, "No. Nothing happened."

When, earlier that very same day, he'd written her this letter.

My fingers tighten around the journal, crushing the edges of the pages. Burning ropes of jealousy coil around my chest as memories from the past week come racing back with new meaning.

All those looks I caught between him and her.

All those trips to track down her relatives.

The smudge on Orca's cheek that morning she was under the truck with Adam.

The way Adam lectured me after he saw us together on the boat.

The way Orca shies away every time I try to kiss her.

Like she's in love with someone else.

My brother.

I slam the journal shut, storming down the hallway and across the house to my parents' bedroom. Mom is vacuuming the floor, the power cord looped over her arm.

"Where's Adam?!"

Mom looks up, turning off the vacuum when she sees the murderous look on my face. "What's the matter?"

"Where's Adam?"

She hesitates, looking like she'd do anything not to answer that question. "He… took Orca home."

"*What?*"

"She wanted to go back—"

"You mean he took her without even letting her say goodbye to me?"

Mom sighs, parking the vacuum and crossing the room to put her hand on my shoulder. "You weren't here, Jack. You were off partying with your friends."

"No, don't give me that bullshit. I know what this is. This is *Adam*. He's wanted to take her back since day one. Now he waits till my back is turned and flies her home just to spit in my face—"

"That's enough," Mom snaps. "Orca is the one who asked him to take her. She would have said goodbye to you if you'd been here. Don't be angry with your brother—"

"Oh, my brother is always the goddamn saint around here, isn't he?" I roar, making Mom bristle. "If you knew what he did to me, you wouldn't be kissing the ground he walks on!"

"What are you talking about?"

I don't answer that one. I'm too angry. I head for the front door, shoving the journal into my jacket pocket.

"Jack, don't go down there! They'll be gone by now."

Too late. I'm already out the door.

I get back in my car and stab the key into the ignition, my hands shaking. I'm breathing fire the whole drive to the port. Knuckles white as I hold the steering wheel in a death grip.

I spot his truck the second I pull into the parking lot. Then I see his plane—docked right where it usually is.

They haven't left yet.

I swing my car to a stop and get out, my head on a swivel. I don't see them anywhere. The docks are empty and so is the cockpit of Adam's plane. I stride up to his hangar, my heart racing in my chest.

Liar, cheater, dirtbag…

All those words are ready to burst out of my mouth as I reach for the doorknob—

I stop dead in my tracks when I see them through the window.

My stomach drops.

Time slows to a crawl.

It's my worst nightmare.

She's sitting on his workbench, and he's kissing her like I've never seen him kiss any woman before. Her legs are wrapped around him, and her fingers are moving through his hair, and she's devouring his lips like she wants to rip his clothes off right here and now.

For a moment, I am frozen in place—jealousy tearing through my chest as I finally see my brother for what he really is:

My rival.

My enemy.

The ropes snap—three, two, one. Suddenly I'm not a man, I'm a monster. Something primal, wild, savage. Anger takes over my whole body in seconds, swallows me up like quicksand, like fire, like the end of the world.

I kick open the door.

"What the hell do you think you're doing?!"

Adam and Orca break apart, whirling to face me. Orca's eyes widen with shock.

Adam takes a step forward, bracing himself like he's about to get hit by a bulldozer. "Jack, listen. It's not what you—"

"So this is what you've been doing behind my back?" I rage, my blood boiling as I storm across the hangar. "I can't believe you—"

Orca jumps off the workbench, throwing herself between us. "Jack! Jack, stop! Don't be angry with him."

"I'm angry with *both* of you," I seethe, my fingers curling into fists. "What the hell kind of game have you been playing with me, Orca?"

"I haven't been playing any game—"

"Don't give me that shit! You may be naive, Orca, but you're not stupid. You made me think you were into me, you let me think I had a chance, and all along, you're screwing around with my brother when I'm not looking? You know, there's a name for girls like you—"

Adam lunges forward, grabbing me by the shirt and shoving me backward. His voice comes out as a throaty growl. "Don't you talk to her like that."

"Oh, look at you, the big hero," I fire back. "Always swooping in to rescue Orca from *danger*. Is that how you made her fall for you? Well, she wouldn't want you if she knew what a coward you really are."

A muscle twitches in Adam's jaw, but he doesn't defend himself. He releases my shirt with a jolt and says, "You're out of line, Jack. Go home. We'll talk about this later."

"Oh, no, we won't. We'll talk about it *now*." I rip the journal out of my pocket and slam it into Adam's chest.

He staggers back, staring at the book in his hands like it's a time bomb.

"I found your letter to her. Remember? The one you wrote back when 'nothing happened' between you two on the island?"

The color drains from Adam's face as he stares at the journal. "I've… been meaning to talk to you about this for a while."

"Sure," I snap. "You only had a hundred opportunities to say something! But I guess it was more fun to watch me make a fool of myself, huh?"

"I'm sorry I didn't say anything sooner. I should have. But for god's sake, *you* should have been smart enough to take a hint."

"Oh, so it's my fault? Of course. Everything is *always* my fault, never yours—"

"Orca hasn't deceived you," Adam bursts out, his eyes blazing. "You're the one who's been deceiving *yourself.* Orca thought you were showing her the world because you cared about her, not because you hoped to get anything out of it."

"I *do* care about her."

"No, you don't," Adam shoots back. "If you really cared, you wouldn't be trying to change her just to suit yourself. You wouldn't ask her to give up her life and her father and everything she's ever known."

"And if *you* really cared about her, you wouldn't be taking her back to that island to be a prisoner again! If you loved her, you'd want her to stay."

Adam shakes his head. "That's not love, Jack. That's selfishness. Have you ever wondered why it never lasts with any of those girls you've been with? Because all you care about is what you can get out of them."

A flash of rage bolts through me, and *that's it*—

"You bastard."

I punch him in the face.

Adam stumbles backward, his hand flying up to his jaw. For a second, I can't believe what I just did.

Orca screams Adam's name, and he pushes her back, out of the way.

I charge at him, swinging for his face—but he grabs me by the shoulders and sends me flying across the room. I crash into the workbench, slamming my face on the edge. Tools clatter to the cement floor. I taste blood on my lips as I straighten up, adrenaline firing through my veins.

I lunge for Adam again, but he blocks my punch, grabs my forearm.

Damn, he's strong—

He drives me back, back, back until I slam into the metal wall with a *thud.* I go for his ribs, but he blocks his free arm down and seizes my other wrist.

"STOP IT!" he roars into my face, nailing my hands to the wall over my head.

He doesn't want to hurt me; I can see it in his eyes. But I haven't even *begun* to hurt him. I struggle under his hold, fighting to get my hands back. Adam doesn't budge, solid as a rock. He's got about forty pounds on me and could do this all day.

"Jack—"

I kick him hard in the shin.

"AGH!"

It's enough to weaken his hold for that one second.

And that's all I need.

With a roar of rage, I jump on his back and tackle him to the ground. We both crash to the cement, rolling over fallen tools as we grapple on the floor. I sputter cusses, struggling to get on top of Adam as he tries to wrestle me into submission.

I hear Orca shouting my name, but I can't stop. I feel like an animal, like I could tear him apart right now and enjoy every second of it. There is nothing but this moment. Blood in my mouth, sweat in my eyes. A monster coming alive under my skin.

I drive my fist into Adam's side, and he starts coughing violently, cradling his ribs.

His broken ribs.

I feel a jolt of regret when I realize what I just did—but it's too late.

Adam's fist slams into my stomach.

Oh, sweet Jesus.

I roll off him, gripping my abdomen as I coil up on the floor, shock waves of pain rocking through me. Paired with my hangover, it's the worst feeling in the world. My head is pounding, my body is shuddering, and I can't breathe—I feel like I'm going to throw up.

"Stop it, both of you!" Orca screams. "Just stop it!"

I look up to find her red-faced and crying.

"How could you?" she yells at me, her voice shredding. "Adam's your brother, not your enemy!"

For a stunned moment, I stare at her, gripping my stomach with one hand, gasping for breath.

Adam crawls to his feet, steadying himself on the workbench. He wipes his bloody lip with the back of his hand and says, "Come on, Orca. Let's go." Without a backward glance, he limps toward the door, wincing with every step.

Orca rushes forward to take his arm, helping him to the door. But before she leaves the hangar, she pauses and looks over her shoulder at me—a smoking battlefield in her eyes. "I thought you were better than this, Jack."

And with that, she walks out.

HOME

orca

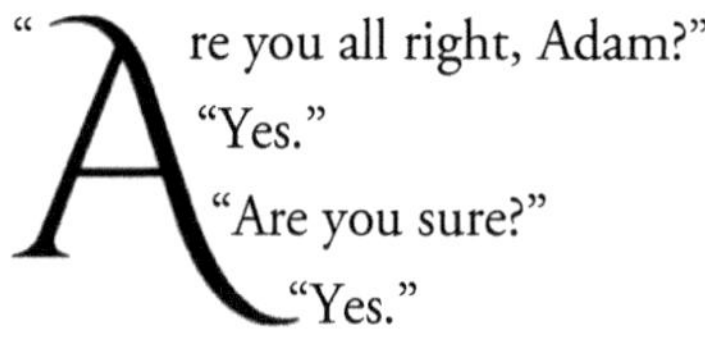

"Are you all right, Adam?"

"Yes."

"Are you sure?"

"Yes."

"You're holding your ribs."

"I'm fine." Adam winces in pain as he limps through the walkaround, slides into the pilot's seat and pulls the door shut behind him. He sighs, tipping his head back against the seat. "My brother sure knows how to hit you where it hurts."

A wave of regret swells through me. "Oh, Adam, I'm so sorry."

"Don't be. It's not your fault."

"But maybe Jack is right. Maybe I did encourage him without meaning to—"

"Orca." He takes my hand firmly. "You did nothing wrong. If anyone is to blame, it's me."

Adam falls silent as he completes the instrument check, and I keep my lips sealed, letting him concentrate. I don't speak until a few minutes later when the plane is rumbling smoothly, propeller spinning as the engine warms up.

"I don't know how I forgot your journal on the bed," I say softly, pressing my eyes shut. "If only I'd been more careful."

"You're not to blame," Adam insists, handing me a set of headphones. "I'm just sorry you had to see us fight."

"Surely grown men can settle their differences without fists."

Adam casts me a look. "I didn't throw the first punch, Orca."

"I know. I watched you; I saw you trying to make him stop. It just… broke my heart to see you two at each other's throats like that."

Adam nods, gently rubbing his swollen jaw. "It certainly wasn't how I wanted Jack to find out."

My heart aches as I watch Adam's hands move over the instruments. Within moments, we are gliding across the water to the widest part of the harbor. After a brief communication through his headset, Adam reaches for the throttle and pushes the lever. The aircraft surges forward, sending up white spray around the floats as beams of bright morning sunlight flash between the spinning propeller blades. We lift gracefully into the sky, and I watch the Otherworld shrink smaller and smaller behind us.

Adam doesn't say a word to me during the whole flight to my island; he just focuses on piloting, frowning intently at the skies ahead. I couldn't speak even if I wanted to—not with my mind still reeling from the brutality I witnessed in the hangar.

Adam said it wasn't my fault, but I know it was. When I go back to the beginning, all this conflict started with me. If I'd never gone to the Otherworld in the first place, Adam and Jack would still be best friends. Inseparable.

I remember the day I watched them embrace on the sunny hillside at the lighthouse—Jack in tears as he gripped fistfuls of his brother's shirt. Those hands couldn't hold Adam tightly enough back then. Now they are bloody and bruised from hitting him.

And it is all my fault.

A tear slips down my cheek as I gaze at the ocean waves shimmering far below us.

I think of the butterfly effect. How something small and seemingly insignificant can spark a sequence of events that lead to a massive disaster.

Chaos.

It is no theory—it's real.

But I don't know which of us is the butterfly.

Was it me when I left the lighthouse?

Or was it Jack when he came to take me to the Otherworld?

Or was it Adam when he first crashed his plane in our waters?

Or was it Papa when he decided to keep me on the island?

Or was it Mama when she left us?

Perhaps we are all butterflies, and the world is our hurricane.

Sooner than I expected, the island comes into view. It looks so small from this perspective—a pocket-sized forest floating on a sea of moving glass. Adam makes a wide turn, tipping the left wing down as we drop altitude. That's when I see the lighthouse standing resolutely on the northernmost tip of our island.

Oh, Papa.

My heart gives a sharp pang of remorse as I remember the day I left and the cross words that passed between Papa and me. I wish I could go back and do it all differently.

We descend, coming to land atop the waves. A spray of whitewater whooshes up around the floats, and we begin to rock and sway on the moving tide. Adam expertly guides the plane to shore, shutting off the engine before we get too close. As we come to a complete stop abreast of the flat gray beach, I look up and see Papa emerge from the lighthouse.

"Perhaps now isn't the right time to speak with my father," I say, turning to lay my hand on Adam's arm. "You should get home and put some ice on that bruise."

Adam shakes his head. "You think just because I got hit a few times, I'd let that stop me?"

"I know you wouldn't," I whisper, cupping his face in my hand. "And I love you for it. But I think I should prepare Papa for this conversation. We might only have one chance to get it right. Just… give me a few days with him."

Adam nods slowly, kissing my forehead. "All right. I'll come back in a few days."

In truth, I never want him to leave my side. But go he must—for however short a time. We both have conflicts to resolve and bonds to rebuild.

I capture Adam's lips in one last kiss, savoring our final moment together. Then I pull myself away. My heart wrenches as I climb down the ladder and step out onto the plane's starboard float, splashing through knee-deep seawater and coming to a stop on the hard gray sand.

Papa is waiting at the top of the grassy knoll, shielding his eyes from the rising sun as he squints at me, as if he can't quite believe I am real.

Oh, Papa.

I race across the beach toward the lighthouse, dodging knotted branches of driftwood as the ground rushes under my feet. When I reach the top of the hill, Papa's arms are open for me. I crash into him and hold him tight, my voice breaking through sobs to beg his forgiveness.

"I'm so sorry, Papa… please forgive me… please…"

He embraces me with a fiercer love than I have ever felt before. And I don't need to hear what he says in reply to my desperate apologies. There is forgiveness in his arms—a fountain of it, pouring from his heart and into mine. He kisses the top of my head as I bury my face in his chest and cry.

I CAN'T DECIDE who is happier to have me back: Papa or Lucius. From the moment I walk through the front door, the sandy mongrel is slathering me in affection, yipping ecstatically—as though he wasn't sure he'd ever see me again. I collapse to my knees and throw my arms around his neck.

Poor, sweet Lucius. He had no way of knowing that I had always intended to come back.

It feels surreal to be home—almost as though the Otherworld was just a startlingly colorful dream that I've awoken from. Nothing has changed in my absence. Papa has kept the house neat and tidy, but there is a lingering sense of loneliness in the crackling fire and the empty rooms, as though everything has been waiting for my return.

It's enough to make me throw my arms around Papa again. "I missed you," I rasp, hugging him tight and breathing in his scent. Salt and sea and earth, my shelter from the storm.

"Oh, my dear girl," Papa says. "I thought you'd never come back to me."

I swallow the ache in my throat, looking up into his face. "I'm so sorry for the way we parted. I realize now how much it must have hurt you to go through that kind of pain all over again."

Papa frowns at me. "Again? What do you mean?"

"I ran away from you," I whisper, blinking back tears. "The same way Mama ran away from you."

He stiffens, his face going pale as a sheet, his gray eyes darting back and forth as he searches for something to say. "I… but—"

"Papa, I saw her. Yesterday. She's living in Seattle, at the top of a skyscraper. She's married and working at a magazine. She wears the ugliest shoes." A pained laugh escapes me, new tears blurring my vision. "Oh, Papa, why didn't you tell me? Was it just too painful for you to talk about?"

"No," Papa says, the sorrow in his eyes so deep it hurts just to look at him. "I didn't tell you because I didn't want it to change the way you felt about yourself." He manages a sad little half-smile, cupping my chin in his hand. "You are such a beautiful, smart, strong young woman. All I've ever wanted was for you to feel loved. Cherished. Priceless. Because that's what you are, my dear girl. When your mother left you behind, she… she made such a mistake. I know it was my fault. I could have been a better husband to her—"

"No, Papa, it wasn't your fault. Mama isn't the right sort of woman for you. She's… empty. That's what I saw when I sat there in her beautiful, cold apartment. She said she had everything she could ever want, but… I could see she had nothing. Nothing that matters."

Papa regards me with a curious look, then leans down to kiss the top of my head. "You are wise beyond your years, Orca."

I murmur a laugh, squeezing his hand. "Only because you're the greatest teacher."

"No," Papa says. "Experience is the greatest teacher. And that's what I've deprived you of, keeping you here. The experience of life—*real* life, with friendships and first love and heartbreak and loss. For so long, I've tried to protect you from all of that. But it wasn't fair of me. And when you left..." He presses his eyes shut, taking a steadying breath. "When you left, I realized that I hadn't learned my lesson with your mother. The more I held onto her, the more she wanted to leave me. And without knowing it, I made the same mistake with you."

I sniff, swiping a rogue tear off my cheek. "I learned something, too, in my time away. I realized how much I need you—and the island and the lighthouse and Lucius and our life here. All of it is so beautiful, so special. I never knew it before. I always imagined the Otherworld to be some sort of mysterious paradise. I always wondered if I belonged there... but I don't. I belong here." I give Papa a weary smile. "You're my home. You always will be."

Papa blinks the tears away from his eyes, pulling me into another long hug. "Thank you, Orca," he rasps into my hair. "Thank you for coming back to me."

Affectionate Friends

jack

As if my hangover wasn't bad enough, I now have the added pleasure of a split lip and the throbbing pain of Adam's uppercut still aching in my stomach.

I head back home to get myself cleaned up, but of course, Mom is right there in the kitchen when I walk through the front door.

Just my luck.

She rushes over when she sees the blood on my jaw. "Jack, what happened? What is this?"

I swat her hand away. "It's nothing. Leave me alone."

"Did you fight with your brother?"

"I don't want to talk about it—"

She grabs my arm, stopping me in my tracks. "Don't you walk away from me, Jack. I want to know what happened."

I look down at the floor, my jaw clenched. "Why don't you ask Adam? You always like his side of the story better than mine."

Mom stares at me, her gaze as sharp as a razor. "I know you're feeling let down right now—"

"You don't know what I'm feeling!" I burst out, yanking my arm out of Mom's grasp. "You don't know what it's like to have a brother who pretends he's your best friend, but meanwhile he goes and sticks a knife in your back! He deserved worse than a punch in the face."

"Jack," Mom gasps, her eyes blazing with holy hellfire, "how could you do such a thing?"

"You don't know what he did—"

"Yes, I *do* know what he did. And he should have spoken up sooner. But that's no excuse to punch your brother in the face—"

"You knew about Orca?" I stare at her, a pit of ice in my stomach. "How long have you known?"

Mom hesitates, her gaze shifting. "I've known there was something between them for a while. Since the day Adam came back from her island."

I scoff. "Unbelievable. And you didn't think to tell me?"

"I was giving him a chance to tell you himself—"

"Does Dad know? Am I the one moron you all play for a fool?!"

"No. Your father doesn't know about any of it."

"Because you kept Adam's dirty little secret for him, huh?" I shake my head, muttering a bitter laugh. "He's always been your favorite. You're always taking his side—"

"That's a lie," Mom snaps. "I would be saying the same thing if it were the other way around! This isn't about favorites. It's about right and wrong."

"Right and wrong? I think you'd better talk to your other son about right and wrong—"

"Adam isn't the one who can't control his temper," Mom argues, crossing her arms over her chest. "He never would have laid a finger on you if you hadn't started it."

"I never would have started it if *he* hadn't betrayed me!" I roar, slamming my hand on the kitchen table. My vision blurs with hot, angry tears as I lower my voice. "He's the one who *started* it, Mom. He's a lying, cheating bastard. And I'll never forgive him as long as I live."

Mom stares at me like I just drove a knife through her chest. She shakes her head, tears glossing in her eyes. "You break my heart, Jackie," she whispers. "You both break my heart."

I turn away from her and storm down the hallway, shutting myself in the bathroom.

The first thing I do is rifle through the medicine cabinet for a bottle of aspirin. I shake four pills into my hand, swallow them, and turn the shower on as cold as it goes. As I tear my shirt off, I catch a glimpse of myself in the mirror. God, I look like hell. Dark circles under my eyes, a smear of dried blood on my jaw, and a nasty bruise darkening my abs where Adam punched me.

He could have done worse. After I slugged him in the face, I half-expected him to ground and pound me. But instead, he was all defense, just trying to make me stop. He didn't want to hurt me, I could tell. And that makes me hate him even more.

Because I wanted to hurt *him*. I enjoyed making him suffer.

It was payback.

But it was wrong.

I know that, deep down.

And I'm ashamed of myself.

MY HEAD IS STILL SPLITTING when I get out of the ice-cold shower and go to my room for a fresh T-shirt. As I walk through the door, I see something that wasn't there last night: a folded square of paper on my pillow with my name written across the front.

I sit on the edge of my bed and unfold the note.

Dear Jack,

I hope you won't be too disappointed when you find this letter. But it's time for me to go back home. Perhaps it's better that we part ways without saying goodbye. This way, I can remember our last happy memory together: dancing to Bryan Adams on top of that yacht you shined up for me.

I want to thank you for showing me the world and giving me so many wonderful memories. You've been such a good friend to me. Ever since that night I first talked to you on the phone, I felt like you knew my soul. You understood my feelings in a way no one else ever has. I treasure your friendship, Jack. And the last thing I want to do is hurt you, but I need to be honest with you.

Adam is the only man I could ever love. I think you already knew that deep down inside. I tried to tell you a few days ago, but you wouldn't listen. I know you didn't want to hear it then, and you probably don't want to hear it now. But it wouldn't be fair if I let you believe a lie.

The world is waiting for you, Jack Stevenson. Go see those mountains, those deserts. I know you'll find yourself somewhere along the way. And someday, you'll meet someone and fall in love with her, and she'll fall in love with you, and she will never, ever let you go.

Thank you for giving me the world and making my dreams come true.

I'll never forget you, Superman.

Your affectionate friend,
Orca

I press my eyes shut, but it's too late—hot tears fall onto the page, smudging her words. *God, it hurts.* Part of me wants to crunch up the letter and throw it away. But it's impossible to be angry at Orca for telling the truth.

I'm not angry at her.

I'm angry at *myself.*

All I can think about is the way she looked after I fought with Adam. The shock and heartbreak twisted on her face. *I thought you were better than this, Jack.*

So much for her last memory of me being a good one.

Maybe she's right.

Maybe deep down, I always knew she loved Adam.

Maybe that's why I was so desperate to make her fall for *me.* Because I didn't want to lose to my brother.

Maybe that's all Orca and I ever were—affectionate friends.

I SHOW UP LATE FOR WORK, but at least this time, I have a good excuse. I find Dad in the marina office, sitting behind the cluttered desk, talking on the phone with someone. As soon as I walk through the door, he says, "He just got here. I'll call you later." And he hangs up.

Of course, Mom would call Dad and tell him everything that happened. Of course, she would pass him the baton on this whole shitshow— the baton to beat me with, that is.

I stand in the doorway with my arms crossed over my chest, waiting to be read the riot act. But Dad only nods toward my split lip.

"Did Adam give you that?"

"Yeah," I say, yanking my shirt up to reveal my bruised abs. "And this."

Dad studies me, his gaze unwavering. "I heard you gave him worse."

"I hope so," I fire back, knowing I'm poking a snake here—but I don't give a damn. "He deserved it, that's for sure."

"So you're not sorry."

"No, sir. I'm *not* sorry."

Dad watches me for a long moment, his gaze drilling into mine.

"You gonna whoop my ass?"

He sighs, gets to his feet, and slowly paces to the other end of the office. "No."

I'm stunned. Why is he not even angry about this? Does he agree with me? Somehow, the possibility of Dad taking my side is more disappointing than getting my ass whooped.

"You're not a child anymore, Jack. As you so often like to remind me."

I stare at him, not sure how to respond. He's being so weird. So unlike Dad, who yells at me for every little thing I do wrong.

"Do you know what Adam did?"

Dad nods slowly. "Yes."

"All this time, he's been keeping the truth from me. It would've been the easiest thing in the world to tell me what was going on with him and Orca, but instead he had to let me make a fool of myself. He saw how things were between me and her, but did he say anything? No, he just let me stay in the dark and let *Orca* think it was A-okay for her to be going out with me while he screwed around with her behind my back!"

Dad remains silent, staring out the dusty window that overlooks the harbor.

"I found out this morning," I continue, my voice rough with bottled-up rage. "And when I went to confront him about it, I walked in on the two of them making out."

"And you responded by beating him up?"

"How would you *expect* me to respond?"

"Like a man."

Somehow, that hits me harder than Adam's uppercut.

Dad turns around to face me, his voice low and serious. "You want to prove you're no longer a child, Jack? You can start by apologizing to your brother."

"Apologize? To *him*?"

"Since you missed your opportunity to be a man earlier."

"But Adam—"

"I don't care what Adam did!" Dad booms, stepping closer. "He's your brother. Your *blood*. Now, I don't know all the details of what happened with this Orca girl, but it seems to me like the whole thing is one big misunderstanding. When you're done with work today, I want you to talk to your brother and sort this thing out like grown men. Is that clear?"

I stare at him, my fists clenched at my sides.

"I said, is that clear?"

"Yeah. Clear as day." I turn away sharply and march back to the door. "What do you want me to work on?"

Dad hesitates before answering, "Got a dozen boats out there that need cleaning."

Of course.

I'm sore just thinking about it. "Fine. I'll get started right away." I turn to leave the office, but Dad stops me.

"Jack."

I freeze, looking over my shoulder at him. The shadow of grief in his eyes startles me more than his rage ever could. It cuts me down to size without a single word. It proves that all he sees when he looks at me is a little boy who can't control his temper.

"While you're out there, I want you to do some thinking. Not about what Adam did wrong, but what *you* did wrong… and how you're going to fix it. Understood?"

I clench my jaw, knuckles white around the doorjamb. "Yes, sir."

KHAOS

adam

"I can't believe Jack did this to you." Mom sighs, handing me a bag of crushed ice wrapped in a dishcloth. "He was so angry when he left to find you and Orca, but I never thought he would do something like this…"

I lean against the refrigerator, gently pressing the compress to my swollen face. "Ow, damn it."

Mom winces *for* me. "Are you all right, sweetheart? Why are you holding your side?"

"Because Jack punched my broken ribs."

Mom sucks in a sharp breath. "Oh, my god—"

"I'm fine," I insist. "Just… sore."

Mom leans on the counter with her face in her hands. There's a moment of silence; then her shoulders start trembling with silent sobs.

"Don't cry, Mom," I say, putting an arm around her.

"I don't understand you boys." She sniffs, her voice thick with tears. "I must have failed miserably as a mother—"

"Oh, stop. You're the best mother in the world. All my life, I've watched you sacrifice for Jack and me. You've always taught us to do the right thing."

"Then how can you fight with each other? How can Jack, of all people—"

"It's my fault. I'm the one who should have been honest with him from the very beginning." I sigh, leaning into the ice pack. "Don't worry about it, Mom. I'll make things right."

WHILE JACK IS AT WORK, I gather some stuff from our room. A blanket, a pillow, a fresh change of clothes, and a couple of books. I inform Mom that I'll be sleeping at my hangar until Jack cools off. She tries to talk me out of it, but I know it's for the best.

I miss the times when our fights were stupid and small. When Jack was little and would forgive me in a heartbeat. Like that time when I was fifteen and he caught me kissing my first girlfriend behind the barn. I was so mad when he stumbled out from his hiding place and started laughing his head off. I yelled at him and called him a snot-nosed brat, which made him run off and lock himself in our room with a "keep out" sign taped to the door. I apologized through the crack and then took him out to the diner and bought him chocolate chip pancakes, and everything was okay again.

But Jack isn't five years old anymore. It will take much more than a simple "sorry" to make this right.

So after I drop off my stuff at the hangar, I drive up to the marina to have a talk with him. Dad has been making him clean boats almost every day, so I know exactly where to find him: in the lot beside the launch ramp, shirtless and sweating in the afternoon sun, a polishing rag in his hand.

He sees me approaching but turns away, climbing up into a sport fisher to begin aggressively wiping everything down. There's a bruise taking shape on his abdomen and a swollen cut on his lip from where he collided with my workbench during our fight this morning. Seeing it makes me feel a twinge of guilt in my stomach.

"Jack, can I talk to you?"

He doesn't look up. He just continues polishing the boat with a furious work ethic that apparently only emerges when he's feeling murderous.

"Did Dad send you out here?" Jack shoots the question over his shoulder, not sparing me a glance.

I shake my head. "No. He didn't."

"Mom, then?"

"I came on my own, Jack. I want to apologize to you. It was wrong of me to keep you in the dark about my feelings for Orca. You're right, I had a hundred opportunities to say something. It was stupid of me, okay? It was a mistake. But I never knew things would turn out like this. When I first met Orca, I *did* fall for her, and I knew she had feelings for me—but I thought she was just infatuated because I was the first man she'd ever met. I told myself I was too old for her, and that in time she would forget me. I figured it was over. But then you brought her here, and when you two started hanging out together, I thought maybe it was for the best; maybe it would be a good thing for her to experience being with someone her own age. I thought maybe she'd fall for you, and it would prove that I was right, and she was just infatuated with me before."

Jack remains silent, his back to me, still polishing the boat with wide, angry strokes.

"I never meant to hurt you or deceive you, Jack. The truth is, I wanted Orca to be free to choose *you* if that's what she decided. That's why I took a step back from the whole situation."

Jack freezes, the muscles in his back tensing. "You were ready to give her up? If she decided she liked me better?"

"Yes."

He scoffs a humorless laugh. "Bullshit."

"What, do you think I'd want to be with a woman who prefers my brother to me? Would *you* want that, Jack?"

It's not until the words are out of my mouth that I realize I've just pulled the pin out of the grenade.

Jack whirls around, his eyes on fire. "You didn't give me much of a choice, did you? There was no way I ever had a shot with her, not when you were schmoozing her behind my back, bending over backward to find her family and be the hero—"

"Why is it always about me?" I interrupt, stepping closer to the boat and lowering my voice. "Why do you always blame me when you don't get what you want?"

"No, I don't."

"Yes, actually, you do. Be honest with yourself, Jack. You wanted Orca in a way that she didn't want you—and that made you angry, maybe even a little jealous. I think you sensed she had feelings for me, which suddenly made the whole thing a competition. Would you have felt the same way if she was in love with some other guy? Or is it because I'm your brother—"

"No shit, it's because you're my brother," Jack bursts out, storming off the boat and closing the distance between us. "I've spent my whole life in your shadow, Adam. And you know what? I didn't mind it. I didn't care when girls at school tried to talk to me just so they could meet *you*. I didn't care when everyone compared my grades to yours or made jokes about me trying to follow in your footsteps. I didn't care, because I worshipped the ground you walked on! I wanted to be like you—I wanted to *be you*. But I can't. No matter how hard I try."

I shake my head, swallowing the knot in my throat. "Jack, I never wanted you to compare yourself to me—"

"Well, too late. Because I do. Every goddamn day. Ask Mom, ask Dad. Ask *Orca*. You're the goalpost, Adam. Do you know how hard that is, to live every day with somebody that everyone wants you to be like?"

"Nobody expects you to be like me, Jack. Nobody but *you*. Stop thinking you're not good enough."

"But I'm not! Am I? Look at me. I'm a failure. I'm stuck here cleaning boats! My head is splitting, and my not-girlfriend just dumped me for my brother, and everyone else hates me—"

"Nobody hates you, Jack."

"You hate me."

"No, I don't—"

"Well, you should!" Jack shouts, his eyes flashing with rage. "What the hell is wrong with you? I beat you up, for Christ's sake! I'm an asshole. All I ever do is let people down." He turns away, vaulting himself back into the boat to continue scrubbing down the vinyl seats. "Mom says I break her heart, Dad treats me like a child, and then you come around here and make me feel even more like a villain by refusing to be mad at me—"

"Jack, would you stop feeling sorry for yourself?"

He barks a bitter laugh. "Oh, I don't feel sorry for *myself*. I feel sorry for all of you. But don't worry—you won't have to put up with me for much longer."

I frown, squinting at him through the sunlight. "What are you talking about?"

Jack doesn't respond. He keeps his gaze lowered on the job at hand, spraying the glass with cleaning solution and wiping it down with a different rag. Silence isn't like him—and neither is this sudden nose-to-the-grindstone attitude toward the job he hates.

I step up to the edge of the boat, my voice low and serious. "Jack, don't do anything stupid, okay?"

He scoffs. "Stupid is all I'm capable of, apparently."

"That's not true—"

"You done lecturing me, Adam? 'Cause I've got a job to finish here, and I'd just as soon be left alone to do it."

I dip my head in a nod, stepping back. "I just want to say I know now I was wrong. And I'm sorry." With that, I turn and walk back across the parking lot to my truck. When I glance over my shoulder, Jack is watching me go.

SCARY LOVE

orca

There is a new driftwood carving on my nightstand: a miniature, beautifully detailed replica of the lighthouse. I turn it over in my hands, tracing a fingertip over the tiny lantern room—the place where Adam Stevenson first kissed me.

It must have taken Papa hours to carve this one.

Golden evening light filters through the window curtains, casting swaying, gauzy shadows over the walls; ocean charts and whale sketches flutter in the sea breeze, paper edges curling from the humidity. Strings of seashells stir and clink together lazily. My driftwood orca pod dives and breaches across the top of my dresser.

I didn't realize how much I'd missed the lighthouse until now. Every small piece of it seems more precious to me—every imperfection a stroke of magic.

All day long, I've been waiting for the right moment to speak with Papa about Adam. I know the subject will be a delicate one. He's bound to resist the idea with many stubborn arguments. So I summon all the patience I can and wait for the ideal moment to arrive.

In the meantime, we share a quiet supper of vegetable stew and freshly baked bread. Lucius sleeps on the floor underneath the kitchen table, snoring contentedly. Papa says my little furry friend hasn't been easy since I left—that he spent every day sniffing around the house and prowling the beach as though he was looking for me. Just imagining it makes me sad, so I stop in the middle of dinner to crawl underneath the table and give Lucius an apologetic hug.

After we wash the dishes, I boil some water for tea. The ocean has swallowed up the sun, and now the shadows of early evening fold over our world. Outside, an orchestra of crickets and tree frogs serenades the forest, cloaked by an indigo twilight.

Once Papa and I are both seated in the living room with ceramic mugs of chamomile-mint tea and the fire crackling on the hearth, I make my confession.

"Papa, there's something I need to tell you. I've been… trying to find the right words."

Papa watches me in the firelight, his gray eyes solemn but softhearted.

"It's about Adam," I begin quietly, looking down at the tea mug cradled in my hands. "I know you disapprove of him after what happened between us when you were away from the lighthouse. I know you forbade me from ever seeing him again, but… He wasn't as dishonorable as you think." I glance back up at Papa, the words rushing out of me now that I've begun. "When Jack first took me to the Otherworld, Adam wanted to bring me straight back here. He tried to convince me to come home and make things right with you. He told me I'd regret it if I let this enmity stand between us. I was too stubborn to see that he was right. I *shouldn't* have left the way I did. But I guess I needed to make a few mistakes before I could see clearly."

An unexpected wave of sadness passes through me as I recall the brokenhearted anger on Jack's face this morning. His words were so cold and hard. *What the hell kind of game have you been playing with me, Orca?*

I press my eyes shut, drawing in a steady breath. "Papa, the truth is, Adam has been nothing but honorable. If you knew what he's really like, you would love him too—I know you would. He's so kind and strong and genuine, and there's something… indescribable between us. I hardly know how to put it into words. It's like the feeling of staring up at the stars from the top of the lighthouse when there's no moon, and the universe feels like it's not just around you, it's *inside* you. The joy is so intense, it almost feels like grief." I laugh softly, a sweet pain squeezing my heart. "That sounds like nonsense, I know."

Papa shakes his head. "It doesn't sound like nonsense, Orca. It sounds like you're in love with him."

I set my tea mug on the coffee table and come to sit beside Papa, taking his calloused hand in mine. "Oh, Papa, I'm so afraid of hurting you again. But I need to be with him. I feel like a part of me was never truly *alive* until I met him." I press a wobbly smile onto my lips, looking at him through the soft light. "I think maybe it was the same way for you and Mama."

Papa pats the back of my hand. "It was. But I didn't feel it just for your mama. I felt it the day you were born." He hums a little laugh, remembrance shining in his eyes. "You know, that was the scariest day of my life. I remember holding you in my arms, thinking: how did my parents do this? It was as though, all of a sudden, my whole world was wrapped up in this tiny, helpless little being. And if anything happened to you, my world could end—just like that." He snaps his fingers. "The funny thing is that fear never goes away. It's always been with me since the day you were born. There's nothing I wouldn't do for you, my girl. No pain I wouldn't endure. No battle I wouldn't fight."

A warm tear slips down my cheek. Papa gently swipes it away with his thumb.

"What is life without that kind of love?" he asks softly. "I have no right to deny you that love, Orca. I know my life would be empty without it. Without you. But still—you shouldn't be tied to your old father through the best years of your life."

"You're not old," I argue. "And I *want* to be tied to you. I have no intention of moving away. Adam and I want to get married and live here on the island—in a little cottage that Adam wants to build for us. We can be neighbors, and I can still help take care of Lucius and the chickens and anything else you need. Adam will help, too."

Papa chuckles. "You have it all planned out, don't you?"

"Just about," I say with a grin. "I haven't picked out the names for our children yet."

Papa raises his eyebrows. "*That* can wait a while."

A laugh bursts out of me, hope overflowing like sunshine in my veins. "Oh, Papa, thank you for understanding." I press a kiss to his cheek. "Adam is coming back in a few days to ask for your permission. You'll say yes, won't you? When can we get married? Next week?"

"Whoa, whoa, whoa. Slow down. A cottage isn't built in a week, my dear girl. And I need to see that this Adam Stevenson is worthy of you before I make any promises."

I blush through a smile. "He *is* worthy, Papa. You'll see."

Never Be Gone

jack

The recruitment office is small and aggressively tidy—empty this late in the day except for the stony-faced officer who sits behind a metal desk, looking over the questionnaire I've filled out.

"You have your wings already, huh?"

"Yes, sir. I've been a licensed pilot for three years now."

The officer nods, looking impressed. "Well, that'll certainly give you a useful head start if you go on to pursue a career as an aviator."

"I want to, sir."

The officer cuts me a no-nonsense look. "That's what every recruit says. But there's much more to being an Air Force pilot than simply *wanting* it."

"Yes, sir."

He staples a few papers together and sets them aside, then passes me a stack of information pamphlets. "I'll start processing your forms right away. If everything looks good, your next step will be to take the Armed Services Vocation Aptitude Battery, the ASVAB, and see what jobs you qualify for. In the meantime, you can learn more about test requirements and career paths in there." He taps the stack of literature, which looks like a test all by itself.

"Thank you, sir. I appreciate your time."

Adam told me not to do anything stupid. But as I step out of that recruitment office, I can't help feeling like this is the first time I *haven't* done something stupid in my whole life.

When I get back in my Mustang and start the engine, "In the Air Tonight" is playing on the radio, and something about it feels meaningful. I drive back home with the windows down, thinking about what Orca wrote in her letter. How she told me I'd find myself somewhere out there. How is it that she's always known me better than I know myself?

I don't know myself.

I don't know who the hell Jack Stevenson is.

But I'm going to find out.

WHEN I GET HOME, Mom informs me that I've missed dinner. I don't care. She and Dad are seated in the living room, the evening news playing quietly on the TV.

"Where have you been?" Mom asks, peering at me over her shoulder.

"Nowhere," I say, stopping at the back of her chair and leaning down to kiss the top of her head.

She frowns, startled by how nice I'm being. "Are you okay?"

"Yeah."

I shuck off my jacket and head for my room, bracing myself for another argument with Adam. But when I open the door and step inside, the room is dark and silent.

Adam's pillow and blankets are gone from his bed. Some other stuff is missing, too—his backpack, his leather bomber jacket, and his aviator shades.

"Jackie?"

I turn around to find Mom standing in the doorway, studying me with a worried look.

"Where's Adam?" I ask.

Mom crosses her arms over her chest. "He's gone, Jack."

Those words sting like a slap. I am instantly thrown back in time to that awful night I stood in this very spot and watched Mom fall apart because she thought Adam was dead. She said those same words that night. *He's gone, Jack.*

I shut my eyes, pushing the memory away. "When did he leave?"

"This morning," Mom says. "I thought you knew."

"No…" I look back to the naked bed. "Where's he staying?"

"His hangar."

I grunt. "Just can't stand being with me anymore, huh?"

"What do you expect after the way you treated him this morning?"

I kick off my shoes, letting one crash into the wall. "Whatever. I don't give a shit."

"Jack."

It's a warning. But Mom is tired; I can see it in her eyes. Tired of arguing. Tired of keeping the peace. Tired of me.

I almost want to tell her that she won't have to put up with me for much longer. I'll be gone too, pretty soon. Hopefully, I'll be halfway around the world where I'm not *Jackie* or even *Jack*, but just *Stevenson.* That's going to feel so weird. I wonder if I'll ever stop thinking, *Who are you talking to, me or Adam?*

"Look, I'm sorry," I grumble, sitting on the edge of my bed. "I'm exhausted, okay? It's been a long day."

"Get some sleep, then." Mom squeezes my shoulder and leaves the room.

I WAKE UP BEFORE DAWN. The moon is still shining through the window. I'm about to reach for my watch when my gaze catches on Adam's bed, empty and monochrome in the moonlight.

The absence of him messes with my head. Like the permanent shadow a picture frame leaves on a wall when it's been hanging there too long and someone takes it down.

The moon was shining bright that night, too. I woke up fast, and the shape of Adam was the first thing I looked for.

My lifeline.

He was sleeping, but I didn't care. I needed him.

I got out of bed and shuffled across the room. Tapped his shoulder. It was like a rock under his white T-shirt. Tap, tap, tap, until finally, he rolled over, waking up. Saw me standing in the moonlight.

"Jack?" His voice was low and husky. "You okay?"

"I had a bad dream."

It wasn't the first time. Second grade came with a lot of bad dreams. But Adam was always there to make it okay. He pulled aside his blankets, and I climbed into bed with him.

For a minute, we just lay there in the moonlight, Adam's arms folded behind his head. At seventeen, he seemed like a superhero—muscles everywhere. Good for beating up bullies, I thought. But this nightmare wasn't about the bullies.

I roll onto my back, forcing my gaze up to the ceiling.

He's still got muscles everywhere. Good for beating up brothers.

But so are mine.

"You want to tell me about it?" Adam asked. His voice was big, like quiet thunder. I felt it through his chest.

At first, I didn't tell him about it. I was afraid if I said it out loud, it might come true. But I could hear his steady breath, in and out. The boom, boom, boom of his heart in his chest.

He wasn't gone. He was here.

"It was about you," I said, my voice shrinking in the dark.

"Me?"

I nodded.

"Did I do something bad?"

I shook my head, my throat tight as I remembered the dream. "You were gone."

"Gone?" Adam said. "Gone at school?"

"No. You were gone for good. That's what Mom said. She was real sad… and I was looking for you everywhere, but I couldn't find you."

Adam heard it in my voice—the fear. I tried to hide it. I didn't want him thinking I was a wimp. But the dream scared me. I couldn't lie, not back then.

"Come on," Adam said and pushed back the blankets. "We gotta be quiet so we don't wake Mom and Dad."

I get out of bed and grab my T-shirt from the floor, pulling it over my head as I step out into the hallway.

The house is dark, noiseless. I try to be silent as I make my way through the kitchen, weaving around the table and chairs. I do pretty good until I get to the front door—that's where I always screw up, making too much noise.

Adam knew how to do it silently. He was like a cat burglar. I couldn't hear when he eased open the front door and stepped out onto the deck.

Outside, the night was cold and clear, our backyard glazed in silver moonlight. Adam sat me on the deck railing, his strong hands holding my shoulders so I wouldn't fall off.

"Look up."

I tip my head back and stare up at the bright white moon. It's almost full, shining like a beacon in the middle of a navy predawn sky.

"What do you see, Jack?"

"The moon?"

"Mm-hmm. And when you don't see the moon, what does that mean?"

"It means there's clouds in the way."

"But the moon is still there, in outer space. Right?"

"Yeah."

"Well, that's how it is with me."

I craned my neck to look up at him. The pale light etched sharp lines of shadow on his face.

"You're the moon?"

He grinned. "I'm always there. Even if you can't see me. Even if stuff comes between us… I'll never be gone. I promise."

"I won't let you be gone," I said.

He laughed and ruffled my hair with his free hand. "You'd better not, little brother."

The moon wavers and blurs as hot tears fill my eyes, stinging when they meet the cold.

I've lost my brother all over again.

And it's my fault.

I let him be gone.

"No," I rasp, my voice a broken whisper. "No, I won't…"

I run down the porch steps and across the driveway to my car. It's not until I'm starting the engine that I realize I'm not wearing any shoes.

I don't care.

My mind is reeling the whole drive to the port. The sky goes from indigo to gray to pale blue. It's almost dawn by the time I pull into the parking lot.

I see his truck right away, parked in its usual spot outside his hangar. I swerve my Mustang to a stop beside it. Kill the engine, get out.

The port is still sleeping—silent and shrouded in early morning fog. I spot Adam standing at the end of the dock, looking out over the harbor.

Even through the fog, fifty feet away, I recognize him.

My brother.

My hero.

My lifeline.

I make my way toward him, tears fogging my vision. Still barefoot, he doesn't even hear my approach until I finally manage to get my voice out.

"Adam!"

He turns and sees me running down the docks, but he doesn't have a chance to say anything before I throw my arms around him.

At first, he's caught off guard. His body goes rigid. Then suddenly, he's hugging me so hard I think my ribs might break. Tears roll down my face as I hold onto him, wishing I could tell him so many things—but I can't get any words past the lump in my throat.

So instead I just stand there hugging him.

Finally, I manage to choke out an apology. "I'm sorry, Adam. I'm sorry I've been such an asshole."

"I'm sorry too, Jack." His voice cracks, raw with emotion. "For everything."

"Well, I forgive you. So shut up about it already."

A surprised laugh rumbles out of him. I feel it in my chest. "You've got one hell of a left hook, little brother."

"And you've got one hell of an uppercut."

Adam sighs, pulling back to give me a weak half-smile.

"Come back home, Adam. Mom won't be able to handle both of us gone."

He frowns at me, clueless. "What do you mean? Where are *you* going?"

I smirk, swiping the leftover tears off my face. I can't tell my brother that I'm joining the military while I stand here crying like a little girl. I suck in a deep breath.

"I've joined the Air Force."

Adam stares at me, shocked. "What?"

"It's what I want," I assure him with a decided nod. "Really. I've thought about it a lot. I've always wanted to travel. And Mom and Dad want me to stop wasting time and pursue a career, so… that solves everything, doesn't it? Maybe someday I'll even become a fighter pilot. Who knows?"

Adam stares at me for a few seconds, taking it all in. "Wow, Jack. That's… sudden."

"I know."

"Crazy."

"I know."

He studies me for a moment, skeptical. "It's gonna be a lot of hard work."

I narrow my eyes. "You calling me lazy?"

"No," he says with a laugh. "You work harder than anyone I know when you want something badly enough. So if you really want this…"

"I do."

Adam nods, clapping a hand firmly on my shoulder. "Then you should go for it." I could swear I see a glint of pride in his eyes.

Seriously, *pride*.

For me.

"Have you told Mom and Dad?"

I shake my head. "Not yet. I wanted you to be there. To back me up."

Adam grins. "I wouldn't miss this for the world."

I TELL THEM OVER BREAKFAST. And sure enough, Mom freaks out.

"Jackie," she says, "this is so rash. You can't be serious."

But I *am* serious, and I prove it by keeping my cool while explaining my reasons to them. In the end, I win. Mom sheds a few tears of irrational fear, but I assure her that nothing bad will happen to me—it's not like there's a war going on.

Dad thinks it's a good idea. There's a look of respect in his eyes as he listens to me explain my plans. I can tell he wasn't expecting this—but he doesn't try to talk me out of it.

"I can't believe they're okay with it," I say to Adam afterward. We're outside on the deck, watching the sky darken as a thunderstorm rolls in from the ocean. "I mean, Mom's always gonna worry—"

"Well, she'd have to be a little mentally unstable *not* to worry at the thought of you as a fighter pilot," Adam says.

I laugh, shaking my head. "You're such a jerk, you know that?"

He smirks, crossing his arms smugly and leaning back against the railing. I look down at the floorboards, a wave of guilt rising in my chest.

"No, actually," I admit in a low voice, "*I'm* the one who's been a jerk. I think I always knew that I was pushing my luck with Orca. Knew she didn't like me, not the way she likes *you*." I sigh a humorless laugh. "I thought that I could *make* her fall for me. But it doesn't work like that, I guess."

A distant rumble of thunder punctuates my statement.

Adam thinks for a silent moment before responding. "When you meet the right woman, you won't have to *make* her love you, Jack. It'll just… happen. Without your say-so. Probably against your will. It'll turn your life upside down, but you won't care because nothing else will matter to you except *her*."

I turn to look at him. "Is that how you feel about Orca?"

He nods.

"I don't think I've ever felt that way for anyone."

"Well, you're only eighteen, Jack. You've got plenty of time."

"Whereas *you* are an old man, getting more ancient by the minute. Better hurry up and marry her before you go gray."

Adam laughs, tipping his head back. "As a matter of fact, I was planning on flying out there tomorrow to ask for her father's permission."

"No kidding. Really?"

He nods.

"Were you going to invite any of us to the wedding or just sneak off and do that when nobody's looking?"

Adam sighs, but he's still smirking. "I didn't say anything because… well, I wanted to give you some time to get used to the idea."

I look down, a knot tightening in my throat. It's not the same jealousy I felt before—it's more like disappointment laced with a shot of second-hand happiness.

"I *do* love her, in a way," I confess quietly. "I want her to be happy. And I want *you* to be happy. If you were any other guy, I'd want to wring your neck. And if she were any other girl, I'd never want to see her again. But the truth is, you two are the best people in my life. And I don't want to lose either one of you." A surprised laugh catches in my throat. "It's weird as hell, but I wouldn't want her to be with anyone else but you."

That's when my cell phone starts ringing in my pocket. I take it out and glance at the screen, but I don't recognize the number. Maybe it's about my enlistment. I pick up the call and say, "Hello?"

At first, there is silence. Then comes a rush of white noise and the frantic voice of Orca. "Jack? Jack, are you there? Can you hear me?"

"Yeah, I'm here, Orca. What's wrong?"

"It's Papa," Orca cries. "He's collapsed, and I don't know what to do. He's not moving. You've got to help me."

HEARTSICK

orca

Dawn arrives in a soft gray hush. I stand on the catwalk outside the lantern room, my fingers curled around the salt-sprayed railing, a western wind tangling my hair as I look out at the expanse of ocean between two worlds.

I feel like Hero, waiting for my Leander to swim home to me. A restless impatience stirs in my heart every time I think of him.

Soon.

There is such promise in that word. Such effervescent hope in the thought of *someday*—not as a wistful daydream, but as a plan.

Someday, I will marry Adam Stevenson. We will build a home by the sea, close to Papa and far away from everyone else. We will live in our own secret world and be so perfectly happy together; we won't need anything but each other.

Someday, Adam will come home to our cottage after a hard day's work, greeted by the warmth of a home filled with light—candles burning, love ballads on my lips, and something sweet baking in the oven.

Someday, our love will spill over in the form of a brand-new life, and I will experience the miracle of a tiny human growing inside me. I'll feel her move and kick, and I'll take Adam's hand and spread it over my belly and ask, *Can you feel that?* Someday I will look into the pink face of a newborn baby and marvel at the fact that Adam and I brought a new person to life. Someday, I'll know what it feels like to hear a child's voice call me *Mama.*

Someday I will understand that complicated paradox of strength and fragility, the feeling of all your love wrapped up in one tiny soul, the fear that it could all be taken away in an instant, the willingness to risk your whole heart anyway.

Someday, I will hear a chorus of laughter from little girls and boys as they chase seagulls through the shallows, their hair glowing in the sunlight, their bare feet splashing through the low tide. Adam's strong arms around me, his bright eyes smiling.

Someday, I will listen to Adam read our children bedtime stories and watch them drift off to sleep, kiss their foreheads, and whisper, "I love you." Adam and I will stay up late to watch the stars together, to find constellations and invent new ones. We'll grow old together, and even if I live for a thousand years, I'll never find words to describe how much I love him.

I FEEL LIGHT AS A FEATHER all morning, singing cheerfully as I tend to the greenhouse, weed the garden, collect eggs from the henhouse, and take a long walk on the beach to gather seashells with Lucius. While I daydream about the future, Lucius trots ahead of me, sniffing piles of kelp and sneezing violently when he gets sand up his nose.

Eventually, I hear thunder rumbling in the distance and look up to find the western sky growing darker by the minute. I whistle for Lucius to come, and we head back toward the lighthouse together.

"Looks like a storm is headed this way," I announce, coming through the back door and brushing the sand off my bare feet. "Papa?"

Silence.

Where is he?

I leave my pile of seashells on the coffee table, heading for the kitchen.

My heart jumps into my throat when I step through the doorway and see him.

"Papa!"

He is collapsed on the floor, his right arm crumpled underneath him, his hand gripping his chest. I rush to his side and drop to my knees.

"Oh god, Papa—what happened?"

I give his shoulder a firm shake, but his eyes remain shut. My stomach lurches as a wave of panic crashes over me. I bring my ear to his mouth, desperate to hear his breath.

Yes.

It is faint but there. He is alive.

"Papa, can you hear me?"

He doesn't stir. My heartbeat thunders in my chest, and I can't breathe, I can't think, I don't know what to do—

Call Adam.

Scrambling to my feet, I shove aside a worried Lucius and frantically run into the living room to grab the satellite phone. I jab at the buttons, recalling the sequence of numbers I typed over and over again to call Jack back when Adam was missing.

The phone rings once, twice, and then—

"Hello?" Jack's voice comes through the speaker with so much static, I'm not sure he's really there at all.

"Jack? Jack, are you there? Can you hear me?"

"Yeah, I'm here, Orca. What's wrong?"

"It's Papa," I say in a rush, tears welling in my eyes. "He's collapsed, and I don't know what to do. He's not moving. You've got to help me."

"Wait, what? Okay, hold on. Just… stay calm. We're coming."

The call disconnects.

I race back to the kitchen and crash to my knees beside Papa, taking his shoulders. "Papa, can you hear me? Papa…" My voice struggles out between sobs until I am gasping for breath, my hands shaking uncontrollably as fear takes over, wrenching my strength away from me. I crumple against Papa, my tears rushing faster.

"Please don't leave me, Papa… I need you."

Though his heart is still beating and his breath is still coming in weak and shallow puffs, I can feel the loss of him like a shadow looming over me. It is a terrible, suffocating feeling—an angry tidal wave, building and crashing, holding me down in the depths.

A rumble of thunder rattles through the sky, vibrating in the walls. Then comes the rain, a deafening *woosh* that cocoons the house and veils the world beyond the windows in a blinding rush of gray.

Will Adam and Jack even be able to fly out here in this storm?

What if they can't see well enough to navigate?

What if they crash because of me?

Papa's hands are growing colder by the minute. I fight back tears as I rub his fingers briskly, my heart breaking at the sight of him so helpless.

"Stay with me, Papa… Stay with me."

THE RESCUE

adam

"This is insane," Jack says from the copilot's seat, his foot tapping nervously on the floor. "Every station is telling pilots to return to safe harbor immediately."

My heart thuds in my chest as I look out at the dark sky ahead, flashing and moaning with distant thunder.

Jack shoots me a look. "Think we should call the coast guard?"

I shake my head. "No. Orca's father might not have much time. We've got to fly out there ourselves." I reach over him to shut off the radio. "It's risky, I know. I'm going to have to fly straight towards that storm and hopefully skirt around the worst of it. Maybe you should stay here—"

"Are you crazy?" Jack bursts out. "I'm not gonna let you go out there by yourself. Remember what happened last time?"

"Mom will kill me if you get hurt—"

"And I'll kill *you* if you go off and crash again!" Jack crosses his arms, sitting back stubbornly in his seat. "I'm coming."

I nod, wrapping my hand around the throttle. "All right."

My pulse races in my ears as I ease the throttle forward, keeping the yoke straight. The engine roars as we rocket over the water's choppy surface, leaving the safety of the harbor behind. I pull the yoke toward me, and we lift into the blackening sky.

I try to focus on flying smoothly, but it's not easy when I'm staring down a thunderstorm. It looks even bigger as we gain altitude—a churning mass of shadow spreading over the water like a curse, flickering with cloud-to-cloud lightning.

Jack is right—we're insane to be flying into deteriorating weather. But I have no other choice.

Orca needs me.

"You're doing good," my brother assures me through his headset.

I manage a dry laugh despite everything. "I've flown in better skies, that's for damn sure." I reach over to snap on the storm lights so I don't get blinded by the lightning. "I'm going to try to fly around the worst of it, then circle back north to land."

Jack gives me a thumbs up.

I watch my compass, fighting crosswinds, retracing my flight path to Orca's island. Jack acts as my second set of eyes, but it's hard to see anything when the rain is falling in violent torrents, pouring over my wings in a noisy *WHOOSH* that sounds like a thousand nails rushing over metal. A bolt of white lightning leaps out of the clouds, followed by a bellow of thunder that I can feel in my chest.

"Do you see that light up ahead?" Jack shouts, pointing out the windshield to a distant beacon piercing through the curtains of rain. "I think it's coming from the lighthouse!"

I maneuver the yoke back to drop altitude. The sea below us is churning and frothing, a hungry monster ready to swallow us up.

I don't look at it.

Instead, I focus on that light shining through the storm, guiding us to our destination. The island is coming up fast, but I need to descend slowly, or else the downdrafts will do my job for me—and crash us straight into the waves. I grasp the lever in the floor and pull it back to lower my flaps for a slower landing. White-capped swells roll underneath us, looking more like mountains as we come down on them.

"Brace yourself!" I yell to Jack, swallowing back my pounding heart as we land—hard.

I jolt forward, nearly smashing my face on the dash and grimacing as the yoke bites into my ribs.

Land rushes up on my port side, a tangle of evergreens swaying in the wind, then a long stretch of gray beach. The swells rock us around like a paper boat—building and crashing so violently I'm afraid we might capsize.

"Christ," Jack says. "Turn, turn, turn!"

I bank hard to the left, cringing as the angry tide scoops up my plane like a surfer in a pipeline and spits us onto the shore.

Seconds later, I hear the *shooooft* of sand underneath us, and the plane lurches to a stop.

We're beached.

We made it.

A stunned laugh rushes out of me. I turn to Jack, who looks just as amazed as I am. He curses loudly and rips off his headphones, slapping me on the shoulder.

"You deserve the pilot of the year award, bro."

I shake my head. "Don't say that till I get us back home alive."

That's when I see Orca racing down the grassy knoll to the beach, rain pouring down on her as she waves to signal us.

"Adam!" She screams my name the moment I climb down the ladder. "Oh god, I was so worried. The storm…"

I jump down to the sand and wrap my arms around her. "It's okay, Orca. I'm here. Where's your father?"

"He's in the house. He's still breathing, but he won't wake up. I don't know what to do!"

The three of us hurry back to the lighthouse, where Mr. Monroe is lying helpless on the kitchen floor. I kneel beside him, saying his name and trying to get him to respond. Orca watches with wide eyes.

"Mr. Monroe," I say, gently shaking his shoulder. "Lawrence, can you hear me?" I press two fingers to the side of his throat, reading his pulse. "Has he had any heart problems in the past?"

Orca shakes her head frantically. "I don't know… If he did, he never told me."

Jack watches me, a thousand questions in his eyes. "What do you think, Adam?"

"I think he must've had some kind of cardiac episode, maybe a heart attack."

"A heart attack?" Orca bursts out.

"He's breathing, Orca. He's alive. But we need to get him to the hospital right away. Jack, help me carry him."

Jack jumps to attention, taking Mr. Monroe's other arm. Together, we carefully hoist him off the floor. Orca remains calm, focusing on the task at hand—opening doors as we carry her father out of the lighthouse and down the beach, where my Beaver is waiting. Orca follows us, and Lucius follows her—undaunted by the rain and thunder. When we reach the plane, Orca scrambles up the ladder and opens the door for us, reaching down to help guide her father's limp body into the backseat. She settles on the bench with his head in her lap.

"Wait!" she bursts out. "We can't leave Lucius!"

While I start the engine, Jack climbs back down the ladder, grabs the dog, and shoves him into the backseat.

Orca thanks him and loops her arm around the dog's neck. "Come here, Lucius. It's okay…"

Outside, the rain is pouring down more violently than before. Jack and I work together to push my plane back toward the angry tide. It takes a lot of heaving and yelling, waves crashing around us until we're both soaking wet—but we successfully thrust the floats off the sand and into the sloshing whitewater.

"Quick, Jack! Get in!" I climb onto the portside float, waiting for Jack to make it to the ladder before I climb up myself and plunge into the cockpit.

Jack slams the hatch door shut behind him, shivering violently, water dripping into his eyes. "You okay, Orca?"

"Yes," she manages, cradling her father's head in her lap. "But we'd better hurry."

PROMISES

orca

The flight to Whidbey is turbulent and frightening, but Adam manages it well. He remains calm even when the rain smothers us in chaotic torrents and when a flash of lightning jumps out of a nearby cloud, as though seeking to strike us out of the sky.

Thunderstorms have always frightened me, even from the safety of the lighthouse. Never did I imagine I would one day find myself *inside* a thunderstorm. It is both surreal and terrifying—it feels like the storm is happening to the whole world.

When we finally land in the harbor at Whidbey Island, Papa has regained a bit of consciousness. He doesn't open his eyes or speak, but he murmurs indistinctly and flinches in pain when Jack and Adam hoist him out of the plane and into the backseat of Adam's truck. I speak to him the whole drive to the hospital, telling him *It's all right. You'll be all right.*

The hospital is a large, sprawling edifice of red brick and tall glass windows that reflect the darkened skies overhead. Adam jolts to a stop outside a door marked **EMERGENCY** in big red letters. Someone rushes out to assist us, and my heart breaks to leave Lucius behind in the truck, looking so forlorn. I plant a kiss on his head and tell him to be good. Adam drives off to find a parking space, and Jack follows me as I rush after Papa, into the hospital.

Inside, I run into a flock of straight-faced men and women in starchy uniforms. They lay Papa out on a gurney, barking orders to each other. A tall, dark-haired woman with gentle eyes tells me not to worry.

"I'm Dr. Reed," she says. "We're going to do whatever we can to help your father. I just need to know if he has any pre-existing conditions."

I shake my head. "I don't know… He never told me about any."

The doctor looks from me to Jack, who stands at my side. "Are you family?"

Jack stiffens. "No, I'm… just a friend."

"Well, why don't you two have a seat and take some deep breaths," Dr. Reed says, gesturing towards an adjacent waiting room lined with stiff-looking chairs. "I'll check back with you really soon, all right?"

I nod slowly, disoriented by the adrenaline now rushing out of me like a fast-receding tide. When Dr. Reed disappears down the hallway, I let out a trembling sigh.

"Are you okay?" Jack whispers, taking me by the shoulders to look into my face. "You're shaking."

I burst into tears and collapse against him.

"Hey, it's all right." Jack wraps his arms around me, and I cry into his chest, and we stay like that for what feels like a long, long time. He rubs his hand over my back in slow, circular movements, his voice finally coming in a broken rasp. "I'm sorry for the way we parted, Orca. I'm sorry for the things I said to you. I was such a jerk. Please forgive me."

A sad little laugh catches in my throat. "Of course I forgive you, Jack. I hope you forgive me, too. I know I hurt you, and that was the last thing in the world I wanted to do…"

"I know," he says softly, his voice a hundred years old. "I read your letter. I know."

I ease back to look into Jack's hazel eyes, my vision still blurry with tears. "You're not upset?" I sniff, swiping at my wet cheeks with the back of my hand. "It's not that I don't love you, Jack. It's just not—"

"You don't have to explain. I understand. And I'm not upset." Jack gives me a lopsided smile. "You couldn't have picked a better man than Adam."

I can see that he means it—without a hint of regret or bitterness.

"Thank you, Jack." I squeeze his hand. "Thank you for being here for me. For helping my father. You'll always be a dear friend to me."

A tiny laugh escapes him. "I'll never forget the great times we had together," he says, an edge of heartbreak in his voice. "I decided to take your advice and go see the world. Who knows, maybe I'll find myself along the way."

"What do you mean?"

"I've joined the Air Force."

"The *military* Air Force?"

Jack nods, grinning like a wonderstruck child.

"Are you going to be a fighter pilot?"

He laughs. "Well, that's the ultimate goal, yeah. But I have a lot of work to do first."

"Oh, Jack." I throw my arms around him again, hugging him tight. "Don't get yourself shot down out there. We'd all be lost without you."

"Don't worry, Orca. It's not like there's a war going on. I kind of wish there was."

I smack his arm. "Don't say that! War is a terrible thing. If women ran the world, there would be no wars at all."

Jack grunts. "Then there wouldn't be a need for fighter pilots. And where would that leave me?"

"Safe."

"I will be safe, Orca. I promise."

I shake my head, drawing back to look him in the face. "You can't make promises like that. Nobody can. Life is fragile—unpredictable. It can be snatched away at any moment, without warning." My voice thickens with tears, a crushing wall of dread rising within me.

Jack places one hand on my shoulder. "Your dad is gonna be okay. He's the most stubborn person in the world, remember? He's not going to give up that easily."

THE NEXT FEW HOURS feel like an eternity. I sit in the waiting room with Adam's arm looped around my shoulders as we wait for news from the doctor. Jack has gone outside to call his parents and let them know what's going on. Adam keeps assuring me that everything will be all right, but I don't feel at ease until Dr. Reed comes in with a gentle smile and says, "Your father's awake. He's asking to see you."

I spring to my feet and follow the doctor down the sterile white hallway to a strange little room crowded with peculiar machines and bright lights. A few medical workers in the same starchy uniforms hover around a rather uncomfortable-looking bed, where Papa lies. He looks older than he ever has, the color drained from his face and his tired eyes scarcely open.

"Papa," I gasp, rushing to his side and taking his hand. "How are you feeling?"

He pulls in a weary breath, not to answer my question but to murmur, "Those… boys…"

A smile blooms over my lips. "They saved you, Papa. I found you collapsed on the kitchen floor, and I didn't know what to do, so I called Jack and Adam for help. They flew out to the island in the middle of an awful storm and rescued you." I kiss his rough, weather-worn knuckles. "Oh, Papa. I was so scared that I'd lost you."

His gray eyes soften with the faintest smile. "My dear girl…"

Tears blur my vision as I squeeze his hand. It feels like my whole world is right here, wrapped up in his touch. He *is* my world, and I almost lost him. It's funny how a moment of blind panic can help you to see more clearly than ever before.

How foolish and selfish I've been.

Too concerned with my own desires and feelings to consider how much suffering I caused Papa. He had been nursing a broken heart all these years, keeping his quiet grief hidden from me, because he could never share his sorrow without adding to mine. If only I had been more understanding, more compassionate. If only I hadn't left him to go to the Otherworld…

If only I hadn't broken his heart all over again.

"Oh, Papa, I'm so sorry," I whisper. "I'm so sorry."

As I stand there holding my father's hand, I realize I would trade a hundred years in the Otherworld for just one more day with him.

OMNIA VINCIT AMOR

adam

"How's your dad?" I ask when Orca returns to the waiting room, her eyes red from crying.

"He's stable. They think he's going to be just fine. It was a mild heart attack, not as bad as it could have been. They want him to stay here for a few days, just to be sure."

"That makes sense," I say with a nod. "You can stay at our house."

"I appreciate the offer, but tonight I want to stay close to Papa. I can sleep in the waiting room, I'm sure."

"Well, then, I'll stay with you."

She looks down at the floor. "Please don't."

"I want to." I slide my arms around her waist and lean down to kiss the top of her head. "I love you."

She pushes me back, fresh tears glazing her eyes. "I mean it, Adam. Don't make this any harder than it has to be."

"What are you talking about?"

Orca crosses her arms over her chest, avoiding eye contact. "We can't be together. Not now."

"Of course we can—"

"No. We can't. I've already caused Papa so much stress and grief. I don't want to make him face any more changes. He needs to recover. And he's going to need my help now more than ever."

"Well, I could help you."

Orca shakes her head. "It's sweet of you to offer, Adam. But you have your own work. Besides, this is something I have to do. To make up for…" She doesn't finish that sentence, but I can see the shadow of guilt creeping onto her face.

"Don't blame yourself, Orca. What's done is done. You can't go back and change the past."

"I wish I could," she confesses, swiping a fallen tear off her face. "I would do everything differently."

"Everything?"

She looks up, meeting my gaze—and our love has never felt more fragile than it does at this moment. Like everything we've built together is dripping with gasoline, and here she is, standing before me with a lit match between her fingers.

"Just this morning, I was dreaming about our future together," Orca says, her voice a thready whisper. "And everything seemed so vivid, so possible, so perfectly planned out in my mind. Now, it's like a fog has rolled in, and I can't even see what tomorrow will look like."

I take a step closer, laying my hands on her shoulders. "You've been through a lot today, Orca. It's perfectly natural to feel scared about the future. But you don't have to worry. Because no matter what, I will be there for you."

She presses her eyes shut, forcing more tears to stream down. "Oh, Adam. I want you more than anything—you know that. But I'm so afraid of losing Papa. The doctor said another attack could kill him, and I don't want to be the cause of that. My leaving has already broken his heart, and I'd never forgive myself if… well, if the worst happened. All because I was too selfish to give up what I wanted for him."

I fall silent, circling my thumb against her shoulder. "I understand how you feel, Orca. But I know nothing would make your father happier than to see *you* happy."

"I can't think about my own happiness right now." Orca takes my hand in hers, squeezing my fingers with the reluctance of a person reaching out the window of a departing train, not ready to say goodbye. "I need to go home with Papa. I need to nurse him back to health; I need to give him that peaceful life we used to have together. And if that means giving you up… that's what I'll do."

She releases my hand and turns away, walking down the hallway toward her father's hospital room. I stand there watching, waiting for her to look back.

But she vanishes around the corner.

She doesn't look back.

Not once.

"CHEER UP," JACK SAYS from the passenger seat of my truck on the drive home. "It's not like her dad is dead or something."

I haven't said a word since we left the hospital. My eyes are on the road, but my thoughts are miles away. The rain has let up, weakening to a post-storm mist blowing in from the coast. Just enough drizzle to make the windshield wipers squeak over the glass. Lucius has managed to climb onto the center console between Jack and me, whimpering for attention.

"Seriously, Adam. You're starting to worry me." Jack scratches the dog's ears, shooting me a look. "If I didn't know any better, I'd think Orca broke up with you."

A pained, miserable laugh comes out on my next breath. "I think she might have."

"What?"

"I said, I think she might have broken up with me."

"No, I mean, *why*? How—what happened?"

I blow out a sigh, rubbing my forehead. "She blames herself for her father's heart attack and doesn't want to take a chance of it happening again. She thinks it would be too much for him to face any changes right now… and she wants to be there for him, even if that means we can't be together."

"She said all that?"

I nod, tapping on the directional and turning down our street. Jack falls into stunned silence for a full minute before he finally speaks.

"What are you going to do?"

I shrug. "I don't know. Give her some time to think, and then… I don't know."

"Time? You can't give her time—that's stupid. You gotta strike while the iron is hot."

"What do you mean?"

"Just do what you were gonna do before. Ask her dad's permission to marry her. Act like nothing's wrong—"

"I can't do that, Jack. It's not what she wants."

"How do you know?"

"Because she asked me to leave," I fire back, my voice rough with cold, hard finality. "She told me not to make this any harder for her."

Jack squints at me as though it gives him a headache to see things from my point of view. Then he bursts out laughing.

"What's funny?"

"You," he says, leaning back and shaking his head. "A couple of weeks ago, you accused me of not knowing when to back off. And you were right. But you know your problem, Adam? You don't know when to push your luck."

"Jack—"

"No. Just shut up and listen to me for a second. You may be older, but you have *way* less experience with girls. The brush-off is a test. Maybe Orca doesn't see it that way because she's so pure and naive, but the same rules apply. She takes a step back, says it's for the best, and now it's up to *you* to prove you're serious. No girl wants you to leave her alone when she says 'Leave me alone'—it's like Morse code for 'How much do you care?'"

Now *I'm* doing mental gymnastics, trying to see it from this perspective. "I don't think that's the case here, Jack—"

"Don't you love her? Aren't you willing to fight for her? 'Cause if not, maybe you don't deserve her."

I hit the brakes, turning to shoot my brother a hard look.

He puts his hands up, shrinking back as if he's afraid of getting punched again. "It's just the truth, man. She's not *my* girlfriend, but that doesn't mean I don't want the best for her."

"I want the best for her, too. That's what I'm trying to do, here."

"And do you really think it's best for you both to go back to being lonely and miserable again? Seriously, think about it. What do you have to lose?"

I pull into the driveway, park my truck, and kill the engine. Jack's question hangs in the air, burning for an answer. Even Lucius seems to be waiting for my response—his big, droopy eyes gazing up at me from the center console.

At last, I shake my head and admit, "Nothing. I have nothing without her."

ALL NIGHT LONG, I can't sleep. Orca's voice haunts me, her words playing back again and again like a broken record.

How she blames herself for her father's heart attack.

How she is willing to give up everything she wants just to keep him safe.

I remember how she looked sleeping beside me just a few nights ago: her long, dark eyelashes against her rosy cheeks, her breathing soft and heavy. I imagine running my fingers through her hair, kissing the sweet hollow of her neck. The thought alone is enough to make everything I feel for her rise to the surface like a fever in my blood.

I would wait forever for her—for *us*.

But at the same time, I feel like I can't wait a single day.

When dawn breaks, I drive back to the hospital, praying Orca will be asleep when I get there. Sure enough, she's curled up on a bench seat in the waiting room with her arm tucked underneath her head. I don't wake her. It's better if she doesn't know that I'm here.

I beg a passing nurse for the favor of seeing Mr. Monroe, and she reluctantly agrees after checking to ensure he's awake and wants to see me.

When I step into the room, I find Mr. Monroe sitting upright in his hospital bed, still weak—but looking stronger than he did yesterday. He glances up when I enter, an unmistakable glint of gratitude in his eyes.

"Mr. Monroe." I pull up a chair and sit beside the bed, facing him. "How are you feeling?"

"Better, thanks to you and your brother. I owe you both a great debt."

I shake my head. "It was the least we could do. Especially after…" I clear my throat, abandoning the rest of that sentence. "Well, I'm just glad we got there in time."

Silence fills the room. Mr. Monroe looks at me like he's expecting me to say something else. Like he knows exactly why I'm sitting here, and his daughter is not.

After a moment, he prompts me. "Is Orca sleeping?"

"Yes, sir. In the waiting room." I lean forward on my knees, clasping my hands together. "I'm sure you're wondering why I wanted to speak with you privately, without Orca around."

"I have a pretty good idea," he says.

I'm not sure how to begin, so I just come right out and say it. "Mr. Monroe, I love your daughter. And she loves me. God knows I don't deserve her love, but I'll endeavor to be worthy of it. I know you're a man of action, not words. So I want to show you—to prove to you—that I'm worthy of her." I straighten up, looking him square in the eyes. "Sir, I'm willing to do whatever it takes to earn your trust… and your consent to marry her."

Mr. Monroe studies me up and down for a long moment. "How old are you, son?"

A stab of insecurity twists in my chest. "Twenty-eight."

He doesn't seem put off by my age. In fact, he seems to take me more seriously after learning it. "So you're not some impetuous boy moved to such a confession by impulse or a mere fleeting emotion."

I shake my head firmly. "No, sir. I mean what I say. I love your daughter. I believe I could make her happy. I want *nothing more* than to make her happy. I think that's something you and I have in common."

Mr. Monroe ponders this for a moment. His gaze slides to the window, where the light of day is beginning to brighten the outside world.

"Last night," I continue, "Orca told me she's resolved to give up the whole idea of us being together. She feels so guilty about what happened to you. She's terrified that it will happen again, and it will be her fault. I don't want to take her away from you, sir. I don't want things to change between the two of you. But I also don't want to see her deny herself the kind of life we could have together… out of guilt or self-punishment."

Mr. Monroe shakes his head. "I don't want that either, son."

"Then let me help. You can't work yourself as hard as you did before; you'll need another man to help out. Orca's set on doing everything herself, but it's going to be too much for her. And yeah, I have a business to run, but I work for myself—I can take days off. With your permission, I'll fly out to the lighthouse and help you with whatever you need. Please give me this chance. Let me show you. Let me prove to you that I'm worthy of her."

Mr. Monroe scrutinizes me for a long moment, considering my offer. "You're right about one thing, young man. My daughter *does* love you." He pauses to murmur a sad laugh. "I've spent my life trying to protect her. Not for her sake alone, but because I couldn't bear the thought of losing her."

"You wouldn't have to lose her—"

"I've lost her already," he says, without a trace of anger or bitterness in his voice. "You will learn one day that there are two kinds of loss. The kind you can see… and the kind you can feel. Orca told me how much she loves you, and I know that she will never be truly happy without you."

A flame of hope reignites in my chest, desperate for his answer.

"I'm willing to let you prove yourself. If you really do love her as you say, you will wait for her."

"Yes, sir. I'd wait forever."

"I don't ask for *forever*," Mr. Monroe returns. "But I do ask for one year. If you can prove your devotion and commitment to her, then after a year, I will give you my blessing."

I can hardly believe what I'm hearing. A year? That's it? Maybe I should be disappointed. Maybe any normal person would argue that a year is too long, that he's being unreasonable. But it's nothing to me.

A year. That's it.

"Thank you, sir."

He looks apprehensive of my smile. "Don't make her any promises you can't keep."

"I won't."

"Remember, Adam—you're taking her heart in your hands. And if you break it…"

"I swear on my life, I will do nothing but prove my love for Orca."

Mr. Monroe is still unsure; I can see it in his eyes. "We'll see."

I shake his hand and say, "Yes, sir. You will see."

THE MAN

orca

After two days, Papa is discharged from the hospital, and Adam flies us back to the lighthouse. Papa sits beside me in the backseat of Adam's plane, with Lucius sprawled at our feet. I watch the Otherworld shrink to a mere rumple of distant land on the horizon, just as it always has been. The weather is fair for our flight—calm seas, bright sun, infinite blue sky—but I find no pleasure in the majesty surrounding me.

When Adam lands the plane at our beach, I want to smother him with kisses and tearful goodbyes. I want to throw my arms around him and never let go.

But I restrain myself. I am no longer that foolish, feckless girl who followed every romantic urge she felt, fulfilled every want at the expense of someone else's need.

I take Papa's arm and walk with him back to the lighthouse. I hear Adam's plane take off, but I don't look back.

I'll never look back.

I'll never long for the Otherworld again.

PAPA HAS BEEN INSTRUCTED not to exert himself lest he bring on another heart attack, so I've forbidden him to do any chores for the foreseeable future.

"I'm strong," I assure him. "I can manage."

"I won't make you a beast of burden, my dear girl."

"But—"

"I've made arrangements already," he says, staring out the kitchen window at the coastline as though seeing it in a whole new light. "A man will be coming out here several times a week to help us with whatever is needed. If he's true to his word, he'll be here on Wednesday. Until then, we will carry on as before."

As before.

What an impossible notion.

Nothing can be as it was before. I realize that over the course of the following days. There was a time when the rhythm of my habits felt as steady and comforting as the tides that lull me to sleep each night. There was a time when I found wonder and delight in ordinary, everyday things. Now I find only reminders of what I have lost.

Days feel impossibly long, nights even longer. I visit the greenhouse every morning, my harvesting basket slung over my shoulders and Lucius trotting at my heels. I walk the beach and see many beautiful shells, but I don't bring any back to my room. I spend hours on my knees in the garden, digging up root vegetables, scrubbing them clean, and preparing them a hundred different ways. I chop firewood until my hands are calloused and my arms sore. Every evening, I sit by the fire with Papa, who has begun to tell me stories about Mama. Stories of when they were first married. How happy and hopeful they both were, eager for the future, dazzled by the unknown.

I know how Mama must have felt during those glorious days of early love. I've *experienced* that feeling—that thrill of hope and possibility, the bliss of not knowing what the future holds but knowing it will be good.

Now, those feelings are just another memory.

Another weight of sorrow in my heart.

I tell myself that time will heal this wound, but it only feels more tender and sore with every passing day. Sometimes I cannot contain the grief and must let myself cry—an emotional indulgence I allow only when I am alone in my room or somewhere far down the beach, out of Papa's sight. I don't want him to know how much I miss Adam. I've caused him too much trouble as it is.

Then, one clear morning, Papa reminds me, "It's Wednesday."

"What's special about Wednesday? Oh, I remember. The man you hired is going to come today and help us with the chores. So I don't become a beast of burden."

Papa smiles, and there's a sparkle in his eyes that I haven't seen in a long time. "That's what he told me, anyway. Let's see if this man keeps his promises."

Around midmorning, I hear the telltale growl of a small aircraft engine. My heart gives an unexpected thud of anticipation, and I have to remind myself: *It's not Adam.*

"I think that must be the man," Papa says, coming into the kitchen. He looks out the window and sees the plane approaching. "Why don't you go out and meet him?"

I frown. "Me? Right now?" I'm in the middle of kneading bread dough, up to my elbows in flour—but Papa doesn't seem to care how busy I am.

"Yes," he says, his voice soft but serious. "Go on."

Reluctantly, I unstring my apron and brush the flour off my hands. Papa remains at the window while I step outside into the soft golden sunshine. A cool breeze rolls off the ocean as I walk out to the grassy knoll overlooking the beach.

When my gaze lands on the floatplane, I stop dead in my tracks.

It's Adam's plane.

It's *Adam.*

My heart jumps out of my chest as he emerges from the cockpit.

No.

Impossible.

I must be imagining him standing there.

But then he takes off his sunglasses and smiles.

"Adam," I rasp, my voice rushing out in a stunned exhale.

As he strides up the beach towards me, it all clicks into place: He's the man Papa asked to come help us—he *invited* Adam to come here. I can't believe it.

I run to him.

My heart races, laughter spilling past my lips as sandy ground flies underneath my bare feet. I run faster than I ever have in my life—everything rushing around me in a blur of sand and sea and deep blue sky. Adam catches me and sweeps me off my feet, twirling me around in the sunlight while I fall on his neck with tears of joy.

Once I've caught my breath, I pull back just enough to look him in the eyes. "You're the man?"

Adam laughs, surprised by the question. He gently presses his forehead against mine and says, "Yes. I'm the man. I'm *your* man. Now and forever, if you'll have me."

My heart feels like it's doubling in size as he leans in and kisses me deeply, his pulse racing under my fingertips. Tears spill from my eyes as I kiss him back, my hands gripping his T-shirt, his hands circling my waist. There are no words big enough to describe the immensity of love I feel in this moment. It is the universe and all its glory, caught between two souls. *Tenens infinitum.*

"I don't understand," I gasp, sinking back down to my feet in the sand. "How did you convince Papa to let you come?"

"I told him that I love you. That I will *always* love you. That I'm willing to do whatever it takes to prove it." Adam reaches up to gently brush a tear off my cheek. "And I *will* prove it. To both of you."

I shake my head. "You don't need to prove it to me. I know you, Adam. I love you with all my heart."

He stares at me for a moment, like he has so many things to tell me and doesn't know what to say first. "Orca, I want us to spend the rest of our lives together. I know you feel the same way. And I don't want you to deny yourself out of guilt or fear—that's no way to live. Your father agrees with me." He breaks into a smile, looking down at my hand interlaced with his. "He said that we have to wait a year; then he'll give us his blessing."

"What are you saying?"

My heart gives a fluttering leap as he gets down on one knee, taking both my hands in his. "Orca Monroe," he begins, a glint of tears in his beautiful blue eyes, "would you do me the honor of becoming my wife?"

All I can do is stare at him. "Your wife?"

Adam nods.

I take his face in my hands and kiss him fiercely. He remains frozen on the sand, unsure what this means—his eyes beg for answers when I ease back to look at his face.

"Yes," I whisper, "I will marry you. And we'll build that cottage by the sea and live happily—" I kiss him fast "—ever—" another kiss "—after."

A wave of passion swells inside me as his lips capture mine. The rest of the world could fall away, and I wouldn't notice—because my whole world is here, in this moment of perfect happiness. As Adam's lips move in a dance with mine, our souls come back together. All the pain of the past vanishes within seconds, and I am left with nothing but a free heart pounding wildly in my chest, spilling over with love for him.

Adam stands and lifts me off my feet, startling a gasp from my lips. I loop my arms around his neck, crying and laughing and showering him with kisses as he carries me back to the lighthouse.

Acknowledgements

Can I tell you a secret? I don't read the acknowledgements in a book as soon as I finish the final chapter. In order to fully absorb the magic of the story, I need a few hours (or perhaps days) to set the finished book aside and come to terms with the fact that this glorious world and its characters were crafted by an author — but not just an author alone. If I tried to embark on this journey all on my own, you would not be holding this book in your hands right now. The truth is, many incredible people have made this novel possible. And I want to thank them personally right now.

First, Katie. Thank you for being my biggest supporter, best friend, and Eshton-twin. You are quite literally the reason this book was written. If you hadn't encouraged me to turn my "lighthouse plot bunny" into an actual novel, I have no idea when these characters would have been brought to life. Thank you for inspiring me to follow my heart and just write it.

My deepest gratitude goes to my mum and dad, for motivating me to chase my dreams and for encouraging me every step of the way. An especially big thank you to Mum, for all those hours you spent helping me with editing, revising, and proofreading, proofreading, proofreading. (I'm glad you were #TeamAdam from the start.)

A ginormous thank you to my amazing editor Jen, for your creativity and diligence, and for making me cry happy-tears while reading your heartfelt emails. I am infinitely grateful for your encouragement, helpful critiques, and for fangirling over Phil Collins with me.

Also, I want to give a big thank you to Brooks Van Norman and Eric Auxier, for generously sharing your aviation and bush pilot expertise with me. Thanks for putting up with endless questions from an aviation enthusiast. Wishing you blue skies and unlimited visibility!

A million thanks to Jackson Hughens for the jaw-droppingly gorgeous cover art and for your wholehearted support of this book. Only a fellow Enneagram One could have the patience to put up with my fastidious tweaks and adjustments to the cover art. You brought my vision to life and always made the collaborative process fun and enjoyable.

Thank you to my dear friend Brooke, for being such a wonderful cheerleader and a kindred spirit—every time I talk to you, I remember that I'm in good company on the indie publishing path! Also thank you to Amy, for reading this book faster than Jack Stevenson runs from responsibility—I'm so grateful for your friendship and your support of all that I do.

None of this would be possible without the WritersLife Wednesday community, who has been writing with me and cheering me on since 2018. Y'all are the real heroes, and I wish I could hug each and every one of you and personally thank you for believing in this book and supporting my journey day after day.

Last but most definitely not least, thank YOU, beautiful reader, for spending your time with this book and for making my author dreams come true.

Rock on,

Abbie

About the Author

ABBIE EMMONS has been writing stories ever since she could hold a pencil. What started out as an intrinsic love for story-telling has turned into her life-long passion. There's nothing Abbie likes better than writing (and reading) stories that are both heart-rending and humorous, with a touch of cute romance and a poignant streak of truth running through them.

Abbie is also a YouTuber, writing coach, filmmaker, big dreamer, and professional waffle-eater. When she's not writing or dreaming up new stories, you can find her with her nose in a book or binge-watching BBC Masterpiece dramas in her cozy Vermont home with a cup of tea.

youtube.com/abbieemmons

facebook.com/abbieeofficial

@makeyourstorymatter